BOOKS BY CARLOS FUENTES

Where the Air Is Clear
The Good Conscience
Aura
The Death of Artemio Cruz
A Change of Skin
Terra Nostra
The Hydra Head
Burnt Water
Distant Relations
The Old Gringo
Myself with Others
Christopher Unborn
*Constancia and Other Stories
for Virgins*

THE DEATH OF
ARTEMIO
CRUZ

THE DEATH OF ARTEMIO CRUZ

Carlos Fuentes

TRANSLATED FROM THE SPANISH BY

Alfred Mac Adam

Farrar, Straus and Giroux

NEW YORK

Library of Congress Cataloging-in-Publication Data
Fuentes, Carlos.
[Muerte de Artemio Cruz. English]
The death of Artemio Cruz / Carlos Fuentes; translated from the
Spanish by Alfred Mac Adam.
p.   cm.
Translation of: La muerte de Artemio Cruz.
PQ7297.F793M813   1991   863—dc20   90-43280

TO C. WRIGHT MILLS

True voice of the United States of America
Friend and companion in Latin America's struggle

La préméditation de la mort est préméditation de la liberté.

MONTAIGNE, *Essays*

Oh, men who come forth into the earth
through a cradle of ice
and who enter through a grave,
behold how you act . . .

CALDERÓN, *The Grand Theater of the World*

Moi seul, je sais ce que j'aurais pu faire . . . Pour les autres, je
ne suis tout au plus qu'un peut-être.

STENDHAL, *The Red and the Black*

. . . of me and of Him and of the three of us
Always three! GOROSTIZA, *Death Everlasting*

Life is worth nothing. Nothing: that's what life is worth.

Mexican popular song

THE DEATH OF
ARTEMIO
CRUZ

I wake up . . . The touch of
that cold object against my penis wakes me up. I didn't
know I could urinate without being aware of it. I keep my
eyes shut. I can't even make out the nearest voices. If I
opened my eyes, would I be able to hear them? . . . But
my eyelids are so heavy: two pieces of lead, coins on my
tongue, hammers in my ears, a . . . a something like tar-
nished silver in my breath. It all tastes metallic. Or mineral.
I urinate without knowing I'm doing it. I remember with
a shock that I've been unconscious—maybe I ate and drank
without knowing it. Because it was just getting light when
I reached out my hand and accidentally knocked the telephone on the floor. Then I just lay there, face down on the
bed, with my arms hanging, the veins in my wrist tingling.
Now I'm waking up, but I don't want to open my eyes.
Even so, I see something shining near my face. Something
that turns into a flood of black lights and blue circles behind
my closed lids. I tighten my face muscles, I open my right
eye, and I see it reflected in the squares of glass sewn onto
a woman's handbag. That's what I am. That's what I am.
That old man whose features are fragmented by the uneven
squares of glass. I am that eye. I am that eye. I am that
eye furrowed by accumulated rage, an old, forgotten, but
always renewed rage. I am that puffy green eye set between

those eyelids. Eyelids. Eyelids. Oily eyelids. I am that
nose. That nose. That nose. Broken. With wide nostrils. I
am those cheekbones. Cheekbones. Where my white beard
starts. Starts. Grimace. Grimace. Grimace. I am that grimace that has nothing to do with old age or pain. Grimace.
My teeth discolored by tobacco. Tobacco. Tobacco. My bre-
bre-breathing fogs the squares of glass, and someone re-
moves the handbag from the night table.

"Look, Doctor, he's just faking . . ."

"Mr. Cruz . . ."

"Even now in the hour of his death he has to trick us!"

I don't want to talk. My mouth is stuffed with old pen-
nies, with that taste. But I open my eyes a little more, and
between my eyelashes I can make out the two women, the
doctor who smells of aseptic things: his sweaty hands, stinking of alcohol, are now tapping my chest under my shirt.
I try to push that hand away.

"Easy now, Mr. Cruz, easy . . ."

No. I am not going to open my mouth, or that wrinkled
line with no lips reflected in the glass. I'll keep my arms
stretched out on top of the sheets. The covers reach my
stomach. My stomach . . . ah . . . And my legs stay spread,
with that cold gadget between my thighs. And my chest
stays asleep, with the same dull tingling that I feel . . . that
. . . I felt when I would sit in one position for a long time
in the movies. Bad circulation, that's all it is. Nothing more.
Nothing more. Nothing serious. Nothing more serious than
that. I have to think about my body. Thinking about your
body wears you out. Your own body. Your body, whole. It
wears you out. Better not to think. There it is. I do think
about this flight of nerves and scales, of cells and scattered
globules. My body, on which the doctor taps his fingers.
Fear. I'm afraid of thinking about my own body. And my
face? Teresa removed the handbag that reflected it. I'm
trying to remember it in the reflection. It was a face broken
by asymmetrical pieces of glass, with one eye very close to

an ear and far away from the other eye, with the grimace spread out on three encircling mirrors. Sweat is pouring down my forehead. I close my eyes again, and I ask, ask that my face and body be given back to me. I ask, but I feel that hand caressing me, and I would like to get away from its touch, but I don't have the strength.

"Feeling better?"

I don't see her. I don't see Catalina. I see farther off. Teresa is sitting in the armchair. She has an open newspaper in her hands. My newspaper. It's Teresa, but she has her face hidden behind the open pages.

"Open the window."

"No, no. You might catch cold and make everything worse."

"Forget it, Mama. Can't you see he's fooling around?"

Ah. I smell that incense. Ah. The murmuring at the door. Here he comes with that smell of incense, with his black cassock, and with the hyssop out in front, a farewell so harsh it's really a threat. Ha, they fell into the trap.

"Isn't Padilla here?"

"Yes, he is. He's outside."

"Have him sent in."

"But . . ."

"First Padilla."

Ah, Padilla, come closer. Did you bring the tape recorder? If you knew what was good for you, you'd have brought it here the way you brought it to my house in Coyoacán every night. Today, more than ever, you should be trying to trick me into thinking that everything's the same as it's always been. Don't disturb the rituals, Padilla. That's right, come closer. They don't want you to.

"Go over to him, so he can see who you are. Tell him your name."

"I am . . . I'm Gloria . . ."

If I could only see her face better. If I could only see her grimace better. She must notice this smell of dead scales; she must be looking at this sunken chest, this gray, messy beard, this fluid running out of my nose, these . . .

They take her away from me.

The doctor checks my pulse.

"I'll have to talk this over with the other doctors on the case."

Catalina brushes my hand with hers. What a useless caress. I can't see her very well, but I try to fix my eyes on hers. I catch her. I hold her frozen hand.

"That morning I waited for him with pleasure. We crossed the river on horseback."

"What's that? Don't try to talk. Don't wear yourself out. I don't understand what you're saying."

"I'd like to go back there, Catalina. How useless."

Yes: the priest kneels next to me. He whispers his words. Padilla plugs in the recorder. I hear my voice, my words. Ay, a shout. Ay, I shout. Ay, I survived. There are two doctors standing in the doorway. I survived. Regina, it hurts, it hurts, Regina, I realize that it hurts. Regina. Soldier. Hug me; it hurts. Someone has stuck a long, cold dagger into my stomach; there is someone, there is someone else who has stuck a blade into my guts: I smell that incense and I'm tired. I let them do as they please. I let them lift me up heavily as I groan. I don't owe my life to you. I can't, I can't, I didn't choose, the pain bends my waist, I touch my frozen feet, I don't want those blue toenails, my new blue toenails, aaaah ayyyy, I survived. What did I do yesterday? If I think about what I did yesterday, I'll stop thinking about what's happening to me now. That's a good idea. Very good. Think yesterday. You aren't so· crazy; you aren't in so much pain; you were able to think that. Yesterday yesterday yesterday. Yesterday Artemio Cruz flew from Hermosillo to Mexico City. Yes. Yesterday Artemio Cruz . . . Before he got sick, yesterday Artemio Cruz . . . No, he didn't get sick. Yesterday Artemio Cruz was in his office and he felt very sick. Not yesterday. This morning. Artemio Cruz. Not sick, no. Not Artemio Cruz, no. Another man. In a mirror hanging across from the sick man's bed. The other man. Artemio Cruz. His twin. Artemio Cruz is sick. The other one. Artemio Cruz is sick. He isn't living. He certainly is living. Artemio Cruz lived. He lived for some years . . . Years he didn't miss, years he didn't. He lived for a few days. His twin. Artemio Cruz. His double. Yesterday Artemio Cruz, the one who only lived a few days before dying, yesterday Artemio Cruz . . . That's me . . . and it's another man . . . Yesterday . . .

Yesterday you did what you do every day. You don't know if it's worthwhile remembering it. You only want to remember, lying back there in the twilight of your bedroom, what's going to happen: you don't want to foresee what has already happened. In your twilight, your eyes see ahead; they don't know how to guess the past. Yes; yesterday you will fly from Hermosillo, yesterday, April 9, 1959, on the Compañía Mexicana de Aviación shuttle, which will depart from the capital of Sonora, where it will be hot as hell, at 9:55 a.m., and will reach Mexico City exactly on time at 4:30 p.m. From your seat on the four-motor plane, you will see a flat, gray city, a belt of adobe and tin roofs. The hostess will offer you a Chiclet wrapped in cellophane—you will remember that in particular because she will be (she has to be, don't think everything in the future tense from now on) a very pretty girl and you will always have a good eye for such things even if your age condemns you to imagine rather than do (you're using words incorrectly: of course, you will never feel condemned to that, even if you can only imagine it). The bright sign NO SMOKING, FASTEN SEAT BELTS will go on just when the plane, entering the Valley of Mexico, abruptly descends, as if it had lost the power to stay aloft in the thin air; then it suddenly leans to the right, and packages, jackets, suitcases will fall and a collective shout will ring out, cut off by a low sob, and the flames will sputter, until the fourth motor on the right wing stops, and everyone goes on shouting and only you stay calm, unmoved, chewing your gum and watching the legs of the hostess, who will run up and down the aisle calming the passengers. The internal fire extinguisher will work and the plane will land with no difficulty, but no one will have realized that only you, an old man of seventy-one, maintained his composure. You will feel proud of yourself, without showing it. You will think that you have done so many cowardly things that it's easy for you to be brave. You will smile and say to yourself no, no, it isn't a paradox: it's the truth and perhaps even a general truth. You will have made the trip to Sonora by car—a 1959 Volvo, license plate DF 712—because some government officials were misbehaving badly and you would have to go all that way just to make sure those people remain loyal, the people you bought—bought, that's right, you will not fool yourself with words from your own annual speeches: I'll convince them, I'll persuade them. No, you'll buy them—and then they'll impose tariffs (another ugly word) on the truckers who carry fish on the Sonora–Sinaloa–Mexico City route. You will give the inspectors ten percent, and because of those middlemen, the fish will be expensive when they reach the city, and your personal profit will be twenty times larger than the original value of the fish. You will try to remember all this, and you will carry out your desire even if all this seems a fit subject for an editorial in your newspaper and you think that, after all, you're wasting your time remembering it. But you will insist, you will go through with it. You will insist. You would like to remember other things, but above all you would like to forget the condition you're in. You will excuse yourself: You're not at home. You will be. They will carry you in a faint to your house, you will collapse in your office; the doctor will come and say that it will take a couple of hours to make the diagnosis. Other doctors will come. They will know nothing and understand nothing.

They will say difficult words. And you will want to imagine yourself. Like an empty, wrinkled wineskin. Your chin will tremble, your breath will be bad, your armpits will smell, everything between your legs will stink. You will be left there, without a bath, without a shave: you will be a storehouse of sweat, irritated nerves, and unconscious physiological functions. But you will insist on remembering what will happen yesterday. You will go from the airport to your office and you will cross a city impregnated with mustard gas because the police will have just broken up a demonstration in Caballito Plaza. You will consult with your editor in chief about the headlines, the editorials, the cartoons, and you will feel satisfied. You will be visited by your U.S. partner, you will point out to him the dangers of these so-called clean-up-the-union movements. Later your administrator, Padilla, will come to your office and tell you that the Indians are agitating and you, through Padilla, will tell the commissioner for communal lands to clamp down on them; after all, that's what you pay him for. You will do a lot of work yesterday morning. The representative of that Latin American benefactor will visit you and you will get the subsidy for your newspaper increased. You will summon your gossip columnist and order her to insert a libel in her column about that Couto who's fighting you in the Sonora business. You will do so many things! And then you will sit down with Padilla to count your assets. That will amuse you a great deal. An entire wall of your office is covered with the diagram of the vast network of businesses you control: the newspaper, the real-estate investments— Mexico City, Puebla, Guadalajara, Monterrey, Culiacán, Hermosillo, Guaymas, Acapulco—the sulphur domes in Jáltipan, the mines in Hidalgo, the logging concessions in Tarahumara, your stock in the chain of hotels, the pipe factory, the fish business, financing of financing, the net of stock operations, the legal representation of U.S. companies, the administration of the railroad loans, the advisory posts in fiduciary institutions, the shares in foreign corporations—dyes, steel, detergents—and one fact that does not appear on the diagram: $15 million deposited in London, New York, and Zurich. You will light a cigarette, despite the doctor's warnings, and you will recite to Padilla the steps that led to this wealth. Short-term loans at high interest to the peasants in the state of Puebla at the end of the Revolution; acquisition of property near the city of Puebla, foreseeing its growth, thanks to the friendly intervention of whichever President happened to be in power at the time; property for subdivisions in Mexico City; acquisition of the metropolitan daily; purchase of mining stocks and the creation of joint Mexican–U.S. corporations in which you were the front man, to comply with the letter of the law; the man on whom U.S. investors depended; intermediary between Chicago, New York, and the Mexican government; manipulation of the bond market to raise or lower prices, sell or buy according to your wish or need; a cozy, tight relationship with President Alemán; acquisition of communal properties stripped from the peasants to create new subdivisions in the cities of the interior; logging concessions. Yes—you will sigh as you ask Padilla for a match—twenty years of confidence, social peace, class collaboration; twenty years of progress after Lázaro Cárdenas's demagoguery; twenty years of protection for the company's interests; twenty years of submissive union leaders and broken strikes. And then you will raise your hands to your stomach, and your head, with its unruly gray hair, will land with a hollow thud on the glass tabletop, and once again, now from up close, you will see that reflection of your sick twin, while all noise pours out of your head, in laughter, and the sweat of all those people envelops you, the flesh of all those people suffocates you, makes you lose consciousness. The reflected twin will join the other, which is you, the old man seventy-one years of age who will lie unconscious between the desk chair and the big metal desk,

and you will be here but not know which facts will get into
your biography and which will be hushed up, hidden. You
will not know. They are vulgar facts and you will not be
the first or only person to possess such a service record.
You will have had a good time. You will have remembered
that. But you will recall other things, other days, you will
have to remember them, too. They are days that, far back,
recent, pushed toward oblivion, etched in memory—meeting and rejection, fleeting love, freedom, anger, failure,
will—were and will be something more than the names you
might give them: days in which your destiny will pursue
you like a bloodhound, will find you, will charge you dearly,
will incarnate you with words and acts, complex, opaque,
adipose matter, woven forever with the other, the impalpable, the substance of your spirit absorbed by matter: a
love of cool quinces, the ambition of growing fingernails,
the tedium of progressive baldness, the melancholy of sun
and desert, the abulia of dirty dishes, the distraction of
tropical rivers, the fear of sabers and gunpowder, the loss
of clean sheets, the youth of black horses, the old age of
an abandoned beach, the discovery of the envelope and the
foreign stamp, the repugnance toward incense, the reaction
to nicotine, the pain of red earth, the tenderness of the
afternoon patio, the spirit of all objects, the matter of all
souls: the sundering of your memory, which separates the
two halves; the solder of life that reunites them once again,
that dissolves them, that pursues them, that finds them.
The fruit has two halves: today they will be united once
again. You will remember the half you left behind: destiny
will find you: you will yawn: no need to remember: you
will yawn: things and their sentiments have frayed, have
fallen in pieces along the road: there, behind, there was a
garden: if you could return to it, if you could find it again
at the end. You will yawn: you haven't moved: you will
yawn: you are on the garden's earth, but the pale branches
deny fruit, the dusty riverbed denies water. You will yawn:

the days will be different, the same, distant current. Soon you will forget need, urgency, surprise. You will yawn: you will open your eyes and see the women there, next to you, with that false solicitude. You will whisper their names: Catalina, Teresa. They will not be able to dissimulate that feeling of being fooled and violated, their irritated disapproval, which will perforce transform itself now into the appearance of concern, affection, grief. The mask of solicitude will be the first sign of that transition your sickness, your appearance, decency, the gaze of another, inherited habit, will impose on them. You will yawn: you will close your eyes: you will yawn: you, Artemio Cruz, him: you will grow in your days with your eyes closed.

(1941: July 6)

He was on his way to the office. The chauffeur drove, and he read the newspaper. Traffic stopped; he raised his eyes. He saw the two ladies enter the shop. Squinting, he watched them, and then the car moved forward, and he went on reading the news about Sidi Barrani and El Alamein, looking at the photos of Rommel and Montgomery. The chauffeur was sweating in the blazing sun and could not turn on the radio to amuse himself; he concluded that going into business with the Colombian coffee growers when the war in Africa began had not been a bad idea, and the ladies walked into the shop and the young woman asked them please to sit down while she went to get the owner (because she knew who the two ladies were, the mother and the daughter, and the owner had ordered her to tell her when they came in). The young woman walked noiselessly on the rug to the back room, where the owner was leaning over her green-leather desk addressing invitations; she dropped the glasses that hung from a silver chain when the young woman walked in to tell her that the lady and her daughter were there. She sighed and said, "Of course, of course, of course, the big day is coming," and she thanked the young woman, neatened her violet-colored hair, pursed her lips, put out her mentholated cigarette. The two women were sitting in the showroom, not saying a word, until the owner appeared, and then the mother, who had strict notions about what was proper, pretended to be in the middle of a conversation which had never begun and said aloud, ". . . but what about that other style that looks much prettier. I don't know about you, but I'd take that one; really, it's very nice, very, very pretty." The young lady nodded in agreement, because she was used to those conversations her mother intended not for her but for the person who was now entering, who extended her hand to the daughter but not to the mother, whom she greeted with an enormous smile, her violet head cocked to one side. The daughter began to move over on the sofa so there would be room for the owner, but the mother stopped her with her eyes and a finger which she shook close to her bosom; the daughter stopped moving and stared pleasantly at the woman with dyed hair, who remained standing and asked if they had decided which style they preferred. The mother said no, not yet, they hadn't made up their minds, that's why they wanted to see all the styles again, because everything else depended on the style they chose, details like the color of the flowers, the bridesmaids' dresses, all that.

"I'm sorry to be such a bother, I wish I . . ."

"But, madam, that's why we're here. It's our pleasure to serve you."

"Well, we just want to be sure."

"But of course."

"We wouldn't want to make a mistake, and then at the last minute . . ."

"You're perfectly right. It's better to choose calmly and carefully, so that later . . ."

"That's right. We want to be sure."

"I'll just tell the girls to get ready."

Since they were alone again, the daughter stretched out her legs; her mother shot her an alarmed gaze and wiggled all her fingers at the same time because she could see her daughter's garters, and she also gestured for her to put some saliva on her left stocking; the daughter looked for and found the place where the silk was split and moistened her index finger with saliva and daubed the spot. "It's just that I'm a little sleepy," she quickly explained to her mother. The lady smiled and patted her daughter's hand as they sat on the pink-brocade sofa, not speaking until the daughter said she was hungry and the mother told her that afterwards they would go to Sanborn's and have something to eat, although she would only watch, she'd been putting on so much weight lately.

"At least you don't have to worry about that."

"Why not?"

"You've still got the figure of a young girl. But later on, be careful. On my side of the family, all the women have good figures when they're young, but after forty they start putting on weight."

"You look fine."

"You don't remember, that's all, you just don't remember. And besides . . ."

"I woke up hungry, and I had a good breakfast."

"Don't worry for now. But later on, watch out."

"Does having a baby make you fat?"

"No, that's not the problem, not at all. A couple of weeks on a diet and you're the same as before. The problem begins after you turn forty."

In the back room, as she got her two models ready, the owner, on her knees, her mouth filled with pins, nervously fluttered her hands and berated the girls for having such short legs. How can women with such short legs ever look good? They should do more exercise, play tennis, go horseback riding, all those things put people in condition, and the girls told her she seemed very annoyed and the owner replied that she was, that those two women got on her nerves. She said the lady would never shake hands with her; the daughter was nicer, but a little absentminded, sitting there like a bump on a log; but, let's face it, they weren't friends of hers and she couldn't say anything, and anyway, as the Americans put it, "the customer is always right," and you've got to walk into the showroom smiling, saying cheese, cheeese, and more cheeeeee. She had to work even if she hadn't been born to work, and she was used to the kind of rich women you see nowadays. Fortunately, on Sundays she could get together with her friends from before, the women she grew up with, and feel she was human at least once a week. They played bridge, she told the girls, and she applauded when she saw they were ready. Too bad about those short legs. She carefully took all the pins out of her mouth and stuck them back into the pincushion.

"Will *he* come to the shower?"

"Who? Your fiancé or your father?"

"Him, Papa."

"How should I know?"

He saw the orange cupola and the fat white columns of the Palacio de Bellas Artes go by, but he looked up higher, where the electric lines came together, came apart, ran—not them, he with his head resting against the gray wool of the seat—parallel or connected to the transformers: the ocher Venetian portal of the Post Office and the leafy sculptures, the full breasts and the emptied cornucopias of the Bank of Mexico. He gently rubbed the silk band on his brown felt hat and jiggled the car's jump seat up and down with his toe; in front of him were the blue mosaics of Sanborn's and the carved blackish stone of the convent of San Francisco. The limousine stopped at the corner of Isabel la Católica, and the chauffeur opened the door, doffing his hat, while he, on the other hand, put on his own, pushing back the strands of hair around his temples which had escaped the hat, as the court of lottery-ticket venders, shoeshine boys, women wrapped in rebozos, and children with snot-encrusted upper lips surrounded him until he passed through the revolving doors and stopped to adjust his tie in front of the vestibule window, and farther along, in the second window, which faced Calle Madero, a man identical to himself, but far away, adjusted the knot of his tie at the same time, with the same nicotine-stained fingers, the same double-breasted suit, but without color, surrounded by beggars, and dropped his hand at the same time that he did and then turned his back on him and walked toward the middle of the street, while he, on the other hand, looked for the elevator, disoriented for an instant.

Once again those outstretched hands depressed her, and she squeezed her daughter's arm to make her walk more quickly into that unreal, hothouse heat, that smell of soaps and cologne and new stationery. She stopped for a moment to look at the beauty products lined up behind the glass and contemplated herself as she narrowed her eyes to peer at the cosmetics arrayed on a strip of red taffeta. She asked for a jar of cold cream ("Theatrical") and two lipsticks of that color, the color of that taffeta, and she tried unsuccessfully to get the right change out of her crocodile bag: "Here, try to find a twenty-peso bill." She picked up her package and her change, and they walked into the restaurant, where they found a table for two. The young lady ordered orange juice and walnut waffles from the waitress dressed in Tehuana costume, and her mother could not resist ordering pound cake with melted butter, and the two of them looked around to see if they knew anyone, and then the young lady asked permission to take off the jacket of her yellow suit because the heat and glare from the skylight were too much for her.

"Joan Crawford," said the daughter. "Joan Crawford."

"No, no. That's not how you say it. Not like that. Cro-for, Cro-for; that's how they say it."

"Crau-for."

"No, no. Cro, cro, cro. The *a* and the *w* come out like an *o*. I think that's how you say it."

"I didn't like the movie very much."

"No, it isn't very good. But she looks wonderful."

"I was really bored."

"But you made such a fuss about going . . ."

"Everybody said it was so good, but it wasn't."

"A way to kill time."

"Cro-ford."

"Yes, I think that's how they say it, Cro-for. I think the *d* is silent."

"Cro-for."

"That's it. Unless I'm mistaken."

The young lady poured syrup over the waffles and cut them into pieces when she was sure every bit would be soaked in syrup. She smiled at her mother each time she filled her mouth with that toasted, syrupy stuff. Her mother did not look at her. One hand played with another, the thumb rubbing the fingertips, seeming to want to pry off the fingernails. She looked at the two hands near her, not wanting to look at the faces: how insistently one hand again took hold of the other and how slowly it explored the other, not missing a single pore. No, they had no rings on their fingers; they must just be going out or something like that. She tried to avert her gaze and concentrate on the puddle of syrup on her daughter's plate, but without wanting to, she went back to the hands of the couple at the next table, successfully avoiding their faces but not their caressing hands. The daughter let her tongue play over her gums, removing bits of waffle and walnut, and then she wiped her lips, staining the napkin red. But before putting on fresh lipstick, she explored for more crumbs and asked her mother for a taste of pound cake. She said she didn't want coffee, it made her so nervous, even if she loved coffee, but not now, she was quite nervous as it was. The lady patted her hand and told her they ought to be going, they had lots to do. She paid the bill, left a tip, and the two women got up.

The American explained how they inject boiling water into the deposits, how the water dissolves them, and the sulphur is brought to the surface by compressed air. He explained the system again, and the other American said they were very pleased with their findings and sliced the air several times with his hand, shaking it quite close to his leathery red face and repeating in Spanish: "Domes good; pyrites bad. Domes good; pyrites bad. Domes good . . ." He drummed his fingers on the glass top of the table and nodded, accustomed to the fact that whenever they spoke to him in Spanish they thought he didn't understand, not because they spoke Spanish badly but because he didn't understand anything well. "Pyrites bad." He removed his elbows from the table as the engineer rolled out the map of the zone. The other man explained that the zone was so rich they could go on mining it at full capacity until well into the twenty-first century; at full capacity, until they exhausted the deposits; at full capacity. He repeated that seven times and then withdrew the fist he'd let fall at the beginning of his sermon right on the green area dotted with triangles that marked the geologist's discoveries. The American winked and said that the cedar and mahogany forests were also enormous and all the profits from that would go—one hundred percent—to the Mexican partner; they, the American partners, would not meddle in his business, although they did advise him to reforest continuously; they had seen forests destroyed everywhere: didn't people realize that those trees were worth money? But that was his affair, because with or without the forests the sulphur domes were there. He smiled and stood up. He stuck his thumbs between his belt and his trousers and seesawed his

unlit cigar between his lips until one of the Americans got
up with a lighted match in his hands. The American brought
the match to the cigar, and he made the man hold it there
until the cigar tip was glowing brightly. He demanded a
payment of $2 million, and they asked him why. After all,
they were happy to bring him in as a full partner for only
three hundred thousand, but no one was going to make a
penny until the investment started to produce. The geologist cleaned his glasses with a small piece of chamois he
kept in his shirt pocket, while the other began to walk from
the table to the window and from the window to the table,
until he repeated that those were his conditions. The $2
million was not an advance or credit or anything like that:
that was how much they owed him for getting the concession for them; without the payment, it might be impossible
to get the concession; over time they would earn back what
they would be giving him now; but without him, without
the front man, as he said in English, apologizing for his
frankness, they would never get the concession to work
those deposits. He pushed a button to call his secretary
and the secretary rapidly read a sheet of figures and the
Americans said okay several times, okay, okay, okay, and
he smiled and offered them whiskey and told them that
they could exploit those sulphur deposits until well into
the next century but that they weren't going to exploit him
for one minute during this one, and they all toasted and
the two Americans smiled as they muttered—just once—
son of a bitch under their breath.

The two ladies strolled arm in arm. They walked slowly
with their heads down and stopped in front of every store
window to say how pretty, how expensive, there's a better
one up the street, look at that one, how nice, until they
got tired and walked into a café, where they picked out a
good table, away from the entrance, where the lottery-
ticket venders peered in and the dry, thick dust swirled,
and far from the lavatories, and they ordered two Canada

Dry orangeades. The mother powdered her face and stared at her amber eyes in the compact mirror, contemplating the progress of the bags that had begun to appear under them, and quickly snapped the cover shut. The two of them observed the bubbling of the soda water mixed with food coloring and waited for the gas to escape before drinking it in little sips. The girl secretly slipped her foot out of her shoe and rubbed her sore toes, and the lady, seated before her orange drink, recalled the separate rooms of the house, separate but contiguous, and the noises that managed to pass through the closed door each morning and each night: someone clearing his throat, shoes falling on the floor, the sound of keys landing on the mantel, the hinges on the closet door that needed oiling, at times even the rhythm of someone's breathing while asleep. A chill ran down her spine. She had gone to the closed door that very morning, walking on tiptoe, and had felt a chill run down her spine. It surprised her to think that all those insignificant, normal sounds were also secret sounds. She had gone back to bed, wrapped herself in the covers, and fixed her eyes on the ceiling, where a fan of round, fleeting lights was spreading: the sparkles created by the shadow of the chestnut tree. She had drunk what remained of her now cold tea and slept until the maid awakened her and reminded her that they had a day full of chores ahead of them. And only now, with that cold glass in her hand, did she remember those first hours of the day.

He leaned back in his desk chair until the screws creaked and asked his secretary: "Is there a single bank that would take such a risk? Is there a single Mexican who believes in me?" He picked up his yellow pencil and pointed it into his secretary's face: let him make a note of it; let him, Padilla, be a witness: no one would take a chance and he was not going to let that wealth rot in the jungle down south; if the gringos were the only ones willing to finance the explorations, what was he supposed to do? The secretary reminded him what time it was, and he sighed and said enough for today. He invited his secretary to lunch. They could eat together. Did he know any new places? The secretary said he did, a new place that specialized in appetizers, very pleasant, very good *quesadillas*—cheese, *flor, huitlacoche*; it was right around the corner. They could go together. He felt tired; he didn't want to go back to the office that afternoon. In point of fact, they ought to be celebrating. Why not? Besides, they had never eaten together. They went out together in silence and walked toward Avenida Cinco de Mayo.

"You're still a very young man. How old are you?"

"Twenty-seven."

"When did you get your degree?"

"Three years ago. But . . ."

"But what?"

"Theory is very different from practice."

"And that makes you laugh? What did they teach you at the university?"

"Lots of Marxism. I even wrote my thesis on surplus value."

"The discipline must be good for you, Padilla."

"But the real world is very different."

"Is that what you are, a Marxist?"

"Well, all my friends were. It was a kind of phase we all went through back then."

"Where is this restaurant?"

"We're almost there, just around the corner."

"I don't like walking."

"It's right over there."

They divided up the packages and walked toward Bellas Artes, where they were to meet the chauffeur. With averted eyes, they walked on, glancing occasionally at the shop windows, attracted as though by antennas. Suddenly the mother clutched the daughter's arm and dropped a package: directly in front of them, two dogs were growling in frozen rage; they pulled apart, they growled, they bit each other's necks until they bled, they ran into the street, they started to fight again, with sharp bites and growls— two street dogs, mangy, foaming at the mouth, a male and a female. The young lady picked up the package and led her mother to the parking lot. They got into the car, and the chauffeur asked if they were going back to Las Lomas, and the daughter said yes, that some dogs had frightened her mother. The lady said it was nothing, she felt fine now: it was all so unexpected and so close to her, but they would come back that afternoon, because they still had lots of shopping to do, lots more shops to visit. The young lady said they still had time, more than a month. Yes, but time flies, said the mother, and your father isn't doing a thing about the wedding, he's leaving all the work to us. In any case, you just have to learn something about social differences, you can't shake hands with everyone you meet. Besides, I want to get this wedding business over with, because I think it'll make your father realize that he's finally reached a certain age. At least it should teach him that. He doesn't seem to understand that he's fifty-two years old. I hope you have children right away. Anyway, it'll be a good lesson for your father to have to sit next to me both during the civil ceremony and during the religious marriage, hear people congratulate him, and see that everyone treats him like a respectable middle-aged man. Maybe all that will have an effect on him, maybe.

I feel that hand touching me and I would like to pull away from it, but I don't have the strength. What useless affection, Catalina. How useless. What can you say to me? Do you think you've finally found the words you never dared to say? Today? How useless. Just keep quiet. Don't allow yourself the luxury of an empty explanation. Be true to the façade you always put on; be true right to the end. Look:

learn from your daughter. Teresa. Our daughter. How hard
it is. What a useless word. Ours. She doesn't pretend.
Before, when I couldn't hear, she probably said to you: "I
hope it's all over soon. Because he's perfectly capable of
pretending to be sick just so he can make our lives miserable." She must have said something like that to you. I
heard something like that when I woke up this morning
from that long, peaceful sleep. I vaguely remember the
drug, the tranquilizer they gave me last night. And you
probably said: "Oh, Lord, I hope he doesn't suffer too
much." You would have wanted to give your daughter's
words a different shade of meaning. And you don't know
what shade of meaning to give the words I whisper:

"That morning I waited for him happily. We crossed the
river on horseback."

Ah, Padilla, come closer. Did you bring the tape recorder? If you knew what's good for you, you'd have brought
it here the way you brought it to my house in Coyoacán
every night. Today, more than ever, you should try to trick
me into thinking that everything's the same. Don't disturb
the rituals, Padilla. That's right, come closer. They don't
want you to.

"No, counselor, we can't permit it."

"It's something we've been doing for years now, ma'am."

"Can't you see how he is by the look on his face?"

"Let me try. Everything's ready. All I have to do is plug
the tape recorder in."

"As long as you take full responsibility . . ."

"Don Artemio . . . Don Artemio . . . I've brought the
recorder this morning . . ."

I nod. I try to smile. Like every other day. A man you
can count on, this Padilla. Of course he deserves my trust.
Of course he deserves a good part of my estate and the
administration of all my property in perpetuity. Who, if
not him? He knows everything. Ah, Padilla. Are you still

storing all the tapes of my conversations in the office? Ah, Padilla, you know everything. I have to pay you well. I'm leaving you my reputation.

Teresa is sitting with the paper open so that it hides her face.

I can feel him coming, with that smell of incense, with his black skirts, with that hyssop out in front, to bid me a farewell that has all the rigor of an admonition; ha, I fooled them; and there's Teresa sniveling over there, and now she takes her compact out of her handbag to powder her nose, so she can start sniveling again. I picture myself at the last moment, the coffin falls into the hole and a multitude of women snivel and powder their noses over my grave. All right; I feel better. I'd feel fine if this stink, my own, didn't rise out of the folds in the sheets, if I couldn't see those ridiculous stains I've put on them . . . Am I really breathing with this spasmodic hoarseness? Is this how I am to receive that black blur and face up to his office? Aaaah. Aaaah. I have to control my breathing . . . I clench my fists, aaah, my facial muscles, and I have that flour-colored face next to me who's come to check the details on the statement that tomorrow or the day after—or never?—will appear in all the newspapers: "With the last rites of the Holy Mother Church . . ." And he brings his clean-shaven face up to my cheeks boiling with gray whiskers. He makes the sign of the cross. He whispers, "Bless me, Father, for I have sinned," and I can only turn my head and grunt while my head fills with all the images I'd like to throw in his face: the night when that poor, filthy carpenter had the pleasure of mounting the shocked virgin who had believed the stories and lies her family told her, who had held white doves between her thighs, thinking that way she'd have a child, the doves hidden between her legs, in the garden, under her skirts, and now the carpenter was mounting her, full of a justified desire, because she must have been very pretty, and he was mounting her, while the intolerable

Teresa's indignant sniveling grows, that pale woman who gleefully desires my final rebelliousness, the motive behind her own final indignation. It's incredible seeing them sitting there, not moving a muscle, no recriminations. How long will it last? I don't feel that bad now. Maybe I'll get better. What a blow! Don't you think? I'll try to put on a good face to see if you can take advantage of it and forget those gestures of forced affection and finally unburden yourselves of the arguments and insults you've got stuck in your throats, in your eyes, in that unattractive humanity which the two of them have become. Bad circulation, that's what it is, nothing more serious than that. Bah. I'm bored just watching them. There should be something more interesting set before half-closed eyes that are seeing for the last time. Ah. They brought me to this house, not to the other. What do you know about that. Such discretion. I'll have to tell Padilla off for the last time. Padilla knows which is my real house. There I could enjoy myself looking at the things I love so much. I would be opening my eyes to gaze at a ceiling of old, burnished beams; right at hand I'd have the gold chasuble that adorns the head of my bed, the candelabrum on my night table, the velvet chair backs, my Bohemian crystal. I'd have Serafín smoking near me, I'd be breathing in that smoke. And she would be dressed up, just the way I've ordered. Beautifully dressed, with no tears, no black rags. There I wouldn't feel so old and worn out. Everything would be arranged to remind me that I am a man who lives, a man who loves, the same as the same as the same as before. Why are these ugly old bitches sitting there like that, just so the phony slobs can remind me that I'm not what I once was? Everything is ready. There in my house everything is ready. They know what to do in situations like this. They keep me from remembering. They tell me that I *am, now*, never that I was. No one tries to explain anything until it's too late. Bah. How can I have any fun here? Of course, I see now that they've set everything up

to make me believe that I come to this bedroom every night
and sleep here. I see that closet with the partly open door,
and I see the outlines of sports jackets I've never worn,
ties without wrinkles, new shoes. I see a desk where they've
piled up unread books, unsigned papers. And this elegant,
disgusting furniture: when did they pull off the dusty
sheets? Ah . . . I see a window. There is a world outside.
A strong wind is blowing, a wind from the plateau that
shakes the thin black trees. I have to breathe.

"Open the window . . ."

"No, no. You might catch cold and make things worse."

"Teresa, your father isn't listening to you . . ."

"He's just faking. He closes his eyes and just fakes."

"Keep quiet."

"Keep quiet."

They will keep quiet. They walk away from the head-
board. I keep my eyes closed. I remember that I went out
to eat with Padilla that afternoon. I've already remembered
that. I beat them at their own game. All this stinks, but at
least it's warm. My body creates warmth. Heat for the
sheets. I beat a lot of them. I beat all of them. That's right,
the blood is flowing nicely through my veins; soon I'll be
better. That's right. It flows warm. It still gives off heat. I
forgive them. They haven't hurt me. It's all right, let them
say or tell what they like. It doesn't matter. I forgive them.
How warm. Soon I'll be better. Ah.

You must feel proud that you could impose your will on
them. Confess it: you imposed yourself so they would let
you in as their equal. You've rarely felt happier, because
from the time you began to be what you are, from the time
you learned to appreciate the feel of fine cloth, the taste
of fine liquors, the scent of fine lotions, all those things that
for the past few years have been your isolated and only
pleasure, from that time on you turned your eyes northward
and lived with the regret that a geographical error kept you

from being part of them in everything. You admire their efficiency, their comforts, their hygiene, their power, their will, and you look around you and the incompetence, the misery, the filth, the languor, the nakedness of this poor country that has nothing, all seem intolerable to you. And what pains you even more is knowing that no matter how much you try, you cannot be like them, you can only be a copy, an approximation, because after all, say it now: was your vision of things, in your worst or your best moments, ever as simplistic as theirs? Never. Never have you been able to think in black and white, good guys versus bad guys, God or the Devil: admit that always, even when it seemed just the opposite, you've found the germ, the reflection of the white in the black. Your own cruelty, when you've been cruel, hasn't it always been tinged with a certain tenderness? You know that all extremes contain their opposites: cruelty and tenderness, cowardice and bravery; life, death. In some way—almost unconsciously, because of who you are, because of where you've come from, because of what you've lived through—you know this, and for that reason you can never resemble them who don't know these things. Does that bother you? Of course it does, it's uncomfortable, annoying. It's much easier to say: this is good and that is evil. Evil. You could never say, "That is evil." Perhaps because we are more forsaken, we do not want to lose that intermediate, ambiguous zone between light and shadow, that zone where we can find forgiveness. Where you may be able to find it. Isn't everyone, in a single moment of his life, capable of embodying—as you do—good and evil at the same time, letting himself be simultaneously led by two mysterious, different-colored threads that unwind from the same spool, so that the white thread ascends and the black one descends and, despite everything, the two come together again in his very fingers? You won't want to think about all that. You will detest me for reminding you of it. You would like to be like them, and now, an old man, you almost achieve that goal. Almost. Only almost. You yourself will block oblivion; your bravery will be the twin of your cowardice, your hatred will have been born from your love, all your life will have contained and promised your death. Therefore, you will not have been either good or evil, generous or selfish, faithful or a traitor. You will let the others affirm your good qualities and your faults; but you yourself, how will you deny that each of your affirmations will be negated, that each of your negations will be affirmed? No one will know about it, except perhaps you. That your existence will be woven of all the threads on the loom, like the lives of all men. That you will have neither too few nor too many chances to make of your life what you wish it to be. And if you become one thing and not another, it will be because, despite it all, you will have to choose. Your choices will not negate the rest of your possible life, all that you will leave behind each time you choose: they will only hone it, hone it to the point that today your choice and your destiny will be one and the same. The coin will no longer have two sides: your desire will be identical with your destiny. Will you die? It won't be the first time. You will have lived so much dead life, so many moments of mere gesticulation. When Catalina puts her ear to the door that separates you and listens to your movements; when you, on the other side of the door, move without knowing you're being listened to, without knowing that someone lives dependent on the sounds and silences of your life behind the door, who will live in that separation? When both of you realize one single word would be enough and yet you keep silent, who will live in that silence? No, you won't want to remember that. You'd like to recall something else; that name, that face the passage of time will wear away. But you will know that if you remember these things, you will save yourself, you will save yourself too easily. You will first remember the things that condemn you, and having been saved there, you will find out that the other, what you think will save you, will be your real condemnation: remembering what you want. You will remember Catalina when she was young, when you met her, and you will compare her with the faded woman of today. You will remember and remember why. You will incarnate what she, and all of them, thought then. You won't know it. You will have to incarnate it. You will never listen to what others say. You will have to live what they say. You will shut your eyes: you will shut them. You will not smell that incense. You will not listen to that weeping. You will remember other things, other days. Days that will reach you at night— your night of eyes shut. You will only recognize them by their voice, never by sight. You will have to give credit to the night and accept it without seeing it, believe it without recognizing it, as if it were the God of all your days: the night. Now you must be thinking that all you'll have to do to have it is to close your eyes. You will smile, despite the pain that reasserts itself. You will try to stretch your legs a little. Someone will touch your hand, but you will not respond to that—what? caress? care? anguish? calculated move? Because you will have created the night with your closed eyes, and from the depth of that ocean of ink, a stone boat—which the hot and sleepy midday sun will cheer in vain—will sail toward you: thick blackened walls raised to protect the Church from Indian attacks and also to link the religious conquest to the military conquest. The rough soldiers, Spanish, the troops of Queen Isabella the Catholic, advance toward your closed eyes with the swelling din of their fifes and drums, and in sunlight you will traverse the wide esplanade with a stone cross at its center and with exterior chapels, the prolongation of the native religion, theatrical and open-air, at its corners. At the top of the church built at the end of the esplanade, the vaults made of *tezontle* stone will rest on forgotten Moorish scimitars, sign of yet one more bloodline imposed on that of the conquistadors. You will advance toward the portal of the early, still Castilian, baroque, already rich in columns wound with profuse vines and aquiline keystones; the portal of the Conquest, severe and playful, with one foot in the old, dead world and the other in the new world that didn't begin here but on the other side of the sea: the new world arrived with them, with a redoubt of austere walls to protect their sensual, happy, greedy hearts. You will go further and will penetrate into the nave of the ship, its Castilian exterior conquered by the macabre, smiling plenitude of this Indian heaven of saints, angels, and indigenous gods. A single, enormous nave will run toward the altar of gilt foliage, somber opulence of masked faces, lugubrious and festive prayer, always urgent, for this freedom, the only one granted, to decorate a temple and fill it with tranquil astonishment, with sculpted resignation, with the horror of emptiness, the terror of the dead times, of those who prolonged the slow deliberateness of free labor, the unique instants of autonomy in color and form, far from that exterior world of whips and branding irons and smallpox. You will walk to the conquest of your new world through a nave devoid of blank spaces: angel heads, luxuriant vines, polychrome flowers, red, round fruits captured in trellises of gold, white saints in chains, saints with astonished faces, saints in a heaven invented by Indians in their own image and likeness: angels and saints wearing the face of the sun and the moon, with the hand to protect harvests, with the index finger of the hounds, with the cruel, unnecessary, alien eyes of the idol, with the rigorous face of the cycles. The faces of stone behind the pink, kindly, ingenuous masks, masks that are, however, impassive and dead: create the night, fill the black sails with wind, close your eyes, Artemio Cruz . . .

(1919: May 20)

His story of Gonzalo Bernal's final moments in the Perales prison opened the doors of the house to him.

"He was always so pure," said Don Gamaliel Bernal, Gonzalo's father. "He always thought that, unless clear thinking determines it, action contaminates us and leads us to betray ourselves. I think that's why he left this house. Well, I believe it in part, because this hurricane swept everyone away, even those of us who never left home. No, what I'm trying to say is that, for my son, moral obligation meant participating in order to explain, to offer coherent ideas, yes, I think he participated to keep this cause from caving in under the test of action, the way all the others have. I don't know, his ideas were very complicated. He preached tolerance. I'm happy to know he died bravely. I'm happy to see you here."

He hadn't simply walked in one day to visit the old man. Beforehand, he had made inquiries in several Puebla towns, spoken with several people, found out what he had to find out. For that reason, he could now listen to the old man's worn-out arguments without blinking an eye, as the old man leaned his head against the polished leather of his chair back, turning his profile into the yellowish light that held the thick dust suffusing the air of the enclosed library. The shelves were so high that Don Gamaliel used a ladder on wheels, which over time had scratched the ocher floors, to reach the tall, thick volumes, French and English texts on geography, fine arts, and natural sciences. To read them, Don Gamaliel had to use a magnifying glass, the one he now held motionless in his silky hands, not noticing that the oblique light passed through the glass and concentrated, burning into the crease of his striped, carefully pressed trousers. Artemio Cruz, on the other hand, did notice it. An uncomfortable silence separated them.

"Please forgive me. May I offer you something? Better yet: stay for dinner."

He opened his hands in a sign of invitation and pleasure, and the magnifying glass fell on the lap of this thin man with flesh stretched over brittle bones, with skull, jowls, and lips spotted with the yellow marks of age.

"I'm not shocked at what's happening," he'd said before, his voice always precise and courteous, sonorous when within those terms, otherwise flat. "What use would all my reading have been to me"—he gestured with the reading glass toward the shelves of books—"if it didn't teach me to understand the inevitability of change? Things change their appearance, whether we like it or not. Why should we stubbornly refuse to see them or long for the past? How much less tiresome it is to accept the unforeseeable! Or should I call it something else? You, Mr. . . . excuse me, I've forgotten your rank . . . yes, Lieutenant Colonel, Lieutenant Colonel . . . I mean, I don't know where you're from, what your profession is . . . I esteem you because you shared my son's final hours . . . Well, you did act, but could you foresee everything? I didn't act and I couldn't either. Perhaps our action and our passivity converge in that, in that both are quite blind and impotent. Although there certainly is a difference . . . don't you think? Ah, well . . ."

He never lost sight of the old man's amber eyes, which were all too intent on creating an atmosphere of cordiality, too self-confident behind that mask of paternal sweetness. Perhaps those aristocratic hand movements, that fixed nobility of his profile, his bearded chin, that attentive cocking of his head, were all natural to him. He thought that even naturalness can be feigned; at times, a mask disguises too well the expressions of a face that does not exist either outside or under it. And Don Gamaliel's mask looked so much like his real face that it was disconcerting to think about the dividing line, the impalpable shadow that might

separate them. He thought all this, and also that one day
he might be able to say it right to the old man's face.

All the clocks in the house chimed at the same instant,
and the old man stood up to light the acetylene lamp on
the rolltop desk. He slowly pushed the top back and fum-
bled through some papers. He picked one up and half
turned toward his visitor's armchair. He smiled, furrowed
his brow, and smiled again as he deposited the paper on
top of the others. Gracefully he raised his index finger to
his ear: a dog was barking and scratching on the other side
of the door.

He took advantage of the fact that the old man had turned
his back toward him to scrutinize him secretly. Not one of
Don Gamaliel's character traits broke the harmonious nobility of his full-length portrait. Seen from the rear, he
walked elegantly, bolt-upright; longish white hair crowned
the old man walking toward the door. Gamaliel Bernal was
troubling—he grew nervous as he thought about it again—
because he was too perfect. It was possible that his courtesy
was nothing more than a natural complement to his naïveté.
The thought annoyed him. The old man made his slow way
to the door; the dog was barking: the fight would be too
easy, could not be savored. But suppose the friendliness
was merely a mask for the old man's cunning?

When the tails of his frock coat stopped swinging and his
white hand had grasped the copper doorknob, Don Gamaliel looked at him over his shoulder with those amber eyes.
His free hand stroked his beard. His look seemed to read
his unknown visitor's thoughts, and his slightly twisted
smile recalled that of a magician about to complete a totally
new trick. If in the old man's gesture the unknown visitor
could understand and accept an invitation to silent complicity, Don Gamaliel's movement was so elegant, so artful,
that he never gave his accomplice the chance to return the
look and seal the tacit agreement.

Night had fallen and the uncertain light of the lamp barely

revealed the golden spines of the books and the silver trim-
ming of the wallpaper that covered the library walls. He
remembered, from when the door of the house had been
opened to him, a long string of rooms that came into view
beyond the old Puebla mansion's main vestibule and went
all the way to the library, with room after room opening
onto the patio with its majolica and its tiles. The mastiff
jumped for joy and licked his master's hand. Behind the
dog appeared the girl dressed in white, a white that contrasted with the crepuscular light stretching out behind her.

She stopped for a second at the threshold, while the dog
leapt toward the unknown man and sniffed at his feet and
hands. Don Gonzalo laughed, took the dog by his red collar,
and muttered a vague excuse. His visitor didn't understand
it. He stood up, buttoning his jacket with the precise movements of military life, straightening it as if he were still
wearing a uniform; he remained still before the beauty of
this young woman, who had not yet passed through the
doorway.

"My daughter, Catalina."

She did not move. The long, smooth chestnut hair that
cascaded down her long, warm neck (even at that distance,
he could see the luster of her nape), her eyes, simultaneously hard and liquid, with a trembling stare, two glass
bubbles: amber like those of her father but franker, less
accustomed to feigning with naturalness, reproduced in the
other dualities of that slim but well-rounded body, in her
moist, slightly parted lips, in her high, taut breasts. Eyes,
lips, hard, smooth breasts alternated between helplessness
and rage. She held her hands together over her thighs and
her narrow waist as she walked, fluttering the white muslin
of her dress, cut full around her solid hips and buttoned
down the back, ending near her thin calves. Toward him
walked a flesh of pale gold, which even now revealed the
faded chiaroscuro of the entire body in its forehead and
cheeks, and she held out her hand, in whose touch he

sought, without finding it, the moisture that would have revealed her emotion.

"He was with your brother during his final hours. I spoke about him to you."

"You were fortunate, sir."

"He told me about the two of you, asked me to visit you. He was a brave man, to the very end."

"He wasn't brave. It's just that he loved all . . . this too much."

She touched her bosom and then quickly withdrew her hand to trace an arc in the air.

"An idealist, yes, very much an idealist," murmured the old man, sighing. "The gentleman will dine with us."

The girl took her father's arm, and he, with the mastiff alongside, followed them through the narrow, damp rooms crammed with porcelain vases and stools, clocks and display cabinets, waxed furniture and large religious paintings of little value. The gilt feet of the chairs and the side tables rested on painted wooden floors devoid of rugs, and the lamps remained unlit. Only in the dining room a grand cut-glass chandelier illuminated the heavy mahogany table and sideboards and a cracked still life in which the pottery and brilliant fruit of the tropics glowed. Don Gamaliel shooed away the mosquitoes flying around the real fruit bowl, less abundant than the one in the painting. Pointing a finger, he invited him to sit down.

Sitting opposite her, he could finally stare directly into the girl's unmoving eyes. Did she know why he was visiting? Did she see in the look in his eyes that sense of triumph, made complete by the woman's physical presence? Could she detect the slight smile of luck and self-assurance? Did she feel his barely disguised intention to possess her? Her eyes expressed only that strange message of hard fatality, seeming to show that she was ready to accept everything but that she would nevertheless transform her acceptance into an opportunity to triumph over

the man who in this silent and smiling way had begun to
make her his own.

She was surprised at the strength with which she suc-
cumbed, the power of her weakness. Immodestly, she
raised her eyes to observe the strong features of the
stranger. She couldn't avoid a clash with his green eyes.
He was not good-looking, certainly not handsome. But the
olive skin of his face, which lent his entire body the same
linear, sinuous energy as his thick lips and the prominent
nerves in his temples, promised something desirable to the
touch, because unknown. Under the table, he stretched
out his foot until he touched the tip of her feminine slipper.
The girl lowered her eyelids, looked at her father out of
the corner of her eye, and moved her foot back. The perfect
host smiled with his usual benevolence, running his fingers
over his glass.

The entrance of the old Indian maid with the rice broke
the silence, and Don Gamaliel observed that the dry season
was ending a bit late this year. Fortunately, the clouds had
begun to gather over the mountains, and the harvest would
be good—not as good as last year, but good. It was odd,
he said, how this old house was always damp, a dampness
that stained the shadowed corners and nurtured the fern
and the bright colors in the patio. It was, perhaps, a good
omen for a family that grew and prospered thanks to the
fruit of the land: established in the valley of Puebla—he
was eating the rice, gathering it on his fork with precise
movements—since the beginning of the nineteenth century
and stronger, true enough, than all the absurd vicissitudes
of a country incapable of tranquillity, enamored of convulsion.

"Sometimes I think the absence of blood and death
throws us into despair. It's as if we feel alive only when
we're surrounded by destruction and executions," the old
man went on in his cordial voice. "But we shall go on, go
on forever, because we have learned to survive, always . . ."

He picked up his guest's glass and filled it with full-bodied wine.

"But there is a price to be paid for surviving," said the guest dryly.

"It's always possible to negotiate the most convenient price . . ."

As he filled his daughter's glass, Don Gamaliel caressed her hand. "It's the finesse with which the negotiations are carried out that matters most. There is no need to frighten anyone, no need to wound sensitive souls . . . Honor should be kept intact."

He felt again for the girl's foot. This time she did not pull her foot back. She raised her glass and stared at the unknown guest without blushing.

"It's important to know how to make distinctions," murmured the old man as he wiped his lips with his napkin. "For example, business is one thing, and religion is something completely different."

"See him there so nice and pious, taking Communion every day with his little girl? Well, that same man stole everything he has from the priests, back when Juárez auctioned off Church property and anybody with a little cash could buy huge tracts of land . . ."

He had spent six days in Puebla before visiting Don Gamaliel Bernal's house. President Carranza had disbanded the troops, and it was then he remembered his conversation with Gonzalo Bernal in Perales and set out on the road to Puebla: a matter of pure instinct, but also the confidence which says that knowing a name, an address, a city in the shattered, chaotic world left by the Revolution is to know a lot. The irony that he should be the one returning to Puebla and not the executed Bernal amused him. It was in a way a masquerade, a sleight-of-hand, a joke that could be played with the greatest seriousness; but it was also proof of being alive, of a capacity to survive and strengthen one's own destiny at the expense of others.

When he reached Puebla, when, from the Cholula road, he could make out, scattered over the valley, the red-and-yellow mushrooms that were the church domes, he was entering doubled, with Gonzalo Bernal's life added to his own, with the destiny of the dead man added onto his, as if Bernal in dying had delegated the possibilities of his unfulfilled life to him. Perhaps the death of others prolongs our life, he thought. But he hadn't come to Puebla to think.

"This year he hasn't even been able to buy seed. His debts have been piling up since last year, when the peasants went in for rebelling and planted the fallow land. They told him that if he didn't give them the land that wasn't being planted, they wouldn't work the land that was. And out of sheer pride he refused, so he was left with no harvest. Before, the Rural Guard would have put the rebels in their place, but now . . . well, another day has dawned.

"And not only that. Even the people who owe him money are getting out of hand. They don't want to pay him another cent. They say that with all the interest he's already charged them they've paid more than enough. See now, Colonel? They all believe things are going to change.

"Ah, but the old man is as stubborn as ever, won't give an inch. He'd rather die than give up whatever it is someone owes him."

He lost the last round of dice and shrugged. He gestured to the bartender for drinks all around, and they all thanked him.

"Who owes money to this Don Gamaliel, then?"

"Well . . . It would be easier to tell you who doesn't, I think."

"Is he friendly with anyone around here? Is there someone he's close to?"

"Sure. Father Páez, right around the corner."

"But didn't he buy all the Church land?"

"Sure . . . but the Father grants eternal salvation to Don

Gamaliel and Don Gamaliel grants salvation on earth to the Father."

The sun blinded them as they stepped into the street.

"Blood will tell, they say. And that gal's sure got good blood."

"Who is that woman?"

"Can't you guess, Colonel? That's our hero's little girl."

Staring at the toes of her shoes, she walked along the old streets laid out like a chessboard. When he could no longer hear the echo of her heels on the paving stones and his steps had raised a cloud of dry, gray dust, he looked toward the walls of the ancient fortress-temple and the almond-shaped stones in its battlements. He crossed the wide esplanade and entered the silent nave. Once again, the footsteps echoed. He walked toward the altar.

The priest was rotund, his skin lifeless; only his coal-black eyes, set deep in his inflamed cheekbones, glowed with life. As soon as he saw the unknown man walking the length of the nave—and he spied on him, hidden behind a large screen, in ancient times a choir for the nuns, who later fled Mexico City, during the liberal Republic—the priest recognized in his movements the unconsciously martial air of a man accustomed to being on guard, accustomed to command and to attack. It was not just the ever so slight deformity of the horseman's lower legs; it was a certain nervous strength in his fist that came from daily contact with pistol and bridle. Even though the man was merely walking with his fist clenched, this was enough for Páez to recognize in him a disturbing power. Up in the nuns' secret place, he concluded that such a man was not there for devotional purposes. He lifted the hem of his cassock and slowly walked down the spiral staircase that led to the abandoned convent. Hem held high, shoulders raised until they almost reached his ears, body black and face white and bloodless, eyes penetrating, he descended with careful

steps. The stairs urgently needed repair; his predecessor
had stumbled in 1910, with fatal consequences. But Remigio Páez, looking like a puffed-up bat, could pierce all
the dark corners of the black, humid, frightening cube. The
darkness and the danger aroused all his senses and made
him reflect: a military man in his church, dressed in civilian
clothes, with no company or escort? Such a sight was too
strange to pass unnoticed. He had, of course, foreseen it.
The battles, the violence, the sacrilege, all of it would pass
(he thought about the order, given barely two years before,
that did away with all the chasubles and all the sacred
vessels), and the Church, everlasting, built to endure eternally, would come to an understanding with the powers of
the earthly city. A military man in civilian clothes . . . with
no escort . . .

Down he came, one hand on the swollen wall, through
which a dark line seeped. The priest recalled that the rainy
season would soon begin. He had already taken it upon
himself, with all his powers, to point it out from the pulpit
and in each confession that he heard: it is a sin, a grave sin
against the Holy Spirit, to refuse to receive the gifts of
heaven; no one can plot against the intentions of Providence, and Providence has ordered things as they are, and
thus people should accept all things; everyone should go
out and work the fields, bring in the crops, deliver the
fruits of the earth to their legitimate owner, a Christian
owner who pays for the obligations of his privilege by
punctually delivering his tithes to Holy Mother Church.
God punishes rebellion, and Lucifer is overwhelmed by
the Archangels Raphael, Gabriel, Michael, Galaliel . . .
Gamaliel.

"And justice, Father?"

"Final justice will be meted out above, my son. Do not
seek it in this vale of tears."

Words, murmured the priest when he rested at last on
the solid floor, shaking the dust off his cassock; words,

miserable strings of syllables that fire the blood and the illusions of those who should be content to pass quickly through this short life and enjoy, in exchange for their mortal trials, eternal life. He crossed the cloister and walked toward a vaulted corridor. Justice! For whom? For how long? Life could be so agreeable for everyone if everyone understood the finality of their destiny and did not go about digging into things, stirring things up, desiring more . . .

"Yes, I believe so; yes, I believe so . . ." repeated the priest in a low voice, and he opened the carved door of the sacristy.

"Admirable work, isn't it?" he said as he approached the tall man standing before the altar. "The monks showed prints and engravings to the native artisans and they turned their own style into Christian forms . . . They say there is an idol hidden behind every altar. If that's so, it must be a good idol, because it no longer demands blood, as the pagan gods did . . ."

"Are you Páez?"

"Remigio Páez," he said with a twisted smile. "And you, General, Colonel, Major . . . ?"

"Just plain Artemio Cruz."

"Ah."

When the lieutenant colonel and the priest said goodbye at the portals of the church, Páez folded his hands over his stomach and watched his visitor walk away. The clear blue morning sharpened and seemed to draw closer the lines of the two volcanoes: the couple consisting of the sleeping woman and her solitary guardian. He squinted: he couldn't stand that bright light. He gave thanks as he observed the black clouds that would soon moisten the valley and extinguish the sun, as they did every afternoon with a punctual gray storm.

He turned his back on the valley and returned to the shade of the convent. He rubbed his hands. The haughtiness and the insults of this upstart did not matter to him. If that was the only way to save the situation and permit Don Gamaliel to spend the last years of his life safe from all danger, it would not be Remigio Páez, Minister of the Lord, who would upset things with a display of indignation and a crusader's zeal. On the contrary: now he patted himself on the back, thinking about the wisdom of humility. If what this man wanted was to humiliate him, Father Páez would listen to him today and tomorrow with his eyes lowered, at times nodding yes, as if painfully accepting the blame this powerful fool cast on the Church. He took his black hat off its hook, set it carelessly on his head of chestnut hair, and headed for the house of Don Gamaliel Bernal.

"Of course he can do it!" affirmed the old man that afternoon, after talking with the priest. "But I wonder what trick he'll use to get in here. He told Father Páez he'd come to see me today. No . . . I'm not sure I understand, Catalina."

She raised her face. She rested a hand on her crocheting, where she was carefully working a floral design. Three years before, they had received the message: Gonzalo was dead. From that day on, father and daughter had grown closer, until they'd transformed that slow passing of the afternoons, as they sat on the wicker patio furniture, into something more than a consolation: into a custom which, according to the old man, would last until he died. What did it matter that yesterday's power and wealth were crumbling; perhaps that was the tribute that had to be paid to time and old age. Don Gamaliel fortified himself in a passive struggle. He would not go out to take control of the peasants, but he would never accept an illegal invasion. He would not demand that his debtors pay back both interest and principal, but they would never get another penny from him.

He was hoping that one day they would come back to him on their knees, when need forced them to abandon their pride. But he would remain steadfast in his own. And now . . . here comes this stranger who promises to give loans to all the peasants at a rate much lower than that demanded by Don Gamaliel. Moreover, he has the effrontery to suggest that the old estate owner hand over all his privileges—and for nothing more than a promise to pay back the fourth part of whatever money can be recouped. Take it or leave it.

"Just as I suspected. His demands won't stop there, either."

"The land?"

"Certainly. He's plotting to take my land from me, don't think he isn't."

As she did every afternoon, she went from one brightly painted cage to another, covering them after observing the nervous movements of the mockingbirds and robins that pecked the seeds and chirped one last time before the sun disappeared.

The old man did not expect a trick of such enormity. The last man to see Gonzalo, his cell mate, the bearer of his last words of love for his father, his sister, his wife, and his son.

"He told me Gonzalo thought about Luisa and the boy before he died."

"Dad. We agreed that we were not going to . . ."

"I didn't tell him a thing. He doesn't know that she remarried and that my grandson has another name."

"You haven't said a word about all that for three years. Why bring it up now?"

"It's true. We've forgiven him, haven't we? I think we should forgive him for having gone over to the enemy. I think we should try to understand him . . ."

"I always thought that every afternoon you and I were forgiving him in silence."

"That's it, that's it. Exactly. You understand me without our having to speak. How comforting that is! You understand me . . ."

Which is why, when that expected, feared guest—because someone, someday, had to appear and say, "I saw him. I met him. He remembered you"—did appear and put forth his perfect pretext, without even mentioning the real problems of the peasant revolt and the suspended payments, Don Gamaliel, after showing him into the library, excused himself and walked rapidly (this old man who thought a measured pace was a sign of elegance) to Catalina's bedroom.

"Fix yourself up. Take off that black dress. Make yourself attractive. Come to the library at seven o'clock sharp."

He said nothing more. She would obey him: this would be the test of all those melancholy afternoons. She would understand. This one trump was left to save the situation. All Don Gamaliel had to do was feel the presence and guess the will of this man in order to understand—or to say to himself—that any delay would be suicidal, that it was difficult to disobey him, that the sacrifice he was demanding was small and, in a way, not really repugnant. He'd been alerted by Father Páez: a tall man, full of vigor, with hypnotic green eyes and a curt way of speaking. Artemio Cruz.

Artemio Cruz. So that was the name of the new world rising out of the civil war; that was the name of those who had come to take his place. Unfortunate land—the old man said, as he returned, slowly once again, to the library and that undesired but fascinating presence—unfortunate land that has to destroy its old possessors with each new generation and put in their place new owners just as rapacious and ambitious as the old ones. The old man imagined himself the final product of a peculiarly Creole civilization, a civilization of enlightened despots. He took pleasure in thinking of himself as a father, sometimes a hard father but always a provider and always the repository of a tradition of good taste, courtesy, and culture.

That's why he'd brought him to the library. There the

venerable—almost sacred—quality of what Don Gamaliel was and symbolized was more in evidence. But the guest did not allow himself to be impressed. The fact that this man had a completely new idea of life, one hammered out on the forge of experience, one that allowed him to put his life on the line because he knew he had nothing to lose, did not escape the keen eye of the old man as he rested his head on the back of the leather chair and squinted to get a better look at his opponent. The stranger didn't even mention the real reasons for his visit. Don Gamaliel realized things would proceed better that way. Perhaps the visitor understood the situation with as much subtlety as he did, although Don Gamaliel's motivation—ambition—might have been stronger. The old man smiled as he remembered that feeling, for him merely a word, the urgent impulse to take advantage of rights won through sacrifice, struggle, wounds, that saber scar on his forehead. Don Gamaliel was not the only one to reach these conclusions. On the silent lips and in the eloquent gaze of the other man was written what the old man, now playing with his magnifying glass, knew well how to read.

The stranger didn't move a muscle when Don Gamaliel walked to his desk to take out that paper, the list of his debtors. So much the better. If things went on this way, they would understand each other perfectly; perhaps it wouldn't be necessary to mention those annoying matters, perhaps everything would be resolved in a more elegant manner. The young military man quickly learned the style of power, Don Gamaliel repeated to himself, and this sense of shared knowledge smoothed the way for the bitter business with which reality forced him to deal.

"But didn't you see how he looked at me?" shouted the girl when the guest had said goodbye. "Didn't you see his lust . . . the filth in his eyes?"

"Yes, yes, of course." The old man calmed his daughter

with his hands. "It's only natural. You may not know it, but you are very beautiful. The problem is, you scarcely ever leave this house. It's only natural."

"I'll never leave!"

Don Gamaliel slowly lit the cigar that stained his thick mustache and the roots of his beard yellow. "I thought you would understand."

"What did Father Páez tell you? He's an atheist! A godless man who has no respect for anything . . . And did you believe that story he made up?"

"Calm down, now. Fortunes are not always made by the godly, you know."

"Did you believe that story? Why did Gonzalo have to die, instead of this person? If the two of them were condemned, in the same cell, why aren't the two of them dead? I know what he's up to, I know: all that claptrap he came here to tell us isn't true. He made it up to humiliate you and so that I . . ."

Don Gamaliel stopped rocking. Everything had been going along so well, so calmly! And now, out of her woman's intuition, came the same objections the old man had already thought up and already rejected as pointless.

"You have the imagination of a twenty-year-old girl." He stood up and extinguished his cigar. "But since you seem to prefer me to be frank, I'll be frank. This man can save us. And that's all that matters . . ."

He sighed and stretched out his arms to touch his daughter's hands. "Think about your father's final years. Don't I deserve a little . . . ?"

"Yes, Father, I haven't said anything . . ."

"And think about yourself."

She lowered her head. "Yes, I understand. I've known something like this would happen ever since Gonzalo left home. If only he were alive . . ."

"But he isn't."

"He didn't think about me. Who knows what he thought about."

Beyond the circle of light cast by the oil lamp that Don Gamaliel held high, along the old, chilly hallways, the girl forced herself to recall those old, confused images. She recalled the tense, sweaty faces of Gonzalo's schoolmates, the long arguments in the room at the back of the house; she remembered her brother's glowing, stubborn, anxious face, his nervous body that sometimes seemed to exist outside reality, his love of comfort, good dinners, wine, books, and his periodic outbursts of rage in which he denounced his own sensual, conformist tendencies. She remembered the coldness of Luisa, her sister-in-law, the violent arguments that turned to silence whenever the "daughter of the house" entered the room; how Luisa's weeping drowned in hysterical laughter when his death was announced to them; how one day she silently departed at dawn when she thought everyone was asleep but the young woman was peeking out from behind the living-room curtains: the hard hand of the man wearing a bowler and carrying a walking stick who took Luisa's hand and helped her and the boy enter the black coach laden with the widow's baggage.

She could only avenge that death—Don Gamaliel kissed her forehead and opened her bedroom door—by embracing this man, by embracing him but denying him the tenderness he would seek in her. By killing him in life, distilling bitterness until he was poisoned. She looked into the mirror, vainly searching for the new features this change should have imprinted on her face. That would be the way for her and her father to avenge Gonzalo's having abandoned them, avenge his idiotic idealism: by giving away this twenty-year-old girl—why did thinking about herself, about her youth, bring her to tears?—to the man who was with Gonzalo during those final hours, hours of which she could have no memory, rejecting self-pity, pouring it out for her dead brother, without a sob of fury, without a tightening of her jaw: if no one explained the truth to her, she would cling to what she thought was the truth. She took off her black stockings. As her fingertips touched her legs, she closed her eyes; she must deny the memory of the rough, strong foot that sought out her own during dinner, flooding her bosom with a strange, uncontrollable feeling. Her body might not be God's creation—she knelt, pressing her laced fingers against her brows—but the creation of other bodies, but her spirit was. She would not allow that body to take a delightful, spontaneous path, to desire caresses, while her spirit demanded she take another. She pulled back the sheet and slipped into bed with her eyes closed. She stretched out her hand to put out the lamp. She put the pillow over her face. She mustn't think about that. No, no, no, mustn't think about it. There was nothing more to say. To say the other name, to tell her father about it. No. No. Humiliating her father was unnecessary. Next month, as soon as possible: and if that man enjoyed Catalina Bernal's fortune, her property, her body . . . what difference did it make . . . Ramón . . . No, not that name, never again. She slept.

"You said it yourself, Don Gamaliel," said the guest when he returned the next day. "It's impossible to stop the course of events. Let's turn over those plots to the peasants; after all, they're only good for dry farming, so no one's going to get much out of them. Let's give out those plots so they can be used only for small-scale farming. You'll see that, to thank us, they'll leave their women to work that dust and come back to take care of our good land. Think about it: you could turn out to be a hero of the agrarian-reform program, and it won't cost you a thing."

Amused, the old man observed him, smiling behind his thick beard. "Have you spoken to her?"

"I have . . ."

She could not contain herself. Her chin trembled when he lifted his hand to raise her closed-eyed face. He was touching that smooth, creamy, rosy skin for the first time. The two of them were surrounded by the penetrating smell of the plants in the patio, herbs suffocated by moisture, the odor of rotten earth. He loved her. As he touched her, he realized he loved her. He had to make her understand that his love was real, even if circumstances said the opposite. He could love her as he had loved once before, the first time: he knew he still possessed that time-proven tenderness. He touched the girl's hot cheeks again. Her rigidity, when she felt that strange hand on her skin, could not hold back the tightly squeezed tears that emerged from her eyelids. "You won't complain, because you will have nothing to complain about," whispered the man as he brought his face close to her lips—which avoided the contact. "I know how to love you . . ."

"We should thank you . . . for having thought of us," she answered in her lowest voice.

He opened his hand to caress Catalina's hair. "You understand, don't you? You are going to live by my side. You'll have to forget many things . . . I promise to respect what is yours . . . You must promise me that never again . . ."

She raised her eyes, narrowing them with a hatred she had never felt before. Her mouth was dry. Who was this monster? Who was this man who knew everything, who took everything, who destroyed everything?

"Don't say it . . ." said the girl as she eluded his embrace.

"I've already had a talk with him. He's a weakling. He didn't really love you. He was frightened from the start."

With her hand the girl cleansed the places he'd touched on her face. "Of course, he's not strong like you . . . He's not an animal, like you . . ."

She wanted to scream when he took her by the arm, smiled, and made a fist. "Your little Ramón is leaving Puebla. You'll never see him again . . ."

He released her. She walked toward the brightly colored cages in the patio: that trill of the birds. One by one, as he looked on, motionless, she opened the painted doors. A robin peeked out and then flew away. The mockingbird hesitated, accustomed to his water and seed. She took him up on her pinkie, kissed his wing, and sent him off. She closed her eyes when the last bird had gone, and allowed the man to take her arm, to lead her to the library, where Don Gamaliel was waiting patiently.

I feel hands that take me under my arms and raise me to make me more comfortable on the smooth cushions, and fresh linen that is like a balm for my body, which is both hot and cold. I feel all this, but when I open my eyes I see before me that newspaper hiding the face of the reader. I think that *Vida Mexicana* is there, will always be there every day, will come out every day, and there will be no human power to stop it. Teresa—who is reading the newspaper—drops it in alarm.

"Is something wrong? Do you feel sick?"

I have to calm her with my hand, and she picks up the newspaper. No. I feel content, perpetrator of a gigantic joke. Perhaps. Perhaps the master stroke would be to leave behind a special will the newspaper would publish, a testament in which I would tell the truth about my honest enterprise in the area of freedom of the press . . . No. I've excited myself and brought back the shooting pain in my stomach. I try to reach out to Teresa, to ask for help, but my daughter is immersed in the newspaper again. Earlier, I had seen the day extinguished beyond the windows and had heard the merciful noise of curtains. Now, in the half light of the bedroom with its high ceilings and oak closets, I can't make out the people standing farthest away. The room is very large, but she's there. She must be sitting stiffly, with her lace handkerchief in her hands, her face devoid of makeup. Perhaps she doesn't hear me when I whisper: "That morning I waited for him happily. We crossed the river on horseback."

The only one listening to me is this stranger I've never seen before, with his smoothly shaven cheeks and black eyebrows. He's asking me to say an act of contrition; I'm thinking about the carpenter and the Virgin, and he's offering me the keys to heaven.

"Well, what would you say . . . in a situation like this . . . ?"

I've caught him by surprise. And Teresa has to ruin everything by shouting: "Leave him alone, Father, leave him alone! Don't you see that there's nothing we can do! He wants to go to hell and die just as he's lived, cold, mocking everything . . ."

The priest holds her back with one arm as he brings his lips close to my ear, almost kissing me: "They don't have to hear us."

And I manage to grunt: "Okay, then, be a man and get these bitches out of here."

He stands up amid the indignant voices of the women and takes them by the arm, and Padilla comes closer. But they don't want that.

"No, counselor, we can't allow that."

"It's customary . . . for years, ma'am."

"Will you take responsibility?"

"Don Artemio . . . I've brought you everything we recorded this morning . . ."

I nod. I try to smile. The same as every day. A man you can count on, this Padilla.

"The outlet is next to the bureau."

"Thanks."

Yes, of course, that's my voice, the voice I had yesterday—yesterday? I can't tell the difference anymore—and I ask Pons, my managing editor—ah, the tape is screeching; adjust it, Padilla, I listened to my voice in reverse: it screeches like a cockatoo's. There I am:

"What do you think about this business, Pons?"

"It's bad, but it'll be a cinch to handle, at least for now."

"Then now's the time to get the paper moving on it, no holds barred, okay? Hit them where it hurts. Don't hold back."

"You're the boss, Artemio."

"Good thing we've prepared our readers for this one."

"They've been talking about it for years now."

"I want to see all the editorials and page one . . . Bring it all over to my house, any time of day or night."

"You know what to do, the same slant for every story. A brazen red plot. Alien infiltration totally foreign to the essence of the Mexican Revolution . . ."

"The good old Mexican Revolution!"

". . . leaders controlled by foreign agents. Tombroni's really got to give it to them; Blanco is to blast them with a column in which he equates the leader with the Antichrist, and the cartoons have to be scathing . . . How are you feeling?"

"Not good. The usual thing. It'll pass. We'd all like to be the men we used to be, right?"

"The men we used to be . . . right."

"Tell Mr. Corkery to step in."

I cough on the tape. I hear the hinges on a door opening and closing. I feel nothing moving in my stomach, nothing, nothing, the gases don't move, no matter how I strain . . . But I see them. They've come in. The mahogany door opens, closes, and the footsteps on the thick rug are soundless. They've closed the windows.

"Open the windows."

"No, no. You could catch cold and complicate everything . . ."

"Open them."

"Are you worried, Mr. Cruz?"

"I am. Sit down, and I'll explain why. Would you like a drink? Wheel the cart over. I don't feel very well."

I hear the little wheels, the clink of the bottles.

"You look okay."

I hear ice falling into the glass, the pressure of soda being siphoned out.

"Look, I'll tell you what's at stake here, in case your people haven't grasped it. Tell the central office that if this so-called union clean-up campaign goes over, we might as well do as the bullfighters do and cut off our pigtails . . ."

"Pigtails?"

"I'll put it as plainly as I can. We're fucked . . ."

"Turn that off!" shrieks Teresa, running over to the tape recorder. "Where do you think you are, don't you have any manners at all?"

I manage to wave my hand, make a face. I miss a few words on the tape.

". . . what these railroad leaders are proposing?"

Someone nervously blows his nose. Where?

". . . explain it to the companies. God forbid they should be so naïve as to think this is a democratic movement—try to see my point of view—aimed at getting rid of some corrupt union bosses. It isn't that."

"I'm all ears, Mr. Cruz."

That's right, it must be the gringo who sneezes. Ah-ah-ah.

"No. No. You could catch cold and complicate everything."

"Open them."

I and not only I, other men, could sniff the breeze for the perfumes of other lands, the aromas drawn out of other noons by the wind. I sniff, I sniff. Far from me, far from this cold sweat, far from these inflamed gases. I made them open the window. I can smell whatever I like, amuse myself by choosing the smells the wind carries: yes, autumn forests; yes, leaves burning; oh, yes, ripe plums; yes, yes, the rotten tropics; yes, hard salt flats, pineapples split open with a machete, tobacco drying in the darkness, the smoke from locomotives, waves on the open sea, pine trees covered with snow; ah, metal and guano. How many tastes that everlasting movement brings and takes away. No, no, they won't let me live: they sit down again, they get up and walk and sit down again together, as if they were a single shadow, as if they couldn't think or act on their own. They sit down again, at the same time, with their backs to the window, to block the movement of air toward me, to suffocate me, to make me close my eyes and remember things and no longer let me see things, touch things, smell things. The damned pair of them, how long will it take them to bring in a priest, speed up my death, wrench confessions out of me? There he is still, on his knees, with his scrubbed face. I try to turn my back on him. The pain in my side stops me. Aaaay. It's almost over. I'll be free. I want to sleep. Here it comes again. Here it is. Aaah-ay. And the women. No, not these women. The women. The ones that love. What? Yes. No. I don't know. I've forgotten the face. By God, I've forgotten that face. No. I shouldn't forget it. Where is it? Ay, it was so pretty, that face, how could I ever forget it. It was mine, how could I ever forget it. Aaah-ay. I loved you, how can I forget you. You were mine, how can I forget you? What did you look like, please, what did you look like? How shall I invoke you? What? Why? Another injection? What? Why? No no no, something else, quick, I remember something else; that hurts, aaah-ay, that hurts, that puts me to sleep . . . that . . .

You will close your eyes, conscious of the fact that your eyelids are not opaque, that even though you close them the light reaches the retina: the sunlight that will stop, framed by the open window, at the same height as your closed eyes, your closed eyes that erase details from vision, that alter brilliance and color but do not eliminate vision itself—the light from the copper penny which will melt in the west. You will close your eyes and think you see more. You will see only what your brain wants you to see, more than what is offered by the world. You will close your eyes and the exterior world will no longer compete with your imaginative vision. You will lower your eyelids, and that immobile, unchanging, constant sunlight will create behind your eyelids another world in movement, light in movement, light that fatigues, frightens, confuses, makes you happy, sad. Behind your closed eyelids, you will know the intensity of a light that penetrates to the depth of that small, imperfect plaque to arouse sentiments contrary to your will, your condition. Nevertheless, you will close your eyes, feign deafness; stop touching something, even if it's the air, with your fingers, imagine an absolute insensibility; halt the flow of saliva across your tongue and palate, overcome the taste of your own self; impede your labored breathing, which will go on filling your lungs, your blood with life, choose a partial death. You will always see, always touch, always taste, always smell, always hear: you will have screamed when they pierced your skin with that needle filled with tranquilizer; you will scream before you feel any pain. The announcement of pain will travel to your brain before your skin actually feels the pain: it will travel to warn you about the pain you will feel, to put you on guard so that you will be aware, so that you will feel the pain more acutely, because awareness weakens us, turns us into victims when we realize that the powers will not consult us, will not take us into account.

There it is: the organs of pain, though slower, will overcome those of reflexive prevention.

And you will feel divided, a man who will receive and a man who will act, sensor man and motor man, man constructed of organs that feel, transmit feeling to the millions of minuscule fibers that spread toward your cerebral cortex, toward that surface on the upper half of the brain which for seventy-one years receives, stores, expends, denudes,

returns the colors of the world, the feel of flesh, the tastes
of life, the smells of the earth, the noises of the air: returning
them to the frontal motor, to the nerves, muscles, and
glands that will transform your body and the fraction of the
exterior world that falls to you.

But in your half sleep the nerve fiber that carries the
light impulse will not connect with the zone of vision. You
will hear color, and you will touch sound, see smells, smell
taste. You will stretch out your arms so as not to fall into
the pit of chaos, to recover the order of your whole life,
the order of the received fact, transmitted to the nerve,
returned to the nerve transformed into an effect and once
again into a fact. You will stretch out your arms and behind
your closed eyes you will see the colors of your mind and
finally you will feel, without seeing it, the origin of the
touch that you hear: the sheets, the light touch of the sheets
between your clenched fingers; you will open your hands
and feel the sweat on your palms and perhaps you will
remember that you were born without lifelines on your
hand, without fortune, life, or love: you were born, you
will be born with a smooth palm, but all you have to do is
be born; after a few hours, that blank surface will be filled
with signs, lines, portents. You will die with your dense
lines worn out, but all you have to do is die for all trace of
your destiny to disappear from your hands after a few hours.

Chaos has no plural.

Order, order: you will cling to the sheets and repeat in
silence, within yourself, the sensations your brain houses,
clarifies. With effort, you will mentally locate the places
that alert you to thirst and hunger, perspiration and chills,
balance and falling. You will find them in the lower brain,
the servant, the domestic who carries out immediate functions and frees the other, the upper brain, for thought,
imagination, desire: child of artifice, necessity, or chance,
the world will not be simple; you cannot know it passively,
allowing things to happen to you; you must think so that a

combination of dangers does not defeat you, imagine so that mere guessing doesn't negate you, desire so that the web of uncertainty doesn't devour you: you shall survive.

You will recognize yourself.

You will recognize others and allow them—her—to recognize you; and you will know that you oppose every individual because each will be one more obstacle keeping you from reaching the objects of your desire.

You will desire: how you would like your desire and the object desired to be the same thing; how you will dream about instant gratification, about the total identification of desire and what is desired.

You will rest with your eyes closed, but you will not stop seeing, you will not stop desiring: you will remember, because that way you will make the desired thing yours: back, back, in nostalgia, you will make yours whatever you desire: not forward, back.

Memory is satisfied desire.

Survive through memory before it's too late.

Before chaos keeps you from remembering.

(1913: December 4)

He felt the moist crook of the woman's knee next to his waist. Her perspiration was always like that, light and fresh: whenever he took his arm from around her waist, he felt the moisture of that crystalline liquid. He stretched out his hand to rub her back slowly and thought he fell asleep: he could stay that way for hours, just caressing Regina's back. When he closed his eyes, he grasped the infinite love in that young body embracing his: a lifetime would not be enough to travel and chart it, he thought, to explore that smooth, undulating geography with its black and pink irregularities. Regina's body waited, and he, without voice

or vision, was spread out on the bed, touching its iron bars
first with the tips of his fingers and then with his toes; he
tried to touch both ends at the same time. They dwelled
within this black crystal: dawn was still far off. The mosquito
netting, weighing nothing, isolated them from everything
outside their own bodies. He opened his eyes. Regina's
cheek came close to his; his matted beard scratched her
skin. The darkness was not enough. Regina's slanted eyes
glowed, half open, like luminous black scars. She took a
deep breath. The girl's hands clasped behind the man's
neck, and once more their profiles joined. The heat of their
thighs fused into a single flame. He breathed: a bedroom
of blouses and starched skirts, quinces cut open on the
walnut table, an extinguished bedside lamp. Closer to him,
the briny smell of the moistened, soft woman. Her nails
made a cat's claw sound on the sheets; her light legs rose
again to entwine the man's waist. Her lips sought out his
neck. Her nipples trembled joyfully when he touched them
with his lips, laughing, pushing aside her long, tangled hair.
Did Regina speak? He felt her breath close to him and he
sealed her lips with his hand. Without tongue or eyes: only
mute flesh abandoned to its own pleasure. She understood
him. She snuggled closer to the man's body. Her hand
descended to the man's sex; his hand felt for her hard,
almost hairless sex: he remembered her standing there naked, young and firm when still but undulating and soft as
she began to walk: when she went to bathe in privacy,
when she closed the curtains, when she fanned the coals
in the brazier. They fell asleep again, each one possessed
by the center of the other. Only their hands, one hand,
moved in sleep, in their smiling sleep.

"I'll follow you."

"Where will you live?"

"I'll slip into each town before you take it. And I'll wait
for you there."

"You'll leave everything behind?"

"I'll bring some clothes. You'll give me money to buy fruit and food, and I'll wait for you. When you get into town, I'll already be there. All I need is something to wear."

That skirt hanging over the chair in the rented room. When she's awake, he likes to touch her and also touch her things: her combs, her little black shoes, her small earrings left on the table. In those moments, he wishes he could give her something more than these days of separation and difficult reunions. An unforeseen command, having to track the enemy, a defeat that forced them to retreat north, had already separated them for weeks on other occasions. But she, like a sea gull, seemed able to read the ebb and flow of the revolutionary tide through the thousand shifts in the fighting and the fortunes of war: if she didn't turn up in the town they'd agreed on, she'd appear, sooner or later, in another. She would go from town to town, asking for his battalion, listening to the answers of the women and the old men left there.

"It's been about two weeks since they passed through here."

"They say there's not a one of them still alive."

"Who knows. They might come back. They forgot a few cannons when they left."

"Watch out for the *federales*, they shoot anyone who helps the rebels."

And they'd end up finding each other again, just as they did now. She would have the room ready with fruit and food, her skirt tossed over a chair. She would wait for him like that, ready, as if she did not want to waste a minute on unnecessary things. But nothing is unnecessary. Seeing her walk, make the bed, loosen her hair, then take off the rest of her clothes, kissing her whole body as she stood there, he kneels, outlines her body with his lips, enjoys the taste of her skin and her fine hair, the moisture of her seashell: gathering in his mouth the tremors of the standing girl who will finally take the man's head in her hands to make him rest, to keep his lips in one place. And, still standing, she will let herself go, squeezing his head with a broken sigh until he feels she is finished and he carries her in his arms to the bed.

"Artemio, will I ever see you again?"

"Never ask that question. Pretend that we've only just met."

She never asked again. She was ashamed of having done it, even once, of having thought that her love could come to an end or be measured by the time used to measure other things. She had no reason to remember where or why she had met this young man, twenty-four years old. It was unnecessary to burden herself with anything more than love and their meetings during the few days of rest, when the troops, having taken one plaza, stopped to heal their wounds, secure their position in the territory wrested from the dictatorship, locate supplies, and plan the next offensive. That was how the two of them decided it, without ever saying anything. They never thought about the danger of war or the time they were apart. If one of them did not show up at the next meeting place, they would go their separate ways without a word: he south, to the capital; she north, to the coasts of Sinaloa, where she had met him and where she let herself be loved.

"Regina . . . Regina . . ."

"Do you remember that rock that stuck out of the sea like a boat of stone? It must still be there."

"That's where I met you. Did you go there often?"

"Every afternoon. A little pool forms between the rocks and you can see yourself in the clear water. I'd go there to look at myself, and one day your face appeared next to mine. At night the stars were reflected in the sea. During the day, you could see the sun burning in it."

"I didn't know what to do that afternoon. We'd been fighting, and suddenly everything stopped: the *federales* gave up, but I was used to living like a soldier. Then I began to remember other things and I found you sitting on that rock. Your legs were wet."

"I wanted it, too. You just appeared next to me, part of me, reflected in the water. Didn't you realize I wanted it, too?"

The dawn was slow in coming, but through a gray veil the two bodies were revealed, joined by the hand, in sleep. He woke up first and watched her. It seemed like the finest thread in the spiderweb of the centuries: it looked like a twin of death: sleep. Her legs drawn up, her free arm over the man's chest, her mouth moist. They liked making love at dawn: for them it was a celebration of the new day. The dusky light barely showed Regina's profile. Within the hour, they would be hearing the sounds of the town. Now there is only the breathing of the dark young woman who sleeps in total serenity, the living part of the world at rest. Only one thing would have the right to interrupt the felicity of that serene body at rest, outlined on the sheet, wrapped up in itself with the smoothness of a moon in mourning. Does he have the right? The young man's imagination leapt past the lovemaking: he contemplated her as she slept as if resting from the loving which would waken her in a few seconds. When is happiness greater? He caressed her breast. Imagine the renewed union; the union itself; the weary joy of memory and then total desire again, augmented by love, by a new act of love: bliss. He kissed Regina's ear and saw her first smile: he brought his face close to hers so he would not miss her first gesture of happiness. He felt her hand playing with him again. Desire flowered within, scattered with heavy drops: Regina's smooth legs again sought Artemio's waist: her full hand knew all: the erection escaped her fingers and woke up at their touch: her thighs parted, trembling, full, and the erect flesh found the open flesh and entered, caressed, surrounded by the eager pulse, crowned by new eggs, squeezed in that universe of soft, amorous skin: the two of them reduced to the meeting of the world, the seed of reason, to the two voices that name things in silence, that within baptize all things: within, when he thinks about everything but this, he thinks, counts things, does not think about everything, all so that this does not end: he tries to fill his head with seas and sand and wind, with houses and animals, fish and crops, all so that this will not end: within, when he raises his face, his eyes closed, and stretches his neck with all the strength of his swollen veins, when Regina loses herself and lets herself be conquered and answers with thick breath, furrowing her brow, her smiling lips saying yes, yes, she likes it, yes, don't stop, go on, yes, it shouldn't end, yes, until she realizes that it all happened at once, one unable to contemplate the other because both were one and uttering the same words:

"How happy I am."

"How happy I am."

"I love you, Regina."

"I love you, my husband."

"Do I make you happy?"

"Don't ever end; how long it lasts; you fill all of me."

While, out on the street, a pail of water splashed over the dust and wild ducks passed by, quacking over the river, and a whistle announced what no one would be able to stop: boots dragging along, the noise of spurs, hooves echoing again, and the smells of oil and lard seeping through doors and houses. He stretched out his hand and felt for the cigarettes in his shirt pocket. She went over to the window and opened it. She stayed there, breathing deep, with her arms open, standing on tiptoe. The circle of gray mountains came closer to the eyes of the lovers as the sun rose. The aroma of the town bakery wafted up and, from farther off, the savor of myrtles tangled with weeds in the rotten ravines. All he saw was her naked body, her open arms that now wanted to take the day by the shoulders and drag it back to bed.

"Want breakfast?"

"It's too early. Let me finish my cigarette first."

Regina's head rested on his shoulder. His long, sinewy hand stroked her hip. Both smiled.

"When I was a little girl, life was beautiful. There were lots of beautiful times. Vacations, holidays, summer days, games. I don't know why, but when I started growing, I began to long for things. When I was a little girl, I didn't. That's why I started to go to that beach. I said it was better to long. I didn't know why I had changed so much that summer, or that I'd stopped being a little girl."

"You still are, you know."

"With you? After all the things we've done?"

He laughed and kissed her, and she bent her knee, pretending to be a bird with folded wings nestled against his chest. She clung to the man's neck, mixing her laughter with feigned tears.

"What about you?"

"I don't remember anymore. I found you and I love you very much."

"Tell me. Why did I know, the moment I saw you, that nothing else would matter anymore? You know, I told myself at that precise instant that I'd have to make a decision. That if you just went away, I'd be wasting my whole life. Did you feel anything like that?"

"Yes, I did. Didn't you think, though, that I was just another soldier looking for some fun?"

"No, no. I didn't even see your uniform. All I saw were your eyes reflected in the water and then I couldn't see my own reflection anymore without yours next to it."

"Honey, sweetheart, go see if we have any coffee."

When they parted that morning like all the mornings of their seven young months of love, she asked if the troops would be pulling out soon. He said he didn't know what the general had in mind. They might have to go after some pockets of defeated *federales* still in the area, but at any rate, they'd be keeping their headquarters in town. There was plenty of water and cattle. It was a good place to stay awhile. They were tired after fighting their way south from Sonora and had earned a rest. At eleven they were to report to their commanders at the plaza.

In every town they passed through, the general would investigate working conditions, reduce the workday to eight hours by public decree, and distribute land to the peasants. If there was a hacienda in the area, he would have the company store burned to the ground. If there were loan sharks—and there were always loan sharks, unless they'd fled with the *federales*—he would rescind all loans. The bad part was that the bulk of the population was under arms and almost all were peasants, so there was no one to enforce the general's decrees. Thus, it was better for them instantly to appropriate the wealth of the rich who remained in each town, and hope the Revolution would triumph, so the land reforms and the eight-hour day would be legalized.

Right now the important thing was to get to Mexico City and depose that drunk Huerta, Don Panchito Madero's assassin. Round and round we go! he murmured as he tucked his khaki shirt into his white trousers. Round and round we go! From Veracruz, where he came from, to Mexico City, and from there north to Sonora, when his teacher Sebastián had asked him to do what the older generation could no longer do: go north, take up arms, and liberate the country. Hadn't even slept with a woman yet, word of honor. But how could he let Sebastián down, the man who had taught him the three things he knew: reading, writing, and hating priests.

He stopped talking when Regina set the coffee down on the table.

"It's boiling hot!"

It was early. They went out on the street with their arms around each other's waists. She wearing her starched skirt, he in his felt hat and white uniform jacket. The cluster of

houses where they were living was near a ravine; the morning glories hung over the void, and a rabbit torn apart by
the teeth of a coyote was rotting in the underbrush. Deep
down, below, a stream ran its course. Regina peered down
to find it, as if hoping to find again the reflected image of
her fiction. Their hands joined; the road to the town clung
to the edge of the canyon, and down from the mountains
came the echoes of thrushes calling to each other. No: the
noise of light hooves, lost in clouds of dust.

"Lieutenant Cruz! Lieutenant Cruz!"

The perpetually smiling face of Loreto, the general's
aide, disappeared behind the sweat and dust coating him,
when he reined in his horse in a dry whinny. "Come
quickly," he said, panting as he wiped his face with a handkerchief. "There's big news: we're moving out right away.
Have you had breakfast? They're serving eggs over at
headquarters."

"Eggs? I've already got mine," he joked, patting his
crotch.

Regina's embrace was an embrace of dust. Only when
Loreto's horse vanished and the dust settled did the whole
woman, clinging to the shoulders of her young lover,
reemerge.

"Wait for me here."

"What can it be?"

"There must be some *federales* wandering around somewhere. Nothing serious."

"I should stay here?"

"Yes. Don't move. I'll be back tonight or early tomorrow
at the latest."

"Artemio . . . Think we'll ever return there?"

"Who knows. Who knows how long this'll go on. Don't
think about it. You know I love you, right?"

"I love you, too. A lot. Forever."

Out in the stables and in the main patio of the headquarters, the troops had received their orders and were

preparing their packs with ritual calm. The cannon rolled along in single file, pulled by white mules with shadows under their eyes; they were followed by ammunition carriages set on rails that ran from the patio to the train station. The cavalry attended to their mounts, removed feed bags, put on bridles, made sure saddles were cinched tightly, and patted the heads of the war horses, so docile and gentle to the men even though they were stained with dust and their stomachs were covered with ticks. Two hundred horses moved slowly past the barracks, spotted, dappled, dusty black. The infantry oiled its rifles and then filed past the smiling dwarf who distributed ammunition. The hats worn by soldiers from the north: gray felt, the brim turned up on one side. Neckerchiefs. Cartridge belts around their waists. Only a few wearing boots: wool trousers, yellow leather shoes or *huaraches*. Striped shirts, collarless. Here and there—on the streets, in the patios, at the station— Yaqui Indian hats hung with leafy twigs: members of the band carrying their music stands in their hands, their metal instruments on their backs. The last swallows of hot water. Pots filled to the brim with beans. Plates of *huevos rancheros*. Shouts come from the station: a flatcar of Mayan Indians was pulling in, to an accompaniment of high-pitched drumming and a flutter of colored bows and primitive arrows.

He made his way through the throng: inside, standing in front of the map hastily nailed to a wall, the general was explaining: "The *federales* are mounting a counterattack at our backs, in territory the Revolution has already liberated. What they want is to cut us off from the rear. At dawn, a scout up in the mountains spotted a thick cloud of smoke rising over the towns occupied by Colonel Jiménez. He reported it, and I remembered that the colonel had collected a big pile of boards and railway ties in each town, which he would burn if he was attacked, to warn us. That's how things stand. We have to split up. Half will go back to the other side of the mountain to help Jiménez. The other half will go out to finish off the groups we defeated yesterday and to make sure that another big offensive doesn't come from the south. We'll only leave a company here. But it doesn't seem likely they'll get this far. Major Gavilán . . . Lieutenant Aparicio . . . Lieutenant Cruz: you head north again."

Jiménez's fires were petering out when, around midday, Artemio Cruz passed the outpost at the mountain pass. From up there he could see the train overflowing with people: it ran without blowing its whistle, carrying mortars and cannon, ammunition boxes and machine guns. The cavalry detachment made its way down the steep slopes with difficulty, and the cannon began to fire on the towns supposedly retaken by the *federales*.

"Let's speed up," he said. "They'll keep firing for about two hours, and then we'll go in to scout."

He never knew why, the moment his horse's hooves reached flat ground, he lowered his head and lost all notion of the finite mission he'd been ordered to carry out. The men with him seemed to vanish, along with the positive feeling of an objective to be reached, and in their place came a tenderness, an inner lament for something lost, a longing to return to Regina's arms and forget it all. It was as if the flaming sphere of the sun had overwhelmed the nearby presence of the cavalry and the distant noise of the bombardment: in place of that real world there was another, a dream world where only he and his love had the right to live, where only they had a reason to save it.

"Do you remember that rock that stuck out of the sea like a boat of stone?"

He gazed at her again, yearning to kiss her, afraid he would wake her, certain that by gazing at her he was making her his. Only one man possesses—he thought—all the secret images of Regina; that man possesses her, and he will never give her up. Contemplating her, he contemplated himself. His hands dropped the reins: all he is, all his love, is embedded in the flesh of this woman who contains both of them. I wish I could go back . . . tell her how much I love her . . . tell her the depth of my feelings . . . so that Regina would know . . .

The horse whinnied and bucked; the rider fell on the hard ground, on the rocks and briars. The grenades of the *federales* rained down on the cavalry, and as he got up in the smoke, all he could see was his horse's chest on fire, the shield that had stopped the flames. Around the fallen body of his own mount, more than fifty horses were rearing senselessly: there was no light above; the sky had moved down one step, and it was a sky of gunpowder no higher than the men. He ran toward one of the low trees: the bursts of smoke hid more than bare branches. Ninety feet away, a forest began; it was low but thick. A chaotic shouting reached his ears. He dove to catch the reins of a riderless horse but threw only one leg over its back. He hid his body behind the horse and whipped it on. The horse galloped and he, head down and eyes blinded by his own tangled hair, desperately held on to the saddle and bridle. The brilliance of the morning finally vanished; the shadow allowed him to open his eyes, part from the animal's flesh, and roll until he hit a tree trunk.

Again he felt as he'd felt before. The confused sounds of war were all around him, but between those near and the far rumble that reached his ears, there was an unbridgeable gap: here the slight trembling of the branches, the slithering of the lizards could be heard quite distinctly. Alone, leaning against the tree trunk, he again felt a sweet, serene life languidly flowing through his veins: a well-being of the body that dispelled any rebellious attempt at thought. His men? His heart beat evenly, without a throb. Would they be looking for him? His arms and legs felt happy, clean, tired. What would they do without him to give them orders? His eyes searched through the roof of leaves for the hidden

flight of some bird. Would they lose all sense of discipline?
Would they, too, run and hide in this providential forest?
But he couldn't go back over the mountain on foot. He
would have to wait here. And what if he was taken prisoner?
He couldn't go on thinking: a moan parted the leaves near
the lieutenant's face, and a man collapsed in his arms. His
arms rejected him for an instant and then held on to that
body from which hung a red, limp rag of torn flesh.

The wounded man rested his head on his comrade's
shoulder. "They're . . . really . . . pouring it . . . on . . ."

He felt the ravaged arm on his back, staining it, dripping
angry blood. He tried to push back the face, which was
twisted with pain: high cheekbones, open mouth, eyes
closed, tangled mustache and beard, short, like his own.
If the man had green eyes, he could be his double . . .

"Is there any way out? Are we losing? Do you know
anything about the cavalry? Have they pulled out?"

"No . . . no . . . They went . . . forward."

The wounded man tried to point with his good arm—
the other, splintered by machine-gun fire—never relaxing
the horrible grimace that seemed to sustain him and prolong his existence.

"They're advancing? How?"

"Water, pal . . . in a bad way . . ."

The wounded man fainted, holding on with a strange
strength full of wordless pleading. The lieutenant bore
that sculpted lead weight on his own body. The tremors of
cannon fire returned to his ears. An uncertain wind shook
the treetops. Again, silence and tranquillity broken by
machine-gun fire. Taking hold of the wounded man's good
arm, he disencumbered himself of the body that had been
tossed over his own. Holding him by the head, he laid him
on the ground, on the knotty roots. He opened his canteen
and took a long drink. He brought it to the lips of the
wounded man: the water ran down his blackened chin. But
his heart still beat: now, on his knees near the wounded

man's chest, he wondered how much longer it would go on beating. He unfastened the man's heavy silver buckle and then turned his back on him. What was happening out there? Who was winning? He stood up and walked into the forest, away from the wounded man.

As he walked, he touched his body, sometimes pushing the lower branches out of the way, but always feeling himself. He wasn't wounded. He did not need help. He stopped by a spring and filled his canteen. A creek, dead before it was really born, ran from the spring and disappeared under the sun just beyond the forest. He took off his uniform jacket and used both hands to douse his chest, his armpits, his burning, dry, raw shoulders, the taut muscles of his arms, the smooth, greenish skin with thick calluses. He wanted to see his reflection in the spring, but the bubbling water made that impossible. This body was not his: Regina had acquired another possession: she had demanded it with each caress. It wasn't his. It was more hers. He had to save it for her. They no longer lived alone and isolated; the walls of separation had fallen; now they were two in one, forever. The Revolution would end; towns and lives would end, but this would never end. It was now their life, the life of both of them. He dried his face. He went out once again on to the plain.

The charge of the revolutionaries came from the plain toward the forest and the mountain. They ran swiftly alongside him while he, disoriented, walked down toward the burning towns. He heard the whips slap the croups of the horses, the dry crack of rifles, and he was alone on the plain. Were they running away? He turned around, raising his hands to his head. He didn't understand. It was essential to leave a site with a clear mission and never lose that golden thread: only then would it be possible to understand what was happening. A moment's distraction and all the chess moves of war would turn into an irrational, incomprehensible game consisting of tattered, abrupt movements devoid of sense. That cloud of dust . . . those furious horses galloping onward . . . that horseman shouting and waving a bare sword . . . that train stopped in the distance . . . that dust cloud coming closer and closer . . . that sun coming closer and closer to his dazed head with each passing minute . . . that sword just barely grazing his forehead . . . that galloping that rushes by him and throws him to the ground . . .

He got up, feeling his wounded forehead. He had to get back to the forest again: it was the only safe place. He staggered. The sun melted his vision and blurred the horizon into crusts, the dry grass, the line of mountains. When he reached the trees, he grabbed a trunk; he unbuttoned his uniform jacket and ripped off his shirt sleeve. He spit on it and put the moist spot on his lacerated forehead. He tied the rag around his head—his head was pounding painfully when the dry branches alongside him splintered under the weight of unknown boots: the soldier belonged to the revolutionary troops and he was carrying a body on his back, a bloody, broken sack with a blood-encrusted arm.

"I found him where the forest begins. He was dying. They blew most of his arm off . . . Lieutenant."

The tall, dark soldier squinted until he could see the insignia. "I think he's gone and died on me. He feels like a dead man."

He put the body down, resting it against the tree. Artemio had done the same thing half an hour, fifteen minutes before. The soldier brought his face close to the wounded man's mouth; he recognized the open mouth, the high cheekbones, the half-closed eyes.

"Yes. He's gone. If only I'd gotten there a little sooner, I might have saved him."

He closed the dead man's eyes with his square hand. He hooked the silver belt buckle, and as he bent his head, he muttered through white teeth: "Damnit, Lieutenant. If there weren't a few brave guys like this one in the world, where would the rest of us be?"

He turned his back on the soldier and the dead man and ran toward the open plain. It was preferable. Even if he neither heard nor saw. Even if the world passed him by like a shadow. Even if all the noises of war and peace—mockingbirds, wind, distant roaring—that persisted were to turn into that single, dull drumming that encompassed all noise and reduced it to sadness. He tripped over a corpse. He bent down, without knowing why, seconds before that voice cut through the deaf drumming of all these noises.

"Lieutenant . . . Lieutenant Cruz."

A hand rested on the lieutenant's shoulder; he raised his face.

"You're badly wounded, Lieutenant. Come with us. The *federales* ran off. Jiménez held the town square. Come back with us to headquarters in Río Hondo. The cavalry really did a job; they multiplied, really. Come on. You don't look so well."

He clasped the officer's shoulders and murmured: "To headquarters. Right, let's go."

The thread was broken. The thread that allowed him to traverse the labyrinth of war without getting lost. Without getting lost: without deserting. He wasn't strong enough to hold the reins. But the horse was tethered to Major Gavilán's saddle during that slow march through the mountains separating the battle plain from the valley where she waits for him. The thread stayed behind. There below, the town of Río Hondo hadn't changed: it was the same jumble of houses he'd left behind that morning, with broken roof tiles and adobe walls, pink, reddish, surrounded by cactuses. He thought he could pick out, next to the green lips of the ravine, the house where Regina must be waiting for him.

Gavilán was trotting in front of him. The afternoon shadows cast the image of the mountain on the tired bodies of the two soldiers. The major's horse stopped for an instant, waiting for the lieutenant's to catch up. Gavilán offered him a cigarette. As soon as the match was out, the horses started trotting again. But by then he'd seen the pain in the major's face and he lowered his head. He deserved it. They'd know the truth about his having deserted under fire, and they'd rip off his insignia. But they wouldn't know the whole truth: they wouldn't know that he wanted to save himself so as to return to Regina's love, nor would they understand if he explained. They also wouldn't know that he'd abandoned the wounded soldier, that he could have saved his life. His love for Regina would compensate for the guilt of abandoning the soldier. That's the way it should be. He lowered his head and thought that for the first time in his life he was experiencing shame. Shame: it wasn't shame that showed in Major Gavilán's clear, direct eyes. The officer rubbed his fuzzy blond beard with his free hand crusted with dust and sun.

"We owe our lives to you and your men, Lieutenant. You halted the enemy's advance. The general will welcome you like a hero . . . Artemio . . . Do you mind if I call you Artemio?"

The major tried to smile. He rested his free hand on the lieutenant's shoulder and went on, laughing dryly. "We've been fighting alongside each other for a long time, and look: we don't even call each other by our first names."

Major Gavilán's eyes asked for some response. The night fell with its incorporeal crystal, and the last glow flashed behind the mountains, now far away, hidden in the darkness, secluded. In the barracks, fires were burning that could not be seen from a distance in the afternoon light.

"The skunks!" exclaimed the major suddenly in a bitter tone. "They made a surprise attack on the town at about one in the afternoon. Naturally, they didn't reach headquarters. But they took their revenge on the outlying areas—their usual tricks. They've promised to take revenge on any town that helps us. They took ten hostages and sent us a message that if we didn't surrender they would hang them. The general replied with mortar fire."

The streets were filled with soldiers, people, stray dogs, and children, as stray as the dogs, crying in doorways. Some fires still burned, and women sat right out in the street on their mattresses, alongside whatever else they had salvaged.

"Lieutenant Artemio Cruz," whispered Gavilán, leaning over to reach the hearing of some soldiers.

"Lieutenant Cruz," ran the murmur from the soldiers to the women.

The people made way for the two horses: the major's bay, nervous in the crowd pressing up against it; the lieutenant's black stallion, his forehead low, letting himself be led by the bay. Hands reached out: the men from the cavalry detachment commanded by the lieutenant. They squeezed his leg in greeting; they motioned toward his forehead, where the blood had seeped through the rag; they muttered congratulations on the victory. They crossed the town. The ravine yawned in the background, and the trees were swaying in the evening breeze. He raised his eyes: the cluster of white houses. He looked for the window; they were all closed. The glare of candles illuminated the entryway to some houses; black groups, wrapped in *rebozos*, were crouched there.

"Don't anyone cut them down!" shouted Lieutenant Aparicio from his rearing horse, using his riding crop to beat back the hands raised imploringly. "We've all got to remember this forever! Everyone's got to know who we're fighting! They make the common people kill their brothers. Take a good look. That's how they killed the Yaquis, because the Yaquis didn't want their land taken from them. The same way they killed the workers at Río Blanco and Cananea, who didn't want to die of hunger. And that's the way they'll kill all of us unless we kick the shit out of them first. Take a good look."

The finger of young Lieutenant Aparicio pointed to the clump of trees near the ravine. The crude henequen ropes still drew blood from the necks; but the open eyes, purple tongues, and limp bodies barely swaying in the wind blowing down from the mountains proved they were dead. The eyes of the onlookers—some lost, some enraged, most with a sweet expression of disbelief, filled with quiet pain—focused on the muddy *huaraches*, a child's bare feet, a woman's black slippers. He dismounted. He came closer. He clutched Regina's starched skirt with a broken, choked sound: it was the first time he'd cried since becoming a man.

Aparicio and Gavilán led him to Regina's room. They made him lie down, cleaned the wound, and replaced the filthy rag with a bandage. After they left, he hugged the pillow, hiding his face. He sought sleep, nothing more, and secretly told himself that perhaps sleep would reunite them, make them as they had been. He knew it was impossible, though here on this bed, with its yellowed mosquito netting, he felt her presence more intensely than when he touched her damp hair, her smooth body, her warm thighs. She was there as she had never been before, more alive than ever in the young man's fevered mind: more herself, more his now than he ever remembered her. Perhaps, during their brief months of love, he'd never seen the beauty of her eyes with such emotion, nor could he have compared them, as he could now, with their brilliant twins—black jewels, the deep, calm sea under the sun, their depths like sand mixed in time, dark cherries from the tree of flesh and hot entrails. He'd never told her that. There had not been time. There had not been time to tell her so many things about their love. There had not been time for a final word. Perhaps if he closed his eyes she would come back, whole, to take life from the desperate caresses that pulsed from his fingertips. Perhaps it would be enough to imagine her, to have her always at his side. Who knows if memory can really prolong existence, entwine their legs, open windows to the dawn, comb her hair, revive smell, noise, touch. He sat up. He felt around in the darkness for the bottle of mescal. But the mescal did not help him forget, as people always say it does; it only made the memories flow quicker.

He would return to the rocks on that beach while the alcohol was setting his stomach on fire. He would return. Where? To that mythical beach that never existed? To that lie about the beloved, to that fiction about a meeting on the beach invented by her so that he would feel clean, innocent, sure of being in love? He threw the glass of mescal to the floor. That's what mescal was really good for: destroying lies. It was a beautiful lie.

"Where did we meet?"

"Don't you remember?"

"No, you tell me."

"Don't you remember that beach? I would go there every afternoon."

"Now I remember. You saw the reflection of my face next to yours."

"Remember now: and then I never wanted to see myself without your reflection next to mine."

"Yes, I remember."

He would have to believe that beautiful lie forever, until the end. It wasn't true: he hadn't gone into that Sinaloa town as he had so many others, looking for the first unwary woman he'd find walking down the street. It wasn't true that the eighteen-year-old girl had been forced onto a horse and raped in silence in the officers' quarters, far from the sea, her face turned toward the thorny, dry hills. It was not true that he'd been forgiven in silence, forgiven by Regina's honorableness, when resistance gave way to pleasure and the arms that had never touched a man joyfully touched him for the first time, her moist mouth open, repeating, as she did last night, yes, yes, she'd liked it, she'd liked it with him, she wanted more, she'd been afraid of such happiness. Regina, with the dreamy, fiery eyes. How she accepted the truth of her pleasure and admitted that she was in love with him; how she invented the story about the sea and the reflection in the calm water to forget what would later, when he loved her, make him ashamed. A whore, Regina, a tasty dish, the clean spirit of surprise, a woman without excuses, without justifications. She didn't know how to be boring; she never annoyed him with painful complaints. She would always be there, in one town or another. Perhaps now the fantasy of an inert body hanging from a rope would vanish, and she would already be in another town. She'd just moved on. Yes: as always. She left without bothering him and went south. She crossed the *federales'* lines and found a little room in the next town. Yes; because she couldn't live without him, nor he without her. Yes. It was just a question of leaving, taking a horse, picking up a pistol, getting on with the offensive, and finding her in the next town when they'd take a rest.

In the darkness, he felt around for his field jacket. He slung his cartridge belts across his chest. Outside, the black horse, the quiet one, was tied to a post. People were still gathered around the victims of the hanging, but he didn't even look in that direction. He got on his horse and galloped to headquarters.

"Where the hell did those bastards go?" he shouted to one of the soldiers on guard.

"They're on the other side of the ravine, sir. They're supposed to be dug in next to the bridge, waiting for reinforcements. Looks like they want to take this town again. Come on in and have something to eat."

He dismounted. Slowly he threaded his way through the bonfires in the patio, the clay pots swinging over the crisscrossed logs. The sound of a woman's hands slapping the dough got louder. He stuck a big spoon into the boiling broth of the tripe stew, took a pinch of onion, some powdered chile and oregano. He chewed the hard, fresh northern-style tortillas; the pigs' feet. He was alive.

He ripped from its rusty iron ring the torch that lit up the entrance to headquarters. He sank his spurs into the black horse's flanks. Those still walking the street jumped out of the way. The surprised horse tried to buck, but he held the bridle tight, spurred the horse, and felt, finally, that the horse understood. It was no longer the horse of the wounded man, the wavering man who had crossed the mountains that afternoon. And it was a different horse, too: it understood. It shook its mane to make sure the man understood: it was a war horse, as furious and swift as its rider. And the rider raised the torch to light the road that wound around the town and led to the bridge over the ravine.

There was another bonfire at the entrance to the bridge. The *federales'* caps glowed with a reddish pallor. But the hooves of the black horse carried all the force of the earth, scattering grass and dust and thorns and leaving a trail of sparks from the torch held on high by the rider, who hurled himself at the post at the bridge, leapt over the bonfire, discharged his pistol into astonished eyes, dark necks, bodies that did not understand, who pushed back the cannons, which could not see in the darkness that he was alone, a rider heading south, to the next town, where someone was waiting for him . . .

"Out of the way, you goddamn sons of bitches!" shout the thousand voices of this one man.

The voice of pain and desire, the voice of the pistol, the arm that torches the boxes of powder and blows up the cannons and stampedes the riderless horses, amid a chaos of whinnies and calls and gunshots that now have a distant echo in the lost voices of the town, in the bell that begins to toll in the reddish church tower, in the pulse of the earth that fears the horses of the revolutionary cavalry, which is now crossing the bridge and finds the destruction, the flight, the spent fires, but they don't find either the *federales* or the lieutenant, he who rides south holding the torch on high, the eyes of his horse burning: riding south, with the thread in his hands, riding south.

I survived. Regina. What was your name? No. You, Regina. What was your name, nameless soldier? I survived. You all died. I survived. Ah, they've left me in peace. They think I'm asleep. I remembered you, I remembered your name. But you have no name. And the two come toward me, holding hands, with their begging bowls empty, thinking they're going to convince me, inspire my compassion. Oh, no. I don't owe my life to you. I owe it to my pride, are you listening? I owe it to my pride. I sent out the challenge. I dared. Virtue? Humility? Charity? Ah, you can live without them, you really can. You can't live without pride. Charity? What good is it? Humility? You, Catalina, what would you have done with my humility? You would have used it to conquer my disdain, you would have abandoned me. I know you forgive yourself, envisioning the sanctity of that sacrament. Ha. If it hadn't been for my money, you wouldn't have waited a second to divorce me. And you, Teresa, if you hate and insult me though I support you, how would you have liked to hate me in misery, insult me in poverty? Imagine yourselves without my pride, pharisees, waiting forever on every corner in town for a bus; imagine yourselves lost in that footsore crowd; imagine yourselves working in some shop, in an office, typing, wrapping packages, imagine yourselves saving up to buy a car on the installment plan, lighting candles to the Virgin to keep up your illusions, making monthly payments on a piece of land, sighing for a refrigerator; imagine yourselves sitting at a neighborhood movie on Saturdays, eating peanuts, trying to find a taxi after the show, eating out once a month; imagine yourselves having to shout that there's no other country like Mexico to feel yourselves alive; imagine yourselves having to feel proud of serapes and Cantinflas and mariachi music and *mole poblano* just to feel alive, ha ha; imagine yourselves having to believe in legacies, pilgrimages, the efficacy of prayer to keep you alive.

Domine, non sum dignus . . .

"Cheers. First, they want to cancel all loans from U.S. banks to the Pacific Railroad. Do you have any idea how much the railroad pays per year in interest on those loans? Thirty-nine million pesos. Second, they want to fire all advisers involved in the railroad rehabilitation program. Do you have any idea how much we make? Ten million a year. Third, they want to fire all of us who administer the U.S. loans to the railroads. Do you have any idea how much you earned and how much I earned last year . . . ?"

"Three million pesos each . . ."

"Exactly. And the thing doesn't end there. Do me a favor and send a telegram to National Fruits Express telling them that these Communist leaders intend to cancel the rental of refrigerator cars, an item that costs the company twenty million pesos a year and brings us a good commission. Cheers."

Ha, ha. That's the way to explain it all. Fools. If I didn't defend their interests . . . fools. Oh, get out of here, all of you. Let me listen. We'll just see if you don't understand me. We'll just see if you don't understand what an arm bent like this means . . .

"Sit down, baby. I'll be right with you. Díaz: just make sure that not a single line about police repression against the agitators gets into the paper."

"But, sir, it looks like somebody died. Besides, it was right in the center of town. It'll be hard . . ."

"No, it won't. Those are orders from above."

"But I know that one of the workers' papers is going to print the news."

"What's gotten into you? Don't I pay you to think? Isn't your source paid to think? Tell the district attorney's office to close down that paper . . ."

How little I need to think. A spark. A spark to give life to this enormous, complex network. Other people need an electric generator, but that would kill me. I need to sail murky waters, communicate over long distances, repel the enemy. Oh, yes. Send this out. I'm not interested.

"María Luisa. This Juan Felipe Couto, as usual, is getting too big for his britches . . . That's all, Díaz. Give me a glass of water, honey. I was saying that he's getting too big for his britches. Just like Federico Robles, remember? But they can't get away with it with me around . . ."

"When do we attack, Captain?"

"With my help, he got the concession to build that highway in Sonora. I even helped him so they'd appropriate a budget three times larger than the actual cost of the work, knowing that the highway was going to pass through those dry-farming plots I bought out of the communal lands. I just found out that the wise guy bought some land out there, too, and now he's planning to move the highway so it passes through his property . . ."

"What a pig! And he looks like such a nice guy."

"So, doll, you know, put a little item in your column about him, mention the upcoming divorce of this distinguished public figure. Go easy, now, we just want to throw a little scare into him."

"Anyway, we have photos of Couto in a cabaret with a blondie who's certainly not Mrs. Couto."

"Hold them in reserve in case he doesn't straighten out."

They say the cells in a sponge are not linked but nevertheless the sponge is one: that's what they say. I remember it, because they say if a sponge is torn apart, the pieces join together again. The sponge never loses its unity, it finds a way to join its cells again, it never dies, ah, it never dies.

"That morning I waited for him with pleasure. We crossed the river on horseback."

"You dominated him and stole him away from me."

He stands up amid the indignant voices of the women and takes them by the arm and I go on thinking about the carpenter and then about his son and about what we might have avoided if they'd just let him go with his twelve PR men, as free as a bird, living off the stories about his miracles, getting free meals, free shared beds for sacred witch doctors, until old age and oblivion defeated him, and Catalina and Teresa and Gerardo sit down in the armchairs at the far end of the room. How long will they wait to call in a priest, hasten my death, squeeze confessions out of me? Oh, how they'd like to know. What fun I'm going to have. What fun, what fun. You, Catalina, would be capable of telling me what you never told me, if that would soften me up so you'd know about you-know-what. Ah, but I know what you'd like to know. And your daughter's pinched face doesn't hide it. It won't be long before that poor fool turns up here and starts bawling, to see if he can finally get something out of all this. Ah, how little they know me. Do they think a fortune like that is going to be wasted among three frauds, among three bats that don't even know how to fly? Three bats without wings: three mice. Who disdain me. Yes. Who cannot avoid the hatred of beggars. Who detest the furs that cover them, who hate the houses they live in, the jewels they show off, because I gave it all to them. No, don't touch me now . . .

"Leave me alone . . ."

"But Gerardo's here . . . dear Gerardo . . . your son-in-law . . . look at him."

"Ah, the idiot."

"Don Artemio . . ."

"Mama, I can't stand it, I can't stand it! I can't!"

"He's ill."

"Bah, I'll get out of this bed one day soon and then you'll
see . . ."

"I told you he was pretending."

"Let him rest."

"I tell you he's pretending! The way he always does, to
make fun of us, the way he always does, always."

"No, no, the doctor says . . ."

"What does the doctor know. I know him better. It's
another trick."

"Don't say anything!"

Don't say anything. That oil. They daub my lips with
that oil. My eyelids. My nostrils. They don't know how
much it cost. They didn't have to decide. My hands. My
icy feet that I can't feel anymore. They don't know. They
didn't have to give everything up. My eyes. They spread
my legs and daub that oil on my thighs.

Ego te absolvo.

They don't know. She didn't speak. She didn't tell.

You will live seventy-one years without realizing it. You
will not stop to think about the fact that your blood cir-
culates, your heart beats, your gallbladder empties itself of
serous liquids, your liver secretes bile, your kidney pro-
duces urine, your pancreas regulates the sugar in your
blood. You haven't caused these functions by thinking about
them. You will know that you breathe, but you will not
think about it, because it doesn't depend on your thoughts.
You will turn your back on it and live. You could have
dominated your functions, feigned death, walked through
fire, endured a bed of broken glass. Simply speaking, you
will live and allow your functions to go about their business
on their own. Until today. Today, when your involuntary
functions will force you to take account of them, will
triumph, and end up destroying your person. You will think
that you breathe each time air labors its way toward your
lungs; you will think that your blood is circulating each

time the veins in your abdomen pulse with that painful presence. They will overcome you because they will force you to take life into account instead of living it. Triumph. You will try to imagine it—it is that lucidity which forces you to perceive the slightest pulsation, all the movements of attraction, of separation, even the most terrible, the movement of that which no longer moves—and within you, in your guts, that serous membrane will cover your abdominal cavity and will wrap itself around your intestines, and the fold of tissue, blood, and lymph vessels that connects the stomach and the intestine with your abdominal walls, that fold of adipose cells, will no longer be irrigated with blood by the thick celiac artery that feeds your stomach and your intestines, that penetrates the base of the fold and descends obliquely to the base of the small intestine after having run behind the pancreas, where it gives rise to another artery that irrigates a third of your duodenum and the mouth of the pancreas; crossing your duodenum, it penetrates your aorta, your inferior vena cava, your right urethra, your genito-femoral nerve, and the veins in your testicles. That artery will last, blotched, thick, red, for seventy-one years without your knowing it. Today you will know it. It's going to stop working. The flow is going to dry up. For seventy-one years that artery will make incredible efforts: over the course of its descent, there comes a moment in which, under pressure from a segment of your spinal column, it will have to move downward and at the same time forward and, abruptly, backward again. For seventy-one years your mesentery artery will, under pressure, survive this test, this death-defying feat. Today it will no longer be able to do so. Today it will no longer withstand the pressure. Today, in the swift, piston-like motion downward, forward, and backward, it will stop, convulsed, congested, a mass of paralyzed blood, a scarlet stone that will obstruct your intestine. You will feel that pulse of growing pressure, you will feel it: it's your blood that has stopped for the first time, that now will not reach the other bank of your life, that stops and congeals within the swirl of your intestine, to rot, stagnate, without reaching the other bank of your life.

And it is then that Catalina will approach you, to ask if you want anything, you who at that instant can attend only to your growing pain, trying to repulse it with your will to sleep, to rest, while Catalina cannot avoid making that gesture, that hand stretched forth which she will quickly withdraw, fearful, and press to her matronly bosom, then extend it again, and this time rest it, trembling, on your forehead. She will caress your forehead and you will not know it; you are lost in the acute concentration of pain. You will not realize that for the first time in decades Catalina has placed her hand on your brow, caressed your forehead, pushing back the sweat-matted gray hair that covers it, and then caressing it again in fear and thankfulness, grateful that tenderness is overcoming fear, in an embarrassed tenderness, ashamed of itself, with a shame that finally seems attenuated by the certainty that you don't realize she is caressing you. Perhaps, as she runs her fingers over your brow, she whispers words that seek to mix with that memory of yours that never ceases, lost in the depth of these hours, unconscious, exempt from your will but fused with your involuntary memory, which slides along the interstices of your pain and repeats now the words you didn't hear then. She, too, will think of her pride. There the spark will be born. There you will hear her, in that common mirror, in that pool that will reflect both your faces, that when you try to kiss will drown both of you in the liquid reflection of your faces. Why don't you look the other way? There you will find Catalina in the flesh. Why do you try to kiss her in the cold reflection of the water? Why doesn't she bring her face to yours; why, like you, does she sink it in the stagnant water and repeat to you now that you are not listening to her, "I let myself go"? Perhaps her hand speaks to you of an excess of freedom that defeats freedom. Freedom that raises an endless tower that does not reach heaven but splits the abyss, cleaves the earth. You will name it: separation. You will refuse: pride. You will survive, Artemio Cruz, you will survive because you will expose yourself to the risk of freedom. You will triumph over the risk and, without enemies, will become your own enemy in order to continue the battle of pride. You've conquered everything else; the only thing left is to conquer yourself. Your enemy will surge forth from the mirror to fight the last battle: the enemy nymph, the nymph of thick breath, daughter of gods, mother of the goatish seducer, mother of the only god to die during the time of man. From the mirror will emerge the mother of the Great God Pan, the nymph of pride, your double, once again your double: your ultimate enemy on the earth whose population has been effaced by your pride. You will survive. You will discover that virtue may well be desirable but only pride is necessary. Yet the hand that at this moment is caressing your brow will reach the end and with its small voice silence the shout of challenges, remind you that only at the end, even if it is at the end, pride is superfluous and humility is necessary. Her pale fingers will touch your feverish brow, will try to ease your pain, will try to say to you today what they did not say to you forty-three years ago.

(1924: June 3)

He didn't hear her say it when she awoke from her fitful sleep. "I let myself go." Lying at his side, her chestnut hair covering her face; and in every fold of her flesh she felt weary moisture, the fatigue of summer. She covered her mouth with her hand and foresaw the new day's vertical sun, the afternoon thundershower, the evening transition

from suffocating heat to coolness. She did not want to remember what happened during the night. She buried her
face in the pillow and said again: "I let myself go."

The cold, clear dawn erased the pride of the night and
came through the half-open window of the bedroom. Once
again it defined the details the darkness had confused in a
single embrace.

"I'm young. I have a right . . ."

She put on her nightgown and fled from the man before
the sun could rise over the line of mountains.

"I have a right. It has the blessing of the Church."

Now, from her bedroom window, she saw in the distance
how the sun crowned Citlaltépetl Mountain. She cuddled
the child in her arms and stayed by the window.

"What weakness. Always when I wake up, this weakness,
this hatred, this disdain I don't really feel . . ."

Her eyes met those of the smiling Indian coming through
the garden gate. He took off his hat and bowed . . .

". . . whenever I wake up and see his body asleep next
to mine . . ."

His white teeth gleamed, especially when he was near
her.

"Does he really love me?"

The boss tucked his shirt into his tight trousers, and the
Indian turned his back on the woman's window.

"Five years have gone by . . ."

"What brings you here so early, Ventura?"

"I let my ears lead me around. Mind if I fill my gourd?"

"Is everything ready in town?"

Ventura nodded, walked to the well, sank his gourd into
the water, took a drink, and filled it again.

"Maybe he himself has forgotten why we were married . . ."

"And where do your ears lead you?"

"To the news that old Don Pizarro hates the sight of
you."

"That I already knew."

"My ears also tell me he's going to take advantage of the goings-on today to get even . . ."

"and now he really loves me . . ."

"Blessed be your ears, Ventura."

"Blessed be my mother, who taught me always to keep them clean and free of wax."

"You know what has to be done."

". . . and loves me and admires my beauty . . ."

The Indian laughed soundlessly, fingered the brim of his tattered hat, and looked toward the terrace with its tile-covered roof, where that beautiful woman was sitting in her rocking chair.

". . . my passion . . ."

Ventura remembered her from years back, always sitting that way, sometimes with her stomach round and huge, at other times thin and silent, always detached from the hustle and bustle of the carts filled with grain, the bawling of the branded bulls, the dry splat of the plums that in summer fell in the orchard planted by the new master around the hacienda's main house. ". . . what I am . . ."

She watched the two men the way a rabbit would measure the distance between itself and a pair of wolves. Don Gamaliel's death left her naked, bereft of the proud defenses she had had during their first months together: her father represented continuity, the old order, hierarchy. Her first pregnancy justified her modesty, her aloofness, her warnings to herself.

"My God, why can't I be the same at night as I am during the day?"

And he, as his eyes turned to follow the Indian's eyes, found his wife's immobile face and thought that during those first years he had been indifferent to her coldness. He himself lacked the will to pay close attention to that secondary world which could not manage to integrate itself, assume its proper form, find its name, feel itelf before saying its name.

". . . at night as I am during the day?"

Another Indian, speaking with even more urgency, sought him out.

("The government don't care nothing for us, Mr. Artemio, sir, so we come to ask you please to lend us a hand."

"Boys, you came to the right man. You're going to have your road, I swear it to you, but on just one condition: that you don't bring your corn to Don Cástrulo Pizarro's mill anymore. Can't you see that the old man refused to give up even an inch of land for reform? Why do him any favors? Bring everything to my mill, and let me market it for you."

"We know you're right, sir, but the problem is that Don Pizarro'll kill us if we do what you say."

"Ventura: give these boys some rifles so they can learn to protect themselves.")

She rocked slowly back and forth. She remembered, counted days, often months, when she never spoke to him. "He's never reproached me for my coldness to him during the day."

Everything seemed to be moving without her taking part in it, and the strong man who got off his horse, his fingers callused, his forehead streaked with dust and sweat, gave her a wide berth as he walked by, whip in hand, to collapse in bed so that he could wake again before dawn and set out, as he did every day, on the long route of fatigue around the land that had to produce, yield, consciously be his pedestal.

"The passion I receive him with at night seems to satisfy him."

Corn-producing land, in the narrow river valley that included the remains of the old Bernal, Labastida, Pizarro haciendas; land that grows the *maguey* that yields the *pulque*, the place where the dry sod begins again.

("Hear any complaints, Ventura?"

"Not to my face, boss, because, as bad as things are, these people are better off now than before. But they realize that you gave them land only good for dry-farming and kept the watered land for yourself."

"What else do they say?"

"That you go on charging interest on the loans you made them, just like Don Gamaliel did before."

"Look, Ventura. Go and explain to them that I'm charging the big landowners like Pizarro and the shop-owners really high interest. But if they feel that my loans are hurting them, we can stop doing business right now. I thought I was doing them a favor . . ."

"No, they don't want that . . ."

"Tell them that in a little while I'm going to foreclose on Pizarro's mortgages, and then I'll give them the bottomland I take from the old man. Tell them to hang on and have faith in me, they'll see.")

He was a man.

"But that fatigue, that worry kept him apart. I never asked for that hasty love he gave me every once in a while."

Don Gamaliel, enamored of the city of Puebla, its society, its comforts, and its plazas, forgot the farmhouse and let his son-in-law take care of everything as he saw fit.

"I accepted, just as he wanted me to. He asked me to set aside all my doubts and arguments. My father. I was bought and had to stay here . . ."

As long as her father was alive, she would make the trip to Puebla every two weeks and spend some time with him, fill his cupboards with his favorite sweets and cheeses, go to Mass with him at the Church of San Francisco, kneel before the mummified body of the Blessed Sebastián de Aparicio, scour the Parián market with him, stroll around the main plaza, cross herself at the great holy-water fonts in front of the cathedral built in Herrera's style, or simply watch her father putter around in the patio library . . .

"Oh yes, of course, he protected me, he was my support."

. . . the arguments in favor of a better life were not totally lost on her, and the world she was used to and loved, her childhood years, had sufficient reality to allow her to return to the country, to her husband, without grief.

"With no voice in the matter, with no point of view, bought, just a mute witness to what he did."

She could imagine herself a casual visitor in that alien world, plucked out of the mud by her husband.

Her real world was in the shady Puebla plaza, in the pleasures of cool linen spread over a mahogany table, the feel of hand-painted china, the silverware, the aroma.

". . . of sliced pears, quince, peach preserves . . ."

("I know you ruined Don León Labastida. Those three buildings of his in Puebla are worth a fortune."

"Look at it from my point of view, Pizarro. All Labastida does is ask for one loan after another, never taking the interest into account. I gave him the rope, but he hung himself."

"You must get some pleasure, seeing all this ancient pride tumble down. But you won't pull the same trick on me. I'm not a Puebla dandy like Labastida."

"You always pay on time and you never borrow beyond what you can reasonably pay back."

"Nobody's going to break me, Cruz. I swear it to you.")

Don Gamaliel felt the proximity of death, and he himself arranged his funeral in every detail and with every luxury. His son-in-law could not refuse him the thousand-pesos cash he demanded. His chronic cough worsened, became like a boiling glass bubble set out in the sun, and soon his chest tightened and his lungs could bring in only a thin, cold breath of air that managed to wend its way through the cracks in that mass of phlegm, irritation, and blood.

"Oh yes, the object of his occasional pleasure."

The old man ordered a coach decorated with silver, covered with a canopy of black velvet, and pulled by eight horses with silver fittings and black plumes. He ordered that he be brought in a wheelchair to the window where he could see the coach and the caparisoned horses pass by, back and forth, before his feverish eyes.

"A mother? What birth takes place without joy and pain?"

He told the young bride to take the four large gold candelabra out of the cabinet and polish them: they were to be set around him both at the wake and at the Mass. He asked her to shave him, because the beard went on growing for several hours after death: only his throat and cheeks, and a few snips with the scissors on his beard and mustache. He should be wearing his starched shirt and his frock coat, and they should poison his mastiff.

"Immobile and mute; out of pride."

He left his land to his daughter and named his son-in-law usufructuary and administrator. It was only in the will that he mentioned him. Her he treated, more than ever, as the little girl who grew up at his side and never once spoke of the death of his son or of his son-in-law's first visit. Death seemed an opportunity piously to set aside all those things and, in a final act, restore the lost world.

"Do I have the right to destroy his love, if his love is true?"

Two days before he died, he gave up the wheelchair and took to his bed. Supported by a mass of pillows, he maintained his elegant erect posture, his silky, aquiline profile. Sometimes he stretched out his hand to make sure his daughter was nearby. The mastiff whimpered under the bed. Finally, his thin lips opened in a spasm of terror, and his hand could no longer reach out. It stayed there, immobile, on his chest. She stood, contemplating that hand. It was the first time she'd witnessed death. Her mother had died when she was very young. Gonzalo had died far away.

"So it's this quietude that's so close, this hand that does not move."

Very few families accompanied the grand coach as it rolled first to the Church of San Francisco and then to the cemetery. Perhaps they were afraid of meeting her husband. He rented out the Puebla house.

"How helpless I felt then. Not even the boy helped. Not even Lorenzo. I began thinking what my life might have been with the man behind bars, the life he cut off."

("Ah, there's old Pizarro sitting in front of the main house of his hacienda with a shotgun in his hands. All he's got left is the house."

"That's right, Ventura. All he's got left is the house."

"He's also got a few boys left who are supposed to be good and who will be loyal to him to the death."

"Right, Ventura. Don't forget their faces.")

One night, she realized she was unintentionally spying on him. Imperceptibly, he began to forget her unaffected indifference during their first years, and she began to seek out her husband's eyes during the gray hours of the afternoon, the slow movements of the man who stretched his legs over the leather hassock or who bent down to light the wood in the old fireplace when it was cold.

"Ah, it must have been a weak look, full of self-pity, begging pity from him; nervous, yes, because I could not control the sadness and helplessness I was left with when my father died. I thought that nervousness was mine alone . . ."

She did not realize that at the same time a new man had begun to observe her with new eyes, eyes of repose and confidence, as if he wanted her to understand that the hard times were over.

("Well, sir, everyone's wondering when you're going to divide up Don Pizarro's land."

"Tell them to hold on for a while. Can't they see that Pizarro hasn't given up yet? Tell them to hold on and keep their rifles ready in case the old man tries something. When things calm down, I'll divide up the land.")

"I'll keep your secret. I know you've been making deals with outsiders to trade Don Pizarro's good land for lots in Puebla."

"The small landowners will give work to the peasants, Ventura. Here, take this, and get some rest . . ."

"Thanks, Don Artemio. I hope you understand that I . . .")

And now that the foundation for their well-being was laid, another man emerged, ready to show her that his strength could also be used for acts of happiness. The night in which their eyes finally stopped to grant each other an instant of silent attention, she thought for the first time in ages about how her hair looked and she brought her hand to her nape with its chestnut tresses.

". . . as he smiled at me, standing by the fireplace, with that, that candor . . . Do I have the right to deny myself the possibility of happiness . . . ?"

("Ventura, tell them to return the rifles to me. They don't need them anymore. Now each one of them has his parcel of land, and most of it belongs either to me or to people who work for me. They have nothing to fear anymore."

"Of course, sir. They agree, and they thank you. Some had dreamed of getting much more, but they'll go along with you; they say they won't bite the hand that feeds them, just to give it a reason to starve them."

"Pick out ten or twelve of the toughest and give them rifles. We don't want malcontents on either side.")

"Afterwards I resented it. I let myself go . . . And I liked it. I felt ashamed."

He wanted to efface all trace of the start of their life together, to be loved without a memory of the act that forced her to take him for a husband. Lying next to his wife, he asked silently—this she knew—that the fingers they entwined at that moment be something more than a temporary response.

"Perhaps I would have felt something more with the

other one; I don't know; I only knew my husband's love; ah, he gave himself with a demanding passion, as if he couldn't live another moment unless he knew I felt the same . . ."

He reproached himself, thinking that appearances were proof against him. How could he make her believe that he'd loved her from the moment he saw her pass by on a street in Puebla, even before he knew who she was?

"But when we're apart, when we sleep, when we begin a new day, I lack whatever it is, the gestures, the way of showing things, that can extend the night's love into everyday life."

He could have told her, but one explanation would have required another, and all explanations would have led to a single day and a single place, a jail cell, one October night. He wanted to avoid that return. He knew that he could do it only by making her his without words; he told himself that flesh and tenderness would speak without words. Then another doubt assailed him. Would this girl understand everything he wanted to say when he took her in his arms? Would she understand the tenderness of his intention? Wasn't her sexual response excessive, fraudulent, learned somewhere? Wasn't any promise of real understanding lost in this woman's involuntary theatrics?

"Perhaps it was modesty. Perhaps it was a desire that this love in the dark be something exceptional."

But he did not have the courage to ask, to speak. He was sure the facts would eventually take control: habit, fatality, need also. Where could she turn? Her only future was at his side. Perhaps that simple fact would make her forget the beginning. He slept next to the woman with that desire, by now a dream.

"I ask forgiveness for having forgotten in pleasure the reasons for my rancor . . . My God, how can I respond to this strength, the glow of these green eyes? What of my own strength, once that ferocious, tender body takes me

in its arms, not asking permission, not begging my pardon
for what I could throw in his face . . . Ah, it's terrible
beyond words; things happen before a word exists for
them . . ."

("It is so silent tonight, Catalina . . . Are you afraid of
breaking the silence? Does it speak to you?"

"No . . . Don't talk."

"You never ask me for anything. Sometimes I'd like . . ."

"I let you talk. You know—the things—that . . ."

"Yes. There's no need to talk. I love you, I love you . . .
I never thought . . .")

She would let herself go. She would let herself be loved;
but when she woke, she would again remember it all and
oppose her silent rancor to the man's strength.

"I won't tell you. You conquer me at night. I conquer
you during the day. I won't tell you. That I never believed
what you told us. That my father knew how to hide his
humiliation behind his courtliness, that courteous man, but
I can avenge him in secret and for the rest of my life."

She would get up, braiding her hair without glancing at
the disarrayed bed. She would light the lamp and pray in
silence, the same way that she would quietly show during
the sunlit hours that she had not been conquered, although
the night, her second pregnancy, her large belly, would
say the opposite. And only in moments of true solitude,
when neither the rancor of the past nor the shame of pleasure occupied her thoughts, was she able to tell herself
with honor that he, his life, his strength,

". . . offer me this strange adventure that fills me with
fear . . ."

It was an invitation to adventure, to plunge into an unknown future in which procedure would not be sanctioned
by the sanctity of custom. He invented and created everything from below, as if nothing had happened before, Adam
without a father, Moses without the Tablets of the Law.

Life wasn't like that, the world ordered by Don Gamaliel wasn't like that.

"Who is he? How did he rise out of himself? No, I don't have the courage to accompany him. I have to control myself. I mustn't weep when I remember my life as a girl. That nostalgia."

She compared the happy days of her childhood with this incomprehensible gallop of hard faces, ambition, fortunes that collapsed or were created from nothing, overdue mortgages, decayed fortunes, pride forced into submission.

("He has reduced us to misery. We cannot see you socially; you are part of what he is doing to us.")

It was true. This man.

"I am hopelessly in love with this man, this man who perhaps really does love me, this man to whom I don't know what to say, this man who brings me from pleasure to shame, from the most depressing shame to pleasure that is most, most . . ."

This man had come to destroy them: he had destroyed them already. She saved her body, but not her soul, by selling herself to him. She passed long hours at the window facing the open fields, lost in contemplation of the shaded valley, sometimes rocking the baby's cradle, waiting for her second child to come, imagining the future this adventurer could offer them. He entered the world the way he entered his wife's body—by overcoming modesty with joy and breaking the rules of decency with pleasure. He sat those men down at his own table, his overseers, peons with shining eyes, people who knew nothing about good manners. He abolished the hierarchy embodied in Don Gamaliel. He turned the house into a stable full of ruffians who talked endlessly about incomprehensible, tedious, unamusing things. He began to receive commissions from his neighbors, to hear himself described in terms of adulation. He should go to Mexico City, to the new congress. They would put him up for office. Who better to represent them? If he and his wife cared to visit the towns in the area on Sunday, they would see how much they were loved and what a shoo-in he would be for the congress.

Ventura bowed his head again before putting on his hat. The peon drove the coach right up to the porch; he turned his back on the Indian and walked to the rocking chair where the pregnant woman was sitting.

"Or is it my obligation to nurture the rancor I feel until the day I die?"

He offered her his hand, and she took it. The rotten fruit burst under their feet; the dogs barked, running around the carriage; and the branches of the plum trees wafted the cool dew. As he helped her into the coach, he squeezed her arm and smiled. "I don't know if I've offended you in some way, but if I have, I beg your forgiveness."

He waited for a few seconds. If only she had shown herself even slightly moved. That would have been enough: a gesture, even if evincing no affection, which would have revealed the barest weakness, the smallest sign of tenderness, of a desire for protection.

"If I could make up my mind, if only I could."

Just as he had at their first meeting, he now moved his hand toward her palm. Once again he touched flesh devoid of emotion. He took the reins; she sat down next to him, opened her blue parasol, and never looked at her husband.

"Take care of the baby."

"I've divided my life into night and day, as if to satisfy two ways of living. For God's sake, why can't I just choose one?"

He stared fixedly toward the east. The road passed by cornfields crisscrossed by lines of water the peasants channeled by hand toward the freshly seeded patches to protect the tiny mounds where the seed was hidden. Hawks soared off in the distance; the green scepters of the *maguey* shot up; machetes labored at cutting incisions in their trunks:

sap. Only a hawk high above could make out the moist, fertile stain that marked the outline of the lands of the new master, lands that had once belonged to Bernal, Labastida, and Pizarro.

"Yes: he loves me, he must love me."

The silvery saliva of the creeks soon ran out, and the exception gave way to the rule: the chalky *maguey* soil. As the coach passed, the workers dropped their machetes and hoes, the drivers whipped their burros; the clouds of dust rose over another kind of earth, suddenly dry. Ahead of the coach, like a black swarm of bees, walked a religious procession which they quickly caught up to.

"I should give him every reason to love me. Doesn't this passion please me? Don't his words of love, his daring, and the proof of his pleasure please me? Even now. Even now that I'm pregnant, he won't leave me alone. Yes, yes, it all pleases me."

The slow advance of the pilgrims stopped them: children dressed in white tunics with gold hems, sometimes with halos of silver paper and wire wobbling over their black heads, holding hands with the women wrapped in *rebozos*, with red cheekbones and glassy eyes, crossing themselves and muttering the ancient litanies—on their knees, feet bare, hands clasped to their rosaries—who held up the man with ulcerated legs who was carrying out his vow, whipping the sinner who rejoiced to receive the lashes on his naked back, his waist cinched with a strap of thorns. The crowns of thorns opening wounds in dark foreheads; the nopal scapularies on hairless chests. The whispers in native language did not rise from the road spattered with red drops which the slow feet flattened and quickly hid: feet with hard soles, callused, accustomed to carrying a second layer of muddy skin. The carriage could not move forward.

"Why haven't I learned to accept all this without feeling a strange weight on my heart, without reservation? I want to understand it as proof that he cannot resist the attraction of my body, and I can only understand it as proof that I have triumphed over him, that I can wrench that love out of him every night and scorn him the next day with my coldness and distance. Why can't I decide? Why do I have to decide?"

The sick pressed slices of onion to their temples or allowed themselves to be stroked by the holy branches the women were carrying: hundreds, hundreds. Only an uninterrupted howl broke the silence beneath their murmuring. Even the slavering dogs with the mangy fur panted softly, running between the legs of the slow-moving crowd that waited for the pink-chalk towers to appear in the distance, the porch tiles, the cupolas with their yellow mosaics. The gourds rose to the thin lips of the penitents, and down their chins ran the thick phlegm of *pulque*. Sightless, wormy eyes, faces stained by ringworm; the shaved heads of sick children; noses pocked by smallpox; eyebrows obliterated by syphilis: the conquistadors' mark on the bodies of the conquered, who moved forward on their knees, crawling, on foot, toward the shrine erected in honor of the god of the god-men, the *teules*. Hundreds, hundreds: feet, hands, signs, sweat, lamentations, bruises, fleas, mud, lips, teeth: hundreds.

"I must decide; I have no other possibility in life than being this man's wife until the day I die. Why not accept him? Yes, it's easy to think it. But not so easy to forget the reasons for my rage. God. God, tell me if I am destroying my own happiness, tell me if I should choose him over my duty as sister and daughter . . ."

The carriage made its difficult way along the dusty road, amid bodies that did not know what haste was, that moved along on their knees, on foot, crawling toward the shrine. The maguey planted along the road prevented them from taking a detour, and the white woman protected herself from the sun with the parasol she held in her fingers. She was rocked softly by the shoulders of the pilgrims: her gazelle eyes, her pink earlobes, the even whiteness of her skin, the handkerchief that covered her nose and mouth, her high breasts behind the blue silk, her big belly, her small, crossed feet, and her velvet slippers.

"We have a son. My father and brother are dead. Why do things past hypnotize me? I should look ahead. I don't know how to decide. Am I going to let events, luck, things beyond my control decide for me? It's possible. God. And I'm expecting another child . . ."

Hands stretched out toward her: first the callused limb of an old, gray-haired Indian, then, quickly, the arms naked under the *rebozos* of the women; a low murmur of admiration and tenderness, a longing to touch her, high-pitched syllables: "Mamita, mamita." The coach stopped, and he jumped up, waving the horsewhip over their dark heads, shouting at them to get out of the way: tall, dressed in black, with his gold-braided hat pulled down to his eyebrows . . .

". . . God, why did you put me in this predicament? . . ."

She took up the reins and drove the horse off to the right, knocking down the pilgrims, until the horse whinnied and reared, breaking clay pots, the crates crammed with squawking hens, which fluttered away. The horse kicked the heads of the Indians on the ground, spun completely around, shining with sweat, the nerves in its neck stretched taut and its eyes bulging out of its head: she felt on her body the sweat, the sores, the muted screams, the vermin, the rising stench of the *pulque*. Standing up, balanced by the weight of her stomach, she snapped the reins over the animal's back. The crowd made way, with tiny shrieks of innocence and shock, arms raised, bodies pressed to the wall of *maguey*, and she sped home.

"Why have you given me this life in which I must choose? I wasn't born for this . . ."

Panting, far now from the pilgrims, they headed for the house lost in the reverberating heat, hidden by the swift height of the fruit trees he'd planted.

"I'm a weak woman. All I ever wanted was a quiet life and for others to make choices for me . . . I can't . . . I can't . . ."

The long tables were set up near the shrine right out in the sun. Dense squadrons of flies flew over the pots of beans, the hard tacos piled up on a tablecloth of newspaper. The pitchers of *pulque* laced with cherries, the dry ears of corn, and the tricolor almond marzipan contrasted sharply with the darkness of the food and the clay pots. The president of the municipality stepped up to the podium, introduced him, praised him to the skies, and he accepted the nomination for the federal congress, arranged months earlier in Puebla and Mexico City with a government that recognized his revolutionary merits, the fact that he'd set a good example by retiring from the army to carry out the mandate of agrarian reform, as well as the excellent service he'd rendered in volunteering to stand in for the not yet reestablished public authority in the region, restoring order at his own cost and risk. The dull, persistent murmur of the pilgrims entering and leaving the shrine was all around them. The pilgrims cried out to their Virgin and their God, they wailed, they listened to the speeches and they drank from the jugs of *pulque*. Someone shouted. Several shots rang out. The candidate never lost his composure, the Indians chewed tacos, and he yielded the floor to another learned colleague from the area, while the Indian drum saluted him and the sun hid behind the mountains.

"Just as I told you," whispered Ventura when the drops of rain began punctually to pelt his hat. "Don Pizarro's killers were there, taking aim at you as soon as you stepped up to the podium."

Hatless, he slipped the coat of corn leaves over his head. "Where are they now?"

"Pushing up daisies." Ventura smiled. "We had 'em surrounded before the speeches began."

He put his foot in the stirrup. "Make sure Pizarro gets some souvenirs."

He hated her when he walked into the whitewashed, naked house and found her alone, rocking, wrapped in her arms, as if the arrival of the man filled her with an intangible chill, as if the man's breath, the dried sweat on his body, the feared tone of his voice all heralded a frozen wind. Her thin, straight nose trembled: he threw his hat on the table and his spurs scarred the brick floor as he walked.

"They . . . frightened me . . ."

He didn't speak. He took off his corn-leaf coat and laid it out near the fireplace. The water hissed, running down the roof tiles. It was the first time she had ever tried to justify herself.

"They asked about my wife. Today was important for me."

"Yes, I know . . ."

"How can I put it . . . We all . . . we all need witnesses of our lives in order to live them . . ."

"Yes . . ."

"You . . ."

"I didn't choose my life!" she shouted, clutching the arms of the rocker. "If you force people to do your bidding, don't demand gratitude, too, or . . ."

"So you did *my* bidding against *your* will? Why do you like it so much, then? Why do you moan for it in bed, when all you do is mope around with a long face afterwards? Who can figure you out?"

"Wretch!"

"Go on, you hypocrite, answer me that, why?"

"It would be the same with any man."

She raised her eyes to face him. She had said it. She preferred to cheapen herself. "What do you know? I close my eyes and give you another face and another name."

"Catalina . . . I've always loved you . . . This isn't my fault."

"Leave me alone. I will be in your hands forever. You've got what you wanted. Take what you've got and don't ask for the impossible."

"Why do you reject me? I know you like me when . . ."

"Leave me alone. Don't touch me. Don't throw my weakness in my face. I swear to you I'll never let myself go with you again . . ."

"But you are my wife."

"Don't come any closer. I won't deprive you. After all, that belongs to you. It's part of your winnings."

"Yes, and you'll have to put up with it for the rest of your life."

"I know what my consolation is. With God on my side, with my children, I'll never lack for solace . . ."

"Why should God be on your side, you fraud?"

"Your insults don't matter to me. I know what my consolation is."

"And just why is it you need consolation?"

"Don't walk away. I need consolation for knowing I live with the man who humiliated my father and betrayed my brother."

"You're going to be sorry, Catalina Bernal. You're making me think I ought to remind you of your father and brother every time you spread your legs for me . . ."

"Nothing you can say can hurt me."

"Don't be so sure."

"Do whatever you like. The truth hurts, doesn't it? You killed my brother."

"Your brother didn't give anyone time to betray him. He wanted to be a martyr. He didn't want to save himself."

"He died and you're here, safe and sound, enjoying his rightful inheritance. That's all I know."

"Well, then, burn. And think about the fact that I'll never give you up, not even when I die, but remember, too, that

I know how to humiliate. You're going to be sorry you didn't realize it . . ."

"Do you think I couldn't see your animal face when you said you loved me?"

"I never wanted you to be separate from me. I wanted you to be part of my life . . ."

"Don't touch me. That's something you will never be able to buy."

"Forget what's happened today. Remember that we're going to live the rest of our lives together."

"Stay away from me. Yes. I think about that. About all those years ahead of us."

"Forgive me, then. I ask you again."

"Will you forgive me?"

"I have nothing to forgive you for."

"Will you forgive me for not being able to forgive you for the oblivion the other man is consigned to, the man I really loved? If I only could remember his face clearly . . . If only I'd had that first love, I could say that I'd lived . . . Try to understand; I hate him more than I hate you, because he let you intimidate him and he never came back . . . Perhaps I'm telling you this because I can't tell it to him . . . Yes, tell me that it's cowardly to think this way . . . I don't know, I . . . I'm weak . . . And you, if you want, can love lots of women, but I'm tied to you. If he had taken me by force, I wouldn't have to remember him and hate him today without being able to recall his face. I was left unsatisfied forever, do you understand me? . . . Listen to me now, don't walk away . . . Since I don't have the courage to blame myself for everything that's happened, and since I don't have him close by to hate, I blame you for every-thing, and I hate you, you who are so strong, because you put up with anything . . . Tell me if you can forgive me that, because I will never forgive you as long as I can't forgive myself and the man who ran away . . . Such a weakling. But I don't even want to think, I don't want to talk. Let me live in peace and ask God's forgiveness, not yours . . ."

"Calm down. I liked your sullen silences better."

"Now you know how things stand. You can hurt me as much as you like. I've even given you the weapon. Now, suddenly, because I want you to hate me, and so all our illusions die all at once . . ."

"It would be simpler to forget everything and start over from scratch."

"That's not the way things work."

The immobile woman remembered her first decision, when Don Gamaliel had told her what was happening. To lose with power. To let herself be victimized and then take her revenge.

"Nothing can stop me, see? Just name one thing that can stop me."

"It's only natural. It just pours out of me."

"No need to nurture it and care for it. It just comes naturally."

"Leave me alone!"

She stopped looking at her husband. The absence of words obliterated the nearness of that tall, dark man with his thick mustache, who felt his brow and his nape weighed down by a pain of stone. That closed mouth, with its grimace of dissimulated scorn, spewed the words it could never say right into his face.

"Do you really think that, after doing all you've done, you still have a right to love? Do you really think that the rules of life can change just so you can get that reward in addition to everything else? You lost your innocence in the outside world. You can't recover it here inside, in the world of feelings. Maybe you once had your garden. I had mine, my little paradise. Now we've both lost it. Try to remember. You can't find in me what you've already sacrificed, what you lost forever by your own actions. I don't know where you come from. I don't know what you've done. I only

know that in your life you lost what you made me lose later:
dreams and innocence. We'll never be the same."

He tried to read those words in his wife's immobile face.
Involuntarily, he felt close to the thought she did not express. Words regained their occult power. Cain: that hor-
rendous word should never, ever have burst from the
woman's lips; even if she'd lost all hope of love, she would
still be a witness—a mute, suspicious witness—to love in
the years to come. He locked his jaw. Only one act could
perhaps rend this knot of separation and rancor. Only a few
words, spoken now or never. If she accepted them, they
could forget and begin again. If she didn't accept them . . .

"Yes, I am alive and here at your side because I let others
die for me. I can talk to you about the ones who died
because I washed my hands of them and shrugged. Accept
me as I am, with these sins, and look at me as a man in
need . . . Don't hate me. Take pity on me, Catalina. I love
you: put my sins on one side of the scale and my love on
the other, and you'll see that my love is much greater . . ."

She didn't dare. She wondered why she didn't dare. Why
didn't she demand the truth from him—even if he was
incapable of telling the truth, conscious as she was that his
cowardice distanced them even more and made him also
responsible for their failed love—so the two of them could
be cleansed of the sin this man ached to share in order to
be redeemed?

"I can't do it alone, alone I just can't do it."

During that brief, intimate minute of silence . . .

"Now I'm strong. My strength is to accept this destiny
without fighting."

. . . he also accepted the impossibility of going back, of
returning . . . She got up, murmuring that the baby was
asleep alone in the bedroom. He was left alone, and he
imagined her, on her knees before the ivory crucifix, carrying out the final act that would detach her completely

"from my destiny and my sin, clinging to your personal

salvation, rejecting this, which should have been ours, even if I offered it to you in silence; now you will not return . . ."

He crossed his arms and walked out into the country night, lifting his head to greet the brilliant company bestowed upon him by Venus, the first star in the celestial vault, now quickly filling with stars. On another night he had looked toward the stars; remembering it gained him nothing. He was no longer that boy, nor were the stars the same ones his boy's eyes had contemplated.

The rain had stopped. The orchard gave off a deep aroma of guava and sloe, plum and apple. He had planted the trees in the garden. He had raised the wall that separated the house and the garden, his intimate domain on the farm.

As his boots sank into the moist earth, he stuck his hands into his pockets and walked slowly toward the gate. He opened it and walked toward the nearby houses. During his wife's first pregnancy, that young Indian girl had occasionally received him with an inert silence and a total absence of questions or demands.

He walked in without knocking, suddenly opening the door of the cabin made of scarred adobe. He took her by the arm, awakening her out of a sound sleep, already feeling the heat of her dark, sleeping body. The frightened girl stared at the master's twisted face, his curly hair falling over his glassy eyes, his thick lips surrounded by disordered, harsh whiskers.

"Come on, don't be afraid."

She raised her arms to put on her white blouse and reached out to pick up her *rebozo*. He led her out. She lowed softly like a lassoed calf. And he raised his face toward the sky, covered tonight with all its lights.

"Do you see that great big star shining over there? Looks like you could touch it, right? But even you know that you'll never touch it. We've got to stay no to the things we can't touch with our hands. Come on; you're going to live with me in the big house."

The girl came into the orchard with her eyes lowered.

Washed by the thunderstorm, the trees glowed in the darkness. The fermented earth filled with heavy odors, and he breathed deeply.

Upstairs in the bedroom, she left the door ajar and got into bed. She lit the night-light. She turned her face to the wall, crossed her arms so her hands were on her shoulders, and tucked up her legs. An instant later, she stretched out her legs and felt for her slippers. She got up and walked the length of the room, raising and lowering her head. Without realizing it, she lulled the child sleeping in his crib. She caressed her stomach. She went back to bed and waited to hear the man's footsteps in the hall.

I let them do what they want, I can't think or desire anymore; I'm getting used to this pain; nothing can last forever without becoming normal. The pain I feel below my ribs, around my navel, in my intestines, is now my pain, a pain that gnaws: the taste of vomit in my mouth is my taste; the swelling of my stomach is my baby, I compare it to giving birth; it makes me laugh. I try to touch it. I run my hand from my navel to my pubis. New. Round. Doughy. But the cold sweat gives way. That colorless face that I manage to see in the asymmetrical mirrors on Teresa's handbag, which passes next to my bed, she never puts down her bag, as if there were thieves in the room. I suffer that collapse. I just don't know. The doctor's gone. He said he was going to get other doctors. He doesn't want to be responsible for me. I just don't know. But I see them. They've walked in. The mahogany door opens and closes, and their footsteps make no noise on the thick carpet. They've closed the windows. With a hiss, they've pulled back the gray curtains. They've entered. Ah, there is a window. There is a world outside. There is this strong plateau wind that shakes the thin black trees. We've got to breathe . . .

"Open the window . . ."

"No, no. You might catch cold and make things worse."

"Open . . ."

"Domine, non sum dignus . . ."

"Fuck God . . ."

"You curse Him because you believe in Him . . ."

Very clever. That was very clever. It calms me down. I don't think about those things anymore. Yes, why would I insult Him if He didn't exist? That does me some good. I'm going to admit all this because if I rebel I concede that those things exist. That's what I'll do. I don't know what I was thinking of. Sorry. The priest understands me. Sorry. I'm not going to let them have their way by rebelling. That's better. I should wear an expression of boredom. That's most appropriate. How much importance all this gets. An event that for the person most concerned, namely me, signifies the end of importance. Yes. That's the way to do it. That's it. When I realize that all of it will cease to have any importance, the others try to make it into the most important thing: pain itself, the salvation of someone's soul. I make this hollow sound through my nose and let them go about their business and I cross my arms over my stomach. Oh, get out, let me listen. Now we'll see if they understand me. Now we'll just see if they don't understand an arm bent like this . . .

". . . they allege that those same cars can be made here in Mexico. But we're not going to allow it, right? Twenty million pesos is a million and a half dollars . . ."

"Plus our commissions . . ."

"The ice isn't going to do that cold of yours any good."

"Just hay fever. Well, I'll be . . ."

"I'm not finished. Besides, they say that the fees charged by the mining companies for freight from the center of Mexico to the frontier are extremely low, that it costs more to ship vegetables than the minerals from our companies . . ."

"Nasty, nasty . . ."

"Of course. You understand that if the fees go up, working the mines won't be cost-efficient . . ."

"Less profit, sure, lessprofitsure, lesslessless . . ."

"Padilla, what's wrong? Padilla. What is that racket?
Padilla."

"The tape ran out. Just a second. I'll just turn it over and
play the other side."

"He's not listening, Mr. Padilla."

Padilla must be smiling his smile. Padilla knows me. I'm
listening, all right. I sure am. Ah, that noise fills my brain
with electricity. The noise of my own voice, my reversible
voice, yes, there it goes, it screeches again and runs backward, squeaking like a squirrel, but it's my voice, and my
name, which has only eleven letters and can be written a
thousand ways: Amuc Reoztrir Zurtec Marzi Itzau Erimor,
but there's a key to that code, a model: Artemio Cruz, ah,
my name, I hear my screeching name, it stops, now it runs
the other way:

"Mr. Corkery, would you be so kind as to communicate
this information to all interested parties in the United
States. They should stir up the newspapers against the
Communist railroad workers in Mexico."

"Sure, if you say they're Commies. I feel it's my duty to
uphold by any means our . . ."

"Sure, sure. It's wonderful that our ideas and our interests are the same, isn't that right? And one other thing:
have a talk with your ambassador, so that he will put some
pressure on the Mexican government, which is just taking
power and is still a little green."

"Oh, we never intervene."

"I'm sorry, I was too brusque. Suggest he study the
matter calmly and then offer his objective opinion, given
his natural concern for the interests of U.S. citizens here
in Mexico. He should explain that we must maintain a
climate favorable to investment, and that with this agitating . . ."

"Okay, okay."

Oh, what a bombardment of signs, words, stimulants for my tired ears. Oh, what exhaustion, oh, what language without language. Oh, but I said it, it's my life, I have to listen to it. Oh, they won't understand my gesture, I can barely move my fingers: I want them to turn it off now, I'm bored, what difference can it make, what a nuisance, what a nuisance . . . I have something to tell them:

"You dominated him and stole him away from me."

"That morning I waited for him with pleasure. We crossed the river on horseback."

"I blame you. You. You're to blame."

Teresa drops the newspaper. Catalina, coming closer to the bed, tells her, as if I can't hear her: "He looks very bad."

"Did he say where it is?" asks Teresa in a lower voice.

Catalina shakes her head. "The lawyers don't have it. It must be handwritten. But he would be capable of dying intestate, anything to make our lives difficult."

I listen to them with my eyes closed, and I dissimulate, dissimulate.

"The priest couldn't get anything out of him?"

Catalina must have shaken her head. I sense that she's on her knees near the head of the bed and that she says in a low, broken voice, "How do you feel? . . . Don't you want to talk a little? . . . Artemio . . . There's a very serious matter . . . Artemio . . . We don't know if you've made out your will. We'd like to know where . . ."

The pain is passing. They don't see the cold sweat pouring down my forehead or my tense immobility. I hear their voices, but it's only now that I can once again make out their silhouettes. Everything's coming back into normal focus, and I can see both of them perfectly, their faces and gestures, and I want the pain to come back to my stomach. I tell myself, I tell myself lucidly that I don't love them, that I never loved them.

". . . We'd just like to know where . . ."

All right, then, bitches, just imagine you're standing in front of a shopkeeper who doesn't give credit, that you're being evicted, that you're up against a shyster lawyer, a thieving doctor, imagine you're from the shitty middle class, bitches, standing on line to buy adulterated milk, to pay property taxes, to get an audience, to get a loan, standing on line to dream you'll do better someday, envying the wife and daughter of Artemio Cruz as they cruise by in their car, envying a house in Las Lomas de Chapultepec, envying a mink coat, an emerald necklace, a trip abroad, imagine yourselves in a world in which I was virtuous, in which I was humble: down below, where I came from, or up above, where I am. Only in those two places, let me tell you, is there any dignity, not in the middle, not in the envy, the monotony, the lines. Everything or nothing: know how I play the game? understand how? everything or nothing, put it all on the black or all on the red, you need balls, see? Balls, putting it all on the line, shooting the works, running the risk of being shot either by the ones on top or by the ones at the bottom. That's what it means to be a man, which is what I've been, not the way you would have wanted, half a man, a man with his little temper tantrums, intemperate shouts, a whorehouse, a saloon man, a postcard macho, no! no! not me! I didn't have to shout at you, I didn't have to get drunk to scare you, I didn't have to smack you around to show you who was boss, I didn't have to humiliate myself to beg your tenderness: I gave you wealth without expecting anything back, tenderness, understanding, and because I didn't demand anything from you, you haven't been able to abandon me, you latched onto my wealth, cursing me probably the way you'd never curse my poor pay packet, but forced to respect me the way you'd never have respected my mediocrity—ah, assholes, conceited bitches, impotent bitches, who had everything money could buy and who still have mediocre minds. If at least you had taken advantage of what I gave you, if at least you had understood what luxury items are for, how they're used: while I had everything, do you hear me? everything that can be bought and everything that can't be bought. I had Regina, do you hear me? I loved Regina, her name was Regina, and she loved me, she loved me without money, she followed me, she gave me life, down below, do you hear me? I heard you, Catalina, I heard what you told him one day:

"Your father; your father, Lorenzo . . . Do you think . . . ? Do you think anyone could approve of . . . ? I don't know, about holy men . . . real martyrs . . ."

Domine, non sum dignus . . .

In the depth of your pain, you will smell that incense which lingers and lingers and you will know, behind your shut eyes, that the windows have been closed as well, that you no longer breathe the cool afternoon air: only the stench of the incense, the trace left behind by the priest who will come to give you absolution, a last rite which you will not request, but which you will nevertheless accept, just so as not to gratify them with your rebelliousness in your last moments. You will want all of this to take place so you won't owe anything to anyone, and you will want to remember yourself in a life that owes nothing to no one. She will stop you, her memory—you will name her: Regina; you will name her: Laura; you will name her: Catalina; you will name her: Lilia—which will summarize all your memories and will oblige you to acknowledge her. But you will transform even that gratitude—you know it, behind each scream of sharp pain—into pity for yourself, in a loss of your loss. No one will give you more in order to take away more from you than that woman, the woman you loved with her four different names: who else?

You will stand fast. You've probably made a secret vow: not to acknowledge your debts. You will have wrapped

Teresa and Gerardo in the same oblivion, an oblivion you will justify because you know nothing about them, because the girl will grow up at her mother's side, far from you, you who will have life only for your son, because Teresa will marry that boy whose face you can never fix in your memory, that vague boy, that gray man who will not waste or occupy the grace period granted to your memory. And Sebastián: you will not want to remember those square hands which pull you by the ears, which spank you with a ruler. You will not want to remember your painful knuckles, your fingers white with chalk dust, the hours standing at the blackboard learning to write, to multiply, to draw elementary things—houses and circles. You will not want to: that is your debt.

You scream and arms hold you down: you want to get up and walk to ease your pain.

You smell the incense.

You smell the enclosed garden.

You think that it's impossible to choose, that no one should choose, that you didn't choose on that day. You let things happen, you weren't responsible, you didn't create either of the moral codes which made their claim on you that day. You couldn't be responsible for options you didn't create. You dream, away from your body which screams and twists, away from that machete jabbed into your stomach until it forces out your tears. You dream about that ordering of life that you yourself created, that you will never be able to reveal because the world will not give you the chance, because the world will offer you only its established tables, its codes in conflict, which you will not dream of, which you will not think about, which you will not live.

The incense will be a smell with time, a smell that talks.

Father Páez will live in your house, will be hidden in the cellar by Catalina: it will not be your fault, it will not be your fault.

You will not remember what you say, you and he, that

night in the cellar. You will not remember if he, if you say it. What's the name of the monster who voluntarily dresses up as a woman, who voluntarily castrates himself, who voluntarily gets drunk on the fictitious blood of a God? who will say that? but who loves, I swear it, because the love of God is great indeed and inhabits all bodies, justifies them. We have our bodies by the grace of God and with his benediction, to give them the minutes of love which life would like to strip from us. Don't feel ashamed, don't feel anything; instead, forget your troubles. It can't be a sin, because all the words and all the acts of our short, hasty love, of today and never of tomorrow, are only a consolation that you and I give each other, an acceptance of the necessary evils of life which later justifies our contrition. After all, how could there be real contrition without the recognition of the real evil in us? How can we understand sin, pardon for which we are to beg on our knees, if beforehand we don't commit sin? Forget your life, let me put out the light, forget everything, and later we will pray together for forgiveness and we will say a prayer that will erase our minutes of love. In order to consecrate this body which was created by God and which says God in every desire, unsatisfied or satisfied, which says God in every secret caress, says God in the gift of the semen God planted between your thighs.

To live is to betray your God. Every act in life, every act that affirms us as living beings, requires that the commandments of your God be broken.

In a whorehouse that night, you will speak with Major Gavilán, with all your old comrades, and you will not remember what they said that night, you will not remember if they say it, if you say it, with the cold voice that will not be the voice of the men, the cold voice of power and self-interest: We want the greatest good for the nation, as long as it's compatible with our personal well-being. Let's be intelligent: we can go far. Let's do what's necessary, not

the impossible. Let's determine once and for all all the acts
of power and cruelty that will be useful to us, in order not
to have to repeat them. Let's scale the benefits so that the
people enjoy every taste they get. We can make a revolution
very quickly, but tomorrow they'll demand more and more
and more, and then we'll have nothing to give if we've
already done and given everything—except, perhaps, our
personal sacrifice. Why die if we aren't going to see the
fruits of our heroism? Let's always keep something in reserve. We are men, not martyrs; everything will be allowed
us if we hold on to power. Lose power and they'll screw
you. Just think how lucky we are: we're young but we're
haloed, wearing the halo of the armed, triumphant Revolution. Why did we fight? to die of hunger? When it's
necessary, force is just. You don't share power."

And tomorrow? We'll be dead, Congressman Cruz. Let
those who follow us make their own deals.

Domine, non sum dignus. Domine, non sum dignus: yes,
a man can speak painfully with God, a man who can forgive
sin because he has committed sin, a priest who has the
right to be a priest because his human misery allows him
to act out redemption in his own body before granting it
to others. *Domine, non sum dignus.*

You reject guilt. You will not be guilty of sins against a
morality you did not create, which you found already made.
You would have wanted

wanted

wanted

wanted

oh, how happy those days were with your teacher Sebastián, whom you will not want to remember anymore.
You sat at his knee, learning those simple things with which
you must begin in order to be a free man, not a slave of
commandments written without your even being con-
sulted. Oh, how happy those apprenticeship days were,
learning the tasks which he taught you so you could earn

a living: days at the forge with the hammers, when your teacher Sebastián would return tired but begin classes only for you, so that you could be something in life and make your own rules, you the rebel, you free, you unique and new. You will not want to remember him. He ordered you, you went to the Revolution: this memory does not leave me, it will not reach you.

You will have no answer for the opposing, imposed codes, you innocent,
you will want to be innocent,
you did not choose on that night.

(1927: November 23)

His green eyes turned toward the window, and the other man asked him if he wanted anything; he blinked and kept his green eyes on the window. The other man, who had been very, very calm until then, tore his pistol out of his belt and slammed it on the table. He felt the shaking of glasses and bottles and reached out his hand, but before he could give a name to the physical sensation that brusque gesture caused in the pit of his stomach—the impact of the pistol on the table, and its effect on the blue glasses and white bottles—the other man was already smiling. An automobile roared down the street, to a chorus of jeers and curses, its headlights illuminating the other man's round head. The other man spun the cylinder in the revolver and showed him that it contained only two bullets; he spun it again, pulled back the hammer, and pointed the barrel directly at his temple. He tried to avert his eyes, but the small room gave him no place to fix his attention: naked walls painted indigo blue, ark *tezontle*-stone floor, tables, two chairs, two men. The other man waited until the green eyes stopped wavering around the room and returned to his hand, the revolver, his temple. The other man smiled, but he was sweating. So was he. In the silence he listened for the tick, tick, tick of the watch he'd put in the right-hand pocket of his vest. Perhaps it was making less noise than his heart, but it was all the same, because the deto-nation of the pistol was already in his ears, beforehand. At the same time, the silence was dominated over all sound, even the possible—not yet actual—sound of the revolver. The other man waited. He watched. The other man squeezed the trigger, and a dry, metallic click was lost in the silence, and, outside, the night went on, uniform and moonless. The other man stood there with the weapon aimed at his temple and began to smile, to laugh aloud: his fat body shook from within, like custard, from within, be-cause outwardly it was motionless. Both remained frozen for some seconds. Again, he breathed the smell of incense that had followed him everywhere since morning; through that imaginary smoke, he made out the other man's face. The other man was still laughing inwardly as he put the pistol back on the table and slowly pushed the weapon toward him with short, yellowed fingers. The turbid mirth in the other man's face might reflect the tears he was hold-ing back; he didn't try to find out. The memory, not yet a memory, of the other man with the gun to his head, the fear in that obese figure, the fear kept in check, wrenched his guts, made his stomach ache, kept him from speaking. If he was found here in this room with the fat man dead, and if charges were pressed against him, it would be all over. He'd recognized his own pistol, which he kept in the dresser drawer; he realized that the fat man was pushing it toward him with his short fingers, its butt wrapped in a handkerchief which might perhaps have slipped out of the other man's hands if he had . . . But even if it didn't slip off, it was a clear case of suicide. Clear to whom? A police commander dies in an empty room, sitting opposite his enemy. Who was getting rid of whom? The other man loosened his belt and drank off his drink in one gulp. Sweat stained his armpits, ran down his neck. The other man's fingers, which looked as though they'd been cropped, insistently pushed the pistol nearer. What would he say? That they had checked him out completely. He'd never squeal, would he? He asked just what it was they'd checked out about him, and the other man said he was fine, that he'd passed; if there was dying to do, he wouldn't falter, but he wasn't going to waste his time going over the same ground again and again, and that was how things stood. If this didn't convince him, well, he didn't know what would. It was proof—the other man told him—that he should come over to their side; or did he think anyone from his side would risk his life to show him how much they wanted him on their side? He lit a cigarette and offered the other man one; the other man lit his own; he brought his lighted match right to the coffee-colored face of the fat man, and the fat man blew it out. He felt surrounded. He balanced his cigarette precariously on the edge of his glass, without noticing that the ashes were falling into the tequila, settling to the bottom. He picked up the pistol. He pressed the muzzle to his temple and felt it had no temperature whatever, although he imagined it should feel cold as he recalled that he was thirty-eight years old, but that fact didn't matter to anyone, not to the fat man and much less to himself.

That morning he had dressed standing in front of the full-length oval mirror in his bedroom, and the incense had reached his nose. He pretended not to smell anything. From the garden, there wafted an odor of chestnuts over the earth, which was dry and clean that month. He saw the strong man with his strong arms, flat stomach, no fat, solid muscles around a dark navel, where the fine hair from his pubis and his stomach ended. He ran his fingers over his cheeks, over his broken nose, and smelled the incense again. He chose a clean shirt from the dresser and did not realize that the revolver was no longer there, and finished dressing and opened the bedroom door. "I don't have time; really, I don't have time. I'm telling you I don't have time."

The garden had been planted with decorative shrubs arranged in horseshoe and fleur-de-lis patterns, with rose-bushes and hedges, and a green fringe surrounded the one-story house, built in Florentine style, with slender columns and stucco friezes above the portal. The exterior walls were pink, and as he passed through the rooms the uncertain morning light isolated the gilt profiles of the chandeliers, the marble statuary, the velvet curtains, the high-backed, brocaded armchairs, the display cabinets, and the gold fillets on the love seats. But he stopped by the side door at the rear of the salon, his hand on the bronze knocker; he did not want to open the door and walk down.

"It belonged to people who went to live in France. We didn't pay anything for it, but restoring it cost a fortune. I said to my husband, I said let me do it all, leave it to me, I know how . . ."

The fat man jumped up from his chair, light, filled with air, and brushed aside the hand that held the pistol: no one heard the shot, it was late and they were alone, yes, perhaps that's why no one heard it, and the bullet lodged in the blue wall while the commander laughed and said that was enough fooling around for now, dangerous fooling around especially. Why bother, when everything could be fixed so easily? So easily, he thought; it's about time for things to be fixed easily; will I ever live a quiet life?

"Why don't you just leave me in peace? Why?"

"But it's the easiest thing in the world, pal. It's up to you."

"Where are we?"

He hadn't come on his own; they'd brought him. And even though they were right in the middle of the city, the driver had got him dizzy: a turn to the left, then a right—the succeeding rectangles of Spanish city planning turned into a labyrinth of imperceptible divisions. It was all imperceptible, like the short, fragile hand of the other man, who snatched away the weapon, always laughing, and sat down again, heavy, fat, sweaty, his eyes flashing fire.

"We're a pair of real motherfuckers, right? Know something? Always choose the biggest motherfuckers for your friends because, if you're on their side, no one's going to fuck you over. Let's have a drink."

They toasted each other, and the fat man said that in this world there are two kinds of people, motherfuckers and assholes, and we have to decide which we're going to be. He went on to say that it would be a shame if he, the congressman, didn't know how to choose when the time came for choosing, because he and his friends were all straight shooters, all good guys, and they were giving everybody a chance to choose, except that not all of them were as smart as the congressman. They thought they were tough guys and started in shooting, when it was so simple to change places, just like that, and be on the right side. Don't tell me this is the first time you ever changed sides . . . Where have you been for the past fifteen years? The other man's voice, fat, like his flesh, whispering, and as terrifying as a snake, lulled him to sleep—that throat made up of contractile rings, lubricated by alcohol and cigars: "Like one?"

The other man stared at him fixedly, and he went on running his fingers over his belt buckle without realizing it. When he did realize it, he moved his fingers away; the silver made him think of the coolness or the heat of the pistol, and he wanted to have his hands free.

"Tomorrow they shoot the priests. I'm telling you as proof of our friendship, because I know for a fact you're not one of those faggots . . ."

They pushed back their chairs. The other man went to the window and rapped his knuckles hard on the glass. He waved and then motioned to the man to get up. The other one stayed at the door while he walked down the fetid stairs, knocking over a garbage can, and everything reeked of rotten orange peels and wet newspapers. The man who had been standing by the door raised a finger to his white hat and showed him that Avenida 16 de Septiembre was over that way.

"What do you think?"

"That we should go over to the other side."

"Not me."

"Well, what do you think?"

"I'm listening."

"Can anyone else hear us?"

"Saturno's a woman you can trust. Not a sound gets out of her house . . ."

"If they don't, then I'll make them . . ."

"We got where we are with the chief, and we'll go down with the chief."

"He's done for. The new boss has him all boxed in."

"So what are you going to do?"

"Put in an appearance with the new guy."

"I'd sooner let' em cut off my ears. Are we men or what?"

"What do you mean?"

"There are lots of ways to do things."

"Maybe, but I don't see any easy way out of this one."

"Right. But you just can't keep saying no to everything."

"I'm not saying no, I'm not saying anything."

"Now it sounds like yes and no at the same time . . ."

"What I say is that we go down like men, with one or the other . . ."

"Wake up, General, sir, it's daybreak."

"Well?"

"Well . . . that's how I see it. Everybody's got his work cut out for him."

"Well, who knows . . ."

"I think I do."

"So you really think our chief's not going anywhere?"

"That's what I think, my opinion."

"Why do you think so?"

"I don't know. It's just how I feel."

"And last but not least, what about you?"

"I'm starting to think the same thing . . ."

"Okay, but when the time comes, just forget we ever had this little talk."

"Who's going to remember, when we didn't say anything?"

"I'm just saying, just in case."

"Just in case, that's what it's all about."

"Shut up, Saturno. Bring us something to drink, go on."

"Just in case, monsieur."

"So we're not going to stick together on this one?"

"Sure we'll stick together, but each guy's got to figure it out for himself."

"The answer's always the same; it's just how you get to it that's different."

"That's it."

"General Jiménez, wouldn't you like something to eat?"

"Everybody's got his story straight, right?"

"Sure, but if somebody squeals . . ."

"Where do you get that stuff, man? We're all pals here."

"Yeah, sure, but then somebody starts thinking about his old gray-haired mama, and then he gets ideas."

"Just in case, as Saturno says . . ."

"Just in fucking case, Colonel Gavilán."

"Just one guy starts thinking . . ."

"One guy starts thinking for himself, and that's it."

"Yeah, but a guy might want to save his skin, right?"

"Skin, yeah, but his honor, too, Congressman, sir."

"His honor, too. Right you are, General."

"So . . ."

"This little meeting never happened."

"Never, never, never."

"But do you think the chief's done for?"

"Which chief, the old one or the new one?"

"The old one, the old one."

Chicago, Chicago, that toddlin' town: Saturno takes the needle off the record and claps her hands. "Girls, girls, line up over here . . ." while he got in the carriage and pulled back the curtains, laughing, and only saw the girls out of the corner of his eyes, dark, but powdered and creamed, with beauty marks drawn on their cheeks, their breasts, next to their lips, their velvet or patent-leather slippers, their short skirts, blue eyelids, and the hand of the bouncer, also powdered: "A little something for me, sir?"

This business was going to turn out fine, he knew it, rubbing his belly with his right hand, stopping in the little garden in front of the whorehouse to breathe in the dew on the lawn, the coolness of the water in its spring of muddy velvet. By now, General Jiménez would have taken off his blue glasses and would be rubbing his dry eyelids, the dry skin flaking off from his conjunctivitis and making his beard snowy. He would be asking for someone to help get his boots off, someone take off his boots, please, because he was tired and because he was accustomed to having someone take off his boots, and everyone would laugh because the general would take advantage of the position the girl was in to lift up her skirt and show her small, round, dark ass covered with lilac silk. The others would rather see the rare spectacle of those eyes that were always hidden, open for once like big, insipid oysters—and all of them, the friends, the brothers, the pals, would stretch out their arms and have their jackets taken off by Saturno's young acolytes, who would be buzzing like bees around the ones in army uniforms, as if they had no idea what might be underneath the uniform, the buttons emblazoned with the eagle and serpent, the gold oak clusters. He'd seen them fuss like that, damp, just barely out of the cocoon, their mestizo arms waving powder puffs in the air, powdering the heads of the friends, brothers, pals leaning back on the beds with their legs spread, their shirts stained with cognac, their temples dripping and their hands dry, while the rhythm of the Charleston filtered through, while the girls undressed them slowly, kissing every part they uncovered, squealing when the men stretched out their fingers. He looked at his fingernails with their white tips; white fingertips were supposedly proof of telling lies, and the half-moon on his thumb, and a dog barked near him. He turned up the lapels of his jacket and walked toward his house, though he'd prefer to go to the other place and sleep in the arms of those powdered bodies and release the acid that had his nerves on edge, that forced him to stand there with eyes open, gazing needlessly at those rows of low gray houses surrounded by balconies decked out with porcelain and glass flowerpots, rows of dry, dusty palm trees on the avenue, needlessly smelling the leftover smell of chillied corn and vinegar dressing.

He ran his hand over his rough beard. He picked through his ring of uncomfortable keys. She would be down there right now—she who went up and down the carpeted stairs without making a sound, who was always frightened to see him walk in. "Oh! What a fright you gave me. I didn't expect you. No, I didn't expect you to be back so soon. I swear I didn't expect you to be back so soon." And he wondered why she went through this act of complicity just to throw his guilt in his face. But complicity and guilt were, at least, words, and their encounters, the attraction that repelled before it began to move them, the rejection, which at times drew them together, were not expressed in words, neither before being born nor after being consummated, because both acts were identical. Once, in the darkness, their fingers touched on the banister, and she squeezed his hand and he lit the lamp so she wouldn't trip, because he didn't know that she was going down the stairs while he was going up, but her face did not reflect the feeling of her hand, and she put out the lamp, and he wanted to call that perversity, but that wasn't the right word for it because habit cannot be perverse, unless it stops being premeditated and exceptional. He knew a soft object, wrapped in silk and linen sheets, an object to be touched because the bedroom lamps were never burning during those moments: only in that moment on the stairs, when she neither hid nor masked her face. It happened only once, which was not necessary to remember but nevertheless wrenched his stomach with a bittersweet desire to repeat it. He thought about it and felt it after it had recurred, when it was repeated that very dawn, and the same hand touched his, this time on the handrail that led to the cellar, although this time no lamp was lit and she merely asked him: "What are you looking for here?" before she recovered herself and repeated in an even tone, "Good heavens, what a fright! I didn't expect you. I swear I didn't expect you so early"— an even tone, with no mockery, and he could only breathe in that almost fleshly smell, that smell with words, with their own musical cadence.

He opened the pantry door and at first could not make him out, because he, too, seemed made of incense. She took the sleeve of her secret guest, who was trying to hide the folds of his cassock between his legs and diffuse the sacred smell by waving his arms, before he realized how useless it all was—her protection, his black gesticulations— and lowered his head in an imitative sign of consummation which must have comforted him and assured him that he was carrying out, for his own satisfaction, if not for that of the witnesses who were in fact looking not at him but at each other, the time-honored motions of resignation. He desired, requested that the man who had just walked in look at him, recognize him. Out of the corner of his eye, the priest saw that the man could not tear his eyes away from the woman, nor could she tear hers from him, no matter how she embraced and shielded the minister of the Lord. For his part, he could feel a spasm in his gallbladder, in the yellowness of his eyes and tongue the promise of a terror which, when the moment came—the next moment, because there would be no other—he would not know how to hide. All he had left, thought the priest, was this moment to accept destiny, but in this moment there were no witnesses. That green-eyed man was asking: he was asking her to ask, to dare to ask, to take a chance on the yes or no of chance, and she could not answer; she could no longer answer. The priest imagined that on another day, in sacrificing this possibility of answering or asking, she had sacrificed, from that day on, this life, the priest's life. The candles highlighted the opacity of his skin, matter that withstands transparency and brilliance; the candles created a black twin for the priest out of the whiteness of his face, neck, and arms. He waited to be asked. He saw the contraction of that neck he longed to kiss. The priest sighed: she would not beg, and all that was left to him, standing before this man with green eyes, was a moment to act out his resignation, because tomorrow he would not be able, it would doubtless be impossible, tomorrow resignation would forget his name and would be named viscera and viscera do not know the words of God.

He slept until noon. Music from an organ-grinder out in the street woke him up, and he did not bother to identify the song. The silence of the previous night—or his mercy of the night and the silence—imposed long-dead moments that cut through the melody, and then, quickly, the slow, melancholy rhythm would begin again to seep through the half-open window before that memory without sound interrupted it once more. The telephone rang, and he picked it up and heard the restrained laughter of the other man, and said:

"Hello."

"We've got him down at the station, Congressman."

"Really?"

"The President has been informed."

"Then . . ."

"You know. A gesture. A visit. No need to say anything."

"When?"

"Come over at about two."

"See you then."

She heard him from the adjacent bedroom and began to weep, clinging to the door, but then she heard nothing and dried her cheeks before sitting down in front of her mirror.

He bought a paper from a newsboy and tried to read it as he drove, but he could only glance at the headlines, which spoke about the execution of those who had made an attempt on the life of the other leader, the candidate. He remembered him in the great moments, the campaign against Villa, during his presidency, when all of them swore their loyalty to him, and he looked at that photo of Father Pro, with his arms wide open to receive the volley of bullets. Passing by him in the street were the white roofs of new automobiles; on the sidewalk, the short skirts and cloche hats of the women, and the balloon trousers of today's lounge lizards, and the shoeshine boys sitting on the ground around the fountain with its ornamental frogs. But it wasn't the city that ran before his glassy, fixed eyes, but the word. He tasted it and saw it in the rapid glances from the sidewalks that met his own; he saw it in the attitudes, the winks, the fleeting gestures, in the bent-over men, in obscene finger signals. He felt dangerously alive, clutching the steering wheel, dizzied by all the faces, gestures, finger-penises on the street, between two swings of the pendulum. He had to do it because, inevitably, the guys who got screwed today would end up screwing him tomorrow. A reflection off the windshield blinded him and he shaded his eyes with his hand: he'd always known how to choose the biggest motherfucker, the emerging leader against the fading leader. The immense square of the Zócalo opened before him with its stands set in the arcades, and the Cathedral bells sounded the deep bronze of two o'clock in the afternoon. He showed his identification card to the guard at the entrance to the Moneda. The crystalline winter of the plateau outlined the ecclesiastical silhouette of old Mexico, and groups of students, now taking exams, walked down Argentina and Guatemala Streets. He parked the car in the patio. He rode the grillwork elevator. He walked through the rosewood-paneled rooms with their shining chandeliers and sat down in the waiting room. Around him, the low voices only rose to utter, as unctuously as possible, those two words:

"Mister President."

"Misser Prisdent."

"Mishter Praisident."

"Congressman Cruz? Please step this way."

The fat man opened his arms to him, and the two of them clapped each other on the back, the waist, rubbed their hips, and the fat man laughed from within, as usual, and outwardly as well, and with his index finger pretended to shoot himself in the head, and laughed again voicelessly, with a silent shaking of belly and dark cheeks. He buttoned—with some difficulty—the collar of his uniform and asked if he'd seen the news, and he said yes, that now he understood the game but that none of it was of the least importance and that he'd come to reiterate his offer of support for the President, his unconditional support, and the fat man asked if he wanted anything, and he talked about some vacant lots on the outskirts of the city that weren't worth much today but that might, in time, be subdivided, and the other man promised to arrange it because, after all, now they were pals, brothers, and the congressman had, wow!, been fighting since 1913, and had a right to live in security, outside the ups and downs of politics. That's what he said to him, and he patted him gently on the arm and again on the back and hips to seal their friendship. The door with gilt handles opened and from the other office emerged General Jiménez, Colonel Gavilán, and other friends who just last night had been at Saturno's and who walked by without seeing him, their heads bowed; and the fat man laughed again and told him that lots of his friends had come to put themselves at the service of the President in this hour of unity, and he ushered him out with a sweeping gesture of his arm.

In the rear of the office, he saw under a greenish light those eyes that had been screwed into the depths of the cranium, those eyes of a tiger on the prowl, and he bowed and said: "I'm at your disposal, Mr. President . . . To serve you unconditionally, I assure you, Mr. President . . ."

I smell that old oil they use to muck up my eyes, my nose, my lips, my cold feet, my blue hands, my thighs, near my sex, and I ask them to open the window: I want to breathe. I push this hollow sound out through my nostrils and I let them do what they wish and I cross my arms over my stomach. The linen of the sheet, its coolness. That is something important. What do they know, Catalina, the priest, Teresa, Gerardo?

"Leave me alone . . ."

"What does the doctor know? I know him better. It's another trick."

"Don't say anything."

"Teresita, don't contradict your father . . . I mean, your mother . . . Don't you see that . . ."

"Ha. You're just as responsible as he is. You because you're weak and a coward, he because . . . because . . ."

"Enough, enough."

"Good afternoon."

"Come this way."

"Enough, for God's sake."

"Keep it up, keep it up."

What was he thinking about? What was he remembering?

". . . like beggars, why does he make Gerardo work?"

What do they know, Catalina, the priest, Teresa, Gerardo? What will their grief, hysterics, or the expressions of sympathy that will appear in the papers matter? Who will have the honesty to say, as I say now, that my only love has been to possess things, their sensual property? That's what I love. The sheet I embrace. And all the rest, what is now passing before my eyes. A floor made of Italian marble, veined in green and black. The bottles that store up the summer of those places. Old pictures with chipped varnish: in a single blotch, they pick up sun- or candlelight and allow us to wander slowly through them with our eyes and our sense of touch as we sit on a white-leather sofa decorated with gold fillet, with a glass of cognac in one hand and a cigar in the other, wearing a light silk tuxedo, our patent-leather slippers resting on a thick, silent carpet made of merino wool. There a man can take possession of landscape and the faces of other men. There, or sitting on the terrace facing the Pacific, watching the sunset and re-iterating with his senses, the most tense, yes, the most delightful, the ebb and flow, the friction of those silver waves on the moist sand. Land. Land that can translate itself into money. Square plots of land in the city on which the forest of construction timbers begins to rise. Green and yellow property in the country, always the best, near the reservoirs, passed over by the roar of the tractor. Vertical property of mountain mines, gray treasure boxes. Machines: that tasty smell of the rotary press as it vomits out its pages in an accelerated rhythm . . .

"Oh, Don Artemio, do you feel okay?"

"It's nothing, just the heat. This glare. What's going on, Mena? How about opening the windows?"

"Right away . . ."

Ah, the noises of the street. Suddenly. It's impossible to tell one from the other. Ah, the noises of the street.

"What can I do for you, Don Artemio?"

"Mena, you know how enthusiastically we defended President Batista, right down to the last moment. But now that he's no longer in power, it's not easy to do. It's even harder, in fact, to defend General Trujillo, even though he's still in power. You represent the two of them, so you'll understand . . . It's hard to make a case for them."

"Don't worry, Don Artemio, I'll see to arranging things. But with so many nuts around . . . And while we're at it, I've brought along a short article that explains the work of the Benefactor . . . Nothing more . . ."

"Good. Leave it to me. Díaz, good thing you came in when you did. Print this on the editorial page with a phony signature . . . Mena, I'll be seeing you. Stay in touch . . ."

In touch. Touch. Stay in touch. In touch with my white lips, ooooh, a hand, give me a hand, oh, another pulse to revive mine, white lips . . .

"I blame you."

"Does that make you feel better? Good. We crossed the river on horseback. We went back to my part of the country. My country."

". . . we'd like to know where . . ."

Finally, finally, they're giving me the pleasure of coming to me on their knees, physically, to ask me for it. The priest hinted at it. It must be that something is going to happen to me soon, for these two to have found their way to my bedside with that tiny tremor I can't help but notice. They're trying to guess what my joke will be, the final joke I've enjoyed so much by myself, the definitive humiliation whose ultimate consequences I won't be able to enjoy, but whose initial spasms delight me right here and now. This may be my last little flame of triumph . . .

"Where . . ." I murmur with so much sweetness, so much secrecy . . . "Where . . . Let me think . . . Teresa, I think I remember . . . Isn't there a mahogany box . . . where I store my cigars . . . ? It has a false bottom . . ."

I don't have to finish. The two of them get up and run to the huge, horseshoe-shaped desk, where they think I sometimes pass away my insomnia-ridden nights reading:

they wish it were so. The two women force open the drawers, they scatter papers, and finally find the ebony box. Ah, so it was there all along. There was another one there. Or someone took it. Their fingers must get the second clasp, hastily sliding it off. But there's nothing there. When was the last time I ate? I urinated a long time ago. But eating. I vomited. But eating.

"The Undersecretary is on the phone, Don Artemio."

They closed the curtains, didn't they? It's nighttime, isn't it? There are plants that need the moonlight to flower. They wait until nightfall. The convolvulus. At that shack there was a convolvulus, at the hut by the river. The flower opened in the afternoon, yes.

"Thank you, miss . . . Hello . . . Yes, this is Artemio Cruz. No, no, no, no, no, reconciliation is impossible. It's a clear-cut attempt to bring down the government. They've already managed to get the unions to abandon the official party en masse; if things go on like this, what will your power base be, Mr. Undersecretary? . . . Yes . . . It's the only way: declare the strike null and void, send in the troops, rough them up, and put the leaders in jail . . . Of course, things are that serious, sir . . ."

Mimosa, too. I remember that the mimosa has feelings; it can be sensitive and modest, chaste and palpitating, alive, the mimosa . . .

". . . yes, of course . . . oh, and one thing more, just to put my cards on the table: if you people show weakness, my associates and I will take our capital out of Mexico. We need guarantees. Listen, what do you think will happen, for example, if in two weeks a hundred million dollars leaves the country? . . . What? . . . No, I do understand. Of course! . . ."

That's it. It's all over. Ah. That's all. Was that all? Who knows. I don't remember. I haven't listened to that tape in a long time. I've been masquerading for a long time, and in fact I'm thinking about things I'd like to eat, yes,

it's more important to think about food because I haven't
eaten for hours, and Padilla disconnects the recorder, and
I've kept my eyes closed and don't know what they can be
thinking or saying—Catalina, Teresa, Gerardo, the child,
no, Gloria went out, she left with Padilla's son, they're
kissing out in the hall, taking advantage of the fact that no
one's there—because I keep my eyes closed and only think
about pork chops, pork roast, barbecue, stuffed turkey, the
soups I like so much, almost as much as I like desserts, oh
yes, I always had a sweet tooth and in this country the
desserts are delicious, candied almond and pineapple, co-
conut and curd, ah, custard too, cakes from Zamora, I think
about those Zamora cakes, candied fruit, red snapper, bass,
filet of sole, I think about oysters and crabs . . .

We crossed the river on horseback. And we reached the
sandbar and the sea. In Veracruz.

. . . mussels and squid, octopus and seviche, I think
about beer, as bitter as seawater, beer, I think about ven-
ison Yucatán-style, I think about the fact that I'm not old,
no, although one day I was, in front of the mirror, and
stinking cheeses, how I love them, I think, I want, how
that relieves me, how it bores me to hear my own exact,
insinuating, authoritarian voice acting out that same role,
always, what a bother, when I could have been eating,
eating: I eat, I sleep, I fornicate, and the rest of it—what?
what? what? who wants to eat sleep fornicate with my
money? You Padilla and you Catalina and you Teresa and
you Gerardo and you Paquito Padilla—is that your name?—
the one who's been chewing on my granddaughter's lips in
the half-light of my room or of this room, you who are still
young, because I don't live here, you are young, I know
how to live well, that's why I don't live here, I'm an old
man, is that right? An old man filled with manias, who has
a perfect right to have them because he screwed himself,
see? He screwed himself screwing everyone else, he chose
just in time, like that night, ah, I've already remembered

it, that night, that word, that woman. Why can't they give
me something to eat? why? Get out: oh, what pain: get out:
motherfuckers.

You will utter it: it's your word, and your word is my word;
word of honor, a word between men: wheel word: mill
word: imprecation, intention, greeting, life project, affili-
ation, memory, the voice of those in despair, liberation of
the poor, order of the powerful, invitation to fight and to
work, epigraph of love, astrological sign, threat, jeer, word
under oath, pal at parties, and when you get drunk, sword
of courage, throne of power, tooth of the cunning, coat of
arms for the race, life preserver when you've reached your
limits, summary of history: Mexico's password: your word:
  Motherfucker
  We're the number-one motherfuckers around here
  Quit fucking around
  Now I'm gonna fuck him up
  Get outta here, you little fucker
  Don't ever let anyone fuck you over
  I fucked the shit out of that bitch
  Fuck you, asshole
  When it's time to fuck, take potluck
  Fuck and the world fucks with you
  I fucked him out of a thousand pesos
  The boss fucked me over
  You could fuck up a free lunch
  Whaddya say we get fucked up
  The Indians really got fucked over
  The Spaniards fucked us up
  The gringos give me a fucking headache
  Viva Mexico, motherfuckers!!!!
Sadness, dawn, toasted, smudged, guava, troubled sleep:
sons of the word. Born of the fucked mother, dead fucked
up, alive because they know how to fuck up others: womb
and shroud, hidden in the fucked mother. She stands up

for us, she deals the cards, she runs the risk, she conceals
our reticence, our double dealing, she reveals our struggles
and our courage, she gets us drunk, shouts, succumbs, lives
in every bed, presides over the rites of friendship, hatred,
and power. Our word. You and I, members of this secret
society: the order of the fucked mother. You are who you
are because you knew how to fuck up other people and not
let yourself get fucked over; you are who you are because
you didn't know how to fuck up other people and you let
yourself get fucked over. The chain of the fucked mother
that binds all of us: one link up, one link down, linked to
all the sons of the fucked mother who preceded us and all
who will follow us. You will inherit the fucked mother
from above; you will bequeath her down below. You are
the son of the sons of the fucked mother; you will be the
father of more sons of the fucked mother. Our word, behind every face, every sign, every tasteless action. Cum of
the fucked mother, prick of the fucked mother, asshole
of the fucked mother: the fucked mother runs your errands,
the fucked mother clears your chest when you've got
whooping cough, you fuck up the fucked mother, the fucked
mother cleans you out, you may not have a mother but
you've always got your fucked mother, she's your buddy,
your partner, your little sister, your piece, your better half:
the fucked mother. You blow your mind with the fucked
mother; you're on top of things with the fucked mother,
you lay some Hiroshima farts with the fucked mother, your
skin puckers with the fucked mother, you put your best
balls forward with the fucked mother: you don't give up
with the fucked mother: you suck the fucked mother's tit.

Where the fuck are you going with the fucked mother?

Oh mystery, oh illusion, oh nostalgia: you think that with
her you can return to the origin: to which origin? Not you:
no one wants to return to the phony golden age, to the
sinister origins, the bestial grunt, the struggle for bear
meat, for the cave, for the flint, return to sacrifice and

madness, to the nameless terror of the origin, the burned fetish, fear of the sun, fear of masks, to the terror of the idols, fear of puberty, fear of water, fear of hunger, fear of being homeless, cosmic terror: fucked mother, pyramid of negations, *teocalli* of horror.

Oh mystery, oh illusion, oh mirage: you think that with her you will walk forward, you affirm yourself: to which future? Not you: no one wants to walk burdened with a curse, with suspicion, frustration, resentment, hatred, envy, rancor, disdain, insecurity, misery, abuse, insult, intimidation, the false pride of *machismo*, corruption, your fucked fucked mother.

Abandon her on the road, murder her with weapons that aren't her own. Let's kill her: let's kill that word that separates us, petrifies us, rots us with its double venom of idol and cross. Let her not be either our answer or our fatality.

Now, while that priest smears your lips, nose, eyelids, arms, legs, and sex in Extreme Unction: pray: let her not be either our answer or our fatality: the fucked mother, sons of the fucked mother, the fucked mother who poisons love, dissolves friendship, smashes tenderness, the fucked mother who divides, who separates, who destroys, who poisons: the cunt bristling with serpents and metal belonging to the mother of stone, the fucked mother: the drunken belch of the priest on the pyramid, of the lord on his throne, of the hierarch in the Cathedral: smoke, Spain and Anahuac, smoke, the fucked mother's stocks, the fucked mother's excrement, the fucked mother's plateaus, the fucked mother's sacrifices, the fucked mother's honors, the fucked mother's slavery, the fucked mother's temples, the fucked mother's tongues. Who will you fuck over today in order to exist? Who tomorrow? Who will you use: the sons of the fucked mother are these objects, these beings that you will transform into objects for your own use, your pleasure, your domination, your disdain, your

victory, your life: the son of the fucked mother is a thing you use: better than nothing
   you get tired
   you don't overcome her
   you hear the murmuring of other prayers which do not listen to your prayer: may it not be either our answer or our fatality: wash the fucked mother off yourself:
   you get tired
   you don't overcome her
   you've been dragging her around your entire life: that thing:
   you're a son of the fucked mother
   of the outrage you washed clean by outraging other men
   of the oblivion you need in order to remember
   of that endless chain of our injustice
   you get tired
   you make me tired; you overcome me; you force me to descend into that hell with you; you want to remember other things, not that: you make me forget that things will be, but never are, never were: you overcome me with the fucked mother
   you get tired
   rest
   dream about your innocence
   say you tried, that you will try: that one day rape will pay you back in the same coin, will turn its other face to you: when you want to ravage as a young man what you should be thankful for as an old man: the day when you realize something, the end of something: a day in which you will awaken—I overcome you—and you will look at yourself in the mirror and will see, at last, that you've left something behind. You will remember it: your first day without youth, first day of a new time. Fix it in your mind, you will fix it as if it were a statue, in order to see it from all sides. You will open the curtains so that an early-morning

breeze can come in. Ah, how it will fill you up, ah, it will make you forget that smell of incense, the smell that pursues you, ah, how the breeze will cleanse you: it will not allow you even to insinuate doubt: it will not lead you to the edge of that first doubt.

(1947: September 11)

He opened the curtains and inhaled the clean air. The early breeze had already come in, shaking those same curtains, as if to announce itself. He looked out: sunrise was the best time of day, the clearest, a daily springtime. Soon the day would be suffocated by the pounding sun. But at seven in the morning the beach across from his balcony glowed with a cool peace and a silent face. The waves barely whispered, and the voices of the few swimmers did not disturb the solitary encounter of the rising sun, the tranquil ocean, and the sand brushed smooth by the tide. He spread the curtains wide and took a deep breath of the clean air. Three small children were walking along the beach with their pails, picking up the night's treasures: starfish, shells, driftwood. A sailboat rocked near the shore; the transparent sky projected itself over the earth through a filter of a paler green. No cars ran along the avenue that separated the hotel from the beach.

He dropped the curtain and walked toward the bathroom with its Moorish-style tiles. He looked into the mirror at that face swollen by a sleep that could hardly be called sleep, it had been so brief, so different. He closed the door quietly. He turned on the water and put the sink plug in. He tossed his pajama top on the toilet seat. He selected a new blade, taking it out of its wax-paper wrapper and inserting it in the gilt razor. Then he dropped it into the hot water, moistened a towel and covered his face with it. The steam clouded the mirror. He cleaned it with one hand while he turned on the fluorescent light above it with the other. He squeezed the tube containing some new American product, brushless shaving cream; he spread the white, refreshing substance over his cheeks, chin, and neck. He scalded his fingers taking the razor out of the water. He frowned, then stretched his cheek flat and began to shave, from top to bottom, very carefully, twisting his mouth. The steam made him sweat; he could feel the droplets running down his ribs. Slowly he shaved himself clean and then rubbed his chin to make sure it was smooth. He turned on the water again to soak the towel and covered his face with it. He cleaned his ears and splashed his face with a stimulating lotion that made him exhale with pleasure. He cleaned the blade and put it back on the razor, returning the razor to its leather pouch. He pulled out the plug and for an instant contemplated the gray stream of soap and whiskers. He studied his features: he wanted to see the same man in the mirror he'd always found there, because after cleaning off the steam that clouded the mirror again, he felt without knowing it—at that early hour, with its insignificant but indispensable chores, its gastric disturbances and indefinite hungers, its undesired smells that permeated the unconscious life of sleep—that even though he looked at himself in the bathroom mirror every day, a long time had gone by since he'd actually seen himself. A rectangle of mercury and glass, the only true portrait of this face with its green eyes, energetic mouth, wide forehead, and prominent cheekbones. He opened his mouth and stuck out his tongue, which looked ragged, covered with white points; then he searched his reflection for the holes where his lost teeth used to be. He opened the medicine chest and took out the dentures that rested at the bottom of a glass of water. He rinsed them quickly, turned his back to the mirror, and put them in. He squeezed the greenish toothpaste on the brush and brushed his teeth.

He gargled, then took off his pajama bottom. He turned on the shower. He checked the water temperature with the palm of his hand and felt the uneven shower on the back of his neck as he rubbed the soap over his thin body with its conspicuous ribs, its flaccid stomach, and its muscles that still managed to conserve a certain nervous tautness, but which now tended to sag in a way he thought grotesque unless he paid false and energetic attention to them . . . and only when he was observed, as he was these days, by impertinent eyes in the hotel and on the beach. He put his face under the shower, turned off the water, and dried himself with the towel. He felt happy again when he doused his chest and underarms with cologne and ran his comb through his curly hair. He took the blue bathing suit and the white polo shirt out of the closet. He put on the Italian sandals made of canvas and string and slowly opened the bathroom door.

The breeze was still billowing the curtains, and the sun had not stopped shining: it would be a genuine shame to waste a day like this. In September, the weather changes so quickly. He glanced over at the bed. Lilia was still sleeping in that spontaneous, free position of hers: her head leaning on her shoulder and her arm stretched over the pillow, her shoulder bare and one knee bent, poking out of the sheet. He walked over to the young body on which that first light was gracefully playing, illuminating the golden down on her arms and the moist corners of her eyelids, her lips, her blond underarms. He bent over to examine the pearls of sweat on her lips and to feel the warmth that rose from this body of a small animal at rest, burned by the sun, innocently lewd. Wishing to turn her over so he could see her body from the front, he reached out his arms. Her half-opened lips closed, and she sighed. He went down to breakfast.

When he finished his coffee, he wiped his lips with his napkin and looked around. It seemed that only children and their nannies had breakfast at this hour. The smooth, still-dripping heads belonged to the ones who hadn't resisted the temptation of a pre-breakfast swim, who were now getting ready, wet bathing suits and all, to go back to the beach, the beach that offered a time without time in which the imagination of each child would impose its own rhythm on the hours, long or short, of castles and walls under construction, of happy preludes to burials, of splashing strolls, and wrestling in the surf, of bodies stretched out without time in the time of the sun, of shrieks in the intangible wrapping of the water. It was strange to see them, at such a tender age, already looking at the hole they'd dug as the bizarre shelter of a fictitious burial, for a sand palace. Now the children were leaving, and the adult hotel guests were coming in.

He lit a cigarette and got ready for the slight vertigo that for the past few months had accompanied his first smoke of the day. He looked far away from the dining room, toward the well-defined curve of the beach that snaked its foamy way from its farthest point on the open sea along the calm half-moon arc of the bay, which was now dotted with sailboats and the growing noise of activity. A couple he knew passed his table, and he waved hello to them. Then he bent his head and inhaled his cigarette again.

The noise level in the dining room rose: forks and knives on plates, teaspoons banged against cups; bottles uncapped and mineral water beginning to bubble, chairs moved, and conversations taking place between couples and among groups of tourists. There was also the growing noise of the surf, which did not resign itself to being overwhelmed by human clamor. From his table, he could see the esplanade of Acapulco's new frontage, which had been hastily erected to provide comfort for the huge influx of travelers from the United States, which the war had taken from Waikiki, Portofino, and Biarritz, and to mask the squalid, muddy land behind it where naked fishermen lived in shacks with their swollen-bellied children, their mangy dogs, streams of sewage, trichinosis, and bacteria. Two ages are always present in this Janus-like community with its double face, so far from what it once was, and so far from what it would like to be.

Seated, he went on smoking, feeling a slight swelling in his legs, which even at eleven o'clock in the morning could not stand this summer clothing. Surreptitiously, he massaged his knee. It must have been the cold inside him, because the morning was bursting into a single round light, and the skull of the sun was burning with an orange plume. And Lilia walked in, her eyes hidden behind dark glasses. He stood up and helped her into her chair. He motioned to the waiter. He took note of the married couple's whispers. Lilia asked for papaya and coffee.

"Get a good night's sleep?"

She nodded, smiled without parting her lips, and patted the man's dark hand, which stood out against the white tablecloth.

"Do you think the Mexico City papers are here yet?" she asked as she cut her slice of papaya into tiny pieces. "Why don't you find out?"

"Right away. But hurry, because we're expected on the yacht at twelve."

"Where will we eat?"

"At the club."

He walked over to the desk. Yes, it was going to be another day like yesterday, with difficult conversations consisting of pointless questions and answers. But the nights, when there were no more words, were a different matter entirely. Why should he ask for more? The wordless contact between them did not require true love, not even the semblance of personal interest. He wanted a girl for his vacation. He got her. On Monday it would all be over, and he'd never see her again. Who could ask for more? He bought the papers and went to his room to put on his flannel slacks.

In the car, Lilia immersed herself in the papers and commented on some movie reviews. She crossed her tan legs and dangled one shoe. He lit his third cigarette of the morning, neglected to tell her that he was the editor of the paper she was reading, and let his mind wander as he read the billboards on the new buildings and observed the strange transition from the fifteen-story hotel and the hamburger joint to the bald mountain that spilled, red-bellied, onto the highway, its guts torn open by a steam shovel.

When Lilia leapt gracefully onto the deck and he tried to keep his balance as he cautiously stepped aboard, the other man was already there. It was he who lent them a hand so they could get off the swaying pier.

"Xavier Adame."

Almost naked, wearing the briefest bathing suit, his face dark, suntan oil glistening around his blue eyes and his bushy, playful brows. He offered his hand with a movement that recalled that of an innocent wolf: audacious, candid, secret.

"Don Rodrigo wondered if you wouldn't mind sharing the boat with me."

He nodded and looked for a spot in the shaded cabin.

Adame was saying to Lilia: ". . . the old boy offered me the use of the boat a week ago and then forgot . . ."

Lilia smiled and spread out a towel on the sun-drenched stern.

"Wouldn't you like something?" the man asked Lilia when the steward appeared with the liquor cart and some snacks.

From her towel, Lilia signaled no with a finger. He pulled the cart over and nibbled on some almonds while the steward made him a gin and tonic. Xavier Adame had disappeared on the canvas roof of the cabin.

The cabin cruiser sailed slowly out of the bay. He put on his cap with the transparent visor and leaned back to sip his drink.

Opposite him, the sun was melting over Lilia. She undid the strap on her bathing suit and exposed her back. Her whole body was a gesture of pure joy. She raised her arms and tied up her brilliant, coppery hair, which had been hanging loose. Her fine sweat ran down her neck, lubricating the soft, round flesh of her arms and the smooth, wide-apart shoulders. He stared at her from deep inside the cabin. She would fall asleep in the same position she'd been in that morning. Resting on one shoulder, with her knee bent. He saw she'd shaved her armpits. The motor started, and the waves spread in two swift crests, raising a salty, even mist which fell on Lilia. The seawater moistened her bathing suit, making it cling to her hips and sink into her backside. Sea gulls flew close to the speeding boat, screeching, as he slowly sucked on his straw. Instead of exciting him, her young body inspired him with restraint, with a kind of malevolent austerity. Sitting on a canvas chair inside the cabin, he played a waiting game with his desires, hoarding them for the silent, solitary night, when their bodies would vanish in the darkness and not be the subject of comparisons. In the night, he would use his experienced hands on her, hands that loved slowness and surprise. He lowered his eyes and looked at those dark hands with their prominent greenish veins, hands that substituted for the vigor and impatience of youth.

They were in the open sea. From the uninhabited coast with its ragged scrub and stone battlements, there rose a burning glare. The yacht turned into the rolling sea and a wave smashed, soaking Lilia's body: she shouted with glee and lifted her breasts, tipped with pink buttons that seemed to hold her hard bosom in place. She lay down again. The steward reappeared with a fragrant platter of peeled plums, peaches, and oranges. He closed his eyes and allowed himself a painful smile, imposed on him by a thought: that sensual body, that slim waist, those full thighs, had hidden within them a cell, tiny as yet: the cancer of time. Ephem-

eral wonder, how would it be different, after the passage
of time, from this body that now possessed her? A corpse
in the sun dripping oils and sweat, sweating away its quick
youth, lost in the blink of an eye, withered capillaries,
thighs that would soften from successive births and from
mere anguished time on earth with its elemental, always
repeated routines, devoid of originality. He opened his
eyes. He stared at her.

Xavier slid down from the roof. He saw the hairy legs,
then the knot of his hidden sex, finally his burning chest.
Yes: he did walk like a wolf as he bent down to enter the
open cabin, taking two peaches off the platter, which had
been left on a tray of ice. Xavier smiled at him and went
out with the fruit in his hand. He squatted in front of Lilia,
with his legs spread in front of the girl's face; he touched
her shoulder. Lilia smiled and took one of the peaches
Xavier was offering, saying words he could not hear, words
drowned out by the motor, the wind, the swift waves. Now
those two mouths were chewing at the same time, and the
juice was dripping down their chins. If at least . . . Yes.
The young man brought his legs together and shifted his
weight so they hung over the port side. He raised his smiling eyes, squinting into the white midday sky. Lilia watched
him and moved her lips. Xavier tried to say something,
moving his arm, pointing toward the coast. Lilia tried to
look in that direction, covering her breasts as she did so.
Xavier came back to her side, and both laughed as he knot-
ted her strap. She sat up with her wet breasts clearly outlined, and shielded her eyes with her hand so she could
see what he was pointing to in the distant line that was a
small beach fallen like a yellow conch shell on the edge of
a thick forest. Xavier stood and shouted an order to the
captain. The yacht turned again and headed toward the
beach. Lilia then joined him on the port side and offered
Xavier a cigarette. They talked.

He saw the two bodies seated side by side, equally dark

and equally smooth, making a single uninterrupted line from their heads to the feet they'd stretched to the water. Immobile but tense with confident expectation; united in their newness, in their barely disguised eagerness to try each other, to reveal themselves. He sipped through his straw and put on his sunglasses, which, along with his visored cap, virtually camouflaged his face.

They talked. They finished sucking their peach pits and might have said: "It tastes good," or it might have been: "I like it . . ."—something no one had ever said before, said by bodies, by presences making their debut in life.

They might have said: "How is it we've never met before? I'm always at the club . . ."

"No, I'm not . . . Come on, let's toss our pits at the same time. One, two . . ."

He watched them toss their pits, laughing a laugh that did not reach him; he saw the power of their arms.

"I beat you!" said Xavier as the pits soundlessly hit the water far from the yacht. She laughed. They settled back again.

"Do you like water skiing?"

"I don't know how."

"Come on, then. I'll give you a free lesson . . ."

What could they be saying? He coughed and pulled the cart over to make himself another drink. Xavier would find out just what sort of couple he and Lilia were. She would tell her petty, sordid story. He would shrug and force her to prefer his wolf's body, at least for one night, just for variety's sake. But as for loving each other . . . loving each other . . .

"All you have to do is keep your arms stiff, see? Don't bend your arms . . ."

"First let me see how you do it . . ."

"Sure. Wait till we get to the little beach."

That's the ticket! Be young and rich.

The yacht stopped a few yards off the half-hidden beach.

Weary, it rocked back and forth and exhaled its gasoline breath, staining the sea of green crystal and white sand. Xavier tossed the skis into the water; then he dove in, came up smiling, and put them on.

"Throw me the towline!"

The girl found the line and tossed it to him. The yacht started to move again, and Xavier rose up out of the water, following in the boat's wake with one arm raised in salute while Lilia contemplated him and he drank his gin and tonic. The strip of water separating the two young people linked them in some mysterious fashion. It united them more than real fornication and fixed them in an immobile nearness, as if the yacht were not cutting through the Pacific, as if Xavier were a statue sculpted now for all eternity but being pulled by the boat, as if Lilia had posed on one, any one, of the waves which in appearance lacked all substance and which rose, broke, died, reconstituted themselves—other, the same—always in motion and always identical, out of time, their own mirrors, mirrors of the waves of our origins, of the lost millennium and of the millennium to come. He sank his body into the low, comfortable chair. What would he choose now? How would he escape from that world of chance packed with needs that elude the control of his will?

Xavier let go of the handle and sank into the sea across from the beach. Lilia dove in without looking, without glancing at him. But her explanation would come. What would it be? Would Lilia explain to him? Would Xavier ask Lilia for an explanation? Would Lilia give Xavier an explanation? When Lilia's head, glittering a thousand strange streaks because of the sun and the sea, appeared in the water next to that of the young man, he knew that no one, no one but he, would dare ask for an explanation; down there, in the calm sea of this transparent anchorage, no one would look for reasons or stop the fatal encounter, no one would corrupt what was there, what had to be. What was

building up between the two young people? This body
sunken into its seat, dressed in a polo shirt, wearing flannel
slacks and a visored cap? This important stare? Down there
the bodies were swimming in silence and the side of the
boat kept him from seeing what was happening. Xavier
whistled. The yacht started up, and Lilia appeared for an
instant on the surface of the water. She fell; the yacht
stopped. Their raucous laughter reached his ears. He'd
never heard her laugh that way. As if she'd just been born,
as if there were no past, always the past, tombstones of
history and of stories, sacks of shame, crimes committed
by her, by him.

By everyone. That was the intolerable word. Committed
by everyone. His bitter grimace could not hold back that
word, which came pouring out. Which broke all the springs
of power and blame, of one man's domination over others,
over someone, over a girl in his power, bought by him, to
bring them into a wide world of common acts, similar des-
tinies, experiences not labeled as personal property. So,
hadn't this woman been branded forever? Wouldn't she
always be a woman occasionally possessed by him?
Wouldn't that be her definition and her fate: to be what
she was because at a given moment she was his? Could
Lilia love someone as if he had never existed?

He stood up, walked toward the stern, and shouted: "It's
getting late. We've got to get back to the club if we're going
to eat on time."

He felt his own face, his entire body, rigid, covered by
a pale starch, when he realized that no one could hear his
shouts. After all, how could two graceful bodies swimming
under the opaline water, parallel to each other and not
touching, as if they were floating in a second level of air,
hear him?

Xavier Adame left them on the dock and returned to the
yacht: he wanted to go on skiing. He said goodbye from
the prow. She waved her blouse, and in her eyes there was

nothing of what he would have wanted to see. Just as, during lunch on the shore of the anchorage under the shelter of palm branches, he would have wanted to see what he did not find in Lilia's chestnut eyes. Xavier hadn't asked. Lilia hadn't told that sad, melodramatic tale which he secretly enjoyed, while he identified the mixed flavors of the vichyssoise. A middle-class couple, with the usual leper, the tough guy, the punisher, the poor fool; divorce and whores. He would have wanted to tell it—and maybe he should have told it—to Xavier. But it was hard for him to remember the story because it had fled from Lilia's eyes this afternoon as if during the morning the past had fled the woman's life.

But the present could not flee because they were living it, sitting on those straw armchairs and mechanically eating the specially ordered lunch: vichyssoise, lobster, Côtes du Rhône, Baked Alaska. She was sitting there, paid by him. He stopped the small forkful of seafood before it reached his mouth: she was paid by him, but she was escaping him. He couldn't have her any longer. That afternoon, that very night, she would look for Xavier, they would meet in secret, they'd already made a date. And Lilia's eyes, lost in the seascape of sailboats and sleeping water, said nothing. But he could get it out of her, he could make a scene . . . He felt he was false, uncomfortable, and went on eating his lobster . . . Now which road . . . A fatal meeting that imposes itself on his will . . . Ah, on Monday it would all be over, he'd never see her again, never feel for her in the dark, naked, sure of finding that reclined warmth between the sheets, he would never again . . .

"Aren't you sleepy?" murmured Lilia when dessert was served. "Doesn't the wine just knock you out?"

"It does. A little. Have some dessert."

"No. I don't want ice cream . . . I need a siesta."

When they got to the hotel, Lilia wiggled her fingers in farewell, and he crossed the avenue and asked a boy to put a chair in the shade of the palms for him. It was hard for him to light his cigarette: an invisible wind that came from nowhere in the hot afternoon insisted on putting out his matches. A few young couples were taking their siesta near him, embracing, some with their legs entwined, others with their heads wrapped in towels. He began to wish Lilia would come downstairs and rest her head on his thin, bony, flannel-covered knees. He suffered or felt wounded, annoyed, insecure. He suffered from the mystery of that love he could not touch. He suffered from the memory of that immediate, wordless complicity, agreed upon right in front of his eyes in gestures that in themselves meant nothing, but in the presence of that man, of that man slumped in his canvas chair, slumped behind his visor, his dark glasses . . . One of the young women lying near him stretched with a languid rhythm in her arms and began to sprinkle a rain of fine sand on her boyfriend's neck. She shrieked when he jumped up, pretending to be mad, and grabbed her around the waist. The two rolled on the sand; she got up and ran; he chased until he caught the panting, excited girl again, and carried her in his arms to the sea. He took off his Italian sandals and felt the hot sand under his feet. He walked the beach, to its end, alone. He walked with his eyes fixed on his own footprints, not noticing that the tide was washing them away and that each new footstep was the sole, ephemeral evidence of itself.

The sun was level with his eyes.

The lovers came out of the water—confused, he couldn't tell how long the prolonged coitus had taken. They could almost be seen from the beach, but they'd been covered by the sheets of the silvery afternoon sea—and that playful display with which they'd entered the water had now become two heads joined in silence, she a splendid dark girl with lowered eyes, young . . . young. The couple stretched out near him again, covering their heads with a towel. They also covered themselves with night, the slow night of the tropics. The black man who rented the chairs began to gather them up. He got up and walked to the hotel.

He decided to take a quick swim in the pool before going up. He walked into the dressing room near the pool and, sitting on a bench, once again took off his sandals. The lockers hid him. Behind him he heard wet footsteps on the rubber mat; breathless voices laughed; they dried their bodies. He took off his polo shirt. From the other side of the lockers there arose the penetrating smells of sweat, cigar smoke, and cologne. A smoke ring wafted toward the ceiling.

"Beauty and the Beast didn't show up today."

"No, they didn't."

"What a piece she is . . ."

"What a waste. That old bird can't cut the mustard."

"He's liable to get a stroke."

"Right. Get a move on."

They went out. He put on his sandals and walked out, putting on his shirt.

He walked up the stairs to his room. There was nothing there to surprise him. There was the bed, in disarray after her siesta, but there was no Lilia. He stood in the middle of the room. The fan was spinning like a vulture on a string. Outside, on the terrace, another night of crickets and fireflies. Another night. He closed the window so the scent wouldn't escape. His senses took in the aroma of recently sprinkled perfume, sweat, wet towels, makeup. Those were not the real names. The pillow, which still showed where her head had been, was a garden, fruit, moist earth, the sea. He moved slowly toward the drawer where she . . . He picked up her silk bra and brought it to his cheek. His whiskers scraped it. He had to be prepared. He had to shower, shave again for tonight. He dropped the bra and walked toward the bath with a different gait, happy once again.

He turned on the light and then the hot water. He tossed

his shirt on the toilet seat. He opened the medicine chest. He saw the things that belonged to both of them: toothpaste tubes, mentholated shaving cream, tortoiseshell combs, cold cream, aspirin, antacid pills, tampons, cologne, blue razor blades, brilliantine, rouge, antispasmodic pills, yellow mouthwash, prophylactics, milk of magnesia, bandages, iodine, shampoo, tweezers, nail clippers, a lip pencil, eye drops, eucalyptus nasal spray, cough syrup, deodorant. He picked up his razor. The blade was clogged with thick chestnut hairs. He paused with the razor in his hand. He brought it to his lips and involuntarily closed his eyes. When he opened them, that old man with bloodshot eyes, gray cheeks, withered lips—who was no longer the other, the reflection he'd learned so well—shot him a grimace from the mirror.

I see them. They've come in. The mahogany door opens and closes and their footsteps on the thick carpet are inaudible. They've closed the windows. They've drawn the curtains with a hiss. I'd like to ask them to open them, to open the windows. There's a world outside. There's a strong wind blowing from the mesa, it shakes the thin black trees. I've got to breathe . . . They've come in.

"Go on over to him, child, let him get to know you. Tell him your name."

She smells good. She has a pretty smell. Ah, yes, I can still make out blushing cheeks, shining eyes, her entire young body, graceful, which comes closer to my bed, taking short steps.

"I'm . . . I'm Gloria."

"That morning I waited for him with pleasure. We crossed the river on horseback."

"See how he ended up? See? Just like my brother. That's how he ended up."

"Feel relieved? Do it."

"*Ego te absolvo.*"

The fresh, sweet rustle of banknotes and new bonds when the hand of a man like me picks them up. The smooth acceleration of a luxury car, custom-built, air-conditioned, with a bar, telephone, soft cushions, and footrests—well priest, well? Up there too, right? That heaven represents power over men, innumerable men with hidden faces, forgotten names: last names from the thousand work lists of the mines, factories, newspapers. That anonymous face which sings me traditional songs on my saint's day, which hides its eyes under its helmet when I visit construction sites, which draws my caricature for the opposition newspapers: well, well? That does exist, that really is mine. That really is what being God is, right? To be feared and hated and whatever, that's really being God, right? Tell me how I save all that and I'll let you go through with your ceremonies, I'll beat myself on the chest, I'll walk on my knees to a sanctuary, I'll drink vinegar and wear a crown of thorns. Tell me how I save all that because the spirit . . .

". . . of the Son and the Holy Ghost. Amen . . ."

He's still there, on his knees, with his washed face. I try to turn my back to him. The pain in my side keeps me from moving. Ooooh. He must be finished by now. I'll be absolved. I want to sleep. Here comes the pain. Here it comes. Ooooooh. And the women. No, not these. Those who love. What? Yes. No. I don't know. I've forgotten that face. By God, I've forgotten that face. It was mine, how could I ever forget it?

"Padilla . . . Padilla . . . Get the story editor and the society-page editor over here."

Your voice, Padilla, the hollow sound of your voice on the intercom . . ."

"Yes, Don Artemio. Don Artemio, we've got an urgent problem here. The Indians are demonstrating. They want to be paid for their forests that were cut down."

"What? How much is it?"

"Half a million."

"Is that all? Tell the commissioner of the *ejido* to get them in line. That's what I pay him for. What next . . ."

"Mena's here, in the waiting room. What should I tell him?"

"To come in."

Ah, Padilla, I can't open my eyes to see you, but I can see your thoughts, Padilla, behind my mask of pain. The dying man is named Artemio Cruz, just Artemio Cruz; only this man is dying, right? no one else. It's like a bit of good luck that wipes out the other deaths. This time, only Artemio Cruz is dying. And that death can take place instead of another, perhaps your own, Padilla . . . Ah. No. I still have things to do. Don't count your chickens yet . . .

"I told you he was faking."

"Let him rest."

"I'm telling you he's faking!"

I see them, from far off. Their fingers quickly get the false bottom open, sliding it out with an air of great expectation. But there's nothing there. I'm waving my arm, pointing toward the oak wall, the long closet that takes up one side of the bedroom. The women run to it, open all the doors, slide all the hangers with their blue suits, with stripes, two-button jackets, made of Irish linen, without remembering that they aren't my suits, that my clothes are in my house, they push aside all the hangers while I point, with the hands I can barely move: perhaps the document is hidden in one of the inside pockets of a suit. Teresa's and Catalina's sense of urgency increases: now they're tearing through things in a fury, throwing empty jackets on the rug, until finally they've looked through all of them and they turn to stare at me. I can't keep a straight face. I'm held up by the pillows, and I breath with difficulty, but my eyes don't miss a single detail. I sense their speed and their covetousness.

I gesture for them to come closer. "Now I remember . . . In a shoe . . . I remember perfectly . . ."

Seeing the two of them down on all fours on the mound of jackets and trousers, digging through shoes, showing me their fat thighs, shaking their asses, panting obscenely— only then does the bitter sweetness cloud my eyes. I bring my hand to my heart and close my eyes.

"Regina . . ."

The grunts of indignation and effort made by the two women fade in the darkness. I move my lips to whisper the name. There isn't much time left for remembering the other, the one she loved . . . Regina . . .

"Padilla . . . Padilla. I want to eat something light . . . I don't feel right in the stomach. Come with me while they're getting this stuff ready . . ."

"What? You choose, build, make, preserve, continue: nothing else . . . I . . ."

"Right. See you soon. Say hello to everyone for me."

"Well put, sir. It'll be easy to smash them."

"No, Padilla, it isn't so easy. Pass me that platter . . . the one with the little sandwiches on it . . . I've seen these people on the march. When they decide something, it's hard to hold them back."

How did the song go? Exiled, I went down south, exiled by the government, and the next year I came back north; oh, those terrible nights I spent without you, without you; not a friend, not a relative to worry about me; only the love, only the love of that woman made me come back . . .

"That's why we have to do something right now, when the bad feelings toward us are just starting, we've got to nip it in the bud. They don't have any organization, and they're putting everything they've got on the line. Come on, come on, have some of these little sandwiches, there's enough for two . . ."

"Useless agitation . . ."

I've got my brace of pistols, they both have ivory butts, and I can shoot it out with the railroad and its scabs. I'm a railroad working girl. My Juan's my pride and joy, I'm in love, you know, with the boy, I'm a railroad working girl. If you see me wearing boots, and you think I'm a soldier girl, well, I'm just a railroad girl, working on the central line.

"It wouldn't be if they were right. But they aren't. But you were a Marxist back when you were a kid, so you must understand these things better. You should be afraid of what's going on. For me, it's a little late . . ."

"Campanela's waiting outside."

What did they say? Did you want to? Hemorrhage? Hernia? Occlusion? Perforation? A volvulus? Involvement of the colon?

Oh, Padilla, I should push the button to make you come in. Padilla, I can't see you because I've got my eyes closed, I have my eyes closed because I no longer believe in that tiny imperfect patch, my retina. What if I open my eyes and my retina no longer perceives anything, no longer communicates anything to my brain? What do I do then?

"Open the window."

"I blame you. The same as my brother."

"Right."

You probably don't know or understand why Catalina, sitting next to you, wants to share that memory with you, that memory she wants to superimpose on all other memories: you here on earth, Lorenzo in the other world? What is it she wants to remember? You with Gonzalo in this prison? Lorenzo without you on that mountain? You probably don't know or understand if you are he, if he might be you, if you lived that day without him, with him, he in your place, you in his place. You will remember. Yes, that last day you and he were together there—he did not live it all in your place or you in his, you were together. He asked you if you were going all the way to the sea together; you were going on horseback; he will ask you where you were going to eat and he told you—he will tell you—papa, he will smile, will raise the arm holding the shotgun and

will go out of the ford with his torso naked, holding the
shotgun and the knapsacks high over his head. She will not
be there. Catalina will not remember that. For that reason
you will try to remember it, in order to forget what she
wants you to remember. She will live locked away and will
tremble when he returns to Mexico City for a few days,
just to say goodbye. She believes him. He won't do it. He
will board a ship in Veracruz, he will go. He would go. She
will have to remember that bedroom where the humors of
sleep struggle to remain even though the air of springtime
wafts in through the open balcony. She will have to remember sleeping in separate beds, different rooms, the
marks left in the mattress, the persistent silhouette of those
who slept in those beds. She will not be able to remember
the mare's croup, similar to two black jewels washed by
the slimy river. You will. As you cross the river, you and
he will make out a ghost on the other shore, a ghost of
earth raised over the misty fermentation of the morning.
That struggle between the dark jungle and the burning sun
will take shape as a double reflection of all things, as a ghost
of the humidity embracing the reverberating sunlight. It
will smell of banana. It will be Cocuya. Catalina will never
know what Cocuya was, is, or will be. She will sit on the
edge of her bed to wait, with a mirror in one hand and a
brush in the other, vaguely depressed, with the taste of
bile in her mouth, deciding to stay that way, sitting, not
looking at anything, unwilling to do anything, telling herself
that this is how scenes always leave her: empty. No: only
you and he will feel the hooves of the horse on the porous
dirt on the bank. As they leave the water, they will feel
the coolness mixed with the broiling of the jungle and they
will look back: that slow river that sweetly swirls the algae
on the other shore. And beyond, at the end of the path
lined with flowering plants, the repainted Cocuya mansion
resting on a shady esplanade. Catalina will repeat, "My
God, I don't deserve this." She will pick up the mirror and

ask herself if that is what Lorenzo will see when he returns, if he comes back: that growing deformity in the chin and neck. Will he notice the disguised wrinkles that begin to run along her eyelids and cheeks? She will see another gray hair in the mirror and pull it out. And you, with Lorenzo at your side, will enter the jungle. You will see your son's naked shoulder in front of you, in the alternating shadows of the mangrove and the fractured rays of the sun that filter through the thick roof of branches. The knotty roots of the trees will break the crust of the earth and will poke out, wild and twisted, all along the path cleared by machete. A path that in a short time will once again be clogged with lianas. Lorenzo will trot along, sitting bolt upright, not turning his head, snapping his riding crop at the mare's flanks to keep off the horseflies. Catalina will repeat to herself that she will have no faith in him, that she will have no faith in him unless she sees him as he was before, as he was as a child, and she will lie back with a moan, her arms spread, tears in her eyes, and will let her silk slippers fall from her feet and she will think about her son, so like his father, so thin, so dark. The dry branches will snap under the hooves, and the white plain will open with its plumes of undulating sugarcane. Lorenzo will spur his horse. He will turn his face back, and his lips will part in a smile that will reach your eyes accompanied by a shout of joy and the raised arm: a strong arm, olive skin, a white smile, like yours when you were young. You will remember your youth through him and through these places, and you will not want to tell Lorenzo how much this land means to you, because doing so might mean extorting his affection. You will remember in order to remember within memory. Catalina, on the bed, will remember the boy kneeling at her side, his head resting on his mother's lap, as she called him the joy of her life, because before he was born she suffered a great deal, and not being able to tell him all, because she had sacred obligations, and the boy looking at her without

understanding: why, why, why? You will bring Lorenzo to
live here so that he can learn to love this land on his own,
without any need on your part to explain the motives behind
your tender labor in reconstructing the burned walls of the
hacienda and reopening the flatlands to agriculture. No
because, without because, because. The two of you will go
out into the sun. You will pick up the wide-brimmed hat
and put it on your head. The wind from your gallop through
the quiet, shimmering air will fill your mouth, eyes, and
head. Lorenzo will take the lead, raising a white cloud along
the road opened between the fields, and behind him, galloping, you will feel sure that both of you are feeling the
same thing. The race opens your veins, makes your blood
flow, sharpens your vision so that you see this wide, vig-
orous land, so different from the highland plateaus, from
the deserts you will get to know, this land parceled out in
huge red, green, and black squares dotted with tall palm
trees, turbid and deep, redolent of excrement and fruit
skin, this land that sends its meanings to your son's aroused,
exalted senses and to your own, you and your son, galloping
swiftly, saving your nerves, the body's forgotten muscles,
from torpor. Your spurs will dig into the bay until he bleeds:
you know that Lorenzo wants to race. His questioning face
will cut through Catalina's voice. She will stop, will wonder
how far he can go, will tell herself that it's only a matter
of time, of repeating the reasons little by little, yes, until
he understands them completely. She sitting in the armchair, he at her feet with his arms folded over his knees.
The earth will echo beneath the hooves. You lower your
head, as if you want to bring it closer to the horse's ear and
spur him on with words, but there is that weight, that
weight of the Yaqui who must be slung face down over the
horse's croup, the Yaqui who will reach out his arm to hang
on to your belt. The pain will put you to sleep. Your arm
and leg will dangle inert, and the Yaqui will still be hanging
on to your waist, moaning, his face flushed. Then you will

come upon the tombstone-shaped crags and you will march along protected by the shadows, in the mountain canyon, reconnoitering hidden rock valleys, deep gorges above abandoned irrigation ditches, roads of thorns and scrub. Who will remember with you? Lorenzo without you on that mountain? Gonzalo with you in this prison?

(1915: October 22)

He wrapped himself in the blue serape because the freezing night wind hissed—as if someone were shaking a sheaf of straw—and negated the vertical heat of the day. They'd spent the night out in the open with no food. Just over a mile from them, the basalt crowns of the mountains shot up, their roots buried in the hard desert. For three days now, the scouting party had been on patrol, never asking where they were going, in which direction, guided only by the captain's instincts. He thought he knew all the tricks and all the routes left to Francisco Villa's tattered retreating columns. Thirty-six miles behind them stood the main body of their troops, only waiting for a galloping messenger from this detachment so they could throw themselves on the remnants of Villa's forces and keep them from joining the fresh troops in Chihuahua. But where were those remnants? The captain thought he knew: in some mountain pass, following the worst road. On the fourth day—today— the detachment was to have plunged into the sierra while the bulk of Carranza's forces would advance toward this place, which he and his men would leave at dawn. Yesterday they ran out of cornmeal. And the sergeant who rode out with the canteens last night, to find the stream coursing through the rocks, which disappeared as soon as it reached the desert, had not found it. Yes, he could see its bed of reddish-veined stone, clean and wrinkled, but it was dry.

Two years before, they'd passed through this same place
during the rainy season, and now, at dawn, only one round
star twinkled over the soldiers' burning heads. They'd made
camp without starting any fires; an enemy scout might see
them from the mountain. In any case, it was unnecessary.
There was no food to cook, and in the immensity of the
desert plains an isolated fire couldn't keep anyone warm.
Wrapped in the serape, he ran his hand over his thin face,
over the wiry beard that had started to cover his chin. Dust
encrusted the corners of his lips, his eyebrows, and the
bridge of his nose. There were eighteen men in the detachment, only a few yards from the captain. Whether he
sleeps or keeps watch, he is always alone, always separated
from his men by a few yards of bare ground. Nearby, the
horses shook their manes in the wind, their black silhouettes standing out against the yellow skin of the desert. He
wanted to go up into the mountains: the spring that gave
rise to the brief, solitary flow of the cool creek was up there.
His body felt tense. Hunger and thirst sank his eyes and
opened them wider, green eyes with a cold, even stare.

The mask of his face, stained with dust, remained fixed
and awake. He was waiting for the first line of dawn to
show itself: the fourth day, according to orders. Almost no
one slept, they were watching him from a distance as he
sat with his knees tucked up, wrapped in the serape, unmoving. Those who tried to close their eyes had to fight
their thirst, hunger, and fatigue. Those who weren't looking
at the captain looked toward the line of horses, all with
their forelocks parted. Their bridles were tied to the thick
mesquite protruding out of the earth like a lost finger. The
tired horses stared at the ground. The sun should be ap-
pearing from behind the mountain about now. It was time.

They were all waiting for the moment when the captain
stood up, tossed aside the blue serape, and revealed himself: his chest covered with cartridge belts, the shining
buckle on his officer's tunic, his pigskin puttees. Without

a word, the detachment got to its feet and went over to the horses. The captain was right: a fan-shaped glow flared up from behind the lowest peaks, casting an arch of light to which unseen birds added a chorus. They kept their distance but they were the real owners of the vast silence of this abandoned land. He signaled to the Yaqui Indian Tobias and said to him, in his own language, "You stay to the back. As soon as we catch sight of the enemy, race back to headquarters."

The Yaqui nodded, putting on his narrow-brimmed hat, which had a round crown and a single red feather stuck in the band. The captain leaped onto his horse, and the line of men began a light trot toward the entrance to the sierra: a canyon with ocher-faced defiles.

There were three bluffs overhanging three passes through the mountain. The detachment headed for the second, the narrowest, along which the horses would have to pass in single file, with the steep cliff wall on one side and the ravine on the other. The path led to the spring; the canteens broadcast their emptiness as they bounced off the men's hips. The clatter of the rocks glancing off the horses' shoes repeated a deep, empty sound which, like the single dry beat of a drum, vanished without an echo down the canyon. Seen from above, the short column of horsemen seemed to be groping its way forward. Only he kept his eyes on the top of the canyon wall, squinting against the sun, letting his horse find the path. At the head of the detachment, he felt neither fear nor pride. He'd left his fear behind, not in his first battles, but in the long series of skirmishes which had made danger normal for him and turned safety into something disturbing. The absolute silence of the canyon secretly alarmed him, and he tightened the reins and flexed the muscles of his right arm and hand so he could swiftly pull out his pistol. He thought he was devoid of arrogance—earlier, because of his fear, and now out of habit. He had no sense of pride when the first bullets whistled past his ear and life like a miracle went on each time another shot missed its mark. He felt only astonishment at the blind wisdom of his body as it avoided danger by standing or crouching, his face hidden behind a tree trunk—astonishment and scorn, when he thought about the tenacity with which his body, faster even than his will, safeguarded itself. He felt no pride when, later, he didn't even hear that pertinacious, all-too-familiar whistle. He lived a dry but controlled dread in those minutes when unforeseen tranquillity surrounded him. He jutted out his jaw in a gesture of doubt.

A soldier's insistent whistle behind him confirmed the danger of this march through the canyon. The whistle was broken by a sudden volley of small-arms fire and a howl he knew only too well: Villa's cavalry was charging down the almost vertical face of the canyon in a suicide attack, while the riflemen dug in on the third bluff fired at his men, whose bleeding horses, enveloped in a din of dust, reared and plunged into the pit of sharp rocks. He was the only one able to look back to see Tobias imitate Villa's men by galloping down the steep slope in a vain attempt to carry out his orders. The Yaqui's horse lost its footing and for an instant flew through the air, until it crashed at the foot of the canyon wall, crushing its rider under it. The howl grew, accompanied by heavy firing; he slipped off the left side of his horse and rolled down the ravine, controlling his fall to the bottom with somersaults and occasional handholds. In his fractured vision, the bellies of the rearing horses pulsated above him, accompanied by the useless shots of the men who'd been surprised on that narrow ledge, where there was no chance to take cover or maneuver the horses. As he fell, clawing at the steep slope, Villa's cavalrymen attacked from the second peak and the hand-to-hand fighting began. Up above, the savage whirlwind of tangled men and crazed horses continued, while down below he was touching the dark floor of the canyon with his bloody hands.

He took out his pistol. Only a renewed silence awaited
him. His strength was completely drained. He dragged
himself forward, his arm and leg in agony, toward a gigantic
rock.

"It's time to give up. Come on out of there, Captain
Cruz."

His throat dry, he answered, "Why? So you can shoot
me? I think I'll stay right here."

But his right hand, numb with pain, could barely hold
the pistol. As he raised his arm, he felt a sharp pain in his
stomach. He fired with his head down because the pain
would not let him lift it. He kept on firing until the trigger
only repeated its metallic clicking. He threw the pistol over
the rock, and the voice from above shouted again: "Come
out with your hands on the back of your neck."

On the other side of the boulder, more than thirty horses
were scattered, dead or dying. Some were trying to lift
their heads; others leaned on a bent leg; most had red bullet
holes in their foreheads, their necks, or their stomachs.
Sometimes on top, sometimes beneath the animals, the
men on both sides had assumed distracted positions: face
up, as if they were trying to drink the thin stream of the
dry creek; face down, hugging the rocks. All dead, except
this man who was groaning, trapped under the weight of
a bay mare.

"Let me bring this man out," he shouted to the group
up above. "He might be one of yours."

How would he do it? With what arms? With what
strength? He had barely bent over to put his hands under
the shoulders of Tobias's trapped body when a bullet whistled past, hitting the boulder. He raised his eyes. The
leader of the winning side—his white officer's hat visible
in the bluff's shadow—halted the firing with a wave of his
hand. Caked sweat, thick with dust, covered his wrists, and
even though one arm could barely move, the other managed to drag Tobias's body with a concentrated will.

Behind him he could hear the swift hooves of Villa's cavalry as they detached themselves from the column to take him. They were almost on him when the Yaqui's broken legs emerged from beneath the animal's body. Villa's men tore the cartridge belts from his chest.

It was seven o'clock in the morning.

By four in the afternoon, when they entered the Perales prison, he wouldn't have any memory of the forced march that Colonel Zagal imposed on his men and the two prisoners to negotiate, in nine hours, the difficult mountain passes and descend into the Chihuahua village. His head was so riddled with pain that he could barely follow the route they took. Seemingly, the harshest. The simplest for someone like Zagal, who had accompanied Pancho Villa on his first raids and had spent twenty years traveling these mountains, memorizing hiding places, passes, canyons, and shortcuts. The mushroom shape of Zagal's hat hid half his face, but his long, clenched teeth were always visible in a smile, framed by a black beard and mustache. Zagal smiled when Cruz was mounted, with great effort, on a horse, and the Yaqui's broken body, face down, was tied on the croup of the animal. He smiled when Tobias stretched out an arm to hold on to the captain's belt. He smiled when the column moved forward, entering a dark mouth, a natural tunnel, which he and the rest of Carranza's men hadn't know about, a shortcut that reduced to an hour what would have been a four-hour gallop on the open road. But he was only half aware of all this. He knew that both sides shot captured officers on the spot, so he wondered why Colonel Zagal was leading him to an unknown destiny.

The pain made him sleep. His arm and leg, badly bruised by the fall, hung inert; the Yaqui still held on to him, moaning, his face flushed. The rock tumulus passed by, one by one, and the men continued on, protected by the shadows at the base of the mountains, entering interior valleys of stone, deep ravines that ended in dry riverbeds, paths camouflaged by thickets and bushes so the column could cross undetected. Perhaps only Pancho Villa's men have really traveled this land, he thought, which was why, before, they had been able to win the string of guerrilla victories that had broken the back of the dictatorship. Masters of surprise, of encirclement, of rapid withdrawal after attack. Exactly the opposite of the tactics taught in military school, the tactics of General Alvaro Obregón, who believed in formal battles on the open plain with precise maneuvers on well-reconnoitered terrain.

"All together and in order. Don't straggle on me," shouted Colonel Zagal, detaching himself from the head of the column and galloping back, swallowing dust and clenching his teeth. "Now that we're out of the mountains, who knows what we'll run into. Everybody on guard; heads down, eyes open for dust clouds; together we see better than I would by myself . . ."

The masses of rock opened wider. The column was on a flat bluff, and the rolling Chihuahua desert, spotted with mesquite, spread out at their feet. The sun was cut by gusts of high wind: a layer of coolness that never touched the burning edges of the desert.

"Let's go by way of the mine so we get down faster," shouted Zagal. "Hold on tight to your pal, Cruz. It's a steep path."

The Yaqui's hand squeezed Artemio's belt. There was more in that pressure than a desire not to fall: an intent to communicate. Artemio lowered his head, patted his horse's neck, and turned toward Tobias's flushed face.

Speaking in his own language, the Indian whispered: "We're going to pass by a mine that was abandoned a long time ago. When we get close to one of the entrances, turn the horse and head him inside. The passages branch off so many times they'll never find you . . ."

He went on patting the horse's neck. Then he raised his head and tried to make out the path they'd take down to the desert and the mine entrance Tobias was talking about.

The Yaqui whispered again: "Forget about me. My legs are broken."

Was it noon? Was it one o'clock? The sun grew heavier and heavier.

A flock of goats appeared on a ridge, and some soldiers fired at them. One goat escaped; another fell off his pedestal and was picked up by a soldier who dismounted, picked up the carcass, and loaded it on his shoulders.

"Hunting season is officially over!" Zagal declared in his hoarse, smiling voice. "You're going to miss those bullets someday, Corporal Payán."

Then, standing up in his stirrups, he spoke to the entire column: "Get one thing through your thick skulls, you bastards: Carranza's troops are right on our ass. Don't anyone waste a single shot. What do you think, that we're on our way south, winning all the way, like before? Well, we aren't. We lost and we're heading north, back where we came from."

"But, sir," whined the corporal in a low voice, "at least now we've got a little something to eat."

"Yeah, and if we don't get out of here, we'll turn into a little something to shit."

The column laughed, and Corporal Payán tied the dead goat behind his saddle.

"No one eats or drinks anything until we get down there," ordered Zagal.

He had his mind fixed on the narrow trails that led down. There, just around the next turn, the open mouth of the mine.

The hooves of Zagal's horse clattered on the narrow-gauge rails protruding a foot or two outside the entrance. It was then that Cruz threw himself off his horse, tumbling down the slope before the surprised rifles could be raised. He fell on his knees in the darkness: the first shots rang out, and Zagal's men began shouting at each other. The sudden cold cleared his head, but the darkness dizzied him. Keep going: his legs ran, forgetting the pain, until he smashed into a boulder. He spread his arms toward two shafts running in different directions. Through one, a strong wind was blowing; out of the other came a shut-in heat. With his arms outstretched, he could feel the different temperatures on the tips of his fingers. He started running again, toward the closed shaft, because it had to be deeper. Behind him, accompanied by the music of jangling spurs, came Villa's men. A match cast an orange glow, and he lost his footing and fell down a vertical shaft, until he felt the dry thud of his body on some rotten beams. Above, the noise of spurs was incessant, and a murmur of voices bounced off the walls of the mine. The man being chased got to his feet painfully; he tried to calculate the dimensions of the place into which he'd fallen and locate the shaft he should follow to get away.

"Better wait here . . ."

The voices above grew louder, as if they were arguing. Then Colonel Zagal's laugh rang out clearly. The voices withdrew. Someone far away whistled: a single, rough whistle to get attention. Other undefinable noises reached his hiding place, heavy sounds that persisted for several minutes. Then nothing. His eyes began to get used to the place: darkness.

"Looks like they've gone. But it might be a trap. Better wait here."

In the heat of the abandoned shaft, he felt his chest, carefully ran his fingers over the ribs he'd hurt in falling. He was in a round space with no exit, no doubt where the miners had stopped digging. A few broken beams lay on the ground; others held up the fragile clay roof. He tested the stability of one of the beams and then sat down again to wait for the hours to pass. One of the beams reached down the hole he'd fallen into: it wouldn't be hard to climb up and make his way back to the entrance. He felt the rents on his trousers and his tunic; his golden insignias were coming loose. And fatigue, hunger, sleepiness. His young body stretched its legs and felt a strong pulse in its thighs. Darkness and rest, slight panting, eyes closed. He thought about the women he would have wanted to know; the bodies of those he did know fled from his imagination. The last one had been in Fresnillo. A prostitute on her day off. The kind that start crying when you ask them where they're from or how they ended up here. The usual question to start up a conversation, because all of them loved to make up stories. Not that one; she just cried. And the war that never ended. Of course, these were the last battles. He crossed his arms over his chest and tried to breathe normally. Once they eliminated Pancho Villa's scattered army, there would be peace. Peace.

"What am I going to do when this is finally over? And why think that it's going to end? I never think that."

Maybe peace would mean good job opportunities. In his crisscrossing over Mexico, all he'd ever seen was destruction. But fields that were despoiled could be planted again. In Bajío, once, he'd seen a beautiful field; alongside, someone could build a house with arcades and flower-covered patios, and tend the crops. To see a seed grow, care for it, watch the plant sprout, harvest the fruit. It would be a good life, a good life . . .

"Don't go to sleep, stay alert."

He pinched his thigh. The muscles in the nape of his neck jerked his head back.

No sounds came from above. He could explore. He grabbed the beam that went up from the hole, and swung his foot to one of the cuts in the wall that ran up. He edged his way, using his good arm and wedging his foot in cut after cut. Finally he was able to grasp the ledge. His head came over the top. He was in the flow of hot air. But now it seemed heavier, even more choked-off than before. He walked to the main gallery. He recognized it because next to the poorly ventilated shaft he'd been in was the other, the one that blew hot air. But beyond, the light no longer came through the entrance. Had night fallen? Had he lost track of time?

His hands felt blindly for the entrance. It wasn't night that had closed it off but Villa's men, who had barricaded it before leaving. They'd sealed him in this tomb with its exhausted veins of ore.

In the nerves of his stomach he felt smashed. He automatically widened his nostrils in an imaginary effort to breathe deeply. He brought his fingers to his temples and rubbed them. The other shaft, the one that blew hot. That wind came from outside, it came up from the desert, the sun whipped it up. He ran toward the second tunnel. His nose led him to that sweet, flowing air, and with his hands braced on the walls he made his way, tripping in the darkness. A drop of water moistened his hand. He brought his open mouth to the wall, searching for the source of the water. Slow, disparate pearls dripped from the roof. He caught another with his tongue; he waited for the third, the fourth. He hung his head. The shaft seemed to end. He sniffed the air. It came from below, he felt it around his ankles. He went down on his knees, feeling with his hands. From that invisible opening, it came from there: the steepness of the shaft gave it more force than it had here at the opening. The stones were loose. He began to pull at them until the wall gave way: a new gallery, glittering with silvery veins, opened before him. He squeezed his body through and realized that he couldn't stand up in this new passage: he would have to crawl. So he dragged himself along, without knowing where this slithering would take him. Gray seams, golden reflections from his officer's bars: only those irregular lights illuminated his slow crawl, like that of a beshrouded snake. His eyes reflected the blackest corners of the darkness, and a thread of saliva ran down his chin. His mouth felt as if it were full of tamarinds:

perhaps the involuntary memory of any fruit recalled stimulates the salivary glands; perhaps the precise messenger of a scent released from a faraway orchard, carried by the mobile desert air, had reached this narrow passage. His newly awakened sense of smell perceived something else. A breath of air. A lungful of air. The unmistakable taste of nearby dirt: unmistakable for someone who had spent such a long time locked up with the taste of stone. The low shaft was descending; now it suddenly stopped and fell, cut off, onto a wide interior space with a sand floor. He dropped down from the high gallery and landed on the soft bed. Some roots had made their way in here. How?

"Yes, now it goes up again. It's light! It looked like a reflection on the sand, but it's light!"

He ran, his chest full of air, toward the opening bathed in sunlight.

He ran without hearing or seeing. Without hearing the slow strumming of the guitar and the voice that sang along with it, the saucy, sensual voice of a tired soldier.

> *Durango girls wear green and white,*
> *Some like to pinch, some like to bite . . .*

Without seeing the small fire over which the carcass of the goat shot back in the mountains was turning, or the fingers that tore off strips of its skin.

Without hearing or seeing, he fell on the first fringe of illuminated ground. How could he see, under the molten sun of three o'clock in the afternoon, Colonel Zagal's hat transformed into a plaster mushroom.

Zagal laughed and offered him his hand. "Get a move on, Captain, you're going to make us late. Just look at the Yaqui over there, eating his head off. And now everybody can use his canteen."

Chihuahua girls are desperate,
they don't know what to do,
They need a man to love them,
I wonder if I'll do . . .

The prisoner raised his face and before looking at Zagal's now relaxed group let his eyes roam the dry landscape of rocks and spiny plants stretching out, wide, silent, and leaden, before him. Then he stood up and walked over to the small camp. The Yaqui fixed his eyes on him. He stretched out his arm, ripped a scorched chunk of meat off the goat's back, and sat down to eat.

Perales.

A town of adobe bricks, scarcely different from any other. Only one of its streets, the one that passed by the town hall, was paved. The others were dirt pounded down by the bare feet of children, the talons of turkeys which preened on street corners, the paws of the pack of dogs that sometimes slept in the sun and sometimes ran around aimlessly, barking. Perhaps one or two good houses, with grand entryways and iron gates and zinc drainpipes: they always belonged to the local moneylender and the political boss (when they weren't one and the same person). But now those figures were fleeing Pancho Villa's swift justice. The troops had taken over both houses and filled the patios—hidden behind the long walls that faced the street like battlements—with horses and hay, boxes of ammunition and tools: whatever Villa's defeated Northern Division had managed to salvage in its march back to its source. The color of the town was gray; only the façade of the town hall boasted a pinkish tone, and that quickly faded on its sides and in the patios into the same gray as the earth. There was a spring nearby, the reason why the town was founded. Its wealth derived from turkeys, chickens, a few dry fields tilled alongside the dusty streets, a pair of blacksmiths, a carpenter's shop, a general store, and a few small businesses set up in houses. It was a miracle anyone survived. People lived in silence. As in most Mexican villages, it was hard to know where the people were hiding. Mornings and afternoons, afternoons and evenings, the blow of an insistent hammer could perhaps be heard, or the wail of a newborn, but it would be difficult to run into a living being on those burning streets. Sometimes the children, small and barefoot, would peer out. The soldiers, too, stayed behind the walls of the abandoned houses or in the patios of the town hall, which was the destination of the weary column.

When they dismounted, a guard detachment approached and Colonel Zagal pointed to the Yaqui. "Lock him up. You come with me, Cruz."

The colonel wasn't laughing now. He opened the door of the whitewashed office, and wiped the sweat off his forehead with his sleeve. He loosened his belt and sat down. The prisoner stood there, staring at him.

"Pull up a chair, Captain, and let's have a nice little chat. Care for a cigarette?"

The prisoner took one, and the flame from the match brought their faces together.

"Well now"—Zagal smiled again—"it's a simple deal. You tell us the plans of the troops chasing us and we'll set you free. I'm talking to you man to man now. We know we're done for, but even so we're going to put up a defense. You're a good soldier and understand what I mean."

"Sure. That's why I won't tell you anything."

"Of course. But actually you wouldn't have to tell us very much. You and all those dead guys back in the canyon were on a scouting mission—anybody could see that. Which means that the rest of your force couldn't be too far away. You even smelled out the route we've been following back north. But since you don't know that pass through the mountain, you would have had to cross the flatland and that takes a few days. Well then: How many men are behind us? Are there troops who've gone ahead by train? What kind of supplies do you have? How much artillery did you bring along? What are your plans? Where are the separate brigades trailing us going to rendezvous? See? I'm not asking for that much. You tell me what I want to know and you go free. Word of honor."

"Since when have you been giving out guarantees?"

"Damn it, Captain, we're going to lose this thing no matter what. I'm being straight with you. The Northern Division has collapsed. It's broken down into small bands that will get lost in the mountains, and even the bands are thinning out, because, as we go along, the men are deserting, going back home to their towns and farms. We're tired. We've been fighting for a long time, ever since we took up arms against Don Porfirio. Then we fought for Madero, then against Orozco and his reds, then Huerta's ragpickers, then you Carranza guys. A lot of years. We're worn out. Our people are like lizards, they're turning the same color as the dirt, they're going back to the shacks they came from, they dress like field hands and wait for the time to start fighting again, even if they have to wait a hundred years. They know we've lost this one, the same way Zapata's men know it down south. You have won. Why should you die when your side's already won? Let us go down fighting. That's all I'm asking. Let us lose with a little honor."

"Pancho Villa's not in this town."

"No. He's up ahead. The men are deserting in droves; there are only a few of us left."

"What kind of guarantees can you give me?"

"We'll leave you here—alive—in the jail until your pals rescue you."

"Sure, if we win. If not . . ."

"If we win, I'll give you a horse so you can get away."

"So you can shoot me in the back when I go."

"Come on . . ."

"No. I've got nothing to say."

"We've got your friend the Yaqui in jail, along with a

lawyer named Bernal, some kind of envoy from Carranza. You can wait with them until the order for your execution comes through."

Zagal stood up.

Neither one took the matter personally. Their feelings had been worn away, effaced by everyday events, by the relentless grind of their blind struggle. They had spoken mechanically, without revealing their true emotions. Zagal asked for information and offered him the opportunity to choose between freedom and execution; the prisoner refused to supply the information. They spoke not like Zagal and Cruz but like gears in two opposed war machines. For that reason, the prisoner received the information about his execution with absolute indifference. An indifference, of course, that obliged him to realize the monstrous tranquillity with which he accepted his own death. Then he, too, stood and set his jaw.

"Colonel Zagal, we've both been following orders for a long time, without giving ourselves the chance to do something like—how can I put it?—something that would say: I'm doing this as Artemio Cruz; I'm doing this on my own, not as an officer in the army. If you have to kill me, kill me as Artemio Cruz. You've already said that all this is coming to an end, that we're all tired. I don't want to die as the last sacrifice in a winning cause, just as you don't want to die as the last sacrifice in a losing cause. Be a man, Colonel, and let me be one. Let's shoot it out with pistols. Draw a line down the patio, and we'll both come out of opposite corners. If you shoot me before I cross the line, you get to finish me off. If I cross it without getting hit, you let me go."

"Corporal Payán!" shouted Zagal, with a glint in his eye. "Take him to his cell."

Then he turned to face the prisoner. "You will get no advance notice of when the execution will take place, so be ready. It might be an hour from now, it might be tomorrow, or even the day after. Just think about what I told you."

The setting sun came through the barred window and outlined in yellow the silhouettes of the other two men, one standing, the other on his back. Tobias tried to murmur a greeting; the other, who paced nervously, came up to him as soon as the cell door screeched and the keys of the corporal of the guard scraped in the lock.

"You're Captain Artemio Cruz? I'm Gonzalo Bernal, envoy of our commander, Venustiano Carranza."

He was wearing civilian clothes, a coffee-colored twill suit whose countrified jacket had a false belt sewn onto it. Artemio looked at him as he looked at all the civilians who tried to come close to the sweaty nucleus of those who did the fighting—he looked at him with a rapid glance of mockery and indifference, until Bernal, wiping his high forehead and blond mustache with a handkerchief, went on: "The Indian is in a bad way. His leg is broken."

The captain shrugged. "For the time he's going to last, it doesn't much matter."

"What do you know?" asked Bernal. He kept the handkerchief over his lips, and his words were muffled.

"They're going to shoot us all. But they won't say when. Did you think we'd be dying of colds?"

"There's no hope our troops will get here first?"

Now it was the captain who stopped—he'd been turning, peering at the roof, the walls, the tiny barred window, the dirt floor: an instinctive search for a means to escape. He looked at the new enemy: the informer planted in the cell.

He asked: "Isn't there any water?"

"The Yaqui drank it all."

The Indian moaned. Cruz approached the coppery face resting against the stone head of the bench that served as both bed and chair. His cheek was next to Tobias's when for the first time, with a force that made him step back, he felt the existence of that face, which had never been more than dark clay, one of the troops, more recognizable in the nervous, rapid wholeness of his warrior's body than in this serenity, this pain. Tobias did have a face; he saw it. Hundreds of white lines—lines of laughter and rage and eyes squinting into the sun—covered the corners of his eyelids and inscribed squares on his wide cheekbones. His thick, protruding lips smiled gently and in his gray narrow eyes there was something like a well of turbid, enchanted, ready light.

"So you made it, too," said Tobias in his own language, which the captain had learned in his daily contact with the troops from the Sinaloa mountains.

He squeezed the Yaqui's sinewy hand. "Yes, Tobias. It's better that you know it now, once and for all: they're going to shoot us."

"It had to be that way. You'd do the same thing."

"Yes."

They remained silent as the sun disappeared. The three men got ready to spend the night together. Bernal paced slowly around the cell: he got up and then sat down on the dirt to scratch some lines in the floor. Outside, in the hall, an oil lamp went on, and they could hear the movement of the jaws of the corporal of the guard. A cold wind sprang up over the desert.

On his feet again, he went to the cell door: thick slabs of rough-cut pine, and a small opening at eye level. On the other side, the plume of smoke from the cigar the corporal was lighting floated up. He closed his hands on the rusty bars and observed his guardian's flat profile. Tufts of black hair sprouted out of his canvas cap and only stopped at his square, beardless cheekbones. The prisoner caught his eye, and the corporal answered by rapidly moving his head and free hand to express a silent "What do you want?" His other hand clutched his carbine in the usual style of those engaged in this kind of work.

"Got your order about tomorrow yet?"

The corporal looked at him with long, yellow eyes. He didn't answer.

"I'm not from these parts. What about you? What kind of place is it?"

"What place?"

"Where they're going to shoot us. What can you see from there?"

He stopped and waved, so the corporal would bring the lamp over.

"What can you see?"

Only then did he remember that he'd always looked ahead, beginning with the night when he'd crossed the mountain and escaped from the old ruined house in Veracruz. From that day on, he'd never looked back. From that day on, he'd willed to know he was alone, with no strength other than his own . . . And now . . . He couldn't resist asking that question—what's it like, what can you see from there—which perhaps was his way of disguising the anxiety of memory, the slope toward an image of leafy ferns and slow rivers, tubular flowers over a shack, a starched skirt and soft hair that smelled of quince . . .

"They'll just take you to the patio out behind here," the corporal was saying, "and what you can see—what did you think it'd be?—is a damn high wall, all pockmarked with bullet holes. We shoot so many people . . ."

"But the mountains. Can't you see the mountains?"

"You know, I swear I don't remember."

"Seen a lot of executions, eh?"

"You said it."

"Maybe the guy who does the shooting can see what's going on better than the guys being shot."

"You mean you've never been in a firing squad?"

(Yes, I've been in firing squads, but without thinking about what the other guy might feel, or that someday it might be my turn. That's why I have no right to ask you anything, right? Like me, you've only killed, without noticing. That's why no one knows what the other guy might feel and no one can tell about it. If the other guy could come back, if he could tell all about hearing shots and feeling them hit his chest and face. If he could tell the truth about all that, it might be that we wouldn't dare to kill anyone ever again; or it might be that dying wouldn't matter to anyone ever again . . . It might be terrible . . . but it might be just as natural as being born . . . What do you and I know?)

"Listen, Captain, you won't be needing your insignia anymore. Give it to me."

The corporal stuck his hand through the bars, and he turned his back on him. The soldier laughed a stifled screech.

Now the Yaqui was whispering in his language. He dragged his feet over to the hard headrest to touch the Indian's fevered brow with his hand and to hear his words. They ran along in a gentle singsong.

"What's he saying?"

"He's telling things. How the government took away the land where his people had always lived, to give it to some gringos. How they fought for their land; how the federal troops came, cut off the men's hands, and chased them into the hills. How they took the Yaqui chiefs up to a bluff, loaded them down with weights, and threw them into the sea."

The Yaqui spoke with his eyes shut. "Those of us who were left were dragged into a long line and from there, from Sinaloa, they made us walk all the way to the other end, to Yucatán."

"How they had to march to Yucatán and the women and the old people and the kids in the tribe were dying. Those who made it to the hemp plantations were sold as slaves, and husbands were separated from wives. How they made the women sleep with the Chinese workers, so they'd forget their language and give birth to more workers . . ."

"I came back, I came back. As soon as I heard the war

had started, I came back with my brothers to fight against the evil."

The Yaqui laughed softly, and Artemio Cruz felt the need to urinate. He stood up, opened the fly of his khaki trousers, found a corner, and listened to the splashing on the dirt. He frowned, thinking of the usual end for brave men, who die with a wet spot on their uniform trousers. Bernal, who had his arms crossed, seemed to be looking through the high bars for a moonbeam on this cold, dark night. Sometimes a persistent hammering from the town reached them; the dogs howled. A few lost, meaningless conversations managed to penetrate the walls. He slapped the dust off his tunic and went to the young lawyer.

"Got any cigarettes?"

"Yes . . . I think so . . . They're somewhere."

"Offer one to the Yaqui."

"I already did. But he doesn't like mine."

"Does he have any of his own?"

"It seems he ran out."

"Maybe the soldiers have cards."

"No. I couldn't concentrate. I think I wouldn't be able to . . ."

"Sleepy?"

"No."

"You're right. There's no need to sleep."

"Think you'll be sorry?"

"What?"

"Sorry, I mean, for ever having slept . . ."

"That's a good one."

"Right. So it's better to remember. They say it's good to remember."

"There's not much life behind."

"Why not? That's the Yaqui's advantage. Maybe that's why he doesn't like to talk."

"Right. No, I don't get you."

"I mean, the Yaqui has a lot to remember."

"Maybe in his language they don't remember the same way we do."

"That march, from Sinaloa. What he told us just now."

"Yes."

" . . . "

"Regina . . ."

"What . . ."

"Nothing. I was just saying names."

"How old are you?"

"I'm just turning twenty-six. What about you?"

"Twenty-nine. I don't have much to remember either. Even though life got pretty hectic all of a sudden."

"When do people start remembering, for instance, their childhood?"

"That's true; it's hard."

"Know something? Just now, while we were talking . . ."

"Yes?"

"Well, I said a few names to myself. Know something? They don't mean anything to me anymore, nothing."

"Sun's coming up."

"Don't take any notice."

"The sweat's pouring down my back."

"Pass me a cigarette. What happened?"

"Sorry. Here. Maybe you don't feel anything."

"That's what they say."

"Who says that, Cruz?"

"The ones who do the killing."

"Does it matter much to you?"

"Well . . ."

"Why don't you think about . . ."

"What? That everything's going to be the same even if they kill us?"

"No. Don't think ahead; think back. I think about all those who've already died in the Revolution."

"Right. I remember Bule, Aparicio, Gómez, Captain Tiburcio Amarillas . . . just a few."

"I'll bet you can't even remember twenty. And not only them. What are the names of all those who died? Not only in this Revolution but in all the wars, and even those who died peacefully, in their beds. Who remembers them?"

"Look. Give me a match."

"Sorry."

"The moon's up now."

"Want to see it? If you stand on my shoulders, you might catch a glimpse . . ."

"No. It's not worth the trouble."

"It's good they took my watch."

"Yes."

"I mean, otherwise I'd be counting the minutes."

"Of course, I understand."

"The night seemed more . . . well, longer . . ."

"This stinking pisshole."

"Look at the Yaqui. Fast asleep. It's good no one showed he was afraid."

"Now, another day stuck in here."

"Who knows. They're liable to walk in any time."

"Not these guys. They like their little game. It's too traditional to be shot at dawn. They're going to play with us."

"He wasn't impulsive?"

"Villa yes. Zagal no."

"Cruz . . . isn't this really absurd?"

"What?"

"Dying at the hands of one of the big bosses, and not believing in any of them."

"Think we'll go all three of us together, or they'll take us out one at a time?"

"Easier in one haul, don't you think? Hey, you're the soldier here."

"Don't you have any tricks up your sleeve?"

"Shall I tell you something? You'll die laughing."

"What is it?"

"I wouldn't tell you if I weren't sure we aren't going to get out of here. Carranza sent me on this mission just so I'd get caught and the other side would be responsible for my death. He got it into his head that he'd rather have a dead hero than a live traitor."

"You, a traitor?"

"Depends on how you look at it. You've only been in battles; you've followed orders and have never had any doubts about your leaders."

"Correct. Our mission is to win the war. Aren't you with Obregón and Carranza?"

"The same way I could have been with Zapata or Villa. I don't believe in any of them."

"So?"

"That's the drama. They're all there is. I don't know if you remember the beginning. It was only a short time ago, but it seems so far away . . . When the leaders didn't matter. When we weren't doing this to raise up one man but to raise up all men."

"Are you trying to get me to find fault with the loyalty of our men? That's what the Revolution's all about, nothing else: being loyal to the leaders."

"Right. Even the Yaqui, who went out to fight for his land, now he's only fighting for General Obregón against General Villa. No—before, it was something else. Before it degenerated into factions. Whenever the Revolution passed through a village, the debts of the peasants were wiped out, the moneylender's property was confiscated, the political prisoners were let out of jail, and the old bosses were run out. But just look at how the people who thought the Revolution was not to puff up leaders but to free the people are being left behind."

"Time will tell."

"No, it won't. A revolution starts in the battlefields, but

once it gets corrupted, even though military battles are still won, it's lost. And we're all to blame. We've let ourselves be divided and directed by the lustful, the ambitious, the mediocre. Those who want a real, radical, intransigent revolution are, unfortunately, ignorant, bloody men. And the educated ones only want half a revolution, compatible with the only thing they really want: to do well, to live well, to take the place of Don Porfirio's elite. That's Mexico's drama. Look at me. I spent my entire life reading Kropotkin, Bakunin, and old Plekhanov, buried in my books since I was a kid, and talk, talk, talk. And when the time comes to make a decision, I have to join up with Carranza, because he's the only one who seems a decent sort, the only one who doesn't scare me. Doesn't that make me sound like a faggot? I'm afraid of the people, of Villa, and of Zapata . . . 'I'll go on being an impossible person as long as the people who are possible today go on being possible' . . . Oh, yeah. Sure, sure."

"You start in with all this now, when you're about to die . . ."

"That's the radical defect in my character: my love of the fantastic, of adventures hitherto unseen, enterprises that open infinite, unknown horizons . . . Oh yeah! Sure, sure."

"Why didn't you say all that when you were out there?"

"I did say it, beginning in 1913, to Iturbe, to Lucio Blanco, to Buelna, to all the honorable military men who didn't try to become big chiefs. That's why they didn't know how to nip Carranza in the bud. I mean, his whole life he's done nothing but turn people against each other and divide them, because if he didn't, who wouldn't take his command from him, the old mediocrity? That's why he promoted mediocrities, the Pablo González types, who'd never put him in the shade. That's how he divided the Revolution, turning it into a factional war."

"And that's why he sent you to Perales?"

"My mission was to convince Villa's men to give up. As if we all didn't know that they're running away in defeat and they're so desperate they shoot every Carranza supporter they can get their hands on. The old man doesn't like getting his hands dirty. He'd rather have the enemy do his dirty work for him. Artemio, Artemio, the leaders haven't been equal to the people and their Revolution."

"So why don't you go over to Villa?"

"Why would I want more of the same? So I could see how long he lasts and then go over to another and then another, until I find myself in another cell waiting for orders for my execution?"

"But you'd save yourself . . ."

"No . . . Believe me, Cruz, I'd like to save myself and go back to Puebla. See my wife, my son. Luisa and little Pancho. And my little sister, Catalina, who depends on me for so much. See my father, my dear old Don Gamaliel, so noble and so blind. I wish I could explain to him why I got involved in all this. He never understood that there are obligations we've just got to see through, even though we know it's all going to fail. For him, the old order was eternal—the haciendas, the camouflaged loan-sharking, all of it . . . I wish there was someone I could ask to go see them and give them a message from me. But no one's getting out of here alive, that I do know. No; it's all a sinister game of musical chairs. We're living among criminals and pygmies, because the big boss only favors midgets who won't stand over him, and the little boss has got to murder the big one to get ahead. A shame, Artemio. How necessary everything that's happening is, and how unnecessary it is to corrupt it. That isn't what we wanted when we started the Revolution of the people in 1913 . . . As for you, you'd better decide. As soon as they eliminate Zapata and Villa, there will be only two bosses left, the two you work for. Which one will you go with?"

"My leader is General Obregón."

"Well, at least you've made a choice. I hope it doesn't cost you your life; I hope . . ."

"You're forgetting that they're going to shoot us."

Bernal laughed in surprise, as if he'd tried to fly, forgetting the chains that held him down. He squeezed the other prisoner's shoulder and said: "This damned mania for politics! Maybe it's an intuition. Why don't you go with Villa?"

He couldn't make out Gonzalo Bernal's face clearly, but in the darkness he could feel the mocking eyes, the know-it-all air of a shyster who never fights but just talks while others win battles. Abruptly, he moved away from Bernal.

"What's the matter?" asked the lawyer, smiling.

He grunted and lit his cigarette, which had gone out. "That's no way to talk," he said between his teeth. "Where do you get this stuff? Am I telling you everything? Well, let me tell you that people who tell everything without being asked really bust my balls, especially when they're going to die any minute. Shut up, Mr. Lawyer, tell yourself whatever you want, but let me die without spilling my guts."

Gonzalo's voice sounded as though sheathed in steel: "Listen, he-man, we are three men sentenced to death. The Yaqui told us his story . . ."

His rage was directed against himself, because he had allowed himself to drift into intimacy and talk, he had opened himself to a man who did not deserve that kind of confidence.

"That was the life of a real man. He had a right to tell it."

"What about you?"

"All I've ever done is fight. If there was more, I don't remember it."

"You loved some woman . . ."

He clenched his fists.

". . . You had a father, a mother; hell, you may even have a son someplace. You don't? I do, Cruz. I do think I had a man's life—I'd like to be free to get on with it. Don't you? Wouldn't you like to be caressing . . . ?"

Bernal's voice broke when Artemio's hands sought him in the darkness, beat him against the wall without a word, with a muffled bellow, his nails stuck into the twill lapels of this new enemy armed with ideas and tenderness, who was merely repeating the secret thoughts of the captain, of the prisoner, his own thoughts: What will happen after our death?

And Bernal went on, despite the fists that pounded him: ". . . If they hadn't killed us before we were thirty? . . . What might have become of our lives? I wanted to do so many things . . ."

Until he, his back covered with sweat, his face close to Bernal's, also murmured: ". . . Everything is going to go on the way it always does, don't you get it? The sun is going to come up, and kids will keep on being born, even if the two of us are dead and buried, don't you get it?"

The two men separated after their violent embrace. Bernal dropped on the floor; Cruz walked toward the cell door, his mind made up: he would tell Zagal a cock-and-bull story, he would ask him to let the Yaqui go and would leave Bernal to his fate.

When the corporal of the guard, humming, led him to the colonel, all he felt was that lost pain for Regina, the sweet and bitter memory he'd hidden, which was now boiling to the surface, asking him to go on living, as if the dead woman needed the memory of a living man to be something other than a body gnawed by worms in an unmarked grave in a nameless town somewhere.

"Don't get any cute ideas about pulling a fast one on us," said Colonel Zagal in his eternally smiling voice. "We're sending two patrols out right now to see if what you're telling us is true, and if it isn't, or if the attack is coming from another direction, make your peace with God and figure you've done nothing more than earn yourself a few more hours of life—at the cost of your honor."

Zagal stretched out his legs and wiggled his stocking toes one after the other. His boots were on the table, worn out and sagging.

"What about the Yaqui?"

"He wasn't part of the deal. Look: the night's drawing long. Why tease these poor bastards with the idea that they're going to live another day? Corporal Payán! . . . Let's send the other two prisoners off to a better life. Take them out of the cell and bring them out back."

"The Yaqui can't walk," said the corporal.

"Who does he think he is, the *cucaracha* in the song? Fine, give him some marijuana," cackled Zagal. "All right, bring him out on a stretcher and prop him up against the wall as best you can."

What did Tobias and Gonzalo Bernal see? The same thing the captain saw, except that he was at a greater elevation, standing next to Zagal on the balcony of the town hall. Down below, the Yaqui was carried out on a stretcher and Bernal walked with his head slumped, and the two were set against the wall between two oil lamps.

A night in which the glow of dawn was slow in showing itself, in which the silhouette of the mountains did not allow itself to be seen, not even when the rifles thundered with reddish blasts and Bernal stretched out his hand to touch the Yaqui's shoulder. Tobias stayed against the wall, held in place by the stretcher. The lamps lit his shattered face, wracked by bullets. They lit only the ankles of Gonzalo Bernal's prone body, out of which flowed rivulets of blood.

"There are your dead," said Zagal.

Another fusillade, distant but heavy, served as a commentary on his words, and immediately a hoarse cannon joined in by blowing away a corner of the building. The shouts of Villa's men rose confusedly to the white balcony, where Zagal was bellowing disarticulate commands:

"They're here! They found us! It's Carranza's men!" And he knocked him down and squeezed his hand—alive once more, concentrated in all its strength—around the butt of the colonel's pistol. He felt the metallic dryness of the weapon in his fingers. He stuck it into Zagal's back and wrapped his right arm around the colonel's neck. He squeezed, keeping him on the ground, his jaws set, his lips foaming. Over the edge of the balcony he could see the confusion down in the execution yard. The soldiers in the squad ran around, trampling the corpses of Tobias and Bernal, kicking over the oil lamps. Explosions rained down on the town of Perales, accompanied by shouts and fire, galloping and whinnying horses. More of Villa's troops came out into the yard, pulling on their jackets and buttoning their trousers. The fallen lamps etched every profile, every belt, every brass button with a golden line. Hands reached out to pick up rifles and cartridge belts. Quickly they opened the stable doors and neighing horses came out on the patio. Their riders mounted and galloped out the gates. Stragglers ran behind the cavalry, and now the patio was deserted. The corpses of Bernal and the Yaqui. Two oil lamps. The shouting faded off into the distance, headed for the enemy attack. The prisoner released Zagal. The colonel remained on his knees, coughing, rubbing his nearly strangled neck. He could barely raise his voice: "Don't give up. I'm here."

And the morning finally showed its blue eyelid over the desert.

The immediate din ceased. Zagal's men ran through the streets toward the siege, their white shirts tinged with blue. Not a murmur rose from the patio. Zagal stood up and unbuttoned his grayish tunic, as if offering his chest. The captain also stepped forward, pistol in hand.

"My offer still stands," he said in a dry voice to the colonel.

"Let's go downstairs," said Zagal, relaxing his arms.

In the office, Zagal picked up the Colt he kept in a drawer.

They walked, both armed, through the cold corridors out to the patio. They divided the rectangular space in two. The colonel moved Bernal's head out of his way with his foot. The captain picked up the oil lamps.

Each man stood in a corner. They moved forward.

Zagal fired first, and his shot pierced Tobias the Yaqui again. The colonel stopped, and a flash of hope lit his black eyes: the other walked forward without firing. The duel was turning into a ritual of honor. The colonel clung—for one second, two seconds, three seconds—to the hope that the other would respect his courage, that the two would meet in the middle of the patio without firing another shot.

They both stopped at the halfway point.

The smile returned to the colonel's face. The captain crossed the imaginary line. Zagal, laughing, was making a friendly gesture with his hand when two quick shots pierced his stomach, and the other man watched him sag and fall at his feet. Then he dropped the pistol on the colonel's sweat-soaked head and stood there, not moving.

The desert wind shook the curly hair over his eyes, the tatters of his tunic stained with sweat, the strips of his leather puttees. Five days' growth of beard bristled on his cheeks, and his green eyes were lost behind eyelids covered with dust and dry tears. Standing there in the patio, a solitary hero surrounded by corpses. Standing there, a hero without witnesses. Standing there, surrounded by abandon while the battle raged on outside the town, with a roll of drums.

He lowered his eyes. Zagal's lifeless arm pointed toward Gonzalo's lifeless skull. The Yaqui was seated, his body against the wall; his back had left a clear outline on the canvas of the stretcher. He knelt next to the colonel and closed his eyes.

Suddenly he stood up and breathed the air he'd wanted to find, thank, and use to give name to his life and his freedom. But he was alone. He had no witnesses. He had no comrades. A muffled shout escaped from his throat, drowned out by steady machine-gun fire in the distance.

"I'm free; I'm free."

He held his fists over his stomach, his face twisted with pain.

He raised his eyes and finally saw what someone sentenced to die at dawn must have seen: the distant line of mountains, the now whitish sky, the patio's adobe walls. He listened to whatever it was someone sentenced to die at dawn must listen to: the chirping of hidden birds, the sharp cry of a hungry child, the strange hammering of the worker in the village, remote from the unvarying, monotonous, lost clamor of the artillery and small-arms fire still raging behind him. Anonymous work, stronger than the clamor, with the certainty that, once the fighting was over, and the dying, and the winning, the sun would shine again, every day . . .

I cannot desire; I let them do whatever they wish. I try to touch it. I run my finger over it, from my navel to my pubis. Round. Puffy. I don't know. The doctor's gone. Said he was going to bring in some other doctors. He doesn't want to be responsible for what happens to me. I don't know. But I see them. They've come in. The mahogany door opens, closes, and their footsteps go unheard on the thick rug. They've closed the windows. They've closed the gray curtains with a hiss. They've come in.

"Go over to him, child . . . so he can recognize you . . . Tell him your name . . ."

She smells good. She smells pretty. Oh yes, now I can make out the blush on her cheeks, her shining eyes, her young, graceful body, which approaches my bed in short steps.

"I . . . I'm Gloria . . ."

I try to whisper her name. I know they don't listen to what I say. For that at least I have to be thankful to Teresa: for having brought her daughter's young body close to me. If only I could make out her face more clearly. If only I could see the expression of disgust on her face. She must be aware of this stench of dead scales, vomit, and blood; she must see this sunken chest, this gray, matted beard, these waxy ears, this fluid I can't keep from pouring out of my nose, this dry saliva on my lips and chin, these unfocused eyes that will have to try to take another look, these . . .

They take her away from me.

"Poor thing . . . She was upset . . ."

"What?"

"Nothing, Papa, just rest."

Someone said she was going out with Padilla's son. How he must kiss her, what words he must say to her, ah, yes, what a blush. They come and go. They touch my shoulder, they nod, they whisper words of encouragement, yes, they don't know that I'm listening in spite of everything: I hear even the remotest conversations, the talk that takes place in the corners of the room, but I don't hear what they say nearby, the words spoken into my ear.

"How does he look to you, Mr. Padilla?"

"He looks bad, very bad."

"He's leaving behind a veritable empire."

"Yes."

"So many years he's spent running his businesses!"

"It'll be hard to find someone to take his place."

"I'll tell you what: the only person fit to fill his shoes is you . . ."

"Yes, I've been so close to him . . ."

"And who would take your place, in that eventuality?"

"Oh, there are so many qualified people."

"So you think there will be quite a few promotions?"

"Certainly. A whole new redistribution of responsibilities."

"Ah, Padilla, come closer. Did you bring the tape recorder?"

"You'll take responsibility?"

"Where Artemio . . . Here it is . . ."

"Yes, sir."

"Be ready. The government is going to intervene in a big way, so you have to be ready to take charge of the union."

"Yes, sir."

"Let me warn you in advance that quite a number of old foxes are getting ready. I've already hinted to the authorities that you're the man we know we can count on. Wouldn't you like a little something to eat?"

"No, thanks, I already ate. Much earlier."

"All right, then, get cracking. Go shake some hands, over in the Ministry of Labor and the Confederation of Mexican Workers—you know what I mean . . ."

"I'll get right on it, boss. You can count on me."

"See you soon, Campanela. Keep a low profile. Be careful. On your toes. Let's go, Padilla . . ."

There. It's finished. Ah. That was everything. But was it? Who knows. I don't remember. I haven't listened to the voices in that recorder for a long time. I've been playing dumb for a while now. Who's touching me? Who is that so close to me? How useless, Catalina. I tell myself: How useless, what a useless caress. I ask myself: What are you going to say to me? Do you think you've finally found the words you never had the courage to say? Ah, so you did love me? Why didn't we ever say it? I loved you. I don't remember anymore. Your caress makes me see you and I don't know, I don't understand why, sitting next to me, you share this memory with me at the end, and this time, without a reproach in your eyes. Pride. Pride saved us. Pride killed us.

". . . for a miserable salary, while he shames us with that woman, while he rubs our noses in his money, he gives us what he gives us as if we were beggars . . ."

They didn't understand. I did nothing for them. I didn't even take them into account. I did it for myself. I'm not interested in these stories. I don't want to remember Teresa and Gerardo. They mean nothing to me.

"Why didn't you demand that he give you your rightful place, Gerardo? You're as responsible as he is . . ."

I have no interest in them.

"Calm down, Teresita, how about trying to understand my point of view? You don't hear me complaining."

"Personality, that's all you needed, but not even that . . ."

"Let him rest."

"Don't start siding with him now! He made no one suffer as much as he made you . . ."

I survived. Regina. What was your name? No. You, Regina. But what was your name, soldier without a name? Gonzalo. Gonzalo Bernal. A Yaqui. A poor little Yaqui. I survived. You died.

"He made me suffer, too. How can I forget it. He didn't even come to the wedding. My wedding, his daughter's wedding . . ."

They never got the point. I didn't need them. I created myself by myself. Soldier. Yaqui. Regina. Gonzalo.

"He destroyed even the things he loved, Mama, and you know it."

"Just stop talking, for God's sake, just stop . . ."

The will? Don't worry: it exists, an officially stamped, notarized document. I don't leave anyone out: why should I leave anyone out, hate anyone? Wouldn't you have secretly thanked me for hating you? Wouldn't it give you pleasure to know that even at the end I thought about you, even if it was to play a trick on you? No, I remember all of you with the indifference of a cold bureaucratic formality, my dear Catalina, my charming daughter, granddaughter, son-in-law: I'm doling out a strange fortune to you, a wealth which you will all ascribe—in public—to my efforts, my tenacity, my sense of responsibility, my personal qualities. Please do so. And remain calm. Forget that I earned that wealth by risking my skin without knowing it in a struggle I didn't try to understand because it wouldn't have helped me to define, to understand, because only those who didn't expect anything from their sacrifices could know and understand it. That's what sacrifice is—am I correct?: to give everything in exchange for nothing. If it isn't, then what should we call giving everything in exchange for nothing? But they didn't offer everything to me. She offered me everything. I didn't take it. I didn't know how to take it. What could her name be?

"Okay. The picture's clear enough. Say, the old boy at the Embassy wants to make a speech comparing this Cuban mess with the old-time Mexican Revolution. Why don't you lay the groundwork with an editorial . . ."

"Yes, yes. We'll do it. How about twenty thousand pesos?"

"Seems fair enough. Any ideas?"

"Sure. Tell him to show the sharp differences between an anarchic, bloody movement that destroys private property and human rights and an orderly, peaceful, legal revolution like Mexico's, a revolution led by a middle class that found its inspiration in Jefferson. After all, people have bad memories. Tell him to praise Mexico."

"Fine. So long, Mr. Cruz, it's always . . ."

Oh, what a bombardment of signs, words, and stimuli for my tired ears. Oh, how tired I am. They will probably not understand my gestures, because I can barely move my fingers: turn it off, it's boring me, what does it have to do with me now? What a bother, what a bother . . .

"In the name of the Father, of the Son . . ."

"That morning I waited for him with pleasure. We crossed the river on horseback."

"Why did you take him away from me?"

I'll bequeath to them all the vain useless deaths, the lifeless names of Regina, the Yaqui . . . Tobias, now I remember, his name was Tobias . . . Gonzalo Bernal, a soldier without a name. And the woman? The other one.

"Open the window."

"No. You might catch cold and make everything worse."

Laura. Why? Why did everything have to happen this way? Why?

You will survive: you will run your finger over the sheets and know that you have survived, despite time and the movements that hem in your fortunes with every passing instant. The line of life is located between paralysis and debauchery. Adventure: you will imagine the greater security, never to move. You will imagine yourself immobile, safeguarded from all danger, chance, uncertainty. Your quietude will not stop time, which runs without you, although you invent it, measure it, time that denies your immobility and submits you to its own danger of extinction: adventurer, you will measure your velocity with the speed of time.

The time you will invent in order to survive, to create the illusion of a greater permanence on earth: the time your brain will create by perceiving that alternation of light and darkness on the clock face of dreams; by retaining those images of placidity threatened by the amassing of concentrated black clouds announcing a thunderclap, the posterity of lightning, the whirlwind discharge of rain, the certain appearance of a rainbow; by listening to the cyclical calls of animals in the forest; by screaming out the signs of time: the howl of wartime, the howl of mourning time, the howl of party time; finally, by saying time, speaking time, thinking the nonexistent time of a universe that knows no time because it never began and will never end: it had no beginning, will have no end, and does not know that you will invent a measure of infinity, a reserve of reason.

You will invent and measure a time that doesn't exist.

You will know, discern, judge, calculate, imagine, foresee, end up thinking that which will have no other reality than that created by your brain, you will learn to control your violence in order to control the violence of your enemies. You will learn to rub two sticks together until they catch fire, because you will have to throw a torch out of your cave to frighten off the beasts which will not make an exception of you, which will not differentiate your flesh from that of other beasts, and you will have to construct a thousand temples, set down a thousand laws, write a thousand books, adore a thousand gods, paint a thousand paintings, construct a thousand machines, dominate a thousand nations, split a thousand atoms in order to throw your flaming torch out of the entrance to your cave again.

And you will do all that because you think, because you will have developed a cluster of nerves in your brain, a thick network capable of obtaining and transmitting information from front to rear. You will survive, not because you are the strongest, but because of the dark luck of an ever colder universe in which only those organisms that know how to maintain their body temperature when that of the environment falls will survive, those organisms that concentrate that frontal mass of nerve tissue and can foresee danger, search for food, organize their movement, direct their swimming in the circular, proliferating ocean teeming with origins. The dead and lost species will stay at the bottom of the sea, your sisters, millions of sisters that did not emerge from the water with their five contractile stars, their five fingers sunk into the other shore, terra firma, the islands of the dawn. You will emerge crossed with amoeba, reptile, and bird, the birds which will launch themselves from the new peaks to smash in the new abysses, learning in failure, while the reptiles already fly and the land grows colder: you will survive with the birds, protected by feathers, clothed in the speed of their heat, while the cold reptiles sleep, hibernate, and finally die, and you will sink your hooves into the hard land, into the islands of dawn, and you will sweat like a horse, and you will climb up the new trees with your constant temperature and descend with your differentiated brain cells, your autonomic nervous system, your constant levels of hydrogen, sugar, calcium, water, and oxygen: free to think beyond your immediate senses and vital necessities.

You will descend with your ten thousand million brain cells, with your electric battery in your head, plastic, mutable, to explore, to satisfy your curiosity, to set yourself goals, to achieve them with a minimum of effort, to avoid difficulties, foresee, learn, forget, remember, connect ideas, recognize forms, to add degrees to the margin left open by necessity, to turn your will away from the attractions and rejections of the physical environment, to seek favorable conditions, to measure reality using the minimum as your criterion, even though you secretly desire the maximum, and not expose yourself to the monotony of frustration.

You will accustom yourself, mold yourself to the requirements of communal life.

You will desire: desire that your desire and the object desired be the same thing; dream of immediate gratification, of the fusion, without division, of desire and that which you desire.

You will recognize yourself.

You will recognize others and allow them to recognize you; and know that you are opposed to each individual because each individual is just one more obstacle between you and your desire.

You will choose, in order to survive you will choose, choose among the infinite mirrors one only, one only, one that will reflect you irrevocably, that will fill other mirrors with a dark shadow, kill them before offering you, once again, those infinite roads of choice.

You will decide, you will choose one of the roads, you will sacrifice the others. You will sacrifice yourself as you choose, will stop being all the other men you might have been, you will wish other men—another man—to carry out for you the life you cut off when you chose: when you chose yes, when you chose no, when you let, not your desire, identical to your freedom, but your intelligence, your self-interest, your fear, and your pride, lead you to a labyrinth.

That day you will fear love.

But you will be able to recover it. You will rest with your eyes closed, but you will not cease to see, not cease to desire, because that is how you will make the desired object yours.

Memory is satisfied desire.

Today, when your life and your destiny are one and the same.

(1934: August 12)

He took a match, struck it, stared into the flame, and touched it to the end of his cigarette. He closed his eyes. He inhaled the smoke. He stretched out his legs and lolled in the armchair. He ran his free hand over its velvet and breathed in the aroma of the chrysanthemums in the crystal vase. He listened to the slow music coming from the phonograph behind him.

"Almost ready."

His free hand felt for the album, which was on the small walnut table to his right. He touched the album cover, read *Deutsche Grammophon Gesellschaft*, and heard the majestic entrance of the cello that faded, reasserted itself, and

finally overtook the violin refrain, relegating it to the chorus's secondary line. He stopped listening. He straightened
his tie and for a few seconds caressed its rich silk, which
rustled under the touch of his fingers.

"Would you like me to fix you a drink?"

He walked to the low liquor cart, replete with bottles
and glasses, picked out a bottle of Scotch and a Bohemian
crystal tumbler. He poured out a jigger of whiskey, dropped
in an ice cube, and added a splash of water.

"Whatever you're having."

He repeated the operation, picked up both glasses,
swished them around to blend the whiskey and water, and
went to the bedroom door.

"One minute more."

"Did you choose it because of me?"

"Yes. Don't you remember?"

"Yes."

"Sorry I'm so slow."

He went back to the armchair. He picked up the album
cover once again and rested it on his knees. *Werke von
Georg Friedrich Handel.* They both went to concerts in
that overheated hall; by chance they were seated next to
each other, and by chance she had heard him comment in
Spanish to a friend about how hot the place was. He asked
her in English for the program and she said certainly in
Spanish. They both smiled. *Concerti grossi, opus 6.*

They made a date for the following month, when they
both had to be in that city, to meet in a café on rue Cau-
martin, near the Boulevard des Capucines, which he would
try to revisit years later without her, and not be able to
find it—wishing he could see it again, order the same
things—a café he remembered having a red-and-sepia de-
cor, with Roman-style banquettes, and a long bar of reddish
wood, not an open-air café, but an open café, without doors.
They drank crème de menthe and water. He ordered it
again. She said that September was the best month, the

end of September, the beginning of October. Indian summer. The end of vacation. He paid the check. She took him by the arm, laughing, taking deep breaths, and they crossed the courtyards of the Palais Royal, walking through the galleries and courtyards, stepping on the first dead leaves, accompanied by pigeons, and they walked into the restaurant with small tables and red backrests and painted walls with inset mirrors: old paint and old varnish—gold, blue, and sepia.

"All ready."

He looked over his shoulder and watched her walk out of the bedroom fastening her earrings to her earlobes, smoothing her soft, honey-colored hair. He held her drink out to her, and she took a sip, wrinkling her nose. She sat in the red chair and crossed her right leg over her left as she raised the glass to eye level. He imitated her movements and smiled at her as she shook something off the lapel of her black suit. The clavichord led the central refrain of that descent, accompanied by the violins. He imagined it as a descent from a height, not as a march forward: a slight, almost imperceptible descent, which, when it touched the earth, became the contrapuntal joy of the low and high tones of the violins. The clavichord, as if it were wings, had only served as a means to descend and touch the earth. Now that the music was on earth, it danced. They looked at each other.

"Laura . . ."

She raised her index finger, and they went on listening. She seated, her glass in her hands; he standing, spinning a celestial globe on its axis, stopping it from time to time to examine the figures traced out in silverpoint on the supposed outline of the constellations: Crow, Shield, Hunting Dogs, Fishes, Altar, Centaur. The needle hung over silence; he walked to the record player, moved the tone arm back, and let it slip into its holder.

"Your apartment turned out very nicely."

"Yes. Funny. There wasn't room for everything."

"It looks fine all the same."

"I had to put the other things into storage."

"If you wanted, you could have . . ."

"Thanks," she said, smiling. "If all I wanted was a big house, I would have stayed with him."

"Do you want to listen to more music, or should we go out?"

"Let's finish our drinks and go out."

They paused in front of that picture. She said she liked it a lot and always came to look at it because of the stopped trains, the blue smoke, the blue-and-ocher houses in the background, the blurred, barely suggested figures. She said she liked the awful tin roof and opaque windows on the Gare Saint-Lazare in Monet's painting a great deal, those were the things she liked about this city, where objects taken separately or examined in detail might not be beautiful but are irresistible taken as a whole. He said that was certainly one interpretation, and she laughed and patted his hand and said he was right, she just liked it, liked all of it, she was happy, and he, years later, went back to see that painting, by then it was in the Jeu de Paume, and the special guide said it was incredible, in thirty years the painting had quadrupled in value, now it was worth thousands, quite incredible.

He went over to her, stopped behind her, rubbed the back of her chair, and then touched Laura's shoulders. She rested her head on the man's hand, rubbed her cheek on his fingers. She sighed, and with a new smile turned and sipped the whiskey. She threw her head back with her eyes closed and swallowed the sip after savoring it between her tongue and her palate.

"We could go back next year. Don't you think so?"

"Yes, we could go back."

"I always remember how we wandered the streets."

"So do I. You'd never gone to the Village. I remember I took you there."

"Yes, we could go back."

"There's something so alive about that city. Remember? You didn't know what it was like to smell the river mixed with the sea. You couldn't place it. We walked to the Hudson and closed our eyes so we could feel it."

He took Laura's hand, he kissed her fingers. The telephone rang, and he stepped forward to answer it. He lifted the receiver and listened to a voice saying over and over again, "Hello, hello, hello? . . . Laura?"

He put his hand over the mouthpiece and held it out to Laura. She left her glass on the little table and walked over to the telephone.

"Hello?"

"Laura? It's Catalina."

"Hi. How are you?"

"Am I interrupting something?"

"I was just on my way out."

"I won't keep you long."

"What is it?"

"Are you really in a hurry?"

"No, not at all. I mean it."

"I think I made a mistake. I should have told you."

"What?"

"Yes, yes. I should have bought your sofa. Now that I've moved into the new house, I realize it. Do you remember the brocade sofa, the one with the embroidery? It would look so nice in the vestibule, because I bought some tapestries, some tapestries to hang in the vestibule, and I think the only thing that would look right in that spot would be your sofa with the embroidery . . ."

"I wonder. Maybe there would be too much brocade."

"No, no. The tapestries are dark and your sofa is light, so they'd make a pretty contrast."

"But you know I'm using that sofa here in the apartment."

"Don't be that way. You've got so much furniture. Didn't you tell me you had to put half of it in storage? You did say that, didn't you?"

"I did, but you have to understand that I arranged the living room just so that . . ."

"All right, think it over. When are you coming to see the house?"

"Whenever you say."

"Don't leave it that way, so vague. Name a day and we'll have tea together and chat."

"Friday?"

"No, Friday I can't, but I can on Thursday."

"Then we'll make it Thursday."

"Just let me say that, without your sofa, the vestibule is just not going to work. I'd almost rather not have a vestibule, you know? It just won't work. An apartment is so much easier to decorate. You'll see when you come over."

"On Thursday."

"Oh, yes, I ran into your husband. He was very polite. Laura, it's a shame, a shame you're going to get divorced. I thought he looked so handsome. You can see he misses you. Why, Laura, why?"

"It's all over now."

"See you Thursday, then. Just the two of us, we'll have a good talk together."

"Yes, Catalina. See you Thursday."

"Bye."

He asked if she wanted to dance and they walked through the Plaza Hotel's potted-palm-lined salons and made their way to the dance floor. He took her in his arms, and she caressed his long fingers, felt the heat in the palm of his hand, rested her head on his shoulder, lifted it, looked into his eyes, he was looking into hers: they were looking at each other, looking at each other, his green eyes, her gray eyes, looking at each other, alone on the dance floor with that orchestra playing a slow blues number, looking at each other, with their fingers, his arm around her waist, slowly turning, that stiff skirt, that skirt . . .

She hung up and looked at him and waited. She walked to the sofa with the embroidery, ran her fingers over it, and again looked at the man. "Would you turn on the light? The switch is right next to you. Thanks."

"She doesn't know anything."

Laura walked away from the sofa and turned to look at it. "No, the light's too bright. I haven't figured out how to arrange the lamps yet. Lighting a big house isn't the same as this . . ."

She felt tired, she sat on the sofa, took a small, leather-bound book off the side table, and leafed through it. She pushed aside her blond hair, which covered half her face, turned toward the light, and in a low voice spoke out what she was reading, her eyebrows raised and a tenuous resignation on her lips. She read, closed the book, and said, "Calderón de la Barca," and, staring at the man, recited from memory: "Is there not to be pleasure someday? God, tell, why did you create flowers if our olfactory sense is not to enjoy the soft aroma of your fragrant scents . . ."

She lay back on the sofa, covering her eyes with her hands, repeating in a precise, tired voice, a voice that did not want to hear itself or to be heard, ". . . if our auditory sense is not to hear them . . . if our eyes are not to see them," and she felt the man's hand on her neck, touching the shining pearls that lay on her bosom.

"I didn't make you do it . . ."

"No, you have nothing to do with it. That started long ago."

"Why did it happen?"

"Oh, maybe I just have too inflated an idea of my own value . . . because I think I have a right to be treated better . . . not as an object, but as a person . . ."

"What about us?"

"I don't know. I just don't know. I'm thirty-five. It's hard
to start over unless someone lends a hand . . . We talked
that night, remember?"

"In New York."

"Yes. We said we ought to get to know each other . . ."

". . . That it was more dangerous to close doors than to
open them . . . But don't you think you know me by now?"

"You never say anything. You never ask me for anything."

"Do you really think I should be asking you for things?
Why?"

"I don't know . . ."

"You don't know. Well, let me spell it out for you. Then
you'll know . . ."

"Maybe."

"I love you. You say you love me. No, you don't want
to understand . . . Give me a cigarette."

He took the pack out of his jacket pocket. He selected
a match and lit it, while she took the cigarette, felt the
paper between her lips, moistened it, with two fingers
removed a few grains of tobacco from her lip, rolled them
in her fingers, casually tossed them away, as she waited.
And he went on looking at her.

"Maybe I'll start taking classes again. When I was fifteen,
I wanted to paint. Later I forgot all about it."

"Aren't we going out?"

"No, we're not going out."

"Want another drink?"

"Yes, make me another."

He took her empty glass from the table, noted the lipstick
smudge on the rim, heard the tinkle of an ice cube against
the crystal, walked to the low table, measured out the
whiskey again, picked up another ice cube with the silver
tongs . . .

"Please, don't add water."

She asked him if it didn't bother him what direction the
girl dressed in white—in white and shadow—standing on

the swing was looking, the girl with the blue braids down her dress. She said there was always something left out of the picture, because the world represented in the picture should be extended, go beyond it, be filled with other colors, other presences, other concerns, because of which the picture was composed and existed. They went out into the September sun. They walked, laughing, under the arcades on the rue de Rivoli, and she told him he ought to see the Place des Vosges, which was perhaps the most beautiful. They hailed a taxi. He spread the subway map out on his knees, and she ran her finger over the red line, the green line, holding on to his arm, her breath very close to his, saying that she loved those names, that she never got tired of saying them, Richard-Lenoir, Ledru-Rollin, Filles-du-Calvaire . . .

He handed her the glass and gave the celestial globe another spin, rereading the names Lupus, Crater, Sagittarius, Pisces, Horologium, Argo Navis, Libra, Serpens. He spun the globe, running his finger on it, touching the cold, distant stars.

"What are you doing?"

"Looking at this globe."

"Ah."

He bent over and kissed her loosened hair; she nodded and smiled.

"Your wife wants this sofa."

"So I hear."

"What do you think? Should I be generous?"

"Do whatever you think best."

"Should I be indifferent? Should I forget she called? I'd rather be indifferent. Sometimes generosity is the worst insult, and not generous at all. Don't you think so?"

"I don't follow you."

"Put on some music."

"What do you want to hear this time?"

"The same album. Put the same album on, please."

He read the numbers on the four sides. He put them in order, pressed the button, let the first record fall, fall with its dry slap on the felt turntable. He smelled that mix of wax, heat from the amplifier tubes, and polished wood, and once again heard the wings of the clavichord, the soft fall toward joy, the clavichord's renunciation, it renounces the air to touch terra firma with the violins—its support, the shoulders of the giant.

"Loud enough?"

"Make it a little louder. Artemio . . ."

"What?"

"I can't go on this way, sweetheart. You have to make up your mind."

"Be patient, Laura. Try to realize . . ."

"Realize what?"

"Don't pressure me."

"Into what? Are you afraid of me?"

"Aren't we doing fine just the way we are? What more do we need?"

"Who knows. Maybe we don't need anything."

"I can't hear you."

"No, don't lower the volume. Listen to me through the music. I'm getting tired of all this."

"I didn't trick you into anything. I didn't pressure you."

"I didn't change you, which is something else. You're not willing."

"I love you like this, the way we've been until now."

"The way we were the first day."

"Yes, that's it."

"But it isn't the first day anymore. Now you know me. Go on."

"Just think for a minute, Laura, please. Those things create real problems. We've got to keep up . . ."

"Appearances? Or is it just fear? Nothing's going to happen, you can be sure that nothing at all will happen."

"We should have gone out."

"No. No more. Raise the volume."

The violins crashed against the windows: the joy, the renunciation. The joy of that forced grimace below those light, shining eyes. He picked up his hat. He walked to the door. He stopped with his hand on the knob. He looked back. Laura, curled up, hugging the pillows, her back turned toward him. He walked out. He closed the door carefully behind him.

I wake up again, but this time screaming. Someone just plunged a long, cold knife into my stomach—someone outside. I couldn't make an attempt on my own life like that. There is someone, some other person who has stabbed an iron rod into my guts. I stretch out my arms, I make an effort to get up, and the hands are there, someone else's arms holding me down, asking me to be calm, saying I should be still, and another finger quickly dials a telephone number, misdials, tries again, misdials again, finally gets the connection, calls for the doctor, quick, right away, because I want to get up and disguise my pain by moving around, and they won't let me—who can they be? who can they be?—and the contractions move up. I imagine them like the coils of a snake, they move up my chest, toward my throat. They fill my tongue, my mouth with ground-up, bitter paste, some old food I forgot and I'm now vomiting, face down, looking vainly for a bowl and not that rug stained by the thick, stinking liquid from my stomach. It doesn't stop, it rends my chest, it's so bitter and tickles my throat, it tickles me horribly. It goes on, doesn't stop, some old digested something with blood, vomited onto the carpet in the bedroom, and I don't have to see myself to sense the pallor on my face, my livid lips, the accelerated rhythm of my heart as my pulse disappears from my wrist. They've stuck a dagger into my navel, the same navel that nourished me once upon a time, once upon a time, and I can't believe what my fingers tell me when I touch that stomach stuck

to my body which isn't really a stomach. It's swollen, inflated, puffed up with gases I can feel moving around, which
I can't expel, no matter how I try: farts that rise up to my
throat and then go back down to my stomach, to my intestines, and I can't expel them. But I can breathe in my
own fetid breath, now that I manage to lean back and feel
that next to me they're hastily cleaning the rug. I smell the
soapy water, the wet rag trying to vanquish the smell of
vomit. I want to get up; if I walk around the room, the pain
will go away, I know it will go away.

"Open the window."

"But he even killed the thing he loved most, Mama, and
you know it."

"Just be quiet. For God's sake, just be quiet."

"Didn't he kill Lorenzo, didn't he . . . ?"

"Shut up, Teresa! Once and for all, just be quiet. You're
killing me."

What . . . Lorenzo? It doesn't matter. It doesn't matter
to me one bit. They can say whatever they like. I know the
things they've been saying, even though they wouldn't dare
say them to my face. Well, let them talk now. They should
take advantage of the opportunity they've got. I took
charge. They never understood. They look at me like statues while the priest anoints my eyelids, my ears, my lips,
my feet, and my hands, anoints me between the legs, near
the penis. Turn on the tape recorder, Padilla.

"We crossed the river . . ."

And she, Teresa, stops me, and this time I do see the
fear in her eyes and the panic on her tight lips devoid of
lipstick, and in Catalina's arms I see the unbearable weight
of words never spoken, words I keep her from speaking.
They manage to lay me down. I can't, I can't, the pain
doubles me up. I have to touch the ends of my toes with
my fingertips to make sure my feet are there, that they
haven't disappeared, they're frozen, already dead, ahhh!
ahhh!, dead already, and only now do I realize that always,

all my life, there was a scarcely perceptible movement in
my intestines, all the time, a movement I recognize only
now because suddenly I don't feel it. It has stopped, it was
wave-like and was with me all my life, and now I don't feel
it, I don't feel it, but I look at my fingernails when I reach
out to touch my frozen feet which I no longer feel, I look
at my brand-new blue, blackish fingernails that I've put on
especially to die, ahhh! it won't go away, I don't want that
blue skin, that skin painted over with lifeless blood, no,
no, I don't want it, blue is for other things, blue for the
sky, blue for memories, blue for horses that ford rivers,
blue for shiny horses and green for the sea, blue for flowers,
but not blue for me, no, no, no, ahhh! ahhh! and I have to
lie back because I don't know where to go, how to move,
I don't know where to put my arms and the legs I don't
feel, I don't know where to look, I don't want to get up
anymore because I don't know where to go, I only have
that pain in my navel, that pain in my stomach, that pain
by my ribs, that pain in my rectum while I uselessly strain,
I strain, tearing myself up, I strain with my legs spread
and I don't smell anything, but I hear Teresa's crying and
I feel Catalina's hand on my shoulder.

I don't know, I don't understand why, sitting next to me,
you're sharing this memory with me at the end, and this
time with no reproach in your eyes. Ah, if you only understood. If we only understood. Perhaps there's another
membrane behind our open eyes and it's only now that
we're breaking through it, to see. The body can send out,
the same way it can receive from the eyes and caresses of
others. You touch me. You touch my hand, and I feel your
hand without feeling my own. It touches me. Catalina pats
my hand. It must be love. I wonder. I don't understand.
Could it be love? We were so used to each other. If I offered
her love, she would respond with reproaches; if she offered
me love, I would respond with pride: perhaps they were
two halves of a single feeling, perhaps. She touches me.

She wants to remember all that with me, only that, and to understand it.

"Why?"

"We crossed the river on horseback . . ."

"I survived. Regina. What was your name? No. You, Regina. What was your name, soldier without a name? I survived. You died. I survived."

"Go over to him, so he can see who you are. Tell him your name . . ."

But I listen to Teresa's sobs, and I feel Catalina's hand on my shoulder, and the rapid, squeaky footsteps of the man who pokes my stomach and sticks his finger in my anus, inserts a hot thermometer reeking of alcohol into my mouth, and the other voices break off and the man who's just arrived says something in the distance, in the depth of a tunnel:

"There's no way to know. It might be a strangulated hernia. It might be peritonitis, it might be a nephritic colon. If that's what it turns out to be, we'll have to inject him with two centigrams of morphine. But that might be dangerous. I think we should get another opinion."

Oh pain that overcomes itself, oh pain, prolonging yourself, until you don't matter, until you become normalcy: oh pain, I couldn't stand being without you, I've grown accustomed to you, oh pain, oh . . .

"Say something, Don Artemio. Speak to us, please. Speak."

". . . I don't remember her, I just don't remember her anymore, of course, how could I forget her . . ."

"Look: his pulse ceases completely when he speaks."

"Give him something, Doctor, don't let him suffer . . ."

"Another doctor will have to see him. It's dangerous."

". . . how could I forget him . . ."

"Just rest now, please. Don't talk anymore. That's right. When did he last urinate?"

"This morning . . . No, two hours ago, without knowing it."

"Did someone save it?"

"No . . . no."

"Put the catheter back on. Save it. We have to run tests on it."

"I wasn't there, so how could I remember to do it?"

Again that cold gadget. Again my lifeless penis inside that metal mouth. I'll learn to live with all this. An attack; an old man my age can have an attack anytime; an attack is nothing out of the ordinary; it'll pass; it has to pass; but there is so little time, why don't they let me remember? Yes, when my body was young; once it was young; it was young . . . Oh, my body is dying of pain, but my brain is full of light: they are separating, I know they are separating: because now I remember that face.

"An act of contrition."

I have a son, I made him: because now I remember that face: where should I take him, where, so he doesn't get away, where, for God's sake, where, please, where?

From the depth of your memory you will cry out; you will lower your head as if to place it next to the horse's ear and spur him on with words. You will feel—and your son will probably feel as well—that fierce, steaming breath, that sweat, those tense nerves, those eyes glassy from strain. Your voices will be lost in the thunder of the hooves, and he will shout: "You've never been able to beat the mare, Papa!" "And who taught you to ride, eh?" "I'm telling you, you'll never be able to beat the mare!" "Let's just see!" "You should tell me all about it, Lorenzo, just as you have until now, just like that . . . just as you have until now . . . You shouldn't be ashamed to tell your mother; no, no, never be embarrassed with me; I'm your best friend, maybe your only friend . . ." She will repeat it that morning, lying in

bed, that spring morning, and she will repeat all the conversations she'd prepared since her son was a child, drain-
ing you out of his life, taking care of him all day long,
refusing to hire a nanny, packing your daughter, as soon
as she turned six, off to Catholic boarding school, so that
all her time would be for Lorenzo, so that Lorenzo would
grow accustomed to that comfortable life devoid of options.
The speed will bring tears to your eyes; you will squeeze
your legs over your horse's flanks, you will throw yourself
violently against its mane, but the black mare will keep
three lengths ahead. You will straighten up, tired; you will
slow down. Seeing the mare and the young rider pulling
away will seem more beautiful to you, the sound of the
hooves lost in the chorus of macaws, in the bleating that
flows down the hillsides. You will have to squint so as not
to lose sight of Lorenzo's mare, which will now leave the
path to trot toward the woods, returning to the riverbank.
No: without difficult options, without the alarming need to
choose, Catalina will say to herself, thinking that in the
beginning you helped her with your indifference, unintentionally, because you belonged to another world, the world
of work and force she came to know when you took Don
Gamaliel's lands away from him, allowing the boy at the
beginning to join the other world of bedrooms in semi-
darkness: a natural slope, a climate of almost nonexistent
exclusions and inclusions created by her between her sacred muttering and her silent dissimulation. Lorenzo's
mare will detour off the path to trot once more toward the
woods, returning to the riverbank. The boy's raised arm
will point east, where the sun came up, toward a lagoon
separated from the bay by a sandbar in the river. You will
close your eyes when you again feel the hot steam rising
toward your face along with the cool shadow that falls on
your head. You will let your horse follow the road on its
own, rocking you on the moist saddle. Behind your closed
eyelids, the shape of the sun and the form of the shadow

will scatter in invisible depths, and the blue phantom of the young, strong figure will stand out. You must have awakened that morning, as you did every day, with expectant joy. "I've always turned the other cheek," Catalina will repeat, the child at her side. "Always, I have always accepted everything. If it weren't for you"—and you will love those astonished, questioning eyes that allow themselves to be led. "One day, I'll tell you everything . . ." You will not be mistaken in bringing Lorenzo to Cocuya from the time he is twelve; you will repeat it: not mistaken. For him alone will you have bought this land, rebuilt the hacienda, left him on it, the child-master, responsible for the harvests, open to the life of horses and hunting, swimming and fishing. You will see him from a distance, on horseback, and you will say to yourself that he is the image of your own youth, slim and strong, dark, his green eyes sunken into high cheekbones. You will breathe in the muddy rot of the riverbank. "One day, I'll tell you everything . . . Your father; your father, Lorenzo . . . Lorenzo: do you really love Our Lord? Do you believe all the things I've taught you? Do you know that the Church is the body of God on earth and that priests are the ministers of the Lord . . . ? Do you believe . . . ?" Lorenzo will place his hand on your shoulder. Each will see the other reflected in his eyes, you will smile. You will grab Lorenzo around the neck; the boy will pretend to punch you in the stomach; you will mess his hair, laughing; you will embrace in a mock but rough, hard-fought, panting struggle until you both collapse on the grass, laughing, out of breath, laughing . . . "My God, why am I asking you this? I have no right, really, I have no right . . . I don't know about holy men . . . about real martyrs . . . Do you think it could be approved? . . . I don't know why I'm asking you . . ." The horses will go home, as tired as you two, and now you will walk, leading them by their bridles, along the sand bridge that leads to the sea, the open sea, Lorenzo, Ar-

temio, to the open sea where Lorenzo will run, agile, toward the waves breaking, around his waist, toward the
green sea of the tropics which will soak his trousers, the
sea guarded by the low flight of sea gulls, the sea that only
pokes its tired tongue onto the beach, the sea that you will
impulsively take in the palm of your hand and raise to your
lips: the sea that tastes like bitter beer, smells like melon,
custard apple, guava, quince, strawberry. The fishermen
will drag their heavy nets toward the sand, you two will
join them, shuck oysters with them, eat crabs and lobsters
with them, and Catalina, alone, will try to close her eyes
and sleep, will await the return of the boy she hasn't seen
now for two years, since he turned fifteen, and Lorenzo,
as he cracks the pink shell of the lobsters and thanks the
fishermen for the slice of lemon they pass him, will ask you
if you ever think about what's on the other side of the sea,
because he thinks all lands resemble each other and that
only the sea is different. You will tell him there are islands.
Lorenzo will say that in the sea so many things happen that
we would have to be bigger, more complete, in order to
live in the sea. Lying back in the sand, listening to the
fishermen's out-of-tune guitar, you would like to explain to
him that years ago, forty or so, something shattered here
so that something else could begin, or something, even
newer, would never begin. Under the misty sun of dawn,
under the blazing, molten sun of midday, on the black paths
and alongside this sea, this one, now tranquil, dense, and
green, there existed for you a ghost, not real but true, that
could . . . It wasn't that—the very truth of those lost possibilities—which upset you so much, what brought you back
to Cocuya hand in hand with Lorenzo, but something—
you will say it with your eyes closed, with the taste of
shellfish in your mouth, with the Caribbean music of Veracruz, the *son*, in your ears, lost in the immensity of this
afternoon—more difficult to express, to think by yourself;
and even though you would like to tell your son, you will

not dare to. He has to understand on his own. You hear him understand, as he settles on his haunches, facing the open sea, his ten fingers spread out, under the overcast, suddenly dark sky: "A ship leaves in ten days. I've already booked passage." The sky and Lorenzo's hand, which turns to receive the first drops of rain, as if he were begging for them: "Wouldn't you have done the same thing, Papa? You didn't stay home. Do I believe in a cause? I don't know. You brought me here, you taught me all these things. It's as if I had relived your life, don't you understand?" "Yes." "Now there is this battle line. I think it's the only one left. I'm going." . . . Oh, that pain, that jab, oh, how you'd like to get up, run, forget the pain by walking it off, working, shouting, giving orders. And they won't let you, they will take you by the arms, they will force you to stay still, they will force you, physically, to keep on remembering, and you will not want to, you do want to, oh, you don't. You will only have dreamed your days: you don't want to know about one day that is more yours than any other day because it will be the only one on which someone will live for you, the only one you can remember in the name of someone; a short day, terror, a day of white poplars, Artemio, your day too, your life too . . . oh . . .

(1939: February 3)

He stood on the flat roof, a rifle in his hands. He was remembering how the two of them went out to the lake to hunt. But the rifle in his hands was rusty, no good for hunting. From the flat roof, the façade of the bishop's palace was clearly visible. All that remained was the façade, a shell without floors or roof. The bombs had destroyed all the rest. Half buried in the rubble, a few old pieces of furniture were also visible. Up the street, a man wearing a butterfly collar and two women dressed in black walked toward them. They were squinting, carrying bundles in their hands, and they took astonished steps as they passed the façade. All he had to do was see them to know they were enemies.

"You there, on the other side of the street!"

He shouted to them from that place on the roof. The man raised his face and the sun on his glasses blinded him. He waved his arm to signal them to cross the street to avoid the dangerous façade, which seemed about to collapse. They crossed, and in the distance the salvos of Fascist artillery resounded—they were hollow when they fell into the depths between mountains and high-pitched when they whistled through the air. Later he sat down on a sandbag. Miguel was next to him. Under no circumstance would he abandon the machine gun. From the roof they saw the town's deserted streets. There were shell holes in the streets, broken telephone poles, and tangled wires— the interminable echo of the salvos and the pam-pam-pam of sporadic small-arms fire, the dry, cold roof tiles: only the façade of the ancient bishop's palace was standing on that street.

"Only one belt left for the machine gun," he informed Miguel, and Miguel responded, "Let's wait until this afternoon. After that . . ."

They leaned back against the wall and lit cigarettes. Miguel wrapped his scarf around his face until it hid his blond beard. The mountains in the distance were covered with snow; the snow had gone down the slopes even though the sun shone brightly. In the morning light, the peaks stood out, seeming to advance toward them. Later, in the afternoon, they would retreat; the trails and pines would disappear. At day's end, there would be only a distant purple mass.

But, that midday, Miguel looked at the sun, squinted, and said, "If it weren't for the artillery and the sniping, you'd say we were at peace. These winter days are beautiful. Look how far down the mountain the snow has come."

He looked at the deep white creases that ran from Miguel's eyelids to his bearded cheeks, like snow drifting down his face. He would never forget those eyes, because in them he'd learned to see joy, courage, rage, and serenity. There had been times when they'd won and then been thrown back again. Sometimes they'd just lost. But the attitude they should all have was already in the creases in Miguel's face before they won or lost. He learned a lot from Miguel's face. The only thing he'd never seen Miguel do was weep.

He crushed his cigarette on the floor and it sent out a shower of sparks. He asked Miguel why they were losing, and Miguel pointed to the mountains on the frontier and said, "Because our machine guns didn't come from over there."

Then Miguel put out his cigarette, too, and began to murmur a song:

> *The four generals, the big four generals,*
> *The big four generals, oh Mama,*
> *Who've attacked us old and young . . .*

And he answered, still leaning back on the sandbags:

> *By Christmas Eve, oh Mama,*
> *They'll surely have been hanged . . .*

They sang to kill time. There were many hours like this one in which they stood guard and nothing happened. So they sang. They never had to say, "Let's sing." And no one ever felt embarrassed to sing in front of the others. Exactly as they laughed for no reason, wrestled, or sang along with the fishermen on the beach near Cocuya. Except that now they sang to bolster their courage, even if the words of the song were a bad joke, because the four generals not only hadn't been hanged but had them surrounded in this town with the mountain frontier in their faces. They had no place to go.

The sun began to fade early, at about four in the afternoon, and he hugged his old rifle with its yellow butt and put on his cap. Like Miguel, he wrapped himself up in his scarf. For the past few days, he'd been wanting to suggest something to him. Even though his boots were worn, they were still holding up; all Miguel had was an old pair of sandals he'd wrapped with rags and bound up with string. He wanted to say they could take turns with the boots: he one day, Miguel the next. But he didn't have the nerve. The wrinkles in that face said he shouldn't. Now they blew on their fingers, because they knew only too well what it meant to spend a night on an open roof. Then, from the far end of the street came a soldier, one of ours, a Republican, running toward us as if he'd popped out of one of the shell holes. He waved his arms and finally fell, face down. Behind him came more Republican soldiers, boots slapping the pockmarked streets. The artillery salvo, which had seemed so far off, suddenly was closer, and from the street below, one of the soldiers shouted: "Weapons, please, give us some guns!"

"Don't stop!" shouted the man leading the soldiers. "Don't make yourself an easy target!"

They passed by at a run, below them, and Miguel and Lorenzo aimed the machine gun at the last of their own soldiers, thinking the enemy would be right on their heels.

"They should be here any time now," he said to Miguel.

"All right, Mexican, do a good job now," said Miguel, holding up the last cartridge belt.

But another machine gun fired first. Two or three blocks away, another hidden machine-gun nest, a Fascist one, had waited for the men to fall back, and now it was raking the street, killing the soldiers. But not their leader, who hit the dirt, shouting: "Get down! You'll never learn!"

He moved the machine gun so he could fire at the hidden enemy gun, and the sun fell behind the mountains. The machine gun shook his entire body, and Miguel whispered, "Balls just aren't enough. Those blond Arabs over there have better weapons."

Because over their heads airplane motors began to buzz. "The Caproni are here."

They fought side by side, but it was so dark they couldn't see each other. Miguel reached out and touched his shoulder. For the second time that day, the Italian planes were bombing the town.

"Let's get out of here, Lorenzo. The Caproni are back."

"Where to? Wait. What about the machine gun?"

"What good is it? We don't have any more ammo."

The enemy machine gun had also fallen silent. Below them, a group of women ran by. They couldn't see them, but they could hear them, because they were singing in loud voices despite the fighting:

> *With Lister and Campesino,*
> *With Galán and Modesto,*
> *With Commander Carlos as our guides,*
> *The army of the people is so brave*
> *It will surely turn the tide . . .*

The voices sounded strange, mixed in with the noise of the bombs, but they were stronger than the bombs: the bombs fell sporadically but the singing never stopped. "And it isn't as if they were warlike voices either, Papa, but the voices of women in love. They were singing to the Republican fighters as if they were their lovers, and up on the roof Miguel and I accidentally touched hands and thought the same thing. That they were singing to us, to Miguel and Lorenzo, and that they loved us . . ."

Then the façade of the bishop's palace collapsed, and
they threw themselves on the ground, covered with dust.
He thought about Madrid when he'd first arrived, about
the cafés filled with people until two or three in the morning, when all they talked about was the war, and how eu-
phoric they all felt and how absolutely sure they'd win, and
he thought how Madrid was still holding out and how the
women of Madrid made curlers out of bomb fragments . . .
They crawled to the stairway. Miguel was unarmed. He
dragged his rifle along. He knew there was only one for
every five soldiers. He decided not to leave it behind.

They walked down the spiral staircase.

"I think a baby was crying in one of the rooms. I'm not
sure, I might have mistaken the air-raid sirens for wailing."

But he imagined the baby there, abandoned. They felt
their way down in the darkness. It was so dark that when
they came out on the street it looked like broad daylight.
Miguel said, "They shall not pass," and the women answered: "They shall not pass!" The night blinded them, and
they must have become disoriented as they walked along,
because one of the women ran after them, saying, "Not
that way. Come with us."

When they got used to the light of night, they found
themselves face down on the sidewalk. The collapsed building shielded them from the enemy machine guns: he
breathed in the dust, but he also inhaled the sweat from
the girls stretched out next to him. He tried to see their
faces. All he saw was a beret and a wool cap, until the girl
who'd thrown herself down at his side raised her face and
he saw her loose chestnut hair whitened by the plaster from
the building, and she said:

"My name's Dolores—Lola."

"I'm Lorenzo. This is Miguel."

"Miguel, that's me."

"We're separated from our group."

"We were in the Fourth Corps."

"How do we get out of here?"

"We'll have to take the long way round and cross the bridge."

"Do you know this place?"

"Miguel knows it."

"Right, I know it."

"Where are you from?"

"I'm Mexican."

"Ah, so it won't be hard to understand each other."

The planes left, and they stood up. Nuri with her beret and María with her wool cap told them their names and they repeated theirs. Dolores was wearing trousers and a jacket; the other two women, overalls and knapsacks. They walked single file down the deserted street, hugging the walls of the tall houses, under dark balconies with their windows open, as if on a summer day. They could hear the interminable sniping, but they didn't know where it came from. A dog barked from an alley, and Miguel tossed a stone at it. An old man, a scarf wrapped around his head, was sitting in his rocker. He didn't look at them as they passed, and they could not understand what he was doing there: was he waiting for someone to come home, or was he waiting for the sun to come up, or what. He didn't look at them.

He breathed deeply. They left the town behind and reached an open field with some bare poplars in it. That autumn no one had raked up the dry leaves and they crackled under their feet. He noticed that the leaves closest to the ground had already turned black from the rains, and he glanced back at the soaking-wet rags wrapped around Miguel's feet. Once again he wanted to offer him his boots, but his comrade was striding along so resolutely on his strong, slim legs that he realized how useless it would be to offer what wasn't needed. In the distance, those dark slopes awaited them. Perhaps then he'd need the boots.

Not now. Now the bridge was there, and beneath it ran a turbulent, deep river. They stopped to stare at it.

"I hoped it would be frozen over"—he gestured angrily.

"Spanish rivers never freeze over," murmured Miguel. "They always run."

"Why did you want it to be frozen?" Dolores asked him.

"Well, that way we could have avoided the bridge."

"Why would we want to do that?" said María, and the three women, the question in their eyes, looked like curious little girls.

"Because bridges are usually mined," said Miguel.

The small group did not move. The swift white river swirling at their feet hypnotized them. They stood stock-still. Until Miguel raised his face, looked toward the mountains, and said: "If we cross the bridge, we can get to the mountains and from there to the border. If we don't cross, we'll be shot . . ."

"Well?" said María, holding back a sob. For the first time, the two men could see her glassy, weary eyes.

"We lost!" shouted Miguel. He clenched his empty fists and walked around as if looking for a rifle on the ground carpeted with blackened leaves. "There's no going back! We've got no planes, no artillery, nothing!"

He did not move. He stood there staring at Miguel until Dolores, Dolores's hot hand, the five fingers she had just taken out of her armpit, clasped the young man's five fingers, and he understood. She sought his eyes, and he saw hers, also for the first time. She blinked, and he saw that her eyes were green, as green as the sea near our land. He saw her with uncombed hair and no makeup, her cheeks red from the cold, her lips full and dry. The other three didn't notice. They walked, she and he, holding hands, and stepped onto the bridge. For a moment, he doubted. She did not. The ten fingers they clasped gave them warmth, the only warmth he'd felt in all those months.

". . . the only warmth I felt in all those months of retreat toward Catalonia and the Pyrenees . . ."

They heard the noise of the river below, and the creak of the bridge's wooden planks. If Miguel and the girls shouted from the other bank, they did not hear them. The bridge grew longer and longer, it seemed to be spanning an ocean and not this rampaging river.

"My heart was beating fast. She must have felt the pounding in my hand, because she put it on her breast, where I could feel the strength of her heart . . ."

Then they walked side by side, and the bridge grew shorter.

On the other side rose something they hadn't seen: a huge, bare elm, beautiful and white. It wasn't covered with snow but with glittering ice. It was so white it glowed like a jewel in the night. He felt the weight of the rifle on his shoulder, the weight of his legs, his leaden feet on the planks; the elm waiting for them seemed so light, luminous, and white.

"I closed my eyes, Papa, and I opened them, afraid that the tree wouldn't be there anymore . . ."

Then their feet touched earth, they stopped, they did not look back, both ran toward the elm, without paying attention to the shouts of Miguel and the two girls, without hearing the running feet of their comrades on the bridge, they ran and embraced the naked trunk, white and covered with ice, they shook it, and pearls of cold fell on their heads. They touched hands, embracing it, and they wrenched themselves from their tree to embrace each other, Dolores and he, so he could caress her brow and she his neck. She stepped back, so he could see her moist green eyes better, her half-open mouth, before she buried her head in the boy's chest, raised her face to give him her lips, before their comrades surrounded them, but not hugging the tree as they had . . .

". . . how warm, Lola, how warm you are, and how much I already love you."

They made camp in the foothills, below the snow line. Miguel and Lorenzo gathered wood and made a fire. Lorenzo sat next to Lola and held her hand once more. María took a dented cup out of her knapsack, filled it with snow, and let the snow melt over the fire. Then she took out a chunk of goat cheese. Nuri pulled some wrinkled Lipton tea bags out of her bosom, and everyone laughed at the face of the English yachtsman smiling on the labels.

Nuri told how they'd packed the tobacco and condensed milk sent by the Americans before Barcelona fell. Nuri was plump and jolly and had worked before the war in a textile factory, but then María started talking, recalling the days when she'd studied in Madrid and lived in the Student Residence and went out on strike against Primo de Rivera and wept at each new play by García Lorca.

"I'm writing to you with the paper resting on my knees as I listen to these girls talk, and I try to tell them how much I love Spain, and the only thing I can think to talk about is my first visit to Toledo, a city I imagined to be the way El Greco painted it—enveloped in a thunderstorm, with lightning flashes and greenish clouds, set over a wide Tagus, a city—how shall I put it?—at war against itself. And I found a city bathed in sunlight, a sunny, silent city with its old fortress bombed out, because El Greco's picture—I try to tell them—is all of Spain, and if the Tagus in the real Toledo is narrower, the Tagus of Spain splits the country apart. That's what I've seen here, Papa. That's what I try to tell them . . ."

That's what he told them, before Miguel told how he'd joined Colonel Asencio's brigade and how hard it had been for him to learn to fight. He told them that everyone in the Republican army was very brave, but they needed more than bravery to win. They had to know how to fight. And amateur soldiers take a long time to understand that there

are rules about security and that it's better to go on living
so as to go on fighting. Moreover, once they learned how
to defend themselves, they still had to learn how to attack.
And when they learned all that, they still had to learn the
hardest lesson of all, how to master themselves, overcome
their habits, their need for comfort. Miguel criticized the
anarchists because, he said, they were defeatists, and criticized the arms merchants who promised weapons to the
Republic they'd already sold to Franco. He said his greatest
sorrow, the one he'd carry to his grave, was that all the
workers of the world had not taken up arms to defend Spain,
because if Spain lost, it was as if all of them lost. He said
that and broke a cigarette in half, giving part of it to the
Mexican. They both smoked, he next to Dolores, and he
passed his to her so she could smoke, too.

They heard heavy artillery in the distance. From their
campsite, they could see a yellowish glow, a fan of dust
rising in the night. "Figueras," said Miguel. "They're shell-
ing Figueras."

They looked out toward Figueras. Lola was next to him.
She didn't speak to all of them. Only to him, in a low voice,
as they watched the far-off dust and listened to the noise.
She said she was twenty-two, three years older than he, so
he pretended to be even older and said he'd already turned
twenty-four. She said she was from Albacete and that she'd
gone to war to be with her boyfriend. They'd studied together—chemistry—and she followed him, but Franco's
Moroccan troops had shot him at Oviedo. He told her he
was from Mexico, and that he lived where it was hot, near
the sea, a place full of fruit. She asked him to tell her about
tropical fruits and laughed at the names she'd never heard
and told him that *mamey* sounded like a poison and *guan-
ábana* like a bird. He told her he loved horses and when
he first came he'd been in the cavalry, but now there were
no more horses, or anything else, for that matter. She told
him she'd never been on a horse; he tried to explain the

pleasure of horseback riding, especially on the beach at dawn, when the air smells of iodine and the north wind is letting up but it's still raining lightly and the foam raised by the horse's hooves mixes with the drizzle, and how he'd ride shirtless, his lips caked with salt. That she liked. She said that maybe he still had the taste of salt on his mouth, and kissed him. The others had gone to sleep next to the fire, which was dying out. He got up to stir it, with Lola's taste fresh in his mouth. He saw that the others had fallen asleep hugging one another to keep warm, and he went back to Lola. She opened his sheepskin-lined jacket, and he clasped his hands around her back, over her rough work shirt, and covered his back with the jacket. She whispered that they should choose a place to meet in case they were separated. He told her they'd meet in a café he knew near the statue of Cybele when they liberated Madrid, and she answered that they'd see each other in Mexico, and he said yes, in the main plaza in the port of Veracruz, under the arches, in the Parroquia Café. They would have coffee and crabs.

She smiled and so did he, and he said he wanted to mess her hair and kiss her and she beat him to it, snatching off his cap and tangling his hair while he slipped his hands under her shirt, caressed her back, sought her unfettered breasts and then he didn't think about anything and neither did she, certainly not, because her voice didn't say words, emptying all her thoughts into that continuous murmur that was thank you I love you don't ever forget me . . .

They clamber their way over the mountain, and for the first time Miguel walks with difficulty, but not because of the climb, even though it's steep. The cold has gotten to his feet, a cold with sharp teeth they all feel in their faces. Dolores leans on her lover's arm, and if he catches a glimpse of her out of the corner of his eye, he can see she's worried, but if he looks her in the eye, she looks back with a smile. All he asks—all any of them asks—is that it not snow. He's the only one with a weapon, and he has only two bullets. Miguel has told them they have nothing to worry about.

"I'm not afraid. The border's on the other side. Tonight we'll be in France, in a house and in bed. We'll have a nice hot meal. I remember you and I think you wouldn't be ashamed, you would have done the same thing I'm doing. You fought, too, and you'd be proud to know that there's always one who goes to war. I know you'd be proud. But now this fight's coming to an end. As soon as we cross the border, this late arrival to the international brigades calls it quits and begins a new life. I'll never forget this one, Papa, because I learned everything I know here. It's simple. I'll tell you everything when I get back. Just now I can't think of the right words."

With one finger, he touched the letter in the inside pocket of his shirt. He couldn't open his mouth in this cold. He was panting. White steam seeped between his clenched teeth. They were moving so slowly. The column of refugees was so long they couldn't see the far end of it. Ahead of them were the carts full of wheat and sausages the peasants were taking to France; the women were carrying mattresses and blankets, the men carrying paintings, chairs, pitchers, mirrors. The peasants said they would plant crops in France. They moved forward slowly. There were children as well, some just infants. The land up in the mountains was dry, harsh, thorny, full of scrub. They were scrabbling their way over the mountain. He felt Dolores's fist at his side and also felt that he had to save her, protect her. He loved her more than he did last night. And he knew that tomorrow he'd love her more than he did today. She loved him as well. There was no need to say it. They liked each other. That's it. We like each other. They already knew how to laugh together. They had things to tell each other.

Dolores left him and ran to María, who had stopped by a boulder, holding her hand to her forehead. She said it was nothing. She suddenly felt so tired. They had to get out of the way of the red faces, the frozen hands, the heavy carts. María repeated that she suddenly felt a little dizzy. Lola took her by the arm, and they started walking again. It was then, yes, then that they heard the noise of a motor coming closer. They stopped. They couldn't find the plane. Everyone looked for it, but the sky was milky. Miguel was the first to see the black wings, the swastika, and the first to shout, "Down! Everybody down!"

Everyone hit the dirt, squeezed between rocks, under the carts. Everyone—except that rifle which still had two bullets in it. And it doesn't fire, rusty damn piece of junk, it doesn't fire no matter how hard he squeezes the trigger, standing there in plain view, until the noise passes over their heads, fills them with that swift shadow and the fusillade that spatters on the ground and ricochets off the rocks . . .

"Down, Lorenzo, get down, you damn fool Mexican!"

Down, down, down, Lorenzo, and those new boots on the dry earth, Lorenzo, and your rifle in the dirt, damn fool Mexican, and a vertigo inside your stomach, as if you were carrying the ocean in your guts, and your face already in the dust with your open green eyes and half asleep, between sun and night, as she screams and you know that, after all, your boots will be of some use to poor old Miguel with his blond beard and white wrinkles, and in a minute Dolores will throw herself on you, Lorenzo, and Miguel will tell her it's useless, crying for the first time, they had better keep going, life is on the other side of the mountains, life and freedom, because that's the way it is, those were the words he wrote: they took the letter with them, they took it out of his stained shirt, she squeezed it in her hands, what heat!, if the snow falls, it will bury him, when you kissed him again, Dolores, clinging to his body, and he wanted to bring you to the sea, on horseback, before touch-

ing his own blood and falling asleep with you in his eyes
. . . how green . . . don't forget . . .

I'd tell myself the truth, if I didn't feel my white lips, if I
weren't doubled over, unable to hold myself together, if I
could bear the weight of the bedclothes, if I didn't stretch
out again, twisted, face down, so I could vomit this phlegm,
this bile: I would tell myself that it wasn't enough to repeat
time and place, pure permanence; I would tell myself that
something more, a desire I never expressed, forced me to
lead him—oh, I don't know, I just can't realize—yes, to
force him to find the ends of the thread I broke, to tie up
the broken ends of my life, to finish off my other fate, the
second part that I could not complete, and all she can do,
sitting there at my side, is ask me:

"Why was it that way? Tell me: why? I raised him for a
different kind of life. Why did you take him away from
me?"

"Didn't he send the very son he'd spoiled to his death?
Didn't he separate him from you and me just to warp his
mind? Isn't all that true?"

"Teresa, your father isn't listening to you . . ."

"He's faking. He closes his eyes and makes believe."

"Quiet."

"Quiet."

I just don't know anymore. But I do see them. They've
come in. The mahogany door opens, it closes, and you can't
hear them walking on the thick rug. They've closed the
windows. They've drawn the curtains with a hiss, the gray
curtains. They've come in.

"I'm . . . I'm Gloria . . ."

The fresh, sweet sound of banknotes and new bonds
when a man like me picks them up in his hand. The smooth
acceleration of a luxury automobile, custom-made, with
climate control, a bar, telephone, with armrests and foot-

rests, what do you say, priest? will it be the same up there, what do you say?

"I want to go back there, to the land . . ."

"Why did it have to be that way? Tell me: why? I raised him for a different kind of life. Why did you take him away?"

And she doesn't realize that there's something more painful than the abandoned body, than the ice and sun that buried it, than its eyes open forever, devoured by the birds. Catalina stops rubbing the cotton over my temples and walks away and I don't know if she's crying. I try to raise my hand to find her; the effort sends shooting pains from my arm to my chest and from my chest to my stomach. Despite the abandoned body, despite the ice and the sun that buried it, despite its eyes open forever, eaten by the birds, there is something worse: this vomit I can't hold back, this need to defecate that I can't hold back yet I can't do it, I can't get these gases out of my puffed-up stomach, I can't stop this diffuse pain, can't find the pulse in my wrist, can't feel my legs now, my blood is exploding, it's pouring inside me, that's right, inside, I know it and they don't and I can't convince them, they don't see it run out my lips, between my legs. They don't believe it, all they say is that I no longer have a temperature, ah, temperature, all they say is collapse, collapse, all they guess is tumefaction, tumefaction of the fluid areas, that's what they say as they hold me down, poke me, talk about marble spots, that's right, I can hear them, violet marble spots on my stomach which I can't feel anymore, I can't see anymore. Despite the abandoned body, despite the ice and sun that buried it, despite the eyes open forever, devoured by the birds, there is something worse: not being able to remember him, being able to remember only through photographs, through objects left in the bedroom, books with notes written in them. But what does his sweat smell of? Nothing catches the color of his skin: I have no thought of it when I can no longer see it or feel it.

That morning I was on horseback.

That I remember: I received a letter with foreign stamps on it.

But to think of it.

Ah, I dreamed, imagined, found out those names, remembered those songs, oh, thank you, but knowing, how can I know? I don't know, I don't know what the war was like, whom he spoke with before dying, the names of the men and women who accompanied him to his death, what he said, what he thought, what he was wearing, what he had to eat that day. I don't know any of it. I invent landscapes, cities, names, and I just don't remember them anymore: Miguel, José, Federico, Luis? Consuelo, Dolores, María, Esperanza, Mercedes, Nuri, Guadalupe, Esteban, Manuel, Aurora? Guadarrama, Pyrenees, Figueras, Toledo, Teruel, Ebro, Guernica, Guadalajara? The abandoned body, the ice and the sun that buried it, the eyes open forever, devoured by the birds.

Oh, thank you for showing me what my life could be.

Oh, thank you for living that day for me.

But there is something more painful.

What? what? That really exists, that really is mine. That's really what it's like to be God, for certain, isn't it?—to be feared and hated and whatever, that's what being God is, really, right? All right, priest, tell me how I can save all that, and I'll let you go through the ceremony, I'll strike myself on the chest, walk on my knees to the sanctuary, drink vinegar and crown myself with thorns. Tell me how to save all that, because the spirit . . .

". . . of the Son and of the Holy Ghost . . ."

There is something more painful.

"No, if that were the case, there would be a soft tumor, but there would also be a dislocation or a partial displacement of one or another of the major organs . . ."

"I'll say it again: it's the valvulae. That pain can only be caused by the twisting of the intestinal folds, which in turn causes the occlusion . . ."

"If that's the case, then we've got to operate . . ."

"Gangrene might be developing right now, and we couldn't do a thing . . ."

"Obviously, there's cyanosis . . ."

"Facies . . ."

"Hypothermia . . ."

"Lipothymia . . ."

Shut up . . . Shut up!

"Open the windows."

I can't move, I don't know where to look, where to go; I don't feel any temperature, only the cold that comes and goes in my legs, but not the cold or heat of everything else, of everything hidden that I never saw . . .

"Poor girl . . . She's had quite a shock . . ."

. . . Shut up . . . I can guess what my face is like, don't say a word . . . I know I've got blackened nails, bluish skin . . . shut up . . .

"Appendicitis?"

"We've got to operate."

"It's risky."

"I'll say it again: a kidney stone. Give him two centigrams of morphine and he'll be all right."

"It's risky."

"He's not hemorrhaging."

Thank you very much. I could have died at Perales. I could have died with that soldier. I could have died in that bare room, sitting across from that fat man. I survived. You died. Thank you very much.

"Hold him down. Bring the basin."

"See how he ended up? Do you see? Just like my brother. That's how he ended up."

"Hold him down. Bring the basin."

Hold him down. He's going. Hold him down. He's vomiting. He's vomiting that taste that he only smelled before.

He can't even turn his head anymore. He vomits face up. He's vomiting over his shit. It's pouring over his lips, down his jaw. His excrement. The women scream. They scream. I don't hear them, but someone has to scream. It's not happening. This is not happening. Someone has to scream so that this won't happen. They hold me down, they keep me still. No more. He's going. He's going without a thing, naked. Without his things. Hold him down. He's going.

You will read the letter, sent from a concentration camp, with foreign stamps, signed Miguel, which will be folded around the other, written hastily, signed Lorenzo. You will receive that letter, you will read: "I'm not afraid . . . I remember you . . . You wouldn't be ashamed . . . I'll never forget this life, Papa, because I learned everything I know here . . . I'll tell you everything when I get back." You will read and you will choose again: you will choose another life.

You will choose to leave him in Catalina's hands, you will not bring him to that land, you will not put him at the edge of his choice; you will not push him into that mortal destiny, which could have been your own. You will not force him to do what you did not do, to ransom your lost life. You will not permit that this time you die on some rocky path and she be saved.

You will choose to embrace that wounded soldier who enters the providential woods, to lay him down, cleanse his wounded arm with water from the tiny spring scorched by the desert, bandage him, stay with him, keep him breathing with your own breath, wait, wait until both of you are found, captured, shot in a town with a forgotten name, like that dusty one, like that one of adobe and thatched roofs: until they shoot the soldier and you, two nameless, naked men buried in the common grave of those sentenced to death, who have no tombstone. Dead at the age of twenty-four, with no more avenues, no more laby-

rinths, no more choices—dead, holding the hand of a nameless soldier saved by you. Dead.

You will say to Laura: yes.

You will say to the fat man in the bare room painted
indigo blue: no.

You will choose to stay with Bernal and Tobias, take your
chances with them, not go to that bloody patio to justify
yourself, to think that by killing Zagal you paid for the
killing of your comrades.

You will not visit old Gamaliel in Puebla.

You will not take Lilia when she comes back that night,
you will not think that you will never again be able to have
another woman.

You will break the silence of that night, you will speak
to Catalina, you will ask her to forgive you, you will speak
to her about those who died for you, you will ask her to
accept you as you are, with your sins, you will ask her not
to hate you but to take you as you are.

You will stay with Lunero on the hacienda, you will never
abandon that place.

You will stay at the side of your teacher Sebastián—what
a man he was, what a man. You will not go out and join
the Revolution in the north.

You will be a peon.

You will be a blacksmith.

You will remain an outsider with all those who remained
outsiders.

You will not be Artemio Cruz, you will not be seventy-
one years old, you will not weigh a hundred and seventy-
four pounds, you will not be five feet eight inches tall, you
will not have false teeth, you will not smoke French cigarettes, you will not wear Italian silk shirts, you will not
collect cuff-links, you will not order your ties from a New
York shop, you will not wear blue, three-button suits, you
will not prefer Irish twill, you will not drink gin and tonic,
you will not have a Volvo, a Cadillac, and a Rambler station

wagon, you will not remember and love that painting by Renoir, you will not eat poached eggs on toast with Blackwell's marmalade, you will not every morning read a newspaper you yourself own, you will not leaf through *Life* and *Paris Match* some nights, you will not be listening to that incantation next to you, that chorus, that hatred which wants to wrench your life away from you before it's time, which invokes, invokes, invokes, invokes what you could have smilingly imagined just a short time ago and which you will not tolerate now.

De profundis clamavi.

De profundis clamavi.

Look at me now, listen to me, shine a light into my eyes, don't put me to sleep in death / Because on the day you eat from his table you will certainly die / Don't rejoice in the death of another, remember that we all die / Death and hell were cast into the pit of flame and this was the second death / That which I fear, that is what comes to me, that which strikes me with terror, that possesses me / How bitter is your memory for the man satisfied with his riches / Have the portals of death opened for you? / Sin came into the world through woman, and because of woman we all must die / Have you seen the portals of the region of darkness? / Your weakness for the poor and the drained of strength is good / And what fruit did they obtain, then? Those for which they now feel shame, because their end is death / Because the appetite of the flesh is death.

Word of God, life, profession of death,
de profundis clamavi, Domine,
omnes eodem cogimur, omnium versatur urna
quae quasi saxum Tantaleum semper impendet
quid quisque vitet, numquam homini satis cautum
   est in horas
mors tandem inclusum protrahet inde caput
nascentes morimur, finisque ab origine pendet

atque in se sua per vestigia volvitur annus
omnia te vita perfuncta sequentur

Chorus, sepulchre; voices, pyre; you will imagine, in the zone of forgetting of your consciousness, those rites, those ceremonies, those twilights: burial, cremation, balm. Exposed at the top of a tower, so that the air, not the earth, will disintegrate you: locked in the tomb with your dead slaves; wept over by paid mourners; buried with your most highly prized objects, your entourage, your black jewels: vigil, guarding,

requiem aeternam dona eis, Domine
de profundis clamavi, Domine

Laura's voice, as she spoke of these things, sitting on the floor with her knees bent, with the small bound book in her hands . . . says that everything can be fatal to us, even that which gives us life . . . she says that since we cannot cure death, misery, ignorance, we would do well, in order to be happy, not to think about them . . . she says that only sudden death is to be feared; which is why confessors live in the houses of the powerful . . . she says be a man, fear death when you're out of danger, not in danger . . . she says the premeditation of death is the premeditation of freedom . . . she says how softly you tread, oh, cold death . . . she says the hours will never forgive you, the hours that are filing down the days . . . she says, showing me the taut knot cut . . . she says is not my door made of double thicknesses of metal? . . . she says a thousand deaths await me, since I expect only my life . . . she says how can man want to live when God wants him to die . . . she says, of what use are treasures, vassals, servants . . .

What use? what use? Let them intone, let them sing, let them wail. They will not touch the sumptuous carving, the opulent inlay, the gold-and-stucco moldings, the vestry dresser of bone and tortoiseshell, the metal plates and door handles, the paneled coffers with iron keyholes, the aromatic benches of *ayacahuite* wood, the choir seats, the baroque crownwork and drapery, the curved chairbacks, the shaped cross-beams, the polychromed corbels, the bronze-headed tacks, the worked leather, the claw-and-ball cabriole feet, the chasubles of silver thread, the damask armchairs, the velvet sofas, the refectory tables, the cylinders and amphora, the beveled game tables, the canopied, linen beds, the fluted posts, the coats of arms and the orles, the merino rugs, the iron keys, the canvases done in four panels, the silks and cashmeres, the wools and taffetas, the crystal and the chandeliers, the hand-painted china, the burnished beams, they will touch none of that. That will be yours.

You will stretch out your hand.

A day, which, nevertheless, will be an exceptional day; three or four years ago; you will not remember; you will remember by remembering; no, you will remember because the first thing that you remember when you try to remember is a separate day, a day of ceremony, a day separated from the rest by red numbers; and this will be the day—you yourself will think it then—on which all the names, persons, words, and deeds of a cycle ferment and make the crust of the earth groan; it will be a night when you will celebrate the New Year; your arthritic fingers will have difficulty grasping the wrought-iron handrail; you will jab your other hand deep into your jacket pocket and descend laboriously.

You will stretch out your hand.

(1955: December 31)

With difficulty, he grasped the wrought-iron handrail. He jabbed his other hand deep into the pocket of his robe and laboriously walked down the stairs, without looking at the niches dedicated to the Mexican Virgins. Guadalupe, Zapopan, Remedios. As the setting sun came through the windows, it bathed in gold the warm silks and the drapery that billowed like silver sails; it reddened the burnished wood of the beams; it illuminated half of the man's face. He was wearing his tuxedo trousers, shirt, and tie: draped in his red robe, he looked like a tired old magician. He imagined his guests repeating the same performances that once upon a time they had put on with unique charm. Tonight, he would be annoyed to recognize the same faces, the same clichés that year after year provided the proper tone for his New Year's Eve party—the feast of St. Sylvester—in his enormous Coyoacán residence.

His footsteps echoed emptily on the *tezontle* floor. Slightly cramped in their black patent-leather slippers, his feet dragged along with that staggering heaviness he could no longer avoid. Tall, rocking on indecisive heels, his barrel chest thrust forward, and his nervous hands with their thick veins dangling at his sides, he slowly made his way along the whitewashed corridors, treading on the thick wool carpeting. He caught sight of himself in the lustrous mirrors and in the crystalware displayed in the colonial breakfronts, as he ran his fingers over the metal plates and door handles, the paneled coffers with iron keyholes, the aromatic benches of *ayacahuite* wood, the opulent marquetry. A servant opened the door of the grand ballroom for him. The old man stopped for the last time in front of a mirror and straightened his bow tie. With the palm of his hand, he smoothed the few curly gray hairs that remained on his high forehead. He squeezed his cheeks to push his false teeth into place, and walked into the room with its shiny floor, a vast expanse decorated with colonial pictures—St. Sebastian, St. Lucy, St. Jerome, and St. Michael. Its glowing cedar floor, from which the rugs had been removed to allow dancing, opened onto the lawns and brick terraces.

At the far end of the room, the photographers were waiting for him, gathered around the green-damask armchair, under the fifty-candle chandelier hanging from the ceiling. The clock on the mantel struck seven; a fire was blazing because it had been so cold the past few days. Two leather hassocks flanked the fireplace. He greeted the photographers with a nod and sat down in the armchair, arranging his stiff shirtfront and his piqué cuffs. Another servant led in the two gray mastiffs with their red dewlaps and melancholy eyes and placed their rough leashes in the master's hands. The bronze studs on the dogs' collars glittered with reflected light. He raised his head, squeezing his dentures back into place. The flashbulbs gave a tone of fresh plaster to his large gray head. As they asked him to strike new poses, he insisted on straightening his hair and running his fingers along the two heavy bags that hung off the sides of his nose and gradually disappeared into his neck. His high cheekbones still had the old hardness, though even they were crisscrossed by a network of wrinkles that began at his eyelids, which seemed to sag more and more every day, as if to protect his eyes, which expressed a combination of amusement and bitterness, their greenish irises hidden in the folds of loose skin.

One of the mastiffs barked and tried to get loose. At the exact moment he was pulled out of his chair by the powerful dog, a flashbulb went off, and his expression of rigid astonishment was captured in the photograph. The other photographers stared severely at the man who had taken the photo. The guilty party pulled the black plate out of his camera and without a word handed it to another photographer.

When the photographers were gone, he reached out his trembling hand and took a filtered cigarette out of the silver box on the rustic table. He had difficulty getting the lighter to work and, nodding all the time, slowly reviewed the hagiography of the old oil paintings, all varnished, all stained by large empty spaces of direct light which effaced the principal details of the pictures but which, by the same token, contributed an opaque relief to the corners with yellow tones and reddish shadows. He ran his fingers over the damask and inhaled the filtered smoke. The servant approached soundlessly and asked if there was anything he wanted. He nodded and asked for a martini, very dry. The servant opened two carved-cedar doors, revealing the built-in, mirrored bar filled with colored labels and bottled liquids, emerald-green opal, red, crystal-clear—Chartreuse, peppermint, aquavit, vermouth, Calvados, Armagnac, vodka, Pernod, Courvoisier, Long John—and the rows of crystal glasses, some thick and squat, others thin and tinkling. He signaled to the servant to go to the cellar and bring up the three wines for dinner. He stretched his legs and thought of the pains he had taken in the construction and comforts of this, his real home. Catalina could live in the mansion in Las Lomas, devoid of personality, identical to the residences of all other millionaires. He preferred these old walls with their two centuries of quarried stone and red *tezontle*, which in a mysterious way brought him closer to events of the past, to an image of the country he did not want to lose completely. Yes, he fully realized that it was nothing but a simulacrum, a wave of the magic wand. Yet the woods, the stone, the wrought iron, the moldings, the refectory tables, the cabinetwork, the cross-pieces in the doors, the panels, the fabric on the chairs—all of it—

returned to him, with just a slight hint of nostalgia, the scenes, the very air, the tactile sensations of his youth.

Lilia whined; but Lilia would never understand. What could a ceiling of antique beams say to such a girl? What could a barred window opaque with rust say to her? What could the sumptuous feel of the chasuble over the fireplace, covered with gold scales and embroidered with silk thread, say to her? What could the aroma of the *ayacahuite* chests say to her? The washed shine of the kitchen with its Puebla tiles, the archbishop's chairs in the dining room . . . ? The mere possession of these things was as rich, as sensual, as sumptuous as that of money and the obvious signs of plenitude. Oh yes, what total pleasure, what absolutely personal pleasure . . . Only once a year did his guests participate in all this, in his celebrated New Year's Eve party, the feast of St. Sylvester . . . A day of multiplied pleasures, because his guests had to accept this as his real home and think of the solitary Catalina, who, at about this time, would be having dinner in the house in Las Lomas accompanied by Teresa and Gerardo . . . He, on the other hand, would introduce Lilia and open the doors to a blue dining room, with blue china, blue linen, blue walls . . . where the wines flow and the platters are brought in piled high with rare meats, rosy fish, savory shellfish, secret herbs, specially made sweets . . .

Why did this moment of rest have to be interrupted? The indolent clumping of Lilia's feet on the floor. Her unpainted nails on the door to the hall. Her face slathered with cold cream. She wanted to know if her pink dress was all right for this evening. She didn't want to be out of place again, as she was last year, and arouse his scornful rage. Oh-ho, already having a little drink, eh? Why didn't he ask her if she wanted one? His distrust was starting to annoy her, with the liquor locked away and that bossy butler who wouldn't let her into the wine cellar. Was she bored? As if he didn't know it. She wished she were old, ugly, so that he'd kick her out once and for all and let her live as she pleased. She can leave whenever she wants? And live on what? Without luxury, without the mansion? Lots of money here, lots of luxury, but no happiness, no fun, not even the right to have a little drink. Of course she loves him. She's told him a thousand times. Women put up with anything; it all depends on how much tenderness they get in return. A woman can get used to a young man or an old one. Of course she's nice to him; what a thing to ask . . . It'll be eight years they've been living together, and he's never made a scene, never chewed her out . . . He just made her . . . But another little fling would do her the world of good! . . . What? Could anyone think she was that dumb? . . . All right, all right, he never knew how to take a joke. Sure, but he realizes how things are . . . No one lasts forever . . . Crow's feet around his eyes . . . Their bodies . . . Except that he was also used to having her around, wasn't that right? At his age, it's hard to start over. No matter how many millions . . . It's work, and you can waste a lot of time hunting down a woman . . . The bitches . . . know so many tricks, they like to take things slow . . . prolong the first stages . . . say no, have doubts, the waiting, the temptation, oh, all that stuff! . . . And make fools of the old men . . . Of course she's more comfortable . . . And she doesn't complain, no, not a chance. He's even flattered that people come to pay their respects every New Year's Eve . . . And she loves him, yes, she swears, she's too used to him . . . But how bored she gets! . . . Let's see, what's the big deal about having a few close friends—women? What's the big deal about going out once in a while to have fun, to . . . have a drink somewhere, once a week . . . ?

He never moved. He never gave her the right to annoy him, and yet . . . a warm, indolent lassitude . . . completely alien to his character . . . made him stay there . . . holding the martini in his hardened fingers . . . listening to the

nonsense spouted out by this woman who grew more vulgar
every day and less, less . . . No, she was still desirable . . .
even if he couldn't stand her . . . How was he going to
keep her in control? . . . Everything he controlled used to
obey him, but now, after a certain inert prolongation . . .
of the strength of his youth . . . Lilia would leave him . . .
It weighed on his heart . . . He couldn't dispel that . . .
that fear . . . There might not be another chance for him
. . . being left alone . . . He laboriously moved his fingers,
his forearm, his elbow, and the ashtray fell on the rug and
spilled the damp yellow butts at one end, a layer of white
dust, gray outside, black inside. He bent down, breathing
hard.

"Don't bend down. I'll just call Serafín."

"Yes."

Perhaps . . . Tedium. But disgust, repulsion . . . Always,
imagining, hand in hand with doubt . . . An involuntary
tenderness made him turn to look at her . . .

She was watching him from the door . . . Spiteful, sweet
. . . Her hair bleached ash-blond, and that dark skin . . .
She, too, could not go back . . . She'd never get him back,
and that made them equal . . . no matter how age or
personality separated them . . . Make a scene, why? . . .
He felt tired. Nothing else . . . No more things, no more
memories, no more names than those he already knew . . .
He again caressed the damask . . . The butts, the spilled
ash did not have a good smell. And Lilia, standing there
with her greasy face.

She at the threshold. He sitting in his damask armchair.

Then she sighed and sauntered to the bedroom, and he
waited, sitting, not thinking about anything until the darkness surprised him by showing him his reflection so clearly
in the glass doors that led to the garden. The boy came in
with his tuxedo jacket, a handkerchief, and a bottle of cologne. Standing up, the old man allowed the servant to
help him into the jacket and then unfolded the handkerchief

so he could sprinkle a few drops of scent on it. When he put the handkerchief into his breast pocket, he exchanged glances with the servant. The boy lowered his eyes. No. Why should he bother to worry what this man might feel?

"Serafín, get rid of these butts right away . . ."

He straightened up, leaning both hands on the arms of the chair. He took a few steps toward the fireplace, caressed the wrought-iron poker from Toledo, and felt the breath of the fire on his face and hands. He stepped forward when he heard the first whispering voices—delighted, admiring—in the entryway. Serafín had just finished cleaning up the mess.

He ordered the boy to stoke up the fire. The Régules walked in just as the boy shifted the logs with the poker and a huge flame shot up. Through the door that led to the dining room came another servant, carrying a tray. Roberto Régules took his drink while the young couple—Betina and her husband, the Ceballos boy—toured the room hand in hand, in ecstasy over the old paintings, the stucco moldings, the carved beams, the polychromed corbels. His back was to the door when the glass smashed on the floor with the tinkle of a broken bell, and Lilia's voice shrieked something in mocking tones. The old man and the guests saw the unmadeup face of the woman, who peeked in, holding on to the door handle: "Haaaapy Neeew Yeear! Don't worry, honey, I'll be okay in an hour . . . and then I'll come down . . . I just wanted to tell you that I'm gonna take it easy next year . . . real easy!"

He walked toward her with his shuffling, laborious gait, and she shouted, "I'm bored watching TV all day . . . honey!"

With each step he took, Lilia's voice rose higher and higher. "I know all the cowboy shows by heart . . . bang-bang . . . the Arizona marshal . . . the Indian camp . . . bang-bang . . . I'm starting to hear those squeaky voices in my dreams . . . honey . . . just drink Pepsi . . . that's all

. . . honey . . . security and comfort; insurance policy . . ."
His arthritic hand slapped her face devoid of makeup,
and her bleached curls fell over her eyes. She stopped
breathing. She turned around and slowly went away, rubbing her cheek. He went back to the Régules and Jaime
Ceballos. He stared fixedly at each one for a few seconds
with his head held high. Régules took a sip of whiskey so
he could hide his face in the glass. Betina smiled and walked
toward her host with a cigarette in her hand, as if asking
for a light.

"Where did you ever find that huge chest?"
The old man stood aside, and Serafín lit a match close
to the girl's face, forcing her to move her head away from
the old man, turning her back on him. At the end of the
corridor, behind Lilia, were the musicians, wrapped in
scarves and shivering with cold. Jaime Ceballos snapped
his fingers and spun on his heels, like a flamenco dancer.

On the table whose legs ended in dolphins, and under
the bronze candelabra: partridges soaking in a bacon-and-
sour-wine sauce, hake wrapped in leaves of tarragon mustard, wild duck in orange glaze, carp surrounded by roe,
Catalonian *bullinada* thick with the smell of olives, coq-au-
vin flambé in Macon, pigeons stuffed with pureed arti-
choke, platters of fresh eel resting on mounds of ice, bro-
chettes of pink lobster in a spiral of lemon skin, mushrooms
and slices of tomato, Bayonne ham, boeuf bourguignon
sprinkled with Armagnac, goose necks stuffed with pork-
liver paté, chestnut puree and fried apple skins with wal-
nuts, onion and orange sauces, garlic and pistachio-nut
sauces, almond and snail sauces. An inaccessible point
glowed in the old man's eyes as he opened a door carved
with cornucopias and fat-buttocked *putti* polychromed long
ago in a Querétaro convent. He opened the doors wide and
emitted a dry, hoarse laugh each time a butler offered a
Dresden plate to one of the one hundred guests, who then
joined in the percussion of knives and forks against the blue

china, the crystal goblets stretched toward the bottles held out by the servants. And he gave the order to draw open the curtains blocking the glass doors to the garden, where bare cherry trees and clean statues of monastic stone cast their shadows: lions, angels, monks, having emigrated from the palaces and convents of the Viceroyalty. The fireworks exploded: huge illusory castles shot into the heart of the winter sky, so clear and so far away; the white and sparkling introduction mixed with the red flight of a fan in which was woven a streak of yellows; fountain of the open scars of the night, festive monarchs flashing their golden medallions on the black backcloth of the night. Behind his closed lips, he laughed that grunted laugh. The empty platters were refilled with more fowl, more seafood, more rare meats. Naked arms circulated around the old man heavily seated in a niche among the old choir chairs, inlaid, carved exuberantly with fantastic crests and baguettes. He sniffed the perfumes, he peered at the overflowing decolletés of the women, the shaved secret of their armpits, their earlobes weighed with jewels, their white necks, and their slim waists where the swirl of taffeta, silk, and gold net began its flight; he breathed in that smell of after-shave lotion and cigarette smoke, lipstick and mascara, feminine slippers and spilled cognac, of labored digestion and nail polish. He raised his glass and stood up; the servant handed him the leashes of the dogs, who would accompany him for the rest of the evening. The shouting of the New Year burst forth: glasses smashed on the floor and arms hugged, squeezed, rose up to celebrate this feast of time, this funeral, this pyre of memory, this fermented resurrection of all facts, while the orchestra played a traditional New Year's Eve tune, "The Swallows," the resurrection of all the facts, words, and things that died in this cycle, to celebrate the preservation of these one hundred lives who held back their questions, men and women, in order to say to each other, at times with tear-filled eyes, that there will never be a

time like this one, the one lived and prolonged during these
instants artificially extended by the bursting of skyrockets
and bells hurled into the sky. Lilia threw her arms around
him as if asking forgiveness. He knew, perhaps, that many
things, many small desires, had to be repressed so that a
single moment of plenitude could be completely enjoyed,
without any prior expense, and that she would thank him
for it: he said it in a whisper. When the violins in the
ballroom began to play "The Poor People of Paris" again,
she, making a face he knew only too well, took him by the
arm. But he refused with a shake of his head and walked,
preceded by his dogs, to the armchair he would occupy for
the rest of the evening, facing the couples . . . He would
amuse himself watching those faces—false, sweet, cunning,
malicious, idiotic, intelligent—thinking about luck, the luck
they all had, they and he . . . faces, bodies, the dances of
free beings, like him . . . They vouch for him, they assure
him as they move lightly over the waxed floor under the
glittering chandelier . . . freeing, blotting them out, his
memories . . . They perversely force him to enjoy this
identity even more . . . liberty and power . . . He wasn't
alone . . . these dancers accompanied him . . . That's
what the warmth in his stomach told him, the satisfaction
in his guts . . . black, carnivalesque escort of powerful old
age, of the gray-haired presence, arthritic, laborious . . .
echo of the persistent, hoarse smile reflected in the movement of those little green eyes . . . recent coats of arms,
like his own . . . some even newer . . . spinning, spinning
. . . he knows them . . . industrialists . . . businessmen . . .
thieves . . . society boys . . . speculators . . . government
ministers . . . deputies . . . newspapermen . . . husbands
. . . fiancées . . . go-betweens . . . lovers . . . The cut-off
words of those who danced by him swirled in the air . . .
    "Yes . . . We'll go after . . . But what about my father . . .
I love you . . . Free? . . . That's what they told me
. . . We've got plenty of time . . . So . . . like that . . .

I'd like to . . . Where? . . . Tell me . . . I'll never go back
. . . Did you really like it? . . . Hard to tell . . . That's
finished . . . cute . . . divine . . . lost everything . . . got
what he deserved . . . Hmmm . . .

    Hmmm! . . . He knew how to tell from their eyes, from
they way they moved their lips, their shoulders . . . He
could tell them what they were thinking . . . He could tell
them who they were . . . He could remind them what their
real names were . . . fraudulent bankruptcies . . . leaks
about currency devaluations . . . price speculations . . .
bank speculations . . . new latifundia . . . editorials at so
much a line . . . inflated contracts for public works projects
. . . a political hanger-on . . . spent every cent his father
left him . . . thievery in state ministries . . . false names:
Arturo Capdevila, Juan Felipe Couto, Sebastián Ibargüen,
Vicente Castañeda, Pedro Caseaux, Jenaro Arriaga, Jaime
Ceballos, Pepito Ibargüen, Roberto Régules . . . And the
violins played and the skirts flew and so did the tuxedo
jackets . . . They won't talk about all that . . . They'll talk
about trips and affairs, houses and cars, vacations and parties, jewels and servants, sicknesses and priests . . . But
they're all there, in the court . . . before the most powerful
. . . make them or break them with a line in the newspaper
. . . force Lilia on them . . . with a little whisper make
them dance, eat, drink . . . feel them when they come
close . . .

    "I had to bring him, just so he could see that painting
of the Archangel, that one, divine . . ."

    "It's what I've always said: only someone with Don Ar-
temio's taste . . ."

    "But how can we ever return the favor?"

    "How right you are never to accept invitations."

    "Everything was just so glorious that I'm speechless;
speechless, speechless, Don Artemio; what wines! And that
duck with the glorious things on it!"

    . . . Turn your face and pay no attention . . . All he

needed were the whispers . . . He didn't want to make it
too clear . . . His senses reveled in the pure murmuring
around him . . . touches, smells, tastes, images . . . Let
them call him, in giggles and whispers, the Mummy of
Coyoacán . . . Let them make fun of Lilia with secret smiles
. . . There they were, dancing before him . . .

He raises his arm: a signal to the orchestra leader. The
music breaks off in mid-song, and everyone stops dancing.
The strings take up an Oriental melody, a path opens in
the crowd, a half-naked woman makes her way from the
door, waving her arms and grinding her hips, until she
occupies the center of the floor. A happy shout. The dancer
writhes with a drum-like rhythm in her waist, her body
smeared with oil, orange lips, white eyelids, and blue
brows. On foot, dancing around a circle, moving her stomach in ever more rapid spasms, she picks out old man
Ibargüen and drags him by the arm to the center of the
floor. She sits him on the ground, arranges his arms so he
looks like the god Vishnu, prances around him while he
tries to copy her gyrations. Everyone smiles. Now she goes
over to Capdevila, forces him to take off his jacket, to dance
around Ibargüen. The host laughs, slumped down in his
damask armchair, fingering his dogs' leashes. The dancer
climbs on Couto's shoulders and urges other women to
imitate her. Everyone laughs. The guffawing horses wreck
their riders' coiffures, and the ladies' faces flush with perspiration. Their skirts wrinkle and slip up above their knees.
Some of the young men try to trip the apoplectic chargers
who battle around the two old dancers and the woman with
her legs spread.

He raised his eyes, as if coming back to the surface after
being carried to the bottom by lead weights. Above the
disarranged hairdos and the waving arms, the clear sky of
beams and white walls, the seventeenth-century canvases,
the angelic carvings . . . And to an attuned ear, the hidden
scurry of immense rats—black fangs, pointed snouts—that

inhabit the eaves and foundations of this ancient convent that once belonged to the Order of St. Jerome. Occasionally, they would scuttle immodestly in the corners of the hall, waiting by the thousands in the darkness above and below the happy revelers . . . waiting, perhaps, for the chance to take them all by surprise . . . infect them with fever and headaches . . . vertigo and cold tremors . . . hard and painful swellings in their thighs and armpits . . . black patches on their skin . . . vomiting blood . . . If he were to raise his arm again . . . so the servants would seal the doors with steel bolts . . . close up the exits from this house filled with amphorae and cylinders . . . beveled panels . . . canopied beds . . . iron keys . . . inlays and chairs . . . doors of double-thick metal . . . statues of monks and lions . . . And the whole crowd of them would have to stay here in quarantine . . . never leave the nave . . . douse themselves with vinegar . . . make bonfires of aromatic wood . . . hang rosaries of thyme on their bodies . . . indolently shoo away the green buzzing flies . . . while he ordered them to dance, live, drink . . . He looked for Lilia in the rolling sea of bodies. She was drinking alone, silently, in a corner, with an innocent smile on her lips, her back turned toward the dancing and the mock-jousts . . . Some men were going out to relieve themselves . . . their hands already on their flies . . . Some women were on their way to powder their noses . . . already opening their evening bags . . . He smiled in his hard way . . . the only reaction this display of joy and munificence provoked: he cackled in silence . . . He imagined them . . . all of them, each one, in a row, standing before the toilet bowls in the floor below . . . all urinating, with their bladders swollen with splendid liquids . . . all shitting out the remains of the food prepared over two days with care, taste, selection . . . all of it alien to this final destiny of the ducks and lobsters, the purees and the sauces . . . ah yes, the greatest pleasure of the entire evening . . .

Soon they were all tired out. The dancer finished her dance and found herself surrounded by indifference. People went back to their conversations, drank more champagne, sat down in the deep couches. Those who had excused themselves were returning, zipping flies, putting compacts back into evening bags. It was running its course. The minor, foreseeable orgy . . . the punctual, programmed exaltation . . . The voices went back to their soft singsong . . . to the classic dissimulation of the Mexican central plateau . . . Those old worries were coming back . . . as if to take revenge for the moment that had passed, the fleeting instant . . .

". . . no, because cortisone makes me break out . . ."

". . . you have no idea of the spiritual exercises Father Martínez is conducting . . ."

". . . just take a look at her: who'd have ever said it; they say they were . . ."

". . . I had to fire her . . ."

". . . by the time Luis gets home, all he wants to do is . . ."

". . . don't, Jaime, he doesn't like it . . ."

". . . she got up on her high horse . . ."

". . . watch a little TV . . ."

". . . who can put up with the kind of maids you get today . . ."

". . . lovers for over twenty years . . ."

". . . how could anyone get the idea of giving that bunch of Indians the vote?"

". . . and his wife all alone in her house; she never . . ."

". . . it's a serious policy matter; we've received the . . ."

". . . I hope the PRI goes right on choosing people . . ."

". . . that's what the President always says in the chamber . . ."

". . . me, I sure would take a chance . . ."

". . . Laura; I think her name's Laura . . ."

". . . only a few of us do any real work . . ."

". . . if I hear another word about that income-tax crap . . ."

". . . for thirty million lazy pigs . . ."

". . . I'll move all my savings to Switzerland . . ."

". . . Commies only understand one thing . . ."

". . . don't do it, Jaime, no one's supposed to bother him . . ."

". . . it's going to be the most incredible deal . . ."

". . . being beaten over the head . . ."

". . . just invest a hundred million . . ."

". . . a divine Dalí . . ."

". . . and get it all back in a couple of years . . ."

". . . the people from my gallery sent it . . ."

". . . or less . . ."

". . . from New York . . ."

". . . for a long time she lived in France; disappointments . . . is what they say . . ."

". . . just us girls are going to get together . . ."

". . . Paris, the city of light, par excellence . . ."

". . . and have a good time . . ."

". . . if you like, we can go to Acapulco tomorrow . . ."

". . . laughing all the way to the bank; the wheels of Swiss industry . . ."

". . . the American ambassador called to warn me . . ."

". . . turn because of those ten billion dollars . . ."

". . . Laura; Laura Rivière; she married again over there . . ."

". . . in the company plane . . ."

". . . we Latin Americans have on deposit there . . ."

". . . no country is safe from subversion . . ."

". . . of course, I read it in *Excélsior* . . ."

". . . I'll tell you: a great dancer . . ."

". . . Rome, the eternal city, par excellence . . ."

". . . but he's not worth a penny . . ."

". . . I made my money the old-fashioned way . . ."

". . . oh, but, darling, it's like the Eucharist dipped in egg . . ."

". . . you tell me why I should pay taxes to a government full of crooks . . ."

". . . they call him the Mummy, the Mummy of Coyoacán . . ."

". . . Darling, a sensational dressmaker . . ."

". . . subsidies for agriculture? . . ."

". . . I'm telling you: he always falls apart when he putts . . ."

". . . poor Catalina . . ."

". . . Yeah? And who's controlling the droughts and the frosts? . . ."

". . . no way around it: without American investments . . ."

". . . they say she was the great love of his life, but . . ."

". . . Madrid, divine; Seville, just lovely . . ."

". . . we'll never get out of this rut . . ."

". . . you know what they say, there's only one Mexico . . ."

". . . turns out it wasn't worth the trouble, understand? . . ."

". . . the lady of the house; if it weren't . . ."

". . . I get back forty-five centavos of every peso . . ."

". . . they give us their money and their know-how . . ."

". . . even before making the loan . . ."

". . . and we still complain . . ."

". . . it was twenty-some years ago . . ."

". . . sure: bosses, venal leaders, whatever you want . . ."

". . . he did everything in white and gold, you'll just die! . . ."

". . . but the good politician doesn't try to reform reality . . ."

". . . why, yes, I have the honor to be the President's friend . . ."

". . . instead, we should take advantage of it, work with it . . ."

". . . from the deals he's got with Juan Felipe, for sure . . ."

". . . he's got tons of charities, but he never talks about them . . ."

". . . I just said to him: The pleasure is all mine . . ."

". . . we all owe each other favors, am I right or am I wrong?"

". . . what she would give to leave him! . . ."

". . . if it were me, I'd be out of there, poor Catalina! . . ."

". . . he talked them down, but it couldn't have been less than ten thousand dollars . . ."

". . . Laura; I think her name's Laura; I think she was very beautiful . . ."

". . . but what do you want, for heaven's sake, women are weak . . ."

The tides of dancing and talk brought them close and carried them away. But now this young man with an open smile and light hair hunkered down next to the old man, balancing a champagne glass in one hand, his other hand on the arm of the chair . . . The young man asked if he would rather he kept his distance, and the old man said, "You've done nothing else all night, Mr. Ceballos . . ." He didn't look at the young man . . . but kept his eyes fixed on the center of the uproar . . . an unwritten law . . . the guests were not to come too close, except to praise the house and the dinner, quickly . . . respect his inviolate territory . . . thank him for his hospitality and entertainment . . . the stage and the seat in the audience . . . Obviously, young Ceballos did not realize . . . "You know? I admire you . . ." He dug into his jacket pocket and pulled out a crushed pack of cigarettes . . . He lit one slowly . . . without looking at the young man . . . who said that only a king could look at people with that kind of disdain, the disdain with which he was looking at them when . . . And he asked if this was the first time he'd ever come to . . . And the young man said yes . . . "Didn't your father-in-law . . . ?" "Of course . . ." "Well, then . . ." "Those rules were made

without consulting me, Don Artemio . . ." He gave in . . .
With languid eyes . . . spirals of smoke . . . he turned to
face Jaime, and the young man stared back without blinking
. . . mischief in his eyes . . . the interplay of lips and jawbone
. . . the old man's . . . the young man's . . . he recognized
himself, ah . . . he disconcerted him, ah . . . "What, Mr.
Ceballos, what did you sacrifice?" . . . I don't understand
. . . he didn't understand, he said he didn't understand
. . . he exhaled a smile through his nostrils . . . "The wound
we suffer when we betray ourselves, my friend . . . Who
do you think you're talking to? Do you really think I'm
fooling myself . . . ?" Jaime held out the ashtray . . . Ah,
they crossed the river that morning on horseback . . . "for
some kind of justification . . . ?" he observed without being
observed . . . "Your father-in-law and other people you
deal with must have . . ." They crossed the river, that
morning . . . "That our wealth is justified, that we've worked
hard to earn it . . . our reward, isn't that right? . . ." She
asked if they would go together to the sea . . . "Do you
know why I'm on top of all these little people . . . why I
control them? . . ." Jaime held out the ashtray; he made a
gesture with his cigarette butt . . . he came out of the ford
with his chest bare . . . "Ah, you came over to me, I didn't
call you . . ." Jaime narrowed his eyes and drank from his
glass . . . "Are you losing your illusions?" . . . She repeated,
"My God, I don't deserve this," raising the mirror, wondering if that is what he'd seen when he came back . . .
Poor Catalina . . . "Because I'm not fooling myself . . ." on
the other bank, they could make out the ghost of land,
right, the ghost . . . "How do you like this party?" . . .
vacilón, qué rico vacilón, cha cha cha . . . The air smelled
of banana. Cocuya . . . "It doesn't matter to me . . ." he
dug his spurs into his horse's flanks; faced him and smiled
. . . ". . . my paintings, my wines, my comforts, which I
control the same way I control all of you . . ." "Do you
think . . . ?" . . . you remembered your youth because of

him and because of these places . . . "Power is its own reward, that's all I know, and to get power you have to be able to do anything . . ." but you didn't want to tell him how much it meant to you, you might have strained his affection . . . "exactly the way your father-in-law and I did it, the way everybody dancing here did it . . ." that morning I waited for him with pleasure . . . "the same way you'll have to do it—if that's what you want . . ." To work with you, Don Artemio, you might perhaps find a place for me in one of your businesses . . . the boy's raised hand pointed east, to where the sun rises, toward the lake . . . "Usually these matters are arranged in a different way . . ." the horses trotted slowly, parting the tangled grass, shaking their manes, raising a scattered foam . . . "your father-in-law would call and insinuate that his son-in-law is . . ." they looked each other in the eye and smiled . . . But, you see, I have other ideals . . . to the ocean, to the open sea, and Lorenzo ran, agile, toward the waves that broke around his waist . . . He accepted things as they are; he became a realist . . . "Yes, exactly right. Just like you, Don Artemio . . ." he asked if he'd ever thought about the other side of the ocean; all land is the same, only the sea is different . . . Just like me! . . . He told him there were islands . . . did he fight in the Revolution, did he risk his hide, was he an inch away from being shot? . . . the sea tasted like bitter beer, smelled like melon, quince, strawberry . . . What? . . . No . . . I . . . A ship leaves in ten days. I've booked passage . . . My friend, you just got here and the party's over. Hurry and pick up the crumbs . . . Wouldn't you do the same thing, Papa . . . on top of forty years because we were baptized in the glory of the Revolution . . . Yes . . . but what about you? Do you think all that can be inherited? How are they going to make it last . . . ? Now there is that front. I think it's the only one left . . . Yes . . . our power? . . . I'm leaving . . . You all showed us how . . . "Bah! I'm telling you, you've come too late" . . . I waited for him with pleasure that morning . . . Others might try to fool me; I've never fooled myself; that's why I'm here . . . they crossed the river on horseback . . . hurry up . . . fill your belly . . . because it's all disappearing . . . he asked if they would go to the sea together . . . What does it matter to me . . . the sea watched over by the low flight of the sea gulls . . . I'll die, and it'll make me laugh . . . the sea that only pokes its tired tongue out on the beach . . . and it will make me laugh to think . . . toward the waves that broke around his waist . . . I keep a world alive for which there are no measures . . . the old man brought his head close to Ceballos's ear . . . the sea that tastes of bitter beer . . . "Shall I confess something to you?" . . . the sea that smells like melon and guava . . . his finger made a dry ping on the young man's glass . . . the fishermen dragging their nets toward the sand . . . "Real power is always born out of revolt . . ." Do I believe? I don't know. You brought me here, showed me all these things . . . And you . . . all of you . . . With his ten fingers outstretched, under the overcast sky, facing the open sea . . . and all of you . . . no longer have what it takes . . .

Again, he looked toward the dance floor.

"So," whispered Jaime, "may I come to see you . . . one of these days?"

"Speak to Padilla. Good night."

The clock in the ballroom struck three times. The old man sighed and snapped the leashes of the sleeping dogs, who instantly pricked up their ears and stood at the same time as he, bracing himself first on the arms of his chair, rose heavily and the music stopped.

He crossed the dance floor amid his guests' expressions of gratitude and the heads turned aside. Lilia made her way toward him: "Excuse me . . ." and she grasped his rigid arm. He with his head held high (Laura, Laura); she with averted eyes, curious. They wended their way along the path opened by the guests, the sumptuous crystalware, the opulent marquetry, the stucco-and-gold moldings, the colonial breakfronts inlaid with bone and tortoiseshell, the metal plates and knockers, the paneled coffers with iron keyholes, the aromatic benches of *ayacahuite* wood, the church choir seats, the baroque crownwork and drapery, the bowed backrests, the carved crossbeams, the poly-chromed corbels, the bronze studs, the embossed leather, the cabriole feet with their claw and ball, the chasubles sewn with silver thread, the damask armchairs, the velvet couches, the cylinders and amphorae, the beveled game tables, the merino-wool carpets, the four-paneled canvases, under the crystal chandeliers, the burnished beams, until they reached the first step of the staircase. Then he caressed Lilia's hand, and the woman helped him, taking him by the elbow, bending, the better to assist him.

She smiled. "You didn't get too tired now, did you?"

He shook his head and again caressed her hand.

I wake up . . . again . . . but this time . . . yes . . . in this car, in this coach . . . no . . . I don't know . . . it runs without any noise . . . it must be that I'm not fully con-scious . . . no matter how wide I open my eyes, I can't make out . . . the objects, people . . . white, luminous ovals spinning around in front of my eyes . . . a wall of milk separates me from the world . . . and the things we touch and the voices of other people . . . I'm apart . . . I'm dying . . . I'm parting . . . no, an attack, an old man my age can have an attack . . . not death, not separation . . . I don't want to say it . . . I want to ask it . . . but I'm saying it . . . if I tried . . . yes . . . now I heard the superimposed noises of the siren . . . it's the ambulance . . . of the siren and my own throat . . . my tight and closed throat . . . my saliva drips through it . . . toward a bottomless pit . . . parting . . . a will? . . . ah, don't worry . . . there's a paper all signed, sealed, witnessed before a notary . . . I didn't forget anyone . . . why would I forget any of you, forgive

any of you . . . ? . . . isn't it delightful for you to think that
right down to the last minute I thought about you to have
my little joke? . . . ah, what a laugh, ah, what a joke . . .
no . . . I remember you with the indifference of a cold
transaction . . . I dole out this wealth they'll say came from
my hard work . . . my tenacity . . . my sense of responsibility
. . . my personal abilities . . . do it . . . calm down . . .
just forget that I earned that wealth, that I risked it, that
I earned it . . . now I give it all in exchange for nothing . . .
isn't that right? . . . what do you call giving everything in
exchange for everything? . . . call it whatever you like . . .
they came back, they didn't give up . . . right, when I think
about it, I smile . . . I mock myself, I mock all you . . . I
mock my life . . . haven't I earned the right? . . . isn't this
the appropriate, the only time to do it? . . . I couldn't mock
myself while I was alive . . . now I can . . . my right . . .
I'll leave you my testament . . . I'll bequeath you those
dead names . . . Regina . . . Tobias . . . Páez . . . Gonzalo
. . . Zagal . . . Laura, Laura . . . Lorenzo . . . so you won't
forget me . . . separated . . . I can think it and ask myself
. . . without knowing it . . . because these last ideas . . .
I know it, too . . . I think, dissimulate . . . run out of my
control, ah, yes . . . as if my brain, my brain . . . asks . . .
the answer comes to me before the question . . . probably
. . . they're the same thing . . . living is another separation
. . . with that mulatto, next to the shack and the river . . .
with Catalina, if we had ever spoken . . . in that jail, that
morning . . . don't cross the sea, there are no islands, it's
not true, I tricked you . . . from the teacher . . . Esteban?
. . . Sebastián? . . . I don't remember . . . he taught me
so many things . . . I don't remember . . . I left him and
went north . . . ah, yes . . . yes . . . yes . . . yes, life would
have been different . . . but only that . . . different . . .
not the life of this dying man . . . no, not dying . . . I'm
telling you no no no . . . an attack . . . an old man, an
attack . . . convalescence, that's it . . . another life . . . the

life of another man . . . different . . . but also apart . . .
oh, what a trick . . . neither life nor death . . . oh, what a
trick . . . on the man's land . . . hidden life . . . hidden
death . . . a fixed period of time . . . no meaning . . . my
God . . . ah, that might be the last piece of business . . .
who's putting his hands on my shoulders? . . . believe in
God . . . yes, a good investment, why not . . . who's making
me lie back, as if I wanted to get up out of here? . . . is
there any other possibility to believe that we go on being
even when we don't believe in it? . . . God God God . . .
all you have to do is repeat a word a thousand times for it
to lose its meaning, be nothing more than a string . . . of
empty . . . syllables . . . God God . . . how dry my lips
are . . . God God . . . illuminate those who are left . . .
make them think of me once . . . in a while . . . make my
memory . . . last . . . I think . . . but I don't see them
clearly . . . I don't see them . . . men and women mourning
. . . that black egg of my sight . . . cracks and I see . . .
that they go on living . . . they go back to their jobs . . .
idleness . . . intrigues . . . without remembering . . . the
poor dead man . . . who hears the shovels digging the moist
. . . earth . . . on his face . . . the sinuous advance . . .
sinuous . . . sinuous . . . sinuous . . . yes . . . sensual . . .
of those worms . . . my throat . . . drips into me like a sea
. . . a lost voice that . . . wants to revive . . . revive . . .
go on living . . . get on with life where it was cut off by
the other . . . death . . . no . . . start over from the beginning . . . revive . . . choose again . . . revive . . . choose
again . . . no . . . how icy my temples feel . . . what blue
. . . nails . . . what a swollen . . . stomach . . . what nausea
. . . from shit . . . don't die senselessly . . . no no . . . ah,
bitches . . . impotent bitches . . . who have had every
object money can buy . . . and a head full . . . of mediocrity
. . . if at least . . . you had understood what those objects
. . . were good for . . . how to use . . . these . . . things . . .
but not even that . . . while I had it all . . . do you hear

me? . . . everything . . . money can buy and . . . everything
it can't buy . . . I had Regina . . . do you hear me? . . . I
loved Regina . . . her name was Regina . . . and she loved
me . . . loved me without money . . . followed me . . .
gave me life . . . down below . . . Regina, Regina . . . how
I love you . . . how I love you today . . . without having
to have you near me . . . how you fill my chest with this
warm . . . satisfaction . . . how . . . you flood me . . . with
your old, forgotten . . . perfume, Regina . . . I remembered
you . . . see? . . . look carefully . . . I remembered you
before . . . I could remember you . . . just as you are . . .
as you love me . . . as I loved you in the world . . . that
no one can take away from us . . . Regina, the world . . .
that I carry with me and save . . . protecting it with my
two hands . . . as . . . if it were a fire . . . a small, living
fire . . . that you gave to me . . . you gave to me . . . you
gave to me . . . I may have taken . . . but I gave to you . . .
oh black eyes; oh dark, aromatic skin, oh black lips, oh dark
love I cannot touch, name, repeat: oh your hands, Regina
. . . your hands on my neck and . . . the oblivion of finding
you . . . the oblivion . . . of all that existed . . . outside
you and me . . . oh Regina . . . without thinking . . . without
speaking . . . existing in the dark thighs . . . of timeless
abundance . . . oh my unrepeatable pride . . . the pride
of having loved you . . . the unanswered challenge . . .
what can the world tell us . . . Regina . . . what could it
add to that . . . what logic could speak . . . to the madness
. . . of our love? . . . what? . . . dove, carnation, convolvulus,
foam, clover, key, chest, star, ghost, flesh: how shall I name
you . . . love . . . how shall I bring you close to . . . my
breath . . . how shall I beg you . . . to give yourself . . .
how shall I caress . . . your cheeks . . . how shall I kiss
. . . your ears . . . how shall I breathe you in . . . between
your legs . . . how shall I say . . . your eyes . . . how shall
I touch . . . your taste . . . how shall I abandon . . . the
solitude . . . of myself . . . to lose myself in . . . the solitude

. . . of ourselves . . . how shall I repeat . . . that I love you
. . . how shall I exile . . . your memory so I can wait for
your return? . . . Regina Regina . . . that stabbing pain is
coming back, Regina, I'm waking up . . . from that half
sleep the sedative induced . . . I'm waking up . . . with
the pain . . . in the center . . . of my guts, Regina, give
me your hand, don't abandon me, I don't want to wake up
and not find you next to me, my love, Laura, my adored
wife, my saving memory, my percale skirt, Regina, it hurts,
my unrepeatable tenderness, my turned-up little nose, it
hurts, Regina, I realize it hurts: Regina, come, so I can
survive again; Regina, exchange your life for mine again;
Regina, die again so I can live; Regina. Soldier. Regina.
Embrace me, both of you. Lorenzo. Lilia. Laura. Catalina.
Embrace me, all of you. No. What ice I feel in my temples
. . . Brain, don't die . . . reason . . . I want to find it . . .
I want . . . I want . . . land . . . nation . . . I loved you
. . . I wanted to go back . . . reason of unreason . . . contemplate from a very high place the life I've lived and then
see nothing . . . and if I don't see anything . . . what reason
to die . . . why die . . . why die suffering . . . why not go
on living . . . the dead life . . . why pass . . . from the
living nothingness to the dead nothingness . . . it runs out
. . . it runs out panting . . . the screech of the siren . . .
pack of dogs . . . the ambulance stops . . . tired . . . couldn't
be more tired . . . land . . . the light enters my eyes . . .
another voice . . .

"Dr. Sabines is operating."

Reason? Reason?

The stretcher slides out of the ambulance. Reason? Who
goes there? Who goes there?

You couldn't be more tired, couldn't possibly be more tired;
it's because you've traveled so far, on horseback, on foot,
in the old trains, and the country just never ends. Will you
remember the country? You will remember it, but it isn't

only one country. It's a thousand countries with a single name. You will know that. You will bring with you the red deserts, the steppes of prickly pears and maguey, the world of the nopal, the belt of lava and frozen craters, the walls with golden church cupolas and stone battlements, the cities of stone and mortar, the cities of red *tezontle*, the towns of adobe, the villages of reed huts, the paths of black mud, the roads of drought, the lips of the sea, the thick, forgotten coasts, the sweet valleys of wheat and corn, the northern pastureland, the lakes of the Bajío region, the tall, slender forests, the branches laden with moss, the white peaks, the black plains, the ports with their malaria and their whorehouses, the calcareous husk of the henequen, the lost, rushing rivers, the gold and silver tunnels, the Indians without a common tongue, Cora tongue, Yaqui tongue, Huichol tongue, Pima tongue, Seri tongue, Chontal tongue, Tepehuana tongue. Huastec tongue, Totonac tongue, Nahua tongue, Maya tongue, the flute and the drum, the contredanse, the guitar and the harp, the feathers, the fine bones of Michoacán, the diminutive flesh of Tlaxcala, the light eyes of Sinaloa, the white teeth of Chiapas, the short-sleeved *huipil* blouses, the bow-shaped combs, the Mixtec tresses, wide *tzotzil* belts, Santa María shawls, Pueblo marquetry, Jalisco glass, Oaxaca jade, the ruins of the serpent, the ruins of the black head, the ruins of the great nose, the tabernacles and the retables, the colors and reliefs, the pagan cult of Tonantzintla and Tlacochaguaya, the old names of Teotihuacán and Papantla, Tula and Uxmal: you carry them with you and they weigh you down, they are very heavy stones for one man to carry: they don't budge and you have them slung around your neck: they weigh you down and they've gotten into your guts . . . they are your bacteria, your parasites, your amoebas . . .

Your land

You will think that there is a second discovery of the land in the hustle and bustle of war, a first footstep over the mountains and canyons that are like a challenging fist in the face of the desperate, slow advance of roads, dams, rails, and telegraph posts. This nature which refuses to be shared or ruled, which wants to go on being in its sharp solitude and gives men for their pleasure only a few valleys, a few rivers—she goes on being the sullen owner of smooth and unreachable peaks, of the flat desert, of the jungles and the abandoned coast. And men, fascinated by that haughty power, stand there with their eyes fixed on her power. If inhospitable nature turns her back on men, men turn their back on the wide, forgotten sea, rotting in its hot fecundity, boiling with lost riches.

You will inherit the land.

You will never again see those faces you saw in Sonora and Chihuahua, faces you saw sleepy one day, hanging on for dear life, and the next furious, hurling themselves into that struggle devoid of reason or palliatives, into that embrace of men which is broken by other men, into that declaration, here I am and I exist with you and with you and with you, too, with all hands and all veiled faces: love, strange, common love that wears itself out on itself. You will say it to yourself, because you lived through it and you didn't understand it as you lived it. Only in dying will you accept it and openly say that, even without understanding it, you feared it each of your days of power. You will fear that the amorous impulse will burst again. Now you will die and will not fear it any longer, because you will not see it. But you will tell the others to fear it: fear the false calm you bequeath them, fear the fictitious concord, the magical patter, the sanctioned greed, fear this injustice that doesn't even know what it is.

They will accept your testament: the respectability you won for them, the respectability. They will give thanks to the lowlife Artemio Cruz because he made them respectable. They will thank him because he did not resign himself to living and dying in a Negro shack. They will thank him because he went forth to risk his life. They will vindicate you because they will no longer have your vindication; they will no longer be able to invoke the battles and the chiefs, as you did, and shield themselves with those battles and leaders to justify plunder in the name of the Revolution and their own glory in the name of the glory of the Revolution. You will think and be astounded: What justification will they find? What obstacle will they overcome? They will not think of it, they will reap the benefits of what you leave them for as long as they can; they will live happily, will put on grieving and grateful faces—in public, you will not ask more of them—while you wait, six feet of dirt on your body; you wait until you feel the rush of feet over your dead face and then you will say:

"They came back. They did not give up."

And you will smile. You will mock them, mock yourself. It's your privilege. Nostalgia will tempt you: that would be the way to beautify the past; you will not do it.

You will bequeath the useless deaths, the dead names, the names of all those who fell, dead, so that your name might live; the names of the men stripped so that your name would have possessions; the names of the men forgotten so that your name would never be forgotten.

You will bequeath this country. You will bequeath your newspaper, the nudges and adulation, the people's awareness lulled by the false speeches of mediocre men. You will bequeath mortgages, you will bequeath a class without class, a power without greatness, a consecrated stupidity, a dwarfed ambition, a clownish commitment, a rotten rhetoric, an institutional cowardice, a clumsy egoism.

You will bequeath them their thieving leaders, their submissive unions, their new latifundia, their U.S. investments, their jailed workers, their monopolizers and their great press, their field hands, their hit men and secret agents, their foreign bank accounts, their slick speculators, their servile congressmen, their adulatory ministers, their elegant subdivisions, their birthdays and commemorations, their fleas and wormy tortillas, their illiterate Indians, their fired laborers, their despoiled mountains, their fat men armed with scuba gear and stocks, their thin men armed with fingernails. Take your Mexico: take your inheritance.

You will inherit the sweet, disinterested faces with no future because they do everything today, say everything today, are the present and exist in the present. They say "tomorrow" because tomorrow doesn't matter to them. You will be the future without being it; you will consume yourself today thinking about tomorrow. They will be tomorrow because they live only today.

Your people.

Your death. You are an animal that foresees its death, sings its death, says it, dances it, paints it, remembers it before dying its death.

Your land.

You will not die without returning.

This village at the foot of the mountain, inhabited by three hundred people and barely visible except for some glimpses of roof tiles among the leaves, which, as soon as the stone of the mountain fixes itself in the earth, curl on the smooth hillside that accompanies the river in its course to the nearby sea. Like a green half-moon, the arc from Tamiahua to Coatzcoalcos will devour the white face of the sea in a useless attempt—devoured in its turn by the misty crest of the mountains, origin and frontier of the Indian plateau—to link itself to the tropical archipelago of graceful undulations and broken flesh. The languid hand of dry Mexico, unchanging, sad, the Mexico of stone cloisters and locked-in dust on the high plateau, the half-moon of Veracruz will have another history, tied by golden strings to the Antilles, the ocean, and, beyond, to the Mediterranean, which in truth will only be conquered by the battlements of the Sierra Madre Oriental. Where the volcanoes join and the silent insignia of the maguey rise up, a world will die which in repeated waves sends its sensual crests from the parting of the Bosporus and the breasts of the Aegean, its splashing of grapes and dolphins from Syracuse and Tunis, its deep wail of recognition from Andalusia and the gates of Gibraltar, its salaam made by a bewigged black courtier from Haiti and Jamaica, its bits and pieces of dances and drums and silk-cotton trees and pirates and conquistadors from Cuba. The black land absorbs the tide. The distant waves will fix on the cast-iron balconies and in the portals of the coffee plantations. The effluvia will die on the white columns of the rural porticoes and on the voluptuous un-dulations of the body and the voice. There will be a frontier here; then the somber pedestal of the eagles and flints will rise. It will be a frontier no one will defeat—not the men from Extremadura and Castile, who exhausted themselves in the first foundation and were then conquered, without knowing it, in their ascent to the forbidden platform that allowed them only to destroy and deform appearances: vic-tims, after all, of the concentrated hunger of statues made of dust, of the blind suction of the lake which has swallowed the gold, the foundations, the faces of all the conquistadors who have raped it; not the pirates who loaded their bri-gantines with shields thrown with a bitter laugh from atop the Indian mountain; not the monks who crossed the Pass of the Malinche to offer new disguises to unshakable gods who had themselves represented in destructible stone but who inhabited the air; not the blacks, brought to the tropical plantations and softened by the depredations of Indian women who offered their hairless sex as a redoubt of victory against the black race; not the princes who disembarked from their imperial galleons and let themselves be fooled by the sweet landscape of palms and nut trees and ascended with their baggage laden with lace and cologne to the pla-teau of bullet-pocked walls; not even the leaders wearing

three-cornered hats and epaulets who in the mute opacity
of the highland found, finally, the exasperating defeat of
reticence, of mute mockery, of indifference.

You will be that boy who goes forth to the land, finds
the land, leaves his origins, finds his destiny, today, when
death joins origins and destiny and between the two, despite everything, fixes the blade of liberty.

(1903: January 18)

He woke up when he heard the mulatto Lunero mutter,
"Drunk again, drunk again," when all the roosters (birds
in mourning, decadent, fallen to the status of rustic servants, their abandoned yards once the pride of this hacienda, where more than half a century earlier they did
battle with the fighting cocks of the region's political boss)
announced the swift tropical morning, which was the end
of the night for Master Pedrito, of yet another solitary drinking bout on the colored-tile terrace of the old, ruined mansion. The master's drunken singing could be heard as far
as the palm-roofed shack where Lunero was already up and
about, sprinkling the dirt floor with water from a pitcher
made somewhere else, whose ducks and painted flowers
once boasted a shiny lacquer finish. Lunero quickly lit a
fire in the brazier to heat up the charal-fish hash left over
from the previous day; poking around the fruit basket, he
picked out the blackest fruit to eat right away, before rot,
the sister of fecundity, softened them and filled them with
worms. Later, when the smoke welling up from under the
tin plate finally awakened the boy, the phlegmy singing
stopped. They could still hear the drunkard's stumbling
footsteps, as they moved farther and farther away, until the
final slam of the door, prelude to a long morning of insom-
nia: face down on the canopied mahogany bed with its bare,

stained mattress, tangled up in the mosquito net, in despair because his supply of rotgut liquor had run out. Before, Lunero recalled, patting the tousled head of the boy, who approached the fire, his too-short undershirt revealing the first shadows of puberty, when the property was big, the shacks stood far from the house and no one would ever know what went on inside unless the fat cooks and young half-breed women who swept up and starched shirts carried their tales to the other world of men roasted in the tobacco fields. Now everything was close, and all that was left of the hacienda, reduced by speculators and by the political enemies of the old, dead master, was the windowless house and Lunero's shack. Inside the house, only the memory of the sighing servants, kept alive by skinny old Baracoa, who went on looking after the grandmother, locked in the blue room in back; in the shack, there was just Lunero and the boy, the only workers left.

The mulatto sat down on the flattened floor and divided the fish, emptying half into the clay bowl and leaving half on the tin plate. He offered the boy a mango and peeled a banana. They began to eat in silence. When the small mound of ashes was finally cold, a thick cloud of perfume from the convolvulus Lunero had planted years before to cover the gray adobe of the walls and to surround the shack with the nocturnal aroma of tuberous flowers drifted through the only opening—door, window, refuge for sniffing dogs, frontier for the red ants held back by a line of lime. They didn't speak. But the mulatto and the boy felt the same happy gratitude at being together, a gratitude they would never mention, never even express in a shared smile, because they weren't there to talk or smile but to eat and sleep and go out together every daybreak, always silent, always weighed down by the tropical humidity, to do the work necessary to go on passing the days and to hand over to the Indian Baracoa the items that each week paid for both the grandmother's food and Master Pedrito's jugs. Those big blue jugs, safeguarded from the heat by woven straw covers and leather handles, were beautiful: potbellied, with short, narrow necks. Master Pedrito would line them up at the entrance to the house, and each month Lunero would go to the village at the foot of the mountain with the pole used on the hacienda to carry pails of water and return with it balanced on his shoulders, the jugs tied on and dangling—the mule they once had was dead. This village at the foot of the mountain was the only center. Inhabited by three hundred people and barely visible except for some glimpses of roof tiles among the leaves which, as soon as the stone of the mountains fixes itself in the earth, curl on the smooth hillside that accompanies the river in its course to the nearby sea.

The boy ran out of the shack and down the path through the ferns in the mango grove. The muddy slope took him, under the sky hidden by red flowers and yellow fruit, to the riverbank where Lunero was clearing a work site with his machete at the spot where the river, still turbulent, began to widen. The mulatto came over to him, buttoning up his denim bell-bottom trousers, a memory of some forgotten sailor fashion. The boy picked up his blue shorts, which had spent the night drying on the circle of rusty iron that Lunero was now approaching. Mangrove bark was lying about, open and smooth, its mouth in the water. Lunero stopped for a moment, his feet sunk in the mud. As it neared the sea, the river breathed more easily and caressed the growing masses of fern and banana. The brush looked higher than the sky because the sky was flat, shimmering low. They both knew what to do. Lunero took the sandpaper and went on smoothing the bark with a strength that danced in the thick sinews of his forearms. The boy brought over a broken, rotten stool and placed it inside the iron circle, which was hanging from a central wooden pole. Out of the ten openings punched through the circle hung ten wicks made of string. The boy spun the circle and then bent over to light the fire under the pot. The melted wax bubbled thickly; the circle spun; the boy poured the wax into the holes.

"Purification Day is coming," said Lunero, through the three nails he held in his teeth.

"When?"

The small fire under the sun brightened the boy's green eyes.

"On the second, Cruz, my boy, on the second. Then we'll sell my candles, not only to the neighbors but to people from farther away. They know our candles are the best."

"I remember last year."

Sometimes the hot wax would spit; the boy's thighs were covered with tiny round scars.

"That's the day the groundhog looks for his shadow."

"How do you know?"

"It's a story that comes from somewhere else."

Lunero stopped and reached for a hammer. He furrowed his dark brow. "Cruz, my boy, could you make canoes all by yourself?"

A big white smile flashed on the boy's face. The green reflections off the river and the moist ferns accentuated his sharp, pale, bony features. Combed by the river, his hair was plastered on his wide forehead and dark nape. The sun gave it copper highlights, but its roots were black. The tones of green fruit ran through his thin arms and strong chest, made for swimming against the current, his teeth shining in the laugh of his body refreshed by the river with its grassy bed and slimy banks. "Yes, I know how. I've watched how you do it."

The mulatto lowered his eyes, which were naturally low, eyes that were serene but searching. "If Lunero goes away, can you take charge of everything?"

The boy stopped turning the iron wheel. "If Lunero goes away?"

"If he has to go."

I shouldn't have said anything, thought the mulatto. He wouldn't say anything, he would just go, the way his kind always went, without saying anything, because he knows and accepts destiny and feels an abyss of reasons and memories between that knowledge and that acceptance and the rejection or acceptance of other men, because he knows nostalgia and wandering. And even though he knew he shouldn't say anything, he knew that the boy—his constant companion—had been very curious, his little head turned to one side, about the man wearing the frock coat who came looking for Lunero yesterday.

"You know, selling candles in town and making more when Purification Day comes; carrying the empty bottles back every month and leaving Master Pedrito his liquor at the door . . . Making canoes and bringing them downriver every three months . . . and handing the gold over to Baracoa, you know, keeping some for yourself, and fishing right here . . ."

The little clearing by the river no longer pulsed with the hiss of the rusty circle or the mulatto's somnambular hammering. Boxed in by the green, the murmur of the swift water grew, water carrying bagasse, trees struck by lightning in nocturnal storms, and grass from the fields upstream. The black-and-yellow butterflies fluttered around as they, too, headed for the sea. The boy dropped his arms and asked the mulatto's fallen face: "You're going away?"

"You don't know everything about this place. In another time, all the land from here to the mountain belonged to these people. Then they lost it. The grandfather master died. Master Atanasio was ambushed and killed, and little by little they stopped planting. Or someone else took their land. I was the last one, and they left me in peace for fourteen years. But my time had to come."

Lunero stopped, because he didn't know how to go on. The silver ripples of water distracted him, and his muscles asked him to get on with his work. Thirteen years before, when they gave him the boy, he thought of sending him down the river, cared for by the butterflies, the way they did with that old king in the white folks' story, and then waiting for him to come back, big and powerful. But the death of Master Atanasio let him keep the boy without even having to fight about it with Master Pedrito, who was incapable of thinking of anything or arguing; without fighting with the grandmother, who lived already locked away in that blue room with lace and chandeliers that tinkled when it stormed, and who would never find out about the growing boy a few yards from her sealed-up madness. Yes, Master Atanasio died at just the right time; he would have had the boy killed; Lunero saved him. The last few tobacco fields passed into the hands of the new master, and all they had left was this little bit of river edge and thickets and what was left of the old house, which was like an empty, cracked pot. He saw how all the workers went over to the lands of the new master and how new men began to come, brought from upstream, to work the new fields, and how men were brought from other towns and hamlets, and he, Lunero, had to invent this work of candles and canoes to earn enough to keep them alive. He began to think that no one would ever take him from that unproductive patch of land, just a tiny plot between the ruined house and the river, because no one would ever notice him, lost among these vegetal ruins with the boy. It took the master fourteen years to notice, but at some time or other his fine-toothed search of the region was bound to turn up this needle in a haystack. And so, yesterday afternoon, the master's agent had ridden up, suffocating in his frock coat, the sweat dripping down his face, to tell Lunero that tomorrow—meaning today— he was to go to the hacienda of the gentleman to the south of the estate, because good tobacco workers were scarce and Lunero had spent fourteen years living off the fat of the land, taking care of a crazy old lady and a drunk. And

Lunero did not know how to tell this to young Cruz, he thought the boy would never understand. The boy had known only work on the bank of the river, the coolness of the water before lunch, trips to the coast, where they gave him fresh crayfish and crabs, and the town nearby, inhabited by Indians who never spoke to him. But in truth the mulatto knew that if he started pulling on one thread in the story, it would all come unraveled and he'd have to start from the beginning and lose the boy. And he loved him—the long-armed mulatto kneeling by the sanded-down bark said to himself. He'd loved him ever since they ran his sister Isabel Cruz off the property and gave him the baby and Lunero fed him in the shack, fed him milk from the old nanny goat, all that remained of the Menchacas' stock, and he drew those letters in the mud that he'd learned when he was a boy, when he served the French in Veracruz, and he taught him to swim, to judge and taste fruit, to handle a machete, to make candles, to sing the songs Lunero's father had brought from Santiago de Cuba when the war broke out and the families moved to Veracruz with their servants. That was all Lunero wanted to know about the boy. And perhaps it was unnecessary to know more, except that the boy also loved Lunero and didn't want to live without him. Those lost shadows of the world— Master Pedrito, the Indian Baracoa, the grandmother— were coming forth like the blade of a knife to part him from Lunero. They were what was alien to the life he shared with his friend, what would part them. That was all the boy thought and all he understood.

"Look, we're running out of wax; the priest will be mad," said Lunero.

A strange breeze made the hanging wicks collide; a startled macaw shrieked out her midday alarm.

Lunero stood up and waded into the river; the net was set halfway into the current. The mulatto dove under and came up with the little net draped over one arm. The boy slipped off his shorts and jumped into the water. As never before, he felt the coolness on every part of his body. He went under and opened his eyes: the crystalline undulations of the first layer of water ran swiftly over a muddy, green bottom. And above, and back—he let himself be carried along like an arrow by the current—was the house he had never entered in all his thirteen years, where the man he'd only seen from a distance and the woman he only knew by name lived. He raised his head from the water. Lunero was already frying the fish and cutting open a papaya with his machete.

Midday had barely passed: the rays of the sun in decline passed through the roof of tropical leaves like water through a sieve, pelting down hard. The time of paralyzed branches, when even the river seemed not to flow. The naked boy stretched out under the solitary palm tree and felt the heat of the sun's rays as they cast the shadow of the trunk and the crown of leaves farther and farther. The sun began its final race; even so, its oblique rays seemed to rise, illuminating his entire body, pore by pore. First his feet, when he leaned back against the naked pedestal. Then his spread legs, his dormant sex, his flat stomach, his chest hardened by the water, his long neck, and his square chin, where the light was opening two deep clefts, like two bows aimed at his hard cheekbones, which framed the clarity of his eyes, lost that afternoon in a deep and tranquil siesta. He was sleeping, and nearby, Lunero, stretched out, face down, was drumming with his fingers on the black frying pan. A rhythm was taking hold of him. The seeming languor of his body at rest was actually the contemplative tension of his dancing arm as it drew concentrated tones out of the utensil. He began to murmur, as he did every afternoon, having recovered the memory of a rhythm that grew ever more rapid, the memory of a childhood song, of a life he no longer lived, when his ancestors crowned themselves, around the silk-cotton tree, with caps decorated with bells and rubbed their arms with liquor: a man would be seated in a chair with his head covered by a white cloth, and everyone drank the mixture of corn and bitter orange down to its black sugar lees. Children were taught that they shouldn't whistle at night:

> *All Yeyé's daughters*
> *like husbands . . . that belong to other women . . .*
> *all of Yeyé's daughters like husbands that belong*
>   *to other women*
> *Allyeyé'sdaughterslike*

The rhythm was taking control of him. He stretched out his arms and touched the edge of the muddy bank, and went on pounding his fingers against it and rubbing his stomach in it and a huge smile flowered on his face and broke his cheeks, which seemed stuck to the wide bones: *likehusbandsthatbelongtootherwomen . . .* The afternoon sun fell on his round, woolly head like hot lead, and he couldn't rise from that position, the sweat pouring off his forehead, his ribs, between his thighs, and his canticle became more silent and deep. The less he heard it, the more he felt it, and the more he glued himself to the earth, as if he were fornicating with it. *Allyeyésdaughters*: his smile was going to explode, the memory of the man with the black frock coat, the one who was going to come *that* afternoon, which is already *this* afternoon; and Lunero was lost in his song and his prostrate dance, which reminded him of the tomb, which reminded him of the French tomb and the women forgotten in the prison of this burnt-out mansion.

Behind, the branches and the ruin of the hacienda mansion he dreams about, dreaming away, the boy bathed in sunlight. Those blackened walls set on fire when the Liberals passed through in the final campaign against the Empire, Maximilian already dead, and found the family which had lent its bedrooms to the Field Marshal of the French forces and opened its larders to the Conservative troops. At the Cocuya hacienda, Napoleon III's troops took on supplies, to go out, their mules loaded with canned food, beans, and tobacco, and destroy Juárez's guerrilla forces. From the mountains, the bands of outlaws harried the French encampments in the flatland and in the forts they held throughout the state of Veracruz. And in the neighborhood of the hacienda, the Zouaves found little bands with guitars and harps that sang *Balajú went off to war and wouldn't bring me along,* cheering up their nights, as did the Indian and mulatto women, who soon gave birth to fairhaired mestizos, mulattos with blue eyes and dark skin named Garduño and Alvarez, who, in fact, should have been called Dubois and Garnier. Yes, on that same afternoon, prostrate in the heat, old Ludivinia, locked forever in the bedroom with its absurd chandeliers—two hanging from the whitewashed ceiling, one left in a corner next to the bed with its fluted posts—and curtains made of yellowed lace, fanned by the Indian Baracoa, who lost her original name only to get this slave name from the plantation's blacks, a name completely incongruous with her aquiline profile and greasy hair: old Ludivinia, her eyes wide open, hums that damned song which, even if she realized she was doing it, she would not remember, but which nevertheless she must enjoy, because it mocks General Juan Nepomuceno Almonte, who was at first a friend of the house and an intimate of the deceased Ireneo Menchaca, Ludivinia's husband, and part of the satanic court. Later, when the Savior of Mexico and great protector of the Menchacas—their lives, their haciendas—tried to come back from the last of his myriad exiles and disembarked and was recovering from an attack of dysentery, he renounced his old loyalties, and Ireneo had him arrested by the French and shipped out again: *San Juan de Nepomu-*

ceno: The Bare Truth. Ludivinia remembers Juan Nepomuceno Almonte, son of the thousand poxy women of the
priest Morelos, and she twists her toothless, sucked-in
mouth when she remembers the burlesque words of that
damned song the followers of Juárez sang when they humiliated General Santa Anna to death: . . . *and what would
you think if some thieves in the night took your old lady
and pulled down her drawers* . . . Ludivinia cackles out
her laugh and gestures to the Indian to fan her more rapidly.
The faded, whitewashed bedroom smelled of the shut-in
tropics, disguised as cold. The old lady liked the moisture
stains on the wall because they made her think of other
climates, those of her childhood before she married Lieutenant Ireneo Menchaca and linked her life and fortune to
those of General Antonio López de Santa Anna and received
from his hand the rich black lands along the river, as well
as other extensive contiguous holdings adjacent to the
mountains and the sea. *Over the sea in France, diddy-dee-
diddy-dee-diddydum, Benito Juárez died, and so did our
freedom.* And now her grimace pursed in disgust, and her
entire face collapsed into a thousand powdered layers, all
held together by a fine net of blue veins. Ludivinia's trembling claw dismissed Baracoa with another gesture and
shook her black silk sleeves and shredded lace cuffs. Lace
and crystal, but not only that: carved poplar tables with
heavy marble tops on which rested clocks under glass
domes, with heavy cabriole feet clutching a glass ball; on
the brick floor, wicker rockers covered with bustles she
never wore again, beveled card tables, bronze nailheads,
chests with inset panels and iron keyholes, oval portraits
of unknown Creoles—rigid, varnished, with puffy side-
burns, chests held high, and tortoiseshell combs—tin
frames for the saints and the Holy Child of Atocha—he in
old, moth-eaten needlepoint which barely retained the first
layer of gold leaf—the bed with its silver foliage and fluted
posts, repository of the bloodless body, nest of concentrated

smells, of sheets stained by running sores, of tufts of stuffing that poked their way through the splitting mattress.

The fire hadn't reached here. Neither did the news of the lost lands, the son killed in ambush, or the boy born in the Negro shacks: the news didn't, but the premonitions did.

"Indian, bring a pitcher of water."

She waited until Baracoa left and then broke all the rules: she parted the curtains and squinted to get a glimpse of what was happening outside. She had seen that unknown boy grow up; she had spied on him from the window, from the other side of the lace. She had seen those green eyes and cackled with joy, knowing herself to be in another young body, she who had etched into her brain the memories of a century, and in the wrinkles of her face disappeared layers of air, earth, and sun. She persisted. She survived. It was difficult for her to get to the window; she practically crawled, eyes fixed on her knees, hands squeezed against her thighs. Her head, covered with patches of white hair, had sunk between her shoulders, which were sometimes higher than the top of her head. But she survived. She was still here, trying, from her unkempt bed, to replicate the gestures of the young, fair-skinned beauty who opened the doors of Cocuya to the long parade of Spanish prelates, French traders, Scots and English engineers, bond salesmen, speculators, and anti-Spanish guerrillas, who all passed through here on their way to Mexico City and the opportunities the young, anarchic nation had to offer: her baroque cathedrals, her gold and silver mines, her *tezontle* and carved-stone palaces, her ecclesiastical businessmen, her perpetual political carnival and her perpetually indebted government, her customs concessions easily arranged for glib foreigners. Those were glorious days for Mexico, when the Menchacas left the hacienda in the hands of their oldest son, Atanasio, so that he might become a man by dealing with workers, bandits, and Indians. They made their way to the central plateau to glitter in the fictitious court of His Most Serene Highness. How was General Santa Anna going to get along without his old pal Menchaca—now Colonel Menchaca— who knew all about fighting cocks and pits and could pass an entire night drinking and recalling the Casamata Plan, the Barradas expedition, the Alamo, San Jacinto, the War of the Cakes, even the defeats perpetrated by the invading Yankee army, to which the Generalissimo alluded with a cynical hilarity, pounding the floor with his wooden foot, raising his glass, and caressing the black hair of Flor de México, the child-bride he'd brought to the nuptial bed when his wife's death rattle was still echoing in the air? There were also days of grief, when the Generalissimo was expelled from Mexico by the Liberals, and the Menchacas went back to their hacienda to defend their property: the thousands of acres heaped on them by the crippled tyrant addicted to cock fighting—acres appropriated without leave from native peasants who either had to stay on as field hands or move to the foot of the mountains; lands cultivated by the new black—and cheap—workers imported from the Caribbean islands, lands swollen by mortgages imposed on all the small landowners in the region. Tomb-like shacks for drying tobacco. Carts piled high with bananas and mangoes. Herds of goats set out to pasture on the low slopes of the Sierra Madre. And in the center of it all, the one-story mansion, with its pink belvedere and stables alive with whinnying, with boats and carriage outings. And Atanasio, the green-eyed son, dressed in white on his white horse, another gift from Santa Anna, galloping over the fertile land, his whip in his hand, always ready to impose his decisive will, to satisfy his voracious appetites with the young peasant women, to defend his property, using his band of imported Negroes, against the ever more frequent incursions of the Juárez forces. *Above all, long live Mexico, long live our Nation, death to the foreign prince . . .* And during the final days of the Empire, when old Ireneo Menchaca was informed that Santa Anna was coming back from exile to proclaim a new Republic, he boarded his black carriage and went to Veracruz, where a boat was waiting for him at the dock. From the deck of the *Virginia*, Santa Anna and his German pirates were signaling Fort San Juan de Ulúa, but no one answered. The port garrison was on the side of the Empire and mocked the fallen tyrant as he paced back and forth under the pennants, desperate, spouting obscenities from his fleshy lips. The sails filled again, and the two old friends played cards in the Yankee captain's cabin; they sailed over a torrid, languid sea, from which they could barely make out the coastline, which was lost behind a veil of heat. From the side of the ship in full dress, the dictator's furious eyes saw Sisal's white silhouette. And the crippled old man walked down the gangplank, followed by his old pal. He issued a proclamation to the inhabitants of Yucatán and once again lived his dream of greatness. Maximilian had just been sentenced to death in Querétaro, and the Republic had a right to count on the services of its natural, its true leader, its monarch-without-a-crown. It was all told to Ludivinia: how they were captured by the commander of Sisal, how they were sent to Campeche and paraded through the streets with their hands in chains, beaten like common criminals by the guards. How they were thrown into a dungeon in the fortress. How that summer, without latrines, swollen with foul water, old Colonel Menchaca died, while newspapers in the United States reported that Santa Anna had been executed by Juárez, as was the innocent Prince of Trieste. A lie: only the cadaver of Ireneo Menchaca was buried in the cemetery opposite the bay, the end of a life of chance and spins of the wheel of fortune, like that of the nation itself. Santa Anna, wearing the permanent grin of an infectious madness, again went into exile.

Atanasio told her, recalled old Ludivinia this hot afternoon, and from that day on, she never left her room. She had them bring her finest possessions there, the dining-room chandelier, the metal-encrusted chests, the most highly varnished pictures. All to wait for a death her romantic mind judged imminent but which had taken thirty-five lost years—nothing for a woman ninety-three years old, born the year of the first revolt, when a riot of clubs and stones was raised by Father Hidalgo in his parish of Dolores and her mother gave birth to her in a house in which terror had bolted the doors. She'd lost her calendars, and this year of 1903 was for her merely a time purloined from the rapid death from grief which should have followed that of the colonel. As if the fire of 1868 never existed: the flames extinguished just as they were reaching the door of the sealed bedroom, while her sons—there was a second, not only Atanasio, but she loved only him—shouted for her to save herself and she piled chairs and tables against the door and coughed in the thick smoke pouring through the cracks. She never wanted to see anyone ever again, only the Indian woman, because she needed someone to bring her food and stitch up her black clothing. She did not want to know more, but only to remember the old times. And within these four walls, she lost track of everything, except the essentials: her widowhood, the past, and, suddenly, that boy who was always running in the distance, right on the heels of a mulatto she didn't recognize.

"Indian, bring a pitcher of water."

But, instead of Baracoa, a yellow specter appeared at the door.

Ludivinia screamed soundlessly and shrank to the back of the bed: her sunken eyes opened wide in horror, and all the husks that made up her face seemed to turn to dust. The man stopped at the threshold and raised a trembling hand. "I'm Pedro . . ."

Ludivinia did not understand. Her trembling kept her from speaking, but her arms managed to wave, to exorcise, to deny in a flutter of black rags, while the pale ghost walked toward her with his mouth open. "Uh . . . Pedro . . . uh . . ." he said, rubbing his sparsely bearded, stained chin, his eyelids blinking nervously. "Pedro . . ."

The paralyzed old woman did not understand what this sluggish man stinking of sweat and cheap alcohol was saying: "Uh . . . There's nothing left, you know? . . . All of it . . . gone to the devil . . . And now . . ." he muttered, with a dry sob, "they're taking away the black; but, Mama, you don't know . . ."

"Atanasio . . ."

"No . . . Pedro." The drunk threw himself on the rocking chair, spreading his legs, as if he'd reached his final port. "They're taking away the black . . . who gives us food . . . yours and mine . . ."

"Not a black; a mulatto; a mulatto and a boy . . ."

Ludivinia was listening, but she did not look at the ghost who had come in to speak to her; no voice which let itself be heard inside the forbidden cave could have a body.

"All right. A mulatto, and a boy . . ."

"Sometimes the boy runs over there, far off. I've seen him. He makes me happy. He's a boy."

"The agent came to tell me . . . He woke me up at dawn . . . They're taking the black away . . . What are we going to do?"

"They're taking a black away? The hacienda is full of blacks. The colonel says they're cheaper and work harder. But if you want one so much, offer a little more for him."

And there they stood, statues of salt, thinking what later they would have wanted to say, when it would be too late, when the boy was no longer with them. Ludivinia tried to focus her gaze on the presence she refused to admit: who could he be, this man who for this purpose, just today, had dusted off his best suit to take the forbidden step? Yes: the batiste shirtfront, stained with mold from its storage in the tropics, the narrow trousers, too tight, too narrow for

the small potbelly of that exhausted body. The old clothes
did not tolerate the truth of the customary sweat—tobacco
and alcohol—and his glassy eyes denied all the affirmation
and bearing his clothes presupposed: the eyes of a drunkard
without malice, remote from all human contact for more
than fifteen years. Ah, sighed Ludivinia, perched on her
disarranged bed, admitting at last that this voice did have
a face, that isn't Atanasio, who was in his virility the extension of his mother. That is the mother, but with whiskers
and testicles—dreamed the old woman—not the mother
as she might have been as a man, as Atanasio was; and for
that reason she loved one son and not the other—she sighed
again—she loved the son who lived firmly rooted in the
place assigned to them on earth, and not the one who, even
after the defeat of their cause, wanted to go on profiting,
up there, in the palaces, from what no longer belonged to
them. She was certain: while everything was theirs, they
had the right to impose their presence on the entire nation;
she doubted: now that nothing was theirs, their place was
within these four walls.

The mother and son contemplated each other, with the
wall of a resurrection between them.

*Have you come to tell me that there is no more land or
greatness for us, that others have taken advantage of us as
we took advantage of the original owners of all this? Have
you come to tell me what I've known in my heart of hearts
since my wedding night?*

*I've come on a pretext. I've come because I no longer
want to be alone.*

*I'd like to remember you as a small boy. I loved you then;
when she's young, a mother should love all her children.
When we get old, we know better. We have to have a reason
for loving someone. Blood is not a reason. The only reason
is blood loved without reason.*

*I wanted to be strong, like my brother. I've used an iron
hand to deal with the mulatto and the boy. I've forbidden*

them to enter the big house. Just as Atanasio did, remember? But in those days there were so many workers. Today, only the mulatto and the boy are left. The mulatto is going.

You've been left alone. You've come looking for me so you won't be alone. You think I'm alone; I see it in your pitying eyes. Fool, always, and weak: not my son, who never asked anyone for pity, but my own image as a young bride. Now it can't be, not now. Now I have my whole life for company, so I can stop being an old woman. It's you who are old if you think the world's come to an end, with your gray hairs and your drunkenness, and your lack of will. Now I see you, now I see you, shitass! You're just the same as when you went to the capital with us; the same as when you thought our power was an excuse to expend it on women and liquor and not a reason to add to it and make it stronger and use it like a whip; the same as when you thought our power had passed without any loss and so you thought you could stay up there without our support when we had to come back down to this burning land, to this fountain of everything, to this hell from which we rose and into which we had to fall . . . It stinks! There's a smell stronger than horse sweat or fruit or gunpowder . . . Have you ever stopped to smell the coupling of a man and a woman? That's what the earth here smells like, the sheets of love, and you never knew it . . . Listen, oh, I caressed you when you were born and gave you my milk and said you were mine, my son, and all I was remembering was the moment when your father made you with all the blindness of a love that was not meant to create you but to give me pleasure: and that's what's left; you have disappeared . . . Out there, listen to me . . .

Why don't you speak? All right . . . all right . . . Don't say a word, just seeing you there looking at me like that is something; something more than a bare mattress and all those sleepless nights . . .

Are you looking for someone? And that boy there outside,

*isn't he alive? I'm suspicious of you; you probably think I
don't know anything, that I don't see anything from here
. . . As if I couldn't sense that there is flesh of my flesh
prowling out there, an extension of Ireneo and Atanasio,
another Menchaca, another man like them, out there, listen
to me . . . Of course he's mine, even though you haven't
sought him . . . Blood answers blood without having to
come near . . .*

"Lunero," said the boy when he woke up from his siesta
and saw the mulatto lying there, worn out, on the muddy
ground. "I want to go into the big house."

Later, when everything would be over, old Ludivinia
would break her silence and go out, like a wingless crow,
to scream along the avenues of fern, her eyes lost in the
underbrush and lifted, finally, to the Sierra; she would raise
her arms toward the human form she hoped to find behind
every branch that slashes her face furrowed with lifeless
veins, blinded by the night she's unaccustomed to in her
cloister of permanently burning candles. And she would
smell that conjunction of the earth and would shout in a
hoarse voice the names she'd forgotten and just recently
learned, she would bite her pale hands out of rage, because
in her heart something—years, memory, the past that was
her life—would tell her that there would still exist a margin
of life beyond her century of memories: a chance to live
and love another being of her blood: something that had
not died with the death of Ireneo and Atanasio. But now,
with Master Pedrito before her, in the bedroom she hadn't
left in thirty-five years, Ludivinia thought she was the center that yoked memory to the beings now around her. Master Pedrito rubbed his unshaven chin and spoke again, this
time aloud. "Mama, you don't know . . ."

The old lady's eyes froze the son's voice in his throat.

*What? That nothing could last? That their strength was
all show, based on an injustice that had to die at the hands
of another injustice? That the enemies we had shot so we*

*could go on being the masters, or the ones whose tongues
were cut out or whose hands were cut off on your father's
orders so that he could go on being the master, that the
enemies from whom your father stole land so he could begin
to be the master were victorious one day and set our house
on fire and took away what wasn't ours, what we had by
force and not by right? That, despite everything, your
brother refused to accept loss and defeat and went on being
Atanasio Menchaca, not up there, far from the scene, like
you, but down here, alongside his servants, facing up to
danger, raping mulattas and Indians, and not, like you,
seducing willing women? That, of your brother's thousand
careless, swift, ferocious couplings, there would remain one
proof, one, one, of his having passed through this land?
That, of all the children scattered by Atanasio Menchaca
over our possessions, one would be born close by? That
the same day his son was born in a Negro shack—as he
should be born, downward, to show once again the strength
of the father—who was Atanasio . . .*

Master Pedrito could not read these words in Ludivinia's
eyes. The old woman's gaze, having left her worn-out face,
wafted like a marble wave over the liquid heat of the bedroom. The man in the tight clothes did not have to hear
Ludivinia's voice.

*Don't reproach me for anything. I'm your son, too . . .
My blood is the same as Atanasio's . . . so why, that
night . . . ? All I was told was: "Sergeant Robaina, from
the old Santa Anna troops, has found what you've been
looking for for so long, Colonel Menchaca's body, in the
Campeche cemetery. Another soldier, who saw where they
buried your father with no marker, told the sergeant when
he was ordered to the port garrison. And the sergeant,
outwitting the commanders, stole Colonel Menchaca's remains at night. Now he's being transferred to Jalisco and
is passing through here and wants to give you the remains.
I'll wait for you and your brother tonight, after eleven, in*

*the clearing about a mile from town, the place where they
had the gallows for hanging rebel Indians." Clever, wasn't
it? Atanasio believed him, as I did; his eyes filled with tears,
he never questioned the message. Why did I ever come to
Cocuya that season? Because I was starting to run out of
money in Mexico City, and Atanasio never refused me anything. He even preferred that I be far away, he wanted to
be the only Menchaca in the area, your only guardian. The
red moon that shines in the hottest time of the year was up
when we got there. There was Sergeant Robaina. We remembered him from when we were kids. He was leaning
against his big horse, his teeth glowing like white rice, just
like his white mustache. We remembered him from when
we were kids. He'd always accompanied General Santa
Anna and was famous as a horse breaker; he'd always
laughed like that, as if he were part of a huge joke. And
there, on the big horse's back, was the filthy sack we were
hoping for. Atanasio hugged him, and the sergeant laughed
as he'd never laughed, he even whistled with laughter, and
that's when the four men came out of the thicket, glowing
in the moonlight, because they were all wearing white. "All
souls in heaven!" shouted the sergeant in his jolly voice.
"Souls in heaven right here for those who aren't satisfied
with having lost a man and go around wanting to get him
back!" And then his face changed, and he went for Atanasio, too. No one took any account of me, I swear. They
just walked forward, looking at my brother, as if I didn't
exist. I don't even know how I managed to get on my horse
and break through that damned circle of four men walking
with machetes in hand, while Atanasio shouted to me in a
hoarse but calm voice: "Go home, brother, and remember
what you take with you." And I felt the butt bouncing off
my knee, but I could no longer see the four men surround-
ing Atanasio, how they first slashed open his legs and then
cut him to pieces, there under the moon, so it could take
place in silence. Where could I go for help on the hacienda*

when I knew he was dead and gone, and besides, he'd been killed by the men who worked for the new headman in the district, who sooner or later had to kill Atanasio to be headman for certain? And from then on, who was going to oppose him? After that, I didn't want to know about the new fence, put up the next day by the man who had defeated us on our own land. What for? The workers went over to him without a word; he couldn't be worse than Atanasio. And as if to warn me to keep my mouth shut, a detachment of federal troops spent a week standing guard over the new boundaries. And for some reason or other, a month later, General Porfirio Díaz visited the new big house in the area. And they didn't even bother to omit their little joke. Along with Atanasio's mutilated body, they gave me some cow bones, a huge skull with horns—which is what the sergeant had in his sack. All I did was hang that shotgun over the door of the house, who knows? maybe as a kind of tribute to poor Atanasio. Really, that night . . . I didn't even realize that I had it on my saddle, even though the butt kept hitting me on the knee on that long gallop, Mama, I swear, it was so long . . .

"No one goes in there," Lunero said, coming out of his dance of terror and anguish, his silent farewell on his last afternoon with the boy. It was probably five-thirty, and the agent wouldn't be late.

"Try running inland," he had said yesterday. "Just try. We've got something better than bloodhounds: all those poor bastards who'd rather turn in a runaway than know that somebody saved himself from their fate."

No: Lunero, imprisoned, after all, by terror and nostalgia, was thinking about the coast. How big the mulatto seemed to the boy when he stood up and looked at the rapid flow of the river toward the Gulf of Mexico! How tall his thirty-three years of cinnamon-colored flesh and pink palms! Lunero's eyes were on the coast, and his eyelids seemed to be painted white, not because of age, which lightens the eyes of people of his race, but out of nostalgia, which is another form of growing old, more ancient, going back. There was the sandbar that broke the flow of the river and stained the first frontier of the sea brown. Farther out, the world of the islands began, and then came the continent, where someone like him could lose himself in the jungle and say he'd returned. He did not want to look back. He breathed deeply and looked toward the sea, as if toward a dream of liberty and plenitude. The boy lost his modesty and ran toward the mulatto. His embrace only reached up to Lunero's ribs.

"Don't go, Lunero . . ."

"Cruz, boy, for God's sake, what else can I do?"

The distressed mulatto patted the boy's hair and could not avoid that moment of happiness, the gratitude, the pain he'd always feared. The boy lifted his face: "I have to speak to them, tell them you can't go . . ."

"Inside?"

"Yes, inside the big house."

"They don't want us there, Cruz. Don't ever go there. Come on, let's get back to work. I won't go for a long time. Who knows if I'll have to go at all."

The murmuring afternoon river received Lunero's body. He dove in to avoid the words and the touch of the boy who had been with him his entire life. The boy went back to candle making and smiled again when Lunero, swimming upstream, imitated the flailing of a drowning man, shot up like an arrow, did a somersault in the water, came up again with a stick in his teeth, and then, on the bank, shook, making funny noises, and finally sat down behind the boy, with the smooth pieces of bark in front of him, and picked up his hammer and nails. He had to consider it again: the agent wouldn't be long. The sun was going down behind the treetops. Lunero fought off thinking what he should be thinking; the edge of bitterness cut through his happiness, now lost.

"Bring me more sandpaper from the shack," he ordered the boy, certain that those were his parting words.

Could he go like that, wearing his everyday shirt and trousers? Why take more? Now that the sun was going down, he would keep watch at the entrance to the house road, so the frock-coated man wouldn't have to go near the shack.

"Yes," said Ludivinia, "Baracoa tells me everything. How we live from the work of the boy and the mulatto. Would you care to acknowledge that? That we eat thanks to them. And you don't know what to do?"

The old lady's real voice was hard to understand; she was so used to muttering to herself that it flowed out with the stillness and gravity of a sulphurous spring.

". . . What your father or brother would have done, gone out to defend the mulatto and the boy, keep them from being taken away . . . If necessary, give up your life so they won't trample us into the dust . . . Are you going to do it, or shall I go, shitass? . . . Bring me the boy! . . . I want to speak to him . . ."

But the boy couldn't distinguish the voices, not even the faces: only the silhouettes behind the lace veil, now that Ludivinia, in a gesture of impatience, ordered Master Pedrito to light the candles. The boy moved away from the window and, walking on tiptoe, sought out the front of the big house, with its columns smeared with soot, with its forgotten terrace, where the hammock of Master Pedrito's bacchanals was hanging. And something else: above the lintel, held up by two rusty hooks, the shotgun Master Pedrito carried on his saddle that night in 1889, which he'd kept ever since, oiled and ready: here in the citadel of his cowardice, because he knew he'd never use it.

The twin barrels shone brighter than the white lintel. The boy crossed by it. What had been the main hall of the hacienda had lost its flooring and roof; the green light of the first hours of evening poured in, illuminating the grass and soot where a few frogs croaked, where pools of rain-water stood stagnant in the corners. From the opposite end of the house—what was left of the old kitchen—appeared the Indian Baracoa, with incredulous eyes. The boy hid his face in the shadow of the hall. He went out on the terrace and brought back a few adobe bricks, which he piled up to reach the shotgun. The voices grew louder. They reached him as a mix of thin fury and stuttered excuses. Finally, a tall shadow left the bedroom: the tails of his frock coat snapped in agitation, and his leather boots thundered on the tiles of the corridor. The boy didn't wait. He knew which path those feet would take; he ran, with the shotgun in his arms, along the path that led to the shack.

And Lunero was already waiting, far from the big house and the shack, in the spot where the red-dirt roads crossed. It was probably seven o'clock. He wouldn't be long in coming now. He peered up and down the highway. The agent's horse would raise a raging dust cloud. But not that distant roar, that double explosion Lunero heard behind him, which for an instant kept him from moving or thinking.

The boy crouched behind the branches with the shotgun in his hands, afraid the steps would find him. He saw the tight boots pass, the lead-colored trousers, and the tails of the frock coat—the same one he'd seen yesterday: he had no doubts when that faceless man walked into the shack and shouted, "Lunero!" And in that impatient voice the boy discerned the irritation and menace he'd noticed yesterday in the attitude of the frock-coated man looking for the mulatto. Who would be looking for the mulatto unless he was going to take him away by force? And the shotgun weighed heavy, with a power that prolonged the boy's silent rage: rage because now he knew that life had enemies and that it was not any longer the uninterrupted flow of river and work; rage because now he would know separation. The trouser-covered legs and the lead-colored frock coat emerged from the shack, and he took aim along the barrel and squeezed the trigger.

"Cruz! Son!" shouted Lunero as he neared Master Pedrito's shattered face, the shirtfront stained red, the false smile of sudden death. "Cruz!"

And the boy, as he came out of the bushes, trembling, had no way to recognize the face drenched in blood and dust, the face of a man he'd always seen from afar, almost undressed, with a jug tipped up and a torn undershirt over a hairless, pale chest. This man was not the other, just as he wasn't the gentleman who came down from Mexico City, elegant and neat: the one Lunero remembered; just as he wasn't the child caressed, sixty years before, by the hands of Ludivinia Menchaca. It was only a face without features, a blood-soaked shirtfront, a stupid grimace. Only the cicadas moved: Lunero and the boy stood still. But the mulatto understood. The master had died for him. And Ludivinia opened her eyes, moistened her index finger on her lips, and put out the candle on her night table. Almost on her knees, she walked to the window. Something had happened. The chandelier had tinkled again. Something had happened. For all eternity. Shaken by the double report. She heard the faraway voices until they faded and the insects started their chorus again. Only the cicadas. Baracoa crouched down in the kitchen; she let the fire go out and trembled to think that the time of gunpowder had returned. Ludivinia, too, stood still, until, in the silence, she was overcome by that thin fury and no longer fit in the enclosed bedroom. She went out stumbling, made smaller by the night sky that appeared through the holes in the burned-out great house—a small worm, white and wrinkled, stretching out her arms in hope of touching a human form that for thirteen years she knew to be close but which only now did she wish to touch and call by name instead of nurturing in thought alone: Cruz, Cruz without a real first or last name, baptized by the mulattoes with the syllables of Isabel Cruz or Cruz Isabel, the mother who was run off by Atanasio: the first woman on the property to give him a son. The old woman was unfamiliar with the night; her legs shook, but she insisted on walking, on dragging herself along with her arms spread, ready to find the last embrace of life. But only a sound of hooves and a cloud of dust approached. Only a sweaty horse which stopped with a whinny when Ludivinia's hunchback form crossed the road, and the agent shouted from the saddle: "Where did the boy and the black go, you stubborn old bitch? Tell me where they went, or I'll set the dogs and men on you!"

"Shitass," she said to the face she couldn't quite see high up on the saddle. "Shitass," she repeated with the snort of the horse near her raised fist.

The whip crossed her back, and Ludivinia fell to the ground as the horse whirled around, covering her with dust, galloping far off from the hacienda.

I know they've pierced my forearm with that needle; I scream before I feel any pain; the herald of that pain travels to my brain before my skin feels it . . . oh . . . to warn me of the pain I will feel . . . to put me on guard so that I realize what's happening . . . so that I feel the pain more intensely . . . because . . . realize . . . weakens . . . turns me into a victim . . . when I realize . . . the powers that will not consult me . . . will not take me into account . . . any longer: the pain organs . . . slower . . . overcome my reflex organs . . . pain which is no longer . . . that of the injection . . . but the same one . . . I know . . . that they're touching my stomach . . . carefully . . . my swollen stomach . . . doughy . . . blue . . . they touch it . . . I can't stand it . . . they touch it . . . with that soapy hand . . . that razor that shaves my stomach, my pubis . . . I can't stand it . . . I scream . . . I must scream . . . they hold me down . . . arms . . . shoulders . . . I shout to them to let me . . .

let me die in peace . . . don't touch me . . . I will not
allow you to touch . . . that inflamed stomach . . . sensitive
. . . like a wounded eye . . . I will not allow . . . I don't
know . . . they stop me . . . they support me . . . my
intestines don't move . . . don't move, now I feel it, now
I know . . . the gases build up, don't escape, are paralyzed
. . . those liquids that ought to flow don't flow anymore . . .
they swell me up . . . I know it . . . I have no temperature
. . . I know it . . . I don't know where they're taking me,
whom I can ask for help, directions, so I can get up and
walk . . . I strain . . . I strain . . . the blood doesn't come
. . . I know it doesn't get to where it should . . . it should
have come out my mouth . . . out of my anus . . . it doesn't
come out . . . they don't know . . . they're guessing . . .
they palpate me . . . they palpate my pounding heart . . .
they touch my pulseless wrist . . . I double up . . . I double
up . . . they take me by the armpits . . . I'm going to sleep
. . . I tell them . . . I ought to tell them before I go to
sleep . . . I tell them . . . I don't know who they are . . .
"We crossed the river . . . on horseback" . . . I smell my
own breath . . . fetid . . . they lay me back . . . the door
opens . . . the windows open . . . I run . . . they push me
. . . I see the sky . . . I see the blurred lights that pass in
front of my eyes . . . I touch . . . I smell . . . I see . . . I
taste . . . I hear . . . they bring me . . . I pass next to . . .
next to . . . along a corridor . . . decorated . . . they bring
me . . . I pass, touching, smelling, tasting, seeing, smelling
the sumptuous carvings—the opulent marquetry—the
moldings made of stucco and gold—the dressers inlaid with
bone and tortoiseshell—the metal plates and door handles—the paneled chests with iron keyholes—the aromatic
benches of *ayacahuite* wood—the choir seats—the baroque
crowns and skirts—the bowed seatbacks—the bronze nailheads—the worked leather—the cabriole claw-and-ball
feet—the damask chairs—the chasubles of silver thread—
the velvet sofas—the refectory tables—the cylinders and

amphorae—the beveled card tables—the canopied, linen-
covered beds—the fluted posts—the shields and orles—the
merino-wool rugs—the iron keys—the paneled paintings—
the silk and cashmere—the wools and taffeta—the crystal
and the chandeliers—the handpainted china—the burnished beams—they will not touch that . . . that will not
be theirs . . . my eyelids . . . I must raise my eyelids . . .
open the windows . . . I turn over . . . big hands . . .
enormous feet . . . I sleep . . . the lights that pass before
my raised eyelids . . . the lights of heaven . . . open up
the stars . . . I don't know . . .

You will be there, on the first ridges of the mountains
behind you, which grow steadily in height and expanse
. . . At your feet, the slope descends, still cloaked in leafy
branches and nocturnal screeching, until it blends in with
the tropical plain, the blue carpet of the night which will
rise, round and encompassing . . . You will stop on the first
platform of rock, lost in the nervous incomprehension of
what has happened, of the end of a life which you secretly
thought eternal . . . The life of the shack covered over by
bell-shaped flowers, of swimming and fishing in the river,
of candle-making, of the company of the mulatto Lunero
. . . But facing your internal convulsion . . . one needle
piercing your memory, another piercing your intuition of
the future . . . this new world of the night and the mountain
will open, and its dark light will begin to make its way in
your eyes, also new, and dyed by what has ceased to be
life in order to become memory, the memory of a boy who
will now belong to the untamable, to something different
from his own powers, to the wideness of the earth . . .
Liberated from the fatality of a single place and birth . . .
enslaved to another destiny, a new, unknown destiny which
looms behind the mountain lit by stars. Sitting down, catch-
ing your breath, you will open to the vast, immediate pan-
orama: the light of the sky crowded with stars will reach

you constantly and forever . . . The earth will spin in its uniform course around its own axis and a controlling sun . . . the earth and moon will revolve around each other, around the opposite body, and both around the shared field of their weight . . . The entire royal court of the sun will move within its white belt and the stream of liquid dust will move before the external conglomerations, around this clear vault of the tropical night, in the perpetual dance of entwined fingers, in dialogue without direction and within the frontiers of the entire universe . . . and the winking light will go on bathing you, the plain, the mountain with a constancy alien to the movement of the star and the turning of the earth, its satellite, other heavenly bodies, the galaxy, the nebula; alien to the frictions, the cohesions, and the elastic movements that unite and compress the power of the world, of the rock, of your own united hands that night in a first exclamation of astonishment . . . You will want to fix your eyes on a single star and gather all its light, that cold light, as invisible as the widest band of light from the sun . . . but that light doesn't allow itself to be felt on human skin . . . You will squint your eyes, and in the night, as during the day, you will not see the true color of the world, forbidden to human eyes . . . You will become confused, distracted, in the contemplation of the white light that penetrates your pupil with a cutting, discontinuous rhythm . . . From all its springs, all the light of the universe will begin its swift, curved flight, bending itself around the fugitive presence of the sleeping bodies of the universe itself . . . By means of the mobile concentration of the tangible, the arcs of light will come together, separate, and create in their rapid permanence the complete contour, the framework . . . You will feel the lights arrive, and at the same time . . . the insignificant tastes of the mountain and the plain: myrtle, papaya, the *huele-de-noche* and the night-shade, the dwarf pineapple, the tulip-laurel, vanilla, the *tecotehue*, the wild violet, the mimosa, the tiger lily . . .

you will clearly see them recede, all of them, farther and farther into the background, in a dizzying ebb of frozen islands . . . ever more distant from the first opening and the first shot . . . The light will run to your eyes; will run at the same time toward the most distant edge of space . . . You will dig your hands into the seat of rock and close your eyes . . . You will again hear the noise of the cicadas close by, the bleating of a lost flock . . . Everything in that eyes-closed instant will seem to move simultaneously forward, backward, and downward to the ground that holds it up . . . the flying buzzard linked to the pull of the deepest turn of the Veracruz River, then later poised on the immobility of a peak, ready for the flight that will rend the constancy of the stars in dark waves . . . And you will feel nothing . . . Nothing seems to move in the night: not even the buzzard will interrupt the quiet . . . The race, the spin, the infinite agitation of the universe will not be felt in your quiet eyes, feet, and neck . . . You will contemplate the sleeping earth . . . All the earth: rocks and mineral veins, the mass of the mountain, the density of the plowed fields, the river's current, men and houses, animals, birds, unknown strata of subterranean fire, they will all oppose the irreversible and imperturbable movement, but they will not be able to resist it . . . You will play with a chunk of rock as you wait for Lunero and the mule: you will toss it down the hill so that for a minute it will possess a swift, energetic life of its own—a small, wandering sun, a diminutive kaleidoscope of double lights . . . Almost as swift as light which gives it contrast; almost immediately a lost speck at the foot of the mountain, while the illumination of the stars continues streaming from its origins, imperceptibly, in absolute speed . . . Your ability to see fades in that lateral precipice into which the stone rolls . . . You will rest your chin on your fist, and your profile will lie on a line with the night horizon . . . You will be the new element of the landscape which will quickly disappear to seek the other

side of the mountain, the uncertain future of its life . . .
But here life will already have begun the next phase, ceas-
ing to be the past. . . . Innocence will perish, not at the
hands of guilt, but at the hands of amorous astonishment . . .
So high, so high, you've never been so high . . . You've
never seen treetops from this angle . . . The accustomed
nearness of the world hugging the river will be only a
fraction of this unsuspected immensity . . . And you will
not feel small as you contemplate and contemplate, in the
serene idleness of uncertainty, the distant cloud banks,
the undulating plane of the earth, and the vertical ascent
of the sky . . . You will feel better . . . orderly and distant
. . . You will not know yourself to be on new ground,
emerged barely a few hours ago from the sea, to smash
mountain chain against mountain chain and crumple itself
like a piece of parchment squeezed by the powerful hand
of the third epoch . . . You will feel tall at the top of the
mountain perpendicular to the fields, parallel to the line of
the horizon . . . And you will sense yourself in the night,
in the lost angle of the sun: in time . . . There, far away,
are those constellations really the way they look to the
naked eye, one next to the other? Or does an uncountable
time separate them? . . . Another planet will revolve above
your head, and the time of the planet will be identical to
itself: the obscure, distant rotation consummates itself, perhaps, in that instant, the only day of the only year, a mer-
curial measurement forever separated from the days of your
years. Now that time will not be yours, just as the present
of the stars you will contemplate again, seeing the past light
of a different, perhaps dead, time, will also not be yours
. . . The light your eyes will see will be only the ghost of
the light that began its journey countless years ago, countless centuries: is that star still alive? . . . It will live as long
as your eyes see it . . . And you will only know that it was
already dead as you looked at it, the future night in which
it ceases to reach your eyes—if it still exists—the light that

really burst forth, in the now of the star, when your eyes contemplated the ancient light and thought to baptize it with your eyes . . . Dead in its origin what will be alive in your senses . . . Lost, burnt out, the wellspring of light that will go on traveling, now without origin, toward the eyes of a boy in a night in another time . . . In another time . . . Time that will be filled with life, actions, ideas, but never be the inexorable flow between the first milestone of the past and the last of the future . . . Time that will exist only in the reconstruction of isolated memory, in the flight of isolated desire, which will be lost once the chance to live is used up, incarnate in this singular individual that you are, a boy, already a moribund old man, who this night links together, in a mysterious ceremony, the tiny insects climbing the stones on the slope and the immense stars that spin silently above the infinite depth of space . . . Nothing will happen in the silent minute of earth, firmament, and you . . . Everything will exist, move, separate in a river of change which in that instant will dissolve it, age, and corrupt everything without a single voice to sound the alarm . . . The sun is burning itself alive, iron is crumbling into dust, aimless energy is dissipating in space, masses are wearing out in radiation, the earth is cooling into death . . . And you will wait for a mulatto and an animal, to cross the mountain and begin to live, to fill time, execute the steps and gestures of a macabre game in which life will advance as life dies; a dance of madness in which time will devour time and no one alive can halt, the irreversible course of death . . . The boy, the earth, the universe: in those three, someday there will be no light, no heat, no life . . . There will be only total, forgotten oneness, nameless, without a man to give it a name: space and time, matter and energy all fused into one . . . And all things will have the same name . . . None . . . But not yet . . . Men are still being born . . . You will still hear Lunero's long "Helloooo" and the sound of horseshoes on

the stone . . . Your heart will still beat in an accelerated
rhythm, because you are conscious that after today the
unknown adventure begins, the world is opening, offering
you its time . . . You exist . . . You are standing on the
mountain . . . You answer Lunero with a whistle . . . You
are going to live . . . You are going to be the meeting point,
the universal order's reason for being . . . Your body has
a reason for being . . . Your life has a reason for being . . .
You are, you will be, you were, the universe incarnate
. . . For you, the galaxies will light up and the sun will burn
. . . All so that you can love and live and be . . . So that
you will find the secret and die without being part of it,
because you will possess it only when your eyes close forever . . . You, standing there, Cruz, thirteen years old, at
the edge of life . . . You, green eyes, thin arms, hair made
coppery by the sun . . . You, friend of a forgotten mulatto
. . . You will hear Lunero's long "Helloooo" . . . You will
compromise the existence of the infinite, bottomless fresh-
ness of the universe . . . You will hear the horseshoes on
the stone . . . In you, the star and the earth touch . . . You
will hear the report of the rifle after Lunero's shout . . .
Above your head will fall, as if returning from a voyage
without origin or end in time, the promises of love and
solitude, of hatred and effort, of violence and tenderness,
of friendship and disillusion, of time and oblivion, of innocence and surprise . . . You will hear the silence of the
night without Lunero's shout, without the echo of the
horseshoes . . . In your heart, open to life, this night; in
your open heart . . .

(1889: April 9)

He, curled unto himself, in the center of those contractions,
he with his head dark with blood, hanging, held by the

most tenuous thread: open to life, at last. Lunero held the
arms of Isabel Cruz or Cruz Isabel, his sister; he closed his
eyes so he wouldn't see what was happening between his
sister's spread legs. He asked her, his face hidden, "Did
you count the days?" And she couldn't answer because she
was screaming, screaming behind closed lips, her teeth
clenched—feeling that the head was coming out now, now
it was coming, while Lunero held her up by the shoulders,
only Lunero, with the pot boiling water on the fire, the
knife, and the rags ready, and he was coming out between
her legs, pushed out by the contractions of the womb, closer
and closer together, and Lunero had to release the shoulders of Cruz Isabel, Isabel Cruz, kneel between her open
legs, receive that moist black head, the sticky little body
tied to Cruz Isabel, Isabel Cruz, the small body finally
separated, received by Lunero's hands, now that the
woman stopped moaning, breathed deeply, exhaled some
foul breath, wiped the sweat off her face, looked for, looked
for him, reached out her arms: Lunero cut the cord, tied
up the end, washed the body, the face, held him close,
kissed him, tried to give him to his sister, but Isabel Cruz,
Cruz Isabel was moaning again in another contraction, and
the boots were approaching the shack where the woman
lay on the dirt floor under the palm roof, the boots were
coming closer and Lunero turned the body face down, he
slapped the baby so he would cry, cry as the boots came
closer: he cried: he cried and began to live . . .

I don't know . . . I don't know . . . if I am he . . . if you
were he . . . if I am the three . . . You . . . I carry you
inside me and you are going to die with me . . . God . . .
He . . . I carried him inside and he is going to die with
me . . . the three of us . . . who spoke . . . I . . . will carry
him inside and he will die with me . . . alone . . .

•

You will no longer know: you will not experience your open heart, tonight, your open heart . . . They say "Scalpel, scalpel" . . . I listen to it, I who go on knowing when you no longer know, before you know . . . I who was he, will be you . . . I listen, in the bottom of the glass, behind the mirror, deep inside, underneath, on top of you and him . . . "Scalpel" . . . They open you up . . . They cauterize you . . . They open your abdominal walls . . . The thin, cold, precise knife parts them . . . They find that liquid in your stomach . . . They part your iliac fossa . . . They find that cluster of irritated, swollen, intestinal loops tied to your mesentery, which is hard and shot through with blood . . . They find that circular plaque of gangrene . . . bathed in a liquid of fetid stench . . . They say, they repeat . . . "Infarct" . . . "mesentery infarct" . . . They look at your dilated, bright-red, almost black intestines . . . They say . . . they repeat, "Pulse" . . . "Temperature," "perforation" . . . Eat, gnaw . . . The hemorrhaged substance runs out of your open stomach . . . They say, repeat . . . "Useless" . . . "useless" . . . all three . . . the coagulation wrenches itself from the black blood . . . will run, will stop . . . stopped . . . your silence . . . your open eyes . . . which cannot see . . . your frozen fingers . . . which cannot feel . . . your black, blue nails . . . your shuddering jaws . . . Artemio Cruz . . . name . . . "Useless" . . . "Heart" . . . "Massage" . . . "Useless" . . . You will no longer know . . . I carried you within and I shall die with you . . . all three . . . We shall die . . . You . . . are dying . . . have died . . . I shall die

Havana, May 1960
Mexico City, December 1961